ACCLAIM FOR SUSANNE ALLEYN'S HISTORICAL FICTION

[*Palace of Justice*] "Alleyn is not only conversant in French history but excels at character development. . . . Her superb series will appeal to readers who want brilliant characterization, an authentic historical setting, and a sense that they are walking the dark streets of Paris with Ravel during the Reign of Terror." (*Library Journal*, starred review)

[*The Cavalier of the Apocalypse*] "Superb . . . Alleyn expertly captures the politics and atmosphere of the period, seamlessly integrating them into a traditional whodunit plot." (*Publishers Weekly*, starred review)

[*A Treasury of Regrets*] "Put her latest on the must-read list." (*Library Journal*, starred review; *Library Journal*'s Best Mysteries of 2007)

[*Game of Patience*] "Alleyn knows her French Revolution, creates a complex brain-teaser of a mystery, and excels in making her characters believable. In short, this book has everything." (*Library Journal*)

[*A Far Better Rest*] "A richly textured, tragic tale that, in the tradition of the best historical novels, brings an era alive through the depiction of human drama." (*Publishers Weekly*)

The Executioner's Heir

A Novel of Eighteenth-Century France

ʒ℧ ℃ʒ

Susanne Alleyn

SPYDERWORT PRESS
ALBANY, NY

For further information, please contact Don Congdon Associates, Inc., 110 William St., Suite 2202, New York, NY 10038, USA. E-mail: dca@doncongdon.com

First paperback edition: September 2013

ISBN-13: 978-1492306795

ISBN-10: 1492306797

10 9 8 7 6 5 4 3 2 1

Spyderwort Press
Albany, New York, USA

To Darline Gay Levy, without whose encouragement nothing might ever have been written.

To Cristína, who's always stood behind this novel.

To Ben, who's been waiting for it for eighteen years.

FOREWORD

Those familiar with the Aristide Ravel novels should be aware that Charles Sanson, the central character of *The Executioner's Heir*, is the same historical figure as the Sanson featured in *Palace of Justice*, but at a much earlier period of his life; while Charles's grown son is the executioner who plays a role in *Game of Patience*.

The French word *parlement*, law court, is not synonymous with the English "parliament," a legislative body, though the two are often confused. Under the ancien régime, a French *parlement* was the supreme court of a region, which served as a court of appeal against lower courts' judgments in both civil and criminal cases; they sometimes also tried important cases of high treason, and criminal cases with aristocratic defendants. The chief parlement was located in Paris, with others in the provinces. All the parlements were abolished in 1790.

Many tiny medieval streets in the heart of Paris disappeared during Baron Haussmann's extensive rebuilding of the city in the 1860s. Many other streets have had their names changed during the past two and a half centuries. All streets and street names mentioned in this novel, however, existed in the eighteenth century.

The quotations at the beginning of each section are drawn from the collection *Maximes et Pensées* by Sébastien Roch Nicolas, called Chamfort (1740?-1794).

CAST OF CHARACTERS

IN PARIS—THE SANSON HOUSEHOLD:

- Charles Sanson
- Jean-Baptiste Sanson, Charles's father, hereditary master executioner of Paris
- Madeleine, Charles's sister
- Jeannette Berger Sanson, Jean-Baptiste's second wife; Charles and Madeleine's stepmother
- Marthe Dubut Sanson, Jean-Baptiste's mother; Charles's grandmother
- Nicolas, Charles's younger half-brother, eldest of Jean-Baptiste's and Jeannette's eight surviving children
- Martin, a half-brother
- Josèphe, a half-sister
- *Jérôme, a servant, chief assistant to Jean-Baptiste Sanson
- *Auguste, Pierre, Olivier, Bastien, servants at the Sanson household and assistant executioners

SANSON ANCESTORS AND FOREBEARS:

- Charles I Sanson (1635-1707), first executioner in the family ("Sanson the First"); great-grandfather of Charles Sanson
- Charles II Sanson (ca. 1681-1726), second executioner in the family; late husband to Marthe Dubut Sanson; father of Jean-Baptiste Sanson; grandfather of Charles Sanson
- Madeleine Tronson (1712-ca. 1742), first wife of Jean-Baptiste Sanson; mother of Charles and Madeleine

- Pierre Jouënne (d. ca. 1685), executioner of Rouen; father-in-law of Charles I Sanson
- Marguerite Jouënne (d. ca. 1681), wife of Charles I Sanson

VISITORS TO THE SANSON HOUSEHOLD:

- Gabriel Sanson, executioner of Reims, Jean-Baptiste's younger brother; Charles's uncle
- Dom Ange-Modeste Gomart, priest and confessor at the prison of the Conciergerie
- Thomas Arthur, Comte de Lally and Baron de Tollendal, general and field marshal of the French army
- Pierre Hérisson, executioner of Melun

PERSONS AND PERSONAGES IN AND ABOUT PARIS:

- Guillaume-François-Louis Joly de Fleury, royal prosecutor-general
- *Zéphire, a dancer, Charles Sanson's mistress
- Jeanne Bécu, a shopgirl of easy virtue, niece to Père Gomart
- *Antoinette Vitry, her friend
- Monsieur and Madame Jugier, farmer of the village of Mont-Martre and his wife
- Marie-Anne Jugier, their eldest daughter
- Christophe de Beaumont, archbishop of Paris

IN FÉROLLES AND BRIE-COMTE-ROBERT:

- François Jean Lefebvre de La Barre, a penniless teenaged aristocrat
- Jacques Lefebvre de La Barre, his elder brother
- Jean-Baptiste Alexandre Lefebvre de La Barre, their father
- Père Jouffroy, parish priest of Férolles
- *Paul, a local urchin

In Abbeville:

- Anne Marguerite Feydeau de Brou ("Madame"), abbess of the convent of Willancourt, cousin to the Lefebvre de La Barre family
- Jacques-Marie-Bertrand Gaillard d'Étallonde, an aristocratic youth, François de La Barre's best friend
- Pierre Dumaisniel de Saveuse de Belleval, another aristocratic youth, a friend of François's
- Marcel de Moisnel, a young orphaned cousin of the Bellevals, a friend of François's
- Louis Douville de Maillefeu, son of the former mayor of Abbeville, a friend of François's
- Père Bosquier, a Dominican monk, priest, and scholar, friend of Madame Feydeau
- Marguerite Becquin de Vercourt, daughter and sole heiress of Abbeville's royal criminal lieutenant
- Joseph de Valines, a murderer
- Nicolas-Pierre Duval de Soicourt, criminal assessor and mayor of Abbeville
- Jean-Clément Hecquet de Roquemont, royal prosecutor at Abbeville
- Lieutenant Merlin, an officer of the Abbeville guard
- Simon-Nicolas Linguet, a lawyer, author, and agitator

Offstage characters in Paris, Abbeville, & elsewhere:

- Robert-François Damiens, a deranged would-be assassin
- Charles de Bourbon-Condé, Comte de Charolais (d. 1760), a distant cousin to the royal family, friendly with Jean-Baptiste Sanson
- Carlo Bertinazzi ("Carlin"), a famous actor of the Comédie-Italienne
- Beauvarlet, a long-term guest at the convent of Willancourt
- President Gaillard de Boëncourt, chief magistrate of the high court of Abbeville, father of Bertrand Gaillard d'Étallonde

- Charles-Joseph Dumaisniel, sieur de Belleval, minor aristocrat, prominent citizen of Abbeville, and great friend of Madame Feydeau; father of Pierre and Charles de Belleval
- Charles Dumaisniel de Belleval, his son; Pierre de Belleval's elder brother
- Etienne Naturé, master at arms and owner of a fencing school in Abbeville
- Voltaire, famous author, playwright, liberal political philosopher, and champion of *causes célèbres*; author of the satirical, anticlerical, banned 1764 book *Le Dictionnaire Philosophique* (*The Philosophical Dictionary*)
- Louis-François-de-Paule Lefebvre d'Ormesson, royal magistrate, former president of the Parlement of Paris; distant cousin to the Lefebvre de La Barre family
- René Nicolas de Maupeou, president of the Parlement of Paris, d'Ormesson's successor

*Fictional character

I

The Paris Title

1754-1757

*Dans l'ordre naturel, comme dans l'ordre social,
il ne faut pas vouloir être plus qu'on ne peut.*

(In the natural order, as in the social order,
one must not desire to be more than one can be.)

—*Suite des Maximes Générales*

1

"This is the sword of justice," Jean-Baptiste told him, lifting it from its long, straw-lined, padlocked crate. "It first belonged to your great-grandfather."

Great-grandfather—the first Charles Sanson in the profession, the first to hold the Paris title, *Master of High Works for the City and Provostry of Paris and Versailles.* His sword was a family heirloom, of sorts, Charles knew, but the kind you didn't boast about.

Engraved near the two-handed hilt, the single word *Iustitia*—Justice—glinted in the light. The gentle spring sunshine spilled through the door into the shadows of the windowless shed, giving murky outlines to other, less graceful objects: coils of rope, oaken planks, leather whips, a brazier, an iron cudgel, a cart wheel.

The sword was three and a half feet long, with a fine, narrow blade kept oiled and gleaming. It was a beautiful thing, if you could manage to forget what it was meant for.

"Go on, take it," his father said. Charles guessed what he'd left unspoken: *You'll have to lift it one day.*

"It's heavy!"

"It has to be. You've been looking through the *Treatise on the Human Skeleton*—don't you remember what neck bones look like? Slicing through them isn't easy."

"No, Father." He balanced the sword in his hands, the point upward, wondering how much it weighed and if his forefathers had found it as intimidating as he did. He would far rather have been back in Jean-Baptiste's library, leafing through the medical and scientific books that his father, his grandfather Charles Sanson the Second, and great-grandfather Charles Sanson the First had collected over the past sixty or seventy years.

"Charles, have you any idea how one beheads a man with a sword?"

The question, almost matter-of-fact, quietly asked, jerked him back to the present. He glanced up at his father, who gazed at him, unsmiling as always.

"You're fourteen now, old enough. You'll have to learn."

"I . . ." Occasionally—before his stepmother hurried him away—he caught sight of Jean-Baptiste practicing with a sword, or a facsimile of one, in a yard well away from the house, beyond the stable where he kept the horses and cart that transported criminals to execution at the Place de Grève. But his father was merely aiming at a standing post or at bundles of straw, a harmless enough pastime, you'd think.

"I suppose you lift it up in the air," he said, groping for words, "and—and chop down—like chopping firewood."

"No," Jean-Baptiste said, taking back the weapon, which Charles willingly relinquished to him. "That's not how it's done. Chopping with an axe on a block—that's a clumsy method. Crude."

No doubt his father expected him to show some respectful, though not unseemly, curiosity about the family profession.

"How do you do it, then?"

"You have to swing it sideways."

"Sideways?"

"Like this." Jean-Baptiste gripped the long hilt in both hands, raised the sword almost to shoulder height and parallel to the ground, and slowly described a wide, horizontal arc at arm's length. The steel glittered, flashing in Charles's eyes, as it swept past.

"The patient kneels in front of you, upright, with his back to you."

Patient?

Charles stifled an uneasy giggle at the euphemism. *Patient*—as though the executioner were a doctor. The final cure for all ills.

Abruptly he imagined himself the executioner's victim (*patient*, Charles), kneeling in a pile of straw, neck bared, awaiting the blow, and the breath seemed to freeze in his lungs.

"You swing the sword about, from high above," his father continued: "like this, high above your shoulder, to get up the speed, and then you must aim just right—"

Awaiting the blow, he thought, *blindfolded, hands tied behind you . . . your heart would race and your breath would come quick and shallow, wouldn't it?*

With an effort Charles balled his fists, closed his eyes for an instant, and turned to face his father, who continued in his usual composed, distant tones.

"—so it passes straight through his neck. It requires strength, control, a keen eye, and steady nerves. You need to know how to do it, and you're strong enough now, I'd judge, to begin practicing with a blade. Only practice will make you skilled at it."

Charles swallowed, glancing covertly at this stranger who was talking so dispassionately about instruments of judicial death and how to use them, this sudden stranger who had once been his father. "I couldn't do that."

"Do . . ."

"I couldn't ever cut somebody's head off."

"I thought so, too, when I was fourteen." Jean-Baptiste laid the sword back in its crate. He rested a hand, for an instant, on Charles's shoulder. Providence had been kind to him, he went on; in all his career, he'd never yet been ordered to behead anyone.

"But should such an unhappy occasion arise, I'm prepared, both in body—to strike a clean blow—and spiritually, as the law's most terrible servant, to take another's life in the name of the law. Fortunately," he added, "we live in a civilized age; the gentry rarely commit capital offenses."

"The gentry?"

"Only people of noble birth are allowed to be beheaded," Jean-Baptiste reminded him, as he shut the crate and secured it with a small padlock wrought—incongruously enough—into an ornate heart. "Always be sure the swords are locked away. I have two here—this one and a spare. The Parlement gave them to my grandfather, sixty years ago, when he assumed the Paris title. They cost six hundred livres each, back in his day, and I hate to think what it would cost now to replace them."

Charles nodded, impressed. Six hundred livres was more than the average workman earned in a year.

Jean-Baptiste gestured him out to the sunshine of the stable-yard, muddy from the spring rain. "Only nobles may be behead-ed," he repeated, as he fished out his keys, "and you must know how to do it yourself, because they have the privilege of being exe-cuted by someone of equivalent rank."

Charles frowned. What was he missing? "Another nobleman?"

"If you find studying the criminal law as tedious as I did when I was your age," Jean-Baptiste said dryly, "you should at least read your history." He locked the shed and joined Charles. "Not another nobleman, no, but nearly so. Only the master executioner may be-head an aristocrat."

Only the master executioner, he went on, an indispensable func-tionary of the high court, who held the royal office and title from the Parlement of Paris—grandly, *Maître des Hautes Œuvres*, Master of High Works—could carry out such a solemn duty; he couldn't delegate it to his lackeys as they did with plebeian hangings.

"And you, as my eldest son, will someday hold the Paris title and you may, one day, be less fortunate than I and have to put some-one to death with your own hands, so—"

"Father? Why are nobles beheaded while ordinary people are hanged?"

"Decapitation is a privilege, Charles. It illustrates the distinc-tion between the high-born and the common masses. It's an honor-able way to die, suitable for a gentleman or gentlewoman."

"Even one who's committed a crime?"

Assault, murder, rebellion, treason, even those?

"Yes, even one who's gone astray and committed some act that's worthy of death. Noble birth implies a tradition of duty and honor, just like our own—and so it's a gentleman's duty, when condemned to die, to hold himself up courageously and maintain the honor of his family name by awaiting the blow without flinching. Ordinary criminals wouldn't have the nerve for it. The dregs of the streets and the slums, they have no noble name or family honor to uphold.

"Imagine," Jean-Baptiste continued, "a common housebreaker, a cutpurse, a brigand, outlaws and cowards all, having the native courage to hold himself still on the scaffold even for a moment or two, while the executioner concentrates on his aim! He'd most likely struggle, or tremble, or even collapse. And that, of course, would spoil the headsman's aim and lead to frightful accidents. It's really to their benefit that the riffraff are hanged."

Charles looked away, feeling a little sick to his stomach, as he usually did when he had to pass the local abattoir on the way to Mass at Saint-Laurent. Its pervasive ooze of filth and stinking stale blood invariably slimed the cobbles and his shoes. If he disliked the thought of innocent animals being slaughtered and butchered nearby for his family's table, how much more repugnant was the prospect of putting human beings to death?

Since his twelfth birthday he'd witnessed at least a dozen executions at Jean-Baptiste's side. *To learn your business*, his father had said. Hanging was humiliating for the victim and Charles had found it unpleasant to watch, but it was reliable, predictable, and passably quick; it was supposed, Jean-Baptiste told him, to snap the neck at once and finish the culprit. If he or she instead strangled to death at the end of the rope, slowly choking while evacuating bladder and bowels, to the mingled amusement, disgust, and indignation of the watching crowds, the executioner's lackeys hadn't done their job properly.

The spring sun was warm on his face. He drew a deep breath, glad to get away from the shed—the one kept locked, where his father kept the tools of his profession, where the children were strictly forbidden to venture—and resolved to light a candle to the Blessed Virgin and pray that he, too, would never have to behead anyone.

"It's a fine afternoon," Jean-Baptiste said. He glanced up at the cloudless sky. "Perhaps we should begin today. You'll start with the dummy sword and get your arms used to supporting the weight at the proper—"

"I'd rather learn about your laboratory," Charles said hastily, eager to examine the rows of dusty bottles and vials, and trying not to think about the executioner's sword at all. "I'd like to learn about medicine and—and curing people." Despite his profession that was both the honor and the curse of the Sanson family, Jean-Baptiste was well known in their outlying parish as a skilled healer, like his father and grandfather before him, with as much expertise in doctoring as many physicians with university degrees.

Jean-Baptiste eyed him for a moment. "How are you getting along with your studies?"

Charles could predict to a hair's breadth that Père Grisel, his tutor, had reported that young Monsieur Sanson had quite a thirst for knowledge, but was an abysmal speller, wrote a poor hand, and had faulty Latin.

"I try my best at Latin. And I know I can't spell. But I like to read anything I can. Natural philosophy, herbalism, anatomy—"

"You're not to spend all your time with those at the expense of history and law."

"No, Father."

Jean-Baptiste's tone was stern, but Charles could tell from a fraction of a smile on his father's lips that he was not altogether displeased with his son's love of learning, whatever branches of knowledge he might be overlooking.

"But I do want to read your scientific books, and learn about medicine."

Jean-Baptiste slipped the key to the shed into his pocket and extracted another. "I see you won't be dissuaded. Very well; the laboratory now, then the wooden sword this afternoon, and no arguments."

Charles grinned and followed him, barely concealing his excitement. Beneath the broad skylight the laboratory was full of mysteries and wonders: a cupboard that held dozens of bottles and small ceramic pots, full of tinctures, syrups, ointments; a shelf of unfamiliar books on botany and anatomy; a brazier for simmering mixtures; and enough mortars and jars of dried herbs to fill an apothecary's shop. Jean-Baptiste pointed at the various articles, explaining, as Charles stared.

A question he'd longed to ask for some years, but had never dared to bring up, hovered at the edge of his memory. Naturally the executioner had frequent contact with corpses. And Jérôme, Jean-Baptiste's chief assistant, a veteran of thirty-five years or more in the profession, had sworn many times that the salve his master prepared would cure anything.

He *would* ask him, for once and for all, when they completed the tour of the outbuilding.

"Father, Jérôme says you know how to make a magic ointment out of hanged men's fat."

He half expected a box on the ear to curb his inquisitiveness, but Jean-Baptiste merely frowned. "Do you believe all the tall tales the servants tell you?"

"Well . . . no."

"Remember, they're not of our class and they haven't had your education."

"It's not true, then?"

It was an ancient superstition, Jean-Baptiste patiently explained, hundreds of years old, that the executioner could mix a magical salve from dead men's fat. Perhaps Sanson the First and his predecessors in the profession, back in less scientific and enlightened centuries, had indeed concocted such a mixture. But he, Jean-Baptiste Sanson, let the men believe such foolishness only because all ignorant people believed it, and wouldn't be convinced otherwise.

"This is the eighteenth century, not the fourteenth, and I won't have you swallowing such nonsense. It's no different from the old wives' tale about a piece of hangman's rope, or a hanged man's bone, bringing good luck. Pagan superstition, not reason."

"But is there a salve—"

"Yes, I prepare one that soothes skin afflictions and small wounds. They all ask me for it, as I'm sure they asked your grandfather and great-grandfather in their time; they believe it'll cure anything ailing them." He retrieved a ceramic jar from a shelf and pulled out the stopper. "But the salve is made from lard mixed with thyme, myrtle, and a few other medicinal herbs: nothing more."

Charles wrinkled his nose at the pungent odor of bitter herbs mingled with pig fat, worse than the rancid reek of cheap tallow candles that smelled like a soap boiler's back alley, and Jean-Baptiste gave him another of his rare smiles. "It does stink to high heaven."

"So you don't take hanged men's fat?"

"Listen to me." He turned Charles around with a firm grip on his shoulder, so that they were face-to-face. "I would never take the fat of a man for such a thing. Never. It's against God's laws to tamper with a human body."

"But don't you dissect bodies?"

"Yes," Jean-Baptiste admitted, "I look inside criminals' dead bodies to see how God created us, so I can understand better how to heal people. So did your grandfather and great-grandfather. But cooking human flesh to render fat for a charm would be much more repugnant to Him. I wouldn't use even a criminal's body for such a purpose; I'm a man of science, not superstition.

"Though a physician from the university," he added, a trace of scorn in his voice, "wouldn't think of touching a corpse himself, even to instruct his students." In the medical schools, he'd been told, the lecturer stood no nearer to the dissection table than necessary to demonstrate with a long pointer, while some grimy-handed minion in a leather apron did the cutting and the pinning.

He left it unsaid, but Charles understood: The executioner could indulge in no such fastidious snobbery.

"The body of the man we hanged on Tuesday is still here. He has a malformed arm. Would you like to see?"

They would have to send him off for burial soon, if the weather stayed warm. Charles nodded. Fresh corpses weren't particularly dreadful; he'd seen them often enough at the gallows. Though religious law forbade dissection of human corpses, the bodies of the executed were an exception; by their crimes they had forfeited the privilege and blessing that all good, law-abiding Christians could claim, burial in consecrated ground. The executioner had the right to the body, clothes, and effects of his victim—*patient*—for his own profit, and could sell cadavers to the medical school if he pleased, or examine them himself.

Jean-Baptiste unlocked a further door at the rear of the laboratory, which led to a room with another north-facing skylight. Something lay covered on a table in the center. He pulled away the sheet. "See here?"

He had already begun to dissect the man's arm; Charles could see how the muscles were laid out and how the bones beneath were crooked. "I expect he broke his arm when he was a child, and it wasn't set properly," Jean-Baptiste continued.

It wasn't horrid at all, but fascinating. Jean-Baptiste knew how to set bones, among many other useful skills more appropriate to a doctor than an executioner.

I'd like to be able to do that, to be like him, Charles thought; and hastily thrust away the image of his father's sword, the headsman's sword that had belonged to three generations of Sansons and someday would belong to him as it had to his forefathers, forever and ever, time without end, amen.

2

Jean-Baptiste's extensive property on Rue d'Enfer was near the edge of Paris, avoiding prying eyes, with few close neighbors but a livery stable and the orchard of an undistinguished monastery. Charles had already heard all the feeble jokes about "Rue d'Enfer": New visitors invariably thought they were being terribly clever and original when they remarked that it was appropriate the executioner and his family should live on a street called Hell or Torment. His tutor had solemnly assured him, however, that "Enfer" had nothing to do with the infernal regions or even with torture, that it was merely a corruption of old Latin from the long-ago days when the Romans built Paris, *via inferior*, lesser street. Such interesting and useless bits of erudition often made daily lessons with Père Grisel more enjoyable than not.

At present, though, he had to concentrate on the other half of his education. He hefted the wooden blade again, with both hands, and held it straight out before him at arm's length, as Jean-Baptiste had taught him. Seven seconds . . . eight . . . nine . . . ten.

He lowered it again, gratefully, muscles aching. Six months ago he'd been barely able to hold the heavy thing in the proper position for five seconds without trembling from wrist to shoulder with the unwieldy weight. Now he could hold it steady for ten and swing it about his head without losing his balance.

He lifted it slowly, above his right shoulder, and brought it whistling down at a sharp angle to the post, his target a two-inch strip of whitewash, three and a half feet from the ground. The wooden sword struck the post with a hollow *thunk* and bounced away, the shock vibrating through his arms.

He grinned at the new dent in the center of the whitewashed strip as he mopped the sweat from his face. As long as you viewed it as a mere test of skill—of strong limbs, a sharp eye, and good aim—then proficiency with the dummy sword was something to be proud of. As for its true purpose . . . well, he wouldn't think about that. Father had never needed to use the sword, had he? If God granted his prayers, neither would he.

"Bull's-eye," said his sister Madeleine, hurrying past the hens scratching for tidbits in the stableyard. "Charlot, can you stop for a minute and go out front?"

"What's the matter?"

She cocked her head, dark hair spilling from beneath her linen cap. "Something's up. Can't you hear?"

"Hear what?" He raised the sword again, uninterested. Wagons rattling, mules braying, and shouting matches between carters were nothing new. Now that he was on a good streak—

"Well, listen! It sounds like trouble."

Charles glanced impatiently toward the house, which was set well back from Rue d'Enfer, behind a high stone wall. Beyond, in the street that was *not* Hell Street, a voice—no, two treble voices were shrilly disputing something. Street brats making trouble again, he guessed. The local boys, respectable householders' sons and beggars' barefoot urchins alike, often thought it a fine joke to loiter together outside (for everybody knew which was the executioner's house) and throw rotten fruit, dead rats, horse manure, or even scraps of offal from the slaughterhouse over the wall.

He reluctantly thrust the wooden sword in the tackroom and shouldered on his waistcoat. "I'll get rid of them."

It was not, he discovered upon reaching the front gate, a clutch of rowdy youths in the road, merely a couple of children—one of them, saints preserve us, his brother Nicolas, yelling like a herring-woman. A small boy was staring him down. Nicolas clenched his fists at his sides, shaking with wounded schoolboy pride, face scarlet with suppressed tears.

"Liar! You take it back! My father's an officer of the high court! He's a gentleman!"

"Well, *my* father says *your* father is the *bourreau*!"

Charles froze. Oh, Lord, was this fair to the poor kid? He was only eight.

His father and stepmother had always taken pains to conceal the family profession from their children; Madeleine and he, the two eldest, had been ordered to say nothing to the little ones until they were "old enough." Among the adults, in commonplace conversation and in their day-to-day activities, no one mentioned where Jean-Baptiste and the lackeys went or what they were up to when they left the house every morning. But now the truth had burst in upon Charles's little brother in an unexpected and disagreeable manner.

"I told my parents I went to your house yesterday," the other boy continued, keeping half a dozen paces between Nicolas and himself. "And when I said it was the big one behind the high wall on Rue d'Enfer, my mother said, 'But that's the hangman's house!' And my father said she was right, it was the house of Sanson, the *bourreau*, and I wasn't to see you ever again because you're Sanson's brat."

Nicolas stared at him a moment, trembling, before fleeing through the gate. Charles imagined his brother felt as if he'd been suddenly stripped naked in the street.

He barked "Be off with you!" at the other boy and followed Nicolas into the house, soon finding him in the kitchen, sobbing into his mother's apron. Jeannette, plump, mild-mannered, perpetually pregnant, stood stroking his hair, saying nothing. After a moment, as the cook—an executioner's sister herself—glanced sympathetically at little Nicolas before returning to her work, Jeannette turned to Charles.

"You'd better fetch your father."

He thought his brother would prefer privacy during the conversation that would surely follow. "I'll take Nico to the study."

A quarter hour later Nicolas calmed, and let Jeannette scrub at his tear-streaked face with a clean rag. Charles took his hand and ushered him to Jean-Baptiste's private chamber. Nicolas would not let go of his hand and so he led the boy inside and lingered by the glass-fronted bookcase where Jean-Baptiste kept his most treasured scientific volumes.

"What happened?" his father asked, beckoning Nicolas to his lap. "Did someone call you names?"

"Some local boy—" Charles began, but Nicolas interrupted him.

"It was Pierre Bonnemain—the boy who came with me to play in the garden yesterday."

Jean-Baptiste glanced at Charles, shaking his head, as if saying *I knew nothing good could come of that.*

"What did he say to you?"

"Horrible lies," Nicolas said, and glared down at the wine-red Turkish carpet as if it, rather than the brat outside, had insulted him, avoiding their father's eyes. "That you were the *bourreau.*"

Charles winced. Brute. Butcher. Hangman. *Bourreau.* It was one thing to discover from your father's own lips, as he and Madeleine had, that your papa was master of an indispensable, honorable, though despised and dreaded profession; but quite another to hear that vile word flung at you, and from one whom you'd thought until then was a friend. *I'd have wept and screamed, too, Nico.* He felt his own face grow hot with anger on his little brother's behalf.

"I am not a *bourreau,*" Jean-Baptiste said. He paused for an instant. "But I won't deny you the truth. Nicolas, that boy was right, to a point. I am the master, or executor, of high works—*maître des hautes œuvres*, the master executioner of Paris."

Nicolas stared at him, speechless.

"What's . . ." he began at last, and stopped.

What, in fact, Charles thought, was the grand-sounding title "executor of high works" supposed to mean, anyway? "Hangman," now—that had at least the virtue of being unambiguous.

"When you're naughty and break a rule," Charles said softly, "Father punishes you, doesn't he?"

Nicolas nodded. No doubt he remembered a not-excessively-hard caning he'd received for climbing to an upper shelf in the larder and stealing—and breaking—a pot of cherry preserves.

"And then your mamma and I hope you've learned your lesson," said Jean-Baptiste.

"Yes, Father."

"Well, you know that God and the king have made rules to protect us all. But many wicked grownup men and women break those rules by stealing, or killing someone, or speaking ill of the king, or blaspheming against the Lord. And they, too, must be punished for what they did, mustn't they?"

"Yes, Father."

Of course Nicolas had heard of public whipping and even of executions by the time he was ten; who hadn't? But you couldn't possibly imagine, Charles thought, that any of the terrifying *bourreaux* who carried them out might be related to you, might be your own papa.

Jean-Baptiste pondered his next words as the boy cuddled into his shoulder, sniffling.

"You see," he said at length, "if people must be punished for breaking the laws, then of course someone must punish them, just as I must birch you and your brothers when you're naughty. Now no decent man would enjoy hurting a fellow human creature, any more than I like whipping my children. But someone must do it for the good of society, even if he doesn't like it, so that law-abiding, God-fearing people will be safe and happy. And the *maître des hautes œuvres* is the man whose solemn task it is to punish criminals in the king's name."

"But isn't that the *bourreau*?"

"No, it's not!" Charles exclaimed, fury at the scorn and cruelty of small boys—and of most of their elders, as well—driving him to interrupt his father. Already, at fourteen, he knew that only the lowest and crudest of those who specialized in applying torture during interrogation, the *questionnaires*, heard the damning word *bourreau* without wincing.

"Charles is right. I'm no *bourreau*, but an officer of the court, with a title, just like the prosecutor-general."

"But why are *you* the ex'cutioner, if you don't like doing it?"

"Because my father was the executioner before me."

Jean-Baptiste paused. Charles knew he was pondering the delicate matter of letting Nicolas realize that his forebears, for the past sixty years and more, had bequeathed their despised but lucrative offices to their sons because an executioner's son couldn't hope to find employment elsewhere.

No, Nico, Charles said silently, *you weren't fated to be a cloth merchant, or a lawyer, or a soldier, or a surgeon; your future, like mine, must be in the business of pain and death.* Nicolas, however, had evidently not attempted to reason that far.

"Father . . ." He still wouldn't meet Jean-Baptiste's eyes. "A *bourreau* kills and hurts people, doesn't he? Why *aren't* you a *bourreau*, then?"

"Many ignorant people call the executioner a *bourreau*. But it means only 'brute' or 'butcher'—words that are an insult to our profession, which is one of duty and honor, never forget that. The executioner is the servant of the king and the high court, the representative of God's justice; he's the avenger of the victim of crime, the avenger of the innocent."

They were silent for a long while, as Nicolas pondered all he had learned and Charles glowered at the gold-stamped leather spine of *Medicinal Herbs of the Île-de-France and Picardy* on Jean-Baptiste's bookshelf.

"Is that why you told me to say my name is Longval?" Nicolas ventured. "Because people don't like us and call us filthy names?"

"Your name *is* Longval. Nicolas-Charles-Gabriel Sanson de Longval. Your grandfather's grandfather was a gentleman: steward to the lord of Longval manor, near Abbeville." Jean-Baptiste stroked Nicolas's cheek. Nicolas summoned up a wan smile; Charles wondered what he was thinking, now that he knew just who was touching him with those tainted hands. (*Bourreau* . . .)

"May I go, Father?"

Jean-Baptiste and Charles exchanged glances as Nicolas hurried from the room.

"Have you been practicing with the wooden sword as I asked you to?" Jean-Baptiste said, at last breaking the silence.

"Yes, Father."

"How are you progressing?"

"My aim's improving. I hit the mark three times today."

"Good." He gestured to the door. "Go on, back to the yard, or your books."

Charles escaped, eager for a wash after sword practice, to find Madeleine sitting on his bed, glancing through the illustrations of wild animals in his book of natural history.

"So did Father explain everything to Nico?"

"As much as he could."

"You and I weren't much older, when Father told us."

But we didn't learn about it from some spiteful little brat who called Father a *bourreau*, did we, he said to himself. He poured cold water into the basin and mopped at his face.

Madeleine closed the book and sat brooding for a moment, chin balanced on fists. Perhaps, he guessed, she was wondering about the heavenly caprices that made some girls princesses and other girls, perhaps cleverer and prettier girls, executioners' daughters.

"Do you ever think about it—about the future?" she said.

"The future?"

"You know, when you . . . take Father's place."

Charles scowled as he reached for a linen towel. All other professions were closed to an executioner's son, forever a pariah, contaminated by associations with torture, death, and corpses; you might as well have been born a Jew. It was inevitable that he, like Jean-Baptiste's three other surviving sons, would have no choice, in reaching manhood, but to become an executioner himself.

"That won't be for a long time. He's not old."

"But you must think about it sometimes."

"Huh. Whenever I go out to practice swinging that sword around."

"*I* think about it," Madeleine said wistfully, "when I see a good-looking boy in the street."

Charles laughed. At fourteen, he could still laugh easily, much of the time. "What's that got to do with it?"

"It's not funny. I want to marry a nice boy someday—and then I remember that even if somebody did like me, eventually he'd find out who my father is." *And then*, she didn't need to add, *and then he wouldn't have anything to do with me.*

"You'll get married someday," Charles said, uninterested in the fantasies of thirteen-year-old girls. "Unless you want to be a nun."

"But I know I'll end up marrying somebody in the profession."

Charles shrugged. They both knew that girls born into the

dynasties that had, by force of circumstance, claimed the title of executioner for their own, rarely found husbands outside the profession; they had as narrow a choice as did princesses.

"Just the way you know you'll be working for Father soon," Madeleine added.

"I'd rather be a doctor. I'd much rather discover what's wrong with people, and cure them, than . . ."

"Poor Charlot," she said, after a lengthy silence. "I wouldn't want to do it, either. But maybe Nico could be Father's assistant. Maybe they could send you away to study medicine, in five or ten years, when the boys are older."

"Nobody would let me into a medical school, once they knew—"

"I mean send you far away, to those German duchies or somewhere. You'd have to learn German, though."

"They speak Latin at the universities. I could manage."

"See? And once you'd got your degree, you could stay there. Where they've never heard of the Sansons. Or the Bergers, or the Jouënnes—"

"Or the Desmorests, or the Hérissons," he interrupted her, laughing again. "Or the Zelles or the Tronsons or the Levasseurs or the Féreys or the Barbiers or the Vermeilles," he continued, rattling off the names of the chief families in the profession; "or any of our thousands of cousins." He cuffed her playfully. "Enough!" She cuffed him back and they collapsed, giggling, on the bed.

3

"Charles," Jean-Baptiste whispered, trying to move his hand. His speech was strangely slurred, like someone speaking through water.

Charles attempted to jostle a cushion beneath his head. "Father . . . Father, please listen to me. Tell me what's the matter. Are you ill?"

He didn't have a fever, didn't have a sign of a wound; and who would wound Father, who would force his way into *this* house?

"I . . . I can't feel my hands . . . my right hand . . ."

Charles sat back on his heels, heart hammering as he racked his memory for clues to Jean-Baptiste's sudden affliction. An ordinary illness he could understand, but not this strange malady that had attacked his tall, robust father without warning, leaving him helpless on the floor of his study.

Above him, Jeannette wrung her hands. She was more than competent at managing the servants and children and keeping the household running smoothly, but she tended to go to pieces in a crisis, whether it was a sudden illness or a shortage of loaves at the baker's.

"What's the matter with him?"

"I don't know."

"But he's been teaching you—"

"Only for a few months!" he exclaimed, wanting to shout at the top of his voice, *What the devil do you want from me?* "You expect me to cure him, and I'm not even fifteen yet!"

"Charles—"

"Mamma, please, *please* stay calm. Where's Grand'mère? Has Jérôme gone for Dr. Lejeune?"

"Yes—but I can't leave Jean-Baptiste like this—"

"Do you want to lose the baby?" His glance slid from her face to the bulge beneath her skirts—her eleventh and Jean-Baptiste's thirteenth; his father was both a good Catholic and a man of sharp appetites. He struggled to his feet, fighting down panic, reeling in mind if not in body. "Go to your bedroom and rest, and keep Grandmother beside you."

As he spoke, the tall figure of his grandmother approached from the passage. He pushed Jeannette toward her.

"What in the name of the saints is all this noise about?" Marthe Dubut Sanson demanded, glancing from Jeannette to Charles to the supine form of her son. "What's the matter, is Jean-Baptiste ill?"

"Jérôme's gone to fetch the doctor. Take Mamma upstairs. And I need some brandy."

She hesitated, unsure whether to follow his instructions, or to remain and tend to her son. "What happened? Did he fall?"

"*Please*, Grand'mère."

"I'll not have a boy giving me orders in my own household!" She took a step toward Jean-Baptiste.

"Grand'mère," Charles said, keeping his voice low, "Father is ill. I don't know what's wrong with him—though it might be an apoplexy." He had already read enough of his father's medical library to come now to the final, dreadful conclusion that what had felled Jean-Baptiste was more than a mere faint. "But if Mamma isn't kept calm, you know she might fall ill herself, and lose the baby."

Marthe scowled but at last led her daughter-in-law out, adding over her shoulder as they disappeared down the passage, "Take care of him, boy."

"Lie quiet, Father," Charles repeated, uselessly. "Lie quiet, the doctor will be here soon." He felt Jean-Baptiste's pulse for the third time, as if it would grow strong again by his wishing for it, but it was weak and irregular. "The doctor's coming."

Madeleine hurried in with a bottle and spoon. "What's the matter with Father?"

"I—he might have had an apoplectic fit."

"Is that serious?"

"People can die from them."

"Father!" Madeleine gasped. She dropped to her knees beside Jean-Baptiste and cradled his head in her arms. "Father, can you hear me?"

Jean-Baptiste's hand quivered. "I'm sorry . . . Charles . . ."

"What should you be sorry about?" He tried to slip a little brandy between his father's pallid lips. "Here, swallow this if you can."

"It's . . . on your head now . . . if I should die . . ."

Voices outside heralded the doctor's arrival as Madeleine burst into tears.

ço   ⁊

"He's not grievously ill," said Dr. Lejeune. "His mind is unaffected, although you'll find him hard to understand."

Charles kept his ear pressed against the keyhole in the passage outside their parents' bedroom, though he stole a quick look at Madeleine, who was hovering beside him. She gave him a half-hearted smile and squeezed his shoulder.

"But?" said Marthe. Jeannette was lying down in the adjoining small bedroom, the maids fussing over her, and Marthe, as usual, had taken charge.

"He's very weak, his right arm is greatly enfeebled, almost paralyzed, and I doubt he'll walk again for some time, if ever."

"I see." Marthe was usually adept at concealing her emotions, but Charles heard the strain in her voice. If Grand'mère was troubled and showed it, then surely disaster was looming, storm clouds were gathering to engulf them all.

"Courage, madame," the polite voice went on, kindly, reassuring. "Once victims of these fits manage to survive the first days—"

"—Which many do not—"

"True, but since your son is only thirty-four, and was strong until today, I think it likely—if God wills it—that he'll prevail."

"You see?" Madeleine whispered, with another squeeze.

"And sometimes, madame, the survivors of apoplectic fits do recover, in time, to be almost as hale as ever. Monsieur Sanson is sure to recover, though it'll require plenty of time and rest."

Footsteps approached the door. Charles scrambled up and fled down the passage with his sister.

"The master executioner can't be a cripple, can he?" Madeleine said once they were safely away.

Charles shook his head. Though it was an unwritten rule, you expected the master at the public scaffold to be a commanding figure, sturdy, strong, a Hercules in an immaculate scarlet coat with fine lace at his throat and wrists, the embodiment of royal authority and God's justice at work. A frail, ill man in a wheeled chair—no, the picture was all wrong, unthinkable.

"So," Madeleine said at last, "who's going to take over?"

Eight days later, Jean-Baptiste was still alive, still speaking, gesturing feebly with his left hand. He could, he managed to croak, at least hold a pen.

The following Thursday, Marthe drew Charles aside after supper. "A word with you, Charles."

He followed her and her candle into Jean-Baptiste's study, hoping that she hadn't disarranged the books and papers. "Grand'mère?"

"You're coming with me tomorrow to the Palais de Justice." She touched her candle to a few others in the candelabrum. "I want you in your best suit of clothes—the brown coat with the green striped waistcoat—so have those lazy servant girls draw you a bath tonight, and be sure you scrub yourself well. And clean your good shoes."

"I don't understand."

"Monsieur Joly de Fleury wishes to take a look at you. Don't forget to polish the buckles!" she added, with a disapproving glance down at his scuffed everyday shoes with their dented steel buckles.

"Monsieur Joly . . . at *me*?" Guillaume-François-Louis Joly de Fleury was the royal prosecutor-general and the most influential magistrate in the land.

"Stop gaping like a halfwit, Charles. Didn't you see the messenger, day before yesterday? He was taking your father's letter of resignation back to the Palais de Justice."

"Resignation!"

"Do you think a man who can barely move his legs—sign his own name, even—is fit to be royal executioner?"

"But Dr. Lejeune said he'd get better—"

"It will take months, perhaps years. That's neither here nor there. What matters is today. He's resigned the duties of his office—at least for the present—and it's vital that the Paris title shouldn't pass out of the family."

"But Uncle . . ." Charles began. Gabriel Sanson lived in Reims, a day's travel by fast postchaise, and visited Rue d'Enfer so often that he was practically a member of his elder brother's household.

Gabriel had sped to Paris to provide support during the crisis and temporarily take over Jean-Baptiste's duties, though he would have to return home eventually, for he had obligations of his own as executioner of Reims. But Charles suspected that Reims, a provincial town one-tenth the size of the capital, made far fewer demands of its *maître des hautes œuvres.* In Reims Gabriel wouldn't be tasked with the almost daily duties—the minor but frequent public chastisements of flogging, branding, and pillorying, and the burning of forbidden books and other undesirable items—of the executioner of Paris, a city teeming with miscreants.

"The title could go to Uncle—"

"Not even to Gabriel. Not when your father has four sons who could succeed him. You're eldest and next in line for it. But you're considerably underage, and Monsieur Joly de Fleury wants to see for himself if you're fit to fill his shoes."

Finally, with a thrill of panic, Charles understood: She had already proposed her solution to the prosecutor-general.

The prospect of someday inheriting Jean-Baptiste's title and duties was something he had preferred not to think about. Inheriting them at the age of fourteen was unimaginable.

"No. *No,* Grand'mère. Not me. Let Uncle Gabriel take over."

"Gabriel's not your father's heir, you are."

"But I don't want it. The position. I—I can't do it."

"Nonsense. You're a strong, healthy, well-schooled lad. Hasn't Jean-Baptiste taken you with him plenty of times to the Halles and the Place de Grève?"

"Yes—"

So you may understand the meaning and gravity of our profession, Jean-Baptiste had told him.

"You know what it's about. All you have to do is give an order now and then; the servants will do the rest. Any ham-fisted fool can lock a felon in the pillory or toss books into a bonfire."

The master's sole duty, Charles knew, on an ordinary day of chastising ordinary culprits, was to oversee and make it legal with his presence. "Yes—but—but—Father never meant me to be—what he is—before I grew up. I'm not fifteen yet."

"Listen, boy." Marthe seated herself in Jean-Baptiste's armchair as if it were a throne. "It's time to remind you of some hard facts. How many brothers and sisters have you?"

"Seven." What had that to do with his predicament?

"Seven brothers and sisters," she repeated. "Seven mouths to feed. Add to those your father's, and your mother's, and mine, and your own. And eight servants. And the baby that's due in two months, if all goes well with Jeannette. Twenty people to be fed and clothed, and the household to be kept up properly. Do you think the money for that grows on pear trees in the orchard? We need your father's salary, and that won't be coming in any longer if he gives away his title."

"But Grand-père left us plenty of property," he protested, with the vague idea that the family had been well provided for, with a healthy income rolling in from rents, annuities, shares in royal funds, and other such sources, in perpetuity. The state, for centuries, had offered a man a wealth of profitable rights, privileges, and incomes in exchange for his services in mutilating and killing those whom the law had condemned, and Jean-Baptiste had always said that his father and grandfather had invested their accumulated fortunes well.

"Father says that he had money invested . . . it brings in . . . I don't know exactly—"

"The income from your grandfather's fortune doesn't go as far as it used to. Expenses, rising prices, a houseful of children to be fed, clothed, and educated—money's not what it once was. And once you touch your capital, you're done for; you should know that, even at your age." Marthe paused for a moment, giving weight to her pronouncement.

"Listen to me: Jean-Baptiste's salary is a fine one and we depend on it to supplement our income. But without it—with such a large family, so many expenses, we'll be struggling to make ends meet, and it can only go downhill from there."

What about keeping up the house and the stables? she continued as Charles listened, eyes cast down, staring numbly at her shoes peeping from beneath her gray woolen gown. What about paying a decent servants' wage, so that we can get the best class of assistants for your father, good clean-living men, and not have to hire drunks and layabouts? What about dowries for your sisters? Madeleine's thirteen already and you can't have her tossed into the market with just her good looks and good cooking, not these days.

"But why can't Uncle Gabriel take over the Paris title, just for now, and live here with us?" Cousin Louis could stay in Reims and be deputy executioner in name there, he thought, trying to work it out—Cousin Louis wasn't much more than nine, but that was someone else's problem—and Uncle Gabriel could come to Paris and be the head of the family until Father recovered. "That would work, wouldn't it?"

"I'll tell you why it won't," said Marthe. "Yesterday, when I called on Monsieur Joly de Fleury, I found him dismissing two men I recognized. They're distant cousins of yours—related to Marguerite Jouënne who married your great-grandfather, if you must know—from Amiens. They'd come to town to steal the Paris title, your father's office, out from under our noses. They know the value of a royal appointment, even if you don't."

She paused to glare at him through the feeble candlelight and he thought it best to nod and murmur, "Yes, Grand'mère."

"I believe old Jouënne and his son had a good chance of winning the post, until they offered Joly a bribe to ensure it. Obviously they'd tried to grease the palm of the only honest official in Paris, for he threw them out."

Charles smiled, despite himself. Marthe let out an exasperated sigh, a sound to which he was well accustomed.

"Gather your wits together, Charles. What I'm trying to tell you is that every clumsy provincial hangman from the back of beyond would give his right hand for the Paris title."

He knew. He'd heard it before, had had it incessantly drummed into him since he was "old enough," initiated into the select company of those who knew about the family profession and never spoke of it. To be the hangman of some little town a hundred leagues from anywhere—that's nothing, that's less than nothing, Marthe would say—but *Paris*! The Paris title is an honor and the proudest of burdens; Paris is where the executioner is only one step away from the high court of the Parlement that sits in the Grand' Chambre, the Golden Hall of the Palais de Justice—the highest court in the land, a finger's breadth from the king.

"Would I have taken your father, twenty-seven years ago," she went on, "and insisted on *his* rights to his father's office, if I didn't see it as something to be held on to with both hands?"

Jean-Baptiste, Charles knew, had been titular executioner of Paris since the age of seven. It was a family legend: A few days after her husband's untimely death, Marthe, still a beautiful woman and striking in her widow's black, had marched her small son into the prosecutor-general's presence to demand that the boy be promised his late father's lucrative post when he was grown; meanwhile, the chief assistant would step in to do the offices. Marthe had later found it politic, when her mourning was over, to marry the chief assistant and ensure for once and for all that everything was safely kept within the family.

"Well? Would I?"

"No, Grand'mère."

"Now what if you refuse to claim the title, and Gabriel applies for it, but loses it to some provincial social climber who has as much right to it as he? Out of the family it goes and that's the end of us—the end of three generations of Sansons to hold the office. Whereas *you*, Charles, you're your father's eldest son and legitimate heir. You have the right to his office over anyone else, and if you step in as his deputy, the transfer is guaranteed. So you're going to take his place or I'll know the reason why."

She paused and stared at him, as if daring him to challenge her.

"And what if I've never wanted to be a *bourreau*?"

In one swift movement Marthe rose from her chair, strode to him, and slapped him. He stumbled backward, gasping, and pressed cold fingers to his smarting cheek.

"Don't you let me hear you say that word again. You insult your father and your whole family." Marthe was the daughter of a master carpenter, not a hangman, but Charles had never heard her speak a single word that might imply she had degraded herself, thirty-nine years before, by allying herself with the Sansons. "Are you ashamed of your father and your forefathers? Is that it?"

"No!"

He saw a dark streak of blood on his fingertips; one of her rings had cut his cheek.

"No, Grand'mère. I'm not ashamed of us. I know it's an honorable profession—and—and that it's useful and—necessary. I just don't want to—do—*that*. I—I want to be a doctor, to treat people like Father, or a surgeon. I want to heal people, help them—not kill them."

"And who do you think will pay you for your services, Dr. Sanson? Do you really think wealthy folk will send for you, or visit your consulting room, when they learn you're the son of the executioner?"

It was the worst possible time, he decided, to bring up the subject of his going abroad to pursue medicine. "Plenty of people come to Father with ailments." Jean-Baptiste had always earned a modest second income from his medical practice, though he charged his poorer patients little or nothing for his services. "Rich people, too. Monsieur de Lally, and the Comte de Charolais himself recommended Father to—"

"Bah! Few enough of them are rich. Most can afford no one else. That's a fine way to live, to take your fees in a broom here, a few eggs there. Your father practices healing out of the goodness of his heart, not to earn a living by it." She seized his collar and jerked him toward her, adding, "I'd like to see you try to support twenty people on what you'd earn as an inexperienced quack doctor, even if you weren't fourteen years old, and could open a consulting room tomorrow.

"We'll have no more talk of this. Now go and clean yourself up."

The royal prosecutor-general's office at the Palais de Justice was very large and very grand, with little cupids peeping out from the moldings at the ceiling, and gilded bas-reliefs of swords and shields and scales of justice gleaming in the spotless white paneling of the *boiseries*. An enormous portrait of Louis XV, splendid in his royal robes, stared down as Charles surreptitiously glanced about him.

The prosecutor-general rose from his desk, imposing in his full wig, even without his judicial robes and chain of office. Gilt rococo festoons ran along the edges of the desk and down the length of its legs. It was almost as big as his bed, Charles realized. Despite his nervousness, he thought that, between the desk and the pair of eight-branched crystal candelabra that stood at either end of it, he'd never seen anything so beautiful. Was this how the great world lived?

"Monsieur prosecutor, this is my grandson Charles Sanson, of whom we spoke." Marthe was resplendent in her best flounced and hooped Sunday gown of dark blue silk with the cascades of lace at bodice and sleeves. She did not curtsy to Joly de Fleury, as most women would have done before such a powerful official as the king's prosecutor. She had always taken fierce pride in being the widow of Paris's master executioner and mother of another, and in public carried herself with the dignity and forbidding hauteur of a dowager duchess.

"Come forward, young man," said the prosecutor-general, beckoning. Charles was hanging back behind Marthe, devoutly wishing he were at home with his books instead of being paraded through the law courts, hair curled and powdered, and turned out in chocolate-brown dress coat and culotte, stiff striped waistcoat, silk stockings, and silver-buckled shoes.

"He's the eldest son of Charles-Jean-Baptiste Sanson, the master executioner," Marthe said. "I request in this emergency, monsieur, that he be confirmed as deputy in his father's office, to which he's heir by right, until my son recovers."

"But this is a boy, Madame Sanson." Joly de Fleury glanced in Charles's direction, sizing him up and, Charles imagined, no doubt finding him wanting. Evidently the prosecutor was unaware that Jean-Baptiste had inherited his position when even younger than Charles.

Charles bowed as Marthe had told him to do when the prosecutor-general looked at him ("Be deferential, boy—remember that he holds your future—all our futures—in his hands"), and nearly stumbled over a gilt and brocade chair behind him. He knew the bruise on his cheekbone, where Marthe had slapped him the day before, was turning purple. *I look as if I'd been in a fistfight*, he thought, like some urchin from Les Halles, and stepped back a pace and tried to be inconspicuous.

"Charles will turn fifteen in a fortnight, monsieur, and he's tall and strong for his years, as you can see—in five years, or less, he'll be as much of a man as you could wish for. He can manage until his father recovers. Meanwhile, what difference does it make? Our servants do all the dirty work."

"In most cases, madame." Joly de Fleury was imagining the scene, Charles guessed, should an inexperienced boy of fifteen be obliged to behead a nobleman with the sword of justice.

"Bah!" Marthe swept aside his objections with a wave of her hand. "What chance is there of that, I'd like to know? And Charles has been practicing his swordsmanship all this past summer. He's a clever lad; he'll manage or I'll know the reason why."

Joly de Fleury turned back to Charles.

"Well, young Sanson, do you think yourself prepared to act as deputy for your father in his solemn office? It's a grave responsibility for one of your age."

The prosecutor-general seemed kinder than Charles had feared he would be. He was almost tempted to blurt out, *No, I'm not, I'm only fourteen and I never wanted anything to do with this*, but knew that Marthe was watching him.

"Yes, monsieur. I'm prepared."

"And you've been to the scaffold and seen the customary chastisements and know what it's all about?"

"Yes, monsieur."

"And do you have the stomach to direct an execution and see a man or woman put to death, perhaps cruelly, according to the dictates of the law?"

"I hope so, monsieur." (Liar—liar.) "I—I've attended hangings, now and then, when my father brought me along to learn my business." He dared a swift glance at Marthe, who was still glaring at him, as if expecting him to add something else. "I c-could do it if I had to."

Couldn't I?

"Very well." Joly de Fleury turned to Marthe. "I think the young man will be satisfactory. I'll have the necessary documents drawn up."

"You're most generous, monsieur." Marthe endeavored to keep the triumph from her expression and look properly grateful.

Now, my boy, the prosecutor-general continued, the situation is this: I can invest you only as your father's primary deputy and guaranteed heir to the post, for not even the Parlement of Paris can legally transfer the office until your father's final retirement, or death. But in fact, if not in name, once the papers are signed and the seals affixed, you will be—by the grace of God and His Majesty—Executor and Master of High Works for the City and Provostry of Paris, and also of Versailles: the most solemn and terrible representative of the king and his justice. Your father has carried out his duties in the position faithfully and well, and I hope you'll not take it lightly.

Joly de Fleury concluded his little speech and beamed benignly at Charles. Another minor problem disposed of. Charles nodded, not trusting his voice, and hurriedly bowed as Marthe sharply inclined her head, signaling to him. ("And you'll remember to bow properly as you've been taught, like a gentleman, or what do we pay a dancing master for?")

He sensed the improvement in her mood as they left the Palais de Justice and crossed the broad courtyard—they called it the Cour du Mai, the May Courtyard, no one seemed to know why. Before hailing a fiacre at the queue of waiting cabs by the tall iron gates, she pointed out Sainte-Chapelle, still the king's private chapel in Paris, where the holiest relic in France, Jesus' own crown of thorns, had been kept in a jeweled reliquary for five hundred years, since the days of St. Louis. She pointed next at the three round medieval towers that faced the quay. "Has Jean-Baptiste taken you there, to the Conciergerie?"

"Not to the Conciergerie, only to the Châtelet." Charles glanced down the street and across the Seine to the equally ancient riverside fortress that held the police courts and the dungeons where petty criminals were locked up until trial. Jean-Baptiste, as part of his regular duties, paid—had paid—a visit every morning to the Châtelet; there he'd inevitably collected various culprits who had been sentenced to flogging, branding, or exposure on the great pillory at the central market of the Halles.

The Conciergerie, Marthe told him as she imperiously gestured at a fiacre to cross over to them, was the prison attached to the law courts, where they kept important prisoners who were about to be tried or punished, or who had an appeal to plead before the Parlement. "Those three towers are part of it. You'll learn your way around it soon enough."

Won't I, though, he thought glumly.

Back at their home on Rue d'Enfer, he found his father, well covered with blankets, sitting in an armchair beside the bedroom fire. Jean-Baptiste listened to his account of the visit to the law courts and pressed his hand.

"I'm sorry th-this should . . . come to you s-s-so early."

"I'll be all right," Charles said, unwilling to upset him.

He thought—hoped?—his father's grip was a little stronger already, although his speech was still labored, and prayed that Jean-Baptiste would quickly recover. Perhaps he wouldn't have to be his deputy for long—and then, perhaps, then he could bring up the subject of studying medicine . . .

The papers from the Palais de Justice arrived two days later by one of the regular messengers, a decent enough fellow who was always ready to flirt charmingly and innocuously with Jeannette or Madeleine, unlike the other one who often looked as if he'd prefer to toss the orders at you for fear of accidentally brushing your hand. Charles slipped out of the house that afternoon and lit a candle for luck at Saint-Laurent, their parish church. Only a handful of people were about at that hour, huddled in their shawls or overcoats against the sunless February chill of the ancient stonework, where vines and frills and fantastic beasts writhed above him. He kept his head down, feeling, though he knew it foolish, as if everyone were looking at him.

Don't be silly, he told himself; ordinarily, when he went out alone, he was just one more teenaged boy in a plain, decent suit of clothes appropriate for the son of any respectable bourgeois. Nobody knew he was the executioner's heir. But he could not help feeling that the few men and women in the church, occupied with their solitary devotions, without warning were going to wheel about and stare at him and point, as they often did with his father, while whispering a few hasty words: Blessed Virgin, preserve us from the *bourreau's* touch.

He quickly muttered a prayer. All men were the same before God, weren't they?

Weren't they?

His first communion had taken place at Saint-Laurent, six or seven years before, with Madeleine, only a year and a week younger than he. It had been a private affair, just the two of them kneeling proud and nervous at the altar rail while the assembled family smiled behind them, applying handkerchiefs to the occasional sentimental tear. Nobody had told them why they hadn't been at Mass with the other children from the parish, but he'd worked it out later, once he knew how the Sansons earned their bread: because, of course, no one wanted their children coming too close to the *bourreau* or his children on any day, least of all that one.

Brute. Butcher. Hangman. *Bourreau.* Look there, that's the *bourreau*, keep away from him, it's bad luck to step into his shadow.

He hastily made the sign of the cross and wondered, as he glanced over his shoulder, *is this what it's going to be like for the rest of my life?*

4

I'll admit it; I was a brat.

What else do you think I could have been?

But I never did what they say I did.

It was always hard luck for us, ever since I could remember. We never had much, because Father never had any get-up-and-go in him; we could see that, even when I was a kid of six or eight. The money kept going out, and it hardly ever came in.

But we managed somehow, kept a respectable household, no matter how poor we were, until Mother died. Then Father just gave up. Then he stopped doing anything except tramping through the woodlands every day and drinking himself stupid every night. He slid farther and farther into debt until all we had left was an estate too rundown to make itself pay, and a moldy old château, and our pride. But you can't eat pride, or buy yourself a place in the world with it.

Hard luck, proud family of Lefebvre de La Barre.

That was when things really started to go downhill: in 'fifty-four, when I was nine and my brother Jacques thirteen, when my mother died, and my father's will to forge on seemed to dry up and disappear with her into her grave. He didn't even go to her funeral. That was for me and Jacques.

"Disgraceful," I overheard some neighbor say, as we shuffled out of the chapel. "He didn't care enough to see his own wife buried?"

We knew better. We knew he'd loved her so much that he couldn't bear the idea of seeing her in her coffin. If he never did see her lying there, stiff and pale, beads wrapped for eternity around bony fingers, he could still drift about the château and not have to face the fact that she was gone. He could keep on telling himself she was just in the next room, just around the corner, just a few footsteps away . . .

We got the worse part of the bargain. As Father spent more and more of his waking hours in a wine-clouded haze, Jacques and I took off to play with the peasant boys and go swimming in the river. Once we were a little older, and Father'd given up even the pretense of going out to the woods to shoot a rabbit for the pot, we'd also go poaching with their fathers so we'd have something on the table at dinner besides boiled turnips and chestnuts—even if it was just a squirrel. The château was big, dark, cold, and nearly empty; the farmers' cottages were jollier. And trapping and fishing with villagers like that old fox Dumont were a lot more fun than moldering at home and watching Father drink himself to death.

All Jacques and I had was each other. My mother had seven children all told, but only the two of us survived—one more way the noble house of Lefebvre de La Barre was going downhill fast. Like the soil, the stock was growing tired, sickly, played out. My great-grandfather had been a famous soldier of the king, governor of New France over in America, well rewarded for his good service, but Jean-Baptiste Alexandre Lefebvre de La Barre, his grandson, my father, in spite of the impressive-sounding name, hadn't inherited his ancestors' vigor. He was content to dream in his library, letting what money he had slip through his fingers, now and then making a stab at some farming that barely paid for itself.

I scarcely knew a world existed outside the little country parish of Férolles and the Thursday market at Brie-Comte-Robert. Paris is only seven leagues away from Brie, but it might as well have been on the moon. Jacques and I grew up out of doors, a couple of little savages in wooden shoes and homespun smocks like our tenants. Not much education: now and then lessons from the curé, Father Jouffroy, who taught us our catechism and our letters, how to read and write, a little Latin and religious history, and a lot of dull moral fables about saints. Nothing else. The world-shaking new philosophy of the Enlightenment hadn't yet shaken anything as far as Férolles-en-Brie.

It wasn't an easy time to be a country noble with nothing but the land to live on. Things were changing and the world was passing us by; you couldn't live on just your rents and dues for long, because the tenants had little enough themselves. Father tried to keep us going by mortgaging the estate and selling the furniture. If he hadn't spent most of the money he raised from it on wine—but what's past is past, and you can't do anything about it.

Sometimes, though, I wonder what my life would have been, if Mother hadn't died when she did. All this would never have happened—or at least it wouldn't have happened to *me*.

5

It was rather pathetic, Charles often thought, that among the crowds who came to stare at public chastisement, the one least eager to be present was the man in charge of the business.

It had already become a routine task, this watching out of the corner of his eye as the assistants flogged and branded petty malefactors or chained them to the pillory, or fed the bonfires that consumed heaps of illegal pornographic or philosophical books. The mundane chores—distasteful but not particularly distressing.

Executions were different, though. He had already attended his share of hangings, when Jean-Baptiste was in charge; but it was much different, oh, so much different, when he, rather than his father, was the one who gave the order, who nodded to Jérôme, directed him to pull the patient off the ladder and then break his neck.

But you can get used to anything, he discovered to his dismayed surprise at the end of his first summer as provisional executioner. Only half a year and he had already grown accustomed to being the official witness to corporal punishment and violent death.

In the middle of the following January, almost a year to the day since his father's apoplectic collapse, the messenger from the criminal court brought him the order he had hoped he would never see, the order for the execution in two days' time of one Michel Ruxton, condemned to be broken alive on the wheel for murder.

He had never seen a breaking, never heard much about them

from Jean-Baptiste except for the brutal fact of their existence. They
were far rarer than hangings, usually ordered two or three times a
year or less, as the edifying, terrifying penalty for the heinous crimes
of parricide, poisoning, and the like. Later, dourly reflecting upon
that glaring gap in his practical education, Charles supposed Jean-
Baptiste had meant well, had wanted to spare him nightmares, by
taking him only to the occasional hanging and not to the spectacle
of a man being smashed, blow by blow, to bloody pulp.

His father, he thought as he stared at the order in his hand,
could have offered him some guidance at such a moment, but Jean-
Baptiste had not spent a night at home on Rue d'Enfer for some
time. After Jeannette's baby, a girl, had been born, was sent off to
the usual wet-nurse at Meaux, and had died a few weeks later, they
had withdrawn to the ancient stone cottage half a day's journey
southeast of Paris. The cottage, a quiet country retreat hidden in
the midst of six acres of meadows and orchards, had been in the
family for fifty years. While old Marthe, with Madeleine's help,
remained to manage the household in town, Jean-Baptiste and
Jeannette had taken to spending weeks at a time at the cottage
with the smaller children, in the hope that the fresh air and
peaceful, rustic life would, in time, cure Jean-Baptiste of his para-
lysis and his grief.

Not long after the messenger had left, Madeleine came up to
Charles's room and found him hunched on the edge of the bed, still
staring at the magistrates' warrant.

"What's the matter? What did he bring you?"

He handed it to her.

"Oh. Oh, Charlot, that's horrible."

"I know." He took back the paper, wanting to crumple it and
fling it on the fire. "I . . . I hope I don't faint." Like the first Charles.
According to family legend, the first Sanson in the profession,
assisting his new wife's father, had collapsed on the scaffold—in
full view of the laughing, jeering crowd—the first time he attended
a breaking.

"Grand'mère said that Great-Grandfather wasn't the master
executioner then, just the chief aide. He was expected to take up
the club himself and do the breaking. Anybody might have fainted.

But that's Jérôme's job; you won't have to do that."

"Oh, that makes me feel much better!" He couldn't look at her. "It's all right, then, is it," he blurted out, "since all I have to do is stand about and give orders to Jérôme, while they torture a man to death in front of me."

"Well, I suppose the man deserves it. He killed someone. What's more, he killed a lawyer—an *avocat au parlement*, no less. A servant of the law, like Father . . . like you."

He gazed at her for a moment. It was all very well for his sister to make excuses; she'd seen only one execution, when Marthe took her three months previously to witness a hanging in order to better understand the profound meaning of the Sanson family's distinctive profession and its service to king and justice. Duty and honor, girl; never forget that.

"Nobody deserves *this*."

He stared once more at the warrant in his hand. He could not help wondering if the wretched Ruxton could possibly have made the man he killed suffer as much as the law had ordered Ruxton to suffer.

"I won't do it. I won't be there."

"But you've got to be!"

"Somebody has to. Not necessarily me." Uncle Gabriel was just downstairs, after all, discussing household business with Grandmother . . . he could stand in for Jean-Baptiste now and then, it was all legal. *If you ever need my help, Charles,* he'd kept declaring, *you know I'll lend a hand.*

Surely Gabriel had overseen a breaking before, and would know what he was supposed to do. He hurried down to the parlor, where his uncle was idly playing the harpsichord while Marthe mended a frayed cuff on the scarlet coat Charles wore when presiding at the scaffold.

"Uncle, could I speak to you for a moment?"

"What's on your mind, Charles?" Gabriel inquired, rising. Charles edged toward the door to the adjoining room.

"I need—"

"Anything you have to say to your uncle," Marthe interrupted, laying the coat aside, "you can say to us both."

"But it's—"

"It's about whatever order young Taillandier brought, isn't it? Well? You'd better get ready."

"It's a decree for a breaking," Charles said, without looking at her.

"Well?"

"I've never seen a breaking, and I don't want to."

"It's all right, Mother," Gabriel said. "The boy's a little young yet to have to endure that. I'll stand in for him. That's what you were going to ask me, eh, Charles?"

Charles nodded. Gratefully he reached out to hand the warrant to his uncle, but Marthe stepped between them and snatched it away.

"This is perfectly straightforward," she said, reading it. Public penance at the cathedral steps, quite as usual. Nine blows. No amputation of the hand, no burning alive, no special instructions. She glanced at him. "Jérôme knows what to do; there's no reason you shouldn't preside."

"But it's horrible!"

"Yes, it's horrible, and it's also the law. It may be the first time for you, but it won't be the last, and you had better get used to it."

"Grand'mère —"

"You'll do your duty as you've been ordered to. No excuses. Now you need to send a message to Guédon, right away."

"Who?"

"The man who builds the scaffolds! You can't conduct a breaking at the gallows. You need a new scaffold, specially built. Go on, then, tell Auguste to run over with a message. Do I have to do everything?"

"Uncle . . ." Charles began. Gabriel frowned and thrust his hands in his pockets.

"I'd take your place if I could, Charles, but this is between you and your grandmother. I'll come along with you, if you want, though I think you'll have to be present."

Charles turned back to Marthe. He had shot up, grown like a mustard plant during the past year and was now five or six inches taller than she.

"Grand'mère, please don't make me do this. I can't watch a man die this way. I'm—I'm not ashamed of who we are," he hastily added as he saw her mouth set in a familiar thin, angry line, "but I'm certainly ashamed of what the magistrates order us to do—when it's—when it's something like this."

"You defy the king's magistrates?" She faced him, eyes hard as granite. "You, the law's servant, want to defy the law?"

"The law's cruel, Grand'mère!"

"And it's not your place to question it!"

"But it's—"

"Never say that again in this house." She hadn't even heard his protest, or made no sign of it. "While you live under this roof, you'll do your duty and carry out your orders—and take pride in being the king's servant."

Duty and honor, boy, he knew she would say next—*your duty to the law and to your family. Duty and honor.*

"No." He drew a deep breath and stood his ground. Someone had to confront her, someday, somehow. "I won't do it. I can't."

She stared at him a moment more, then sighed and turned away. "Very well. You won't do it. Gabriel, you're in charge after all. You'd better go and tell the men to prepare."

She was actually giving in? He began to relax. Marthe swept over to the small writing-desk in a corner of the parlor and seated herself.

"I must write to Jean-Baptiste and tell him that his eldest son refuses to do his duty and carry out what the law has decreed."

Charles stared. "No!"

"He'll have to know."

He opened his mouth to retort, furious, and checked himself. Could he let such news distress Jean-Baptiste, perhaps upset him so much that his frail condition would deteriorate further?

"Grand'mère, *please.*"

She paused, quill halfway to the inkwell. "This is your choice, Charles. But your father is still officially the master. And if you're no longer willing to be his deputy, then we may need to transfer the provisional title to Nicolas."

His little brother, who was barely eleven? The scheming witch. And he was a naïve fool, wasn't he, to think that he, at fifteen, could beat her at her own game. He crumpled the decree in his fist and turned away.

"Stop, Grand'mère. Stop it. You win."

The morning sky hung low over the cathedral, bleak as lead.

"'I repent,'" the prison confessor prompted the condemned man, who knelt bareheaded and barefoot on the cobblestones in the icy winter breeze, a noose around his neck.

"I repent my crime," the man dully echoed him. The flame on the tall candle he held, a faint spark in the daylight, wavered in the wind from the river that found its way through the huddled houses to the west doors of Nôtre-Dame. "I have broken God's law with the crime of murder. I have offended the king's law by murdering a servant of the king's justice. I repent all my crimes and my sins." He paused, shuddering with cold.

Charles shivered in sympathy for the prisoner, reciting the formula of the *amende honorable* at the steps of the cathedral, as law and custom demanded. A few snowflakes drifted down on the wind, stinging his cheeks.

"I have most grievously . . ." Père Gomart murmured, again prompting the condemned man.

"I . . . I have most grievously offended and I beg pardon of God, the king, and Justice. I—I pray to God for mercy."

"May God have mercy on your soul, my son."

"Come on, up you get," Jérôme said, striding forward. They were all cold and wanted the beastly job over with. He seized the man under the arm and hoisted him up. Charles took his other arm and together they led him back to the waiting tumbril, the priest following.

Only a quarter hour now; only a few turns of the wheels to the Place de Grève, until the patient would begin to die, screaming.

The tools for a breaking were simple: a cart wheel, a man-sized wooden X-cross lying flat on the scaffold, and an iron bar. Gabriel stayed below to direct the men while Charles took his usual, ceremonial place at the corner of the scaffold, above the waiting crowd that had gathered, and turned away, already feeling queasy. Although his presence was an essential formality that made the execution legal, there was, he told himself, no law obliging him to watch the proceedings.

Jérôme and the other assistants hustled the patient up the steps, where he sank to his knees, praying with Père Gomart. The crowd prayed loudly with them; some began to sing the *Salve Regina*.

"May God have mercy on you."

After pulling off the dangling noose and the long, coarse shirt that criminals wore for their public penance, they stripped him of his remaining clothing to his underbreeches and bound him on the cross so that he lay spread-eagled, limbs stretched taut. He made little attempt to resist, lips moving in prayer as the priest held a crucifix before his eyes.

The crowd sang "Amen." At last Charles dared to look up in the hush, only to find that the assistants were standing ready about the cross and Jérôme, holding the iron cudgel in his hands, was watching him.

Of course he had to signal them to begin. He managed a single nod and turned away again, pulling his coat tightly about his shoulders as he attempted to avoid the spectators' stares.

That man is a murderer, he reminded himself with a quick glance at the patient, and tried to imagine what Jean-Baptiste would say to him: *He stabbed an officer of the court, Charles, and he deserves his punishment. The executioner is the avenger of crime's victim and of the innocent, the representative of both the king's justice and God's.* Why should the murderer die easily when the man he stabbed wasn't so fortunate?

A howl of pain assaulted his ears, hard upon the dull thud of the iron bar, smashing flesh and cracking bone.

"One," chanted the crowd. Jérôme raised the bar again and stood motionless, silently counting out some necessary stretch of time between each blow, drawing out the pain and the entertainment.

Two . . .

"This new *bourreau*'s much younger and handsomer than the

old," a buxom young wife near the front of the crowd remarked to her friend, over the noise. Charles flushed scarlet and wished he could die of shame.

It wouldn't be quite so horrible, he thought, trying not to listen to the voices below, if they could all wear hoods or masks, hide their faces as the headsmen did in the picture of the execution of King Charles I of England in one of his history books. But the French executioner, the master, when presiding at the scaffold, had always shown his face to the world. He was expected to wear a fine suit of clothes befitting his rank and his royal office, with a three-cornered hat, hair curled and powdered, lace on his sleeves and cravat, white silk stockings, and silver buckles to his high-heeled shoes, just like everyone else of his station.

Except, of course, the *bourreau* was never just like everyone else.

By the time Jérôme had shattered the four limbs with a blow each, the wretch was screaming, sobbing, begging God, between labored, ragged breaths, to let him die quickly. The priest wiped away the sweat on the man's blood-spattered forehead and loudly prayed for him while the sparse crowd jeered and shouted.

. . . Five . . .

Charles huddled into his overcoat, trembling from more than the January chill and the softly falling snow, and turned his gaze firmly away from the shrieks. Below him, a tall, cloaked woman shouldered her way through the spectators until she stood directly in front of him.

"Don't look away!"

With a thrill of horror, he recognized Marthe.

"Don't disgrace your family! Be a man!"

She remained at the front of the crowd, glaring at him, as if ordering him not to flinch. Wouldn't it be a greater disgrace if he showed himself to be an insensible brute at the age of not-quite-sixteen?

Six.

I am not a monster, rejoicing in pain and death!

I am not a monster, he repeated; though he was not so sure about his grandmother. He clenched his teeth and prayed that he wouldn't faint, or vomit. Madeleine would never let him hear the end of it if he acquitted himself no better than had Charles Sanson the First.

... Seven ...

Nine blows.

It was all part of the orders, Gabriel had explained to him the night before. The magistrates decreed how many blows were to be struck before the final crushing blow across the chest that could burst the heart and collapse the lungs, or before one of the men—if a legal decree of *retentum* permitted it—secretly and mercifully garrotted the patient. Four blows—one on each limb—and then strangulation was usual, but eight blows or more was for an exceptionally wicked murder, like parricide or killing an officer of the law or the courts.

... Eight ...

The crowd echoed his silent count, singing out "Nine!" in a triumphant roar as the club crashed down on the heaving ribs and a fine mist of blood settled on the film of snow around them.

At last they untied Ruxton and bound him, shattered and bleeding, to the horizontal cart wheel atop a post where he would lie in blinding pain fifteen feet above the crowd, his face to the sunless January sky and to the crows that circled overhead, scenting death. There would be no quick end today: *To be exposed on a cart wheel, his face to the heavens, for as long as it pleases God to grant him life,* the sentence concluded.

Usually they died within the half hour, Gabriel said; but sometimes it pleased God to keep them alive for twenty hours or more in the rain or the snow, while the crows landed on them to peck out their eyes, and the spectators treated it all as an edifying, cautionary diversion that cost nothing to attend.

Charles was shivering uncontrollably by the time Gabriel brought him home. Madeleine, with a steaming bowl of broth on a tray, slipped into his room a quarter hour later to find him hunched on the bed, hugging his knees, staring at the floor.

"Do you want to eat anything?"

"No."

"Was it awful?" She set down the tray on his writing table.

"It was horrible. But I didn't faint." He grimaced. "I can still hear him screaming."

"He did kill a man."

"I kept telling myself that. He killed someone . . . but he stabbed him, he didn't smash him up and let him die for hours. How long does it take you to die from a stab wound?"

He shivered again. "It's not right. Grand'mère can go on about duty and honor—our sacred duty to carry out the magistrates' orders—but the orders are unjust. So what does that make me?"

"Oh, Charlot," his sister sighed. She gave him a fierce hug and sat back, gazing at him. "It makes you better than they are."

"That's not much comfort."

The door opened without warning and Marthe swept inside, glancing from one to the other of them. "You're not sick, are you?"

He reluctantly rose to his feet. "No, Grand'mère."

"You'll be yourself by tomorrow, I expect."

"Yes, Grand'mère."

"You did well enough today," she added, her gaze softening.

"Did I?"

"You conducted yourself in a professional manner."

He could think of nothing to say in reply. At last he muttered "I try, Grand'mère," and sat down again. Marthe gestured at the tray.

"Eat your soup before it's cold."

He tried a spoonful as Marthe left and found, to his discomfort, that he had a hint of an appetite.

"I think you ought to go into Paris sometimes and amuse yourself," Madeleine said the following Saturday.

Charles almost smiled. Madeleine had a habit of speaking of the vibrant center of the city, a mile and a half away, twenty-five minutes' brisk walk, as if it were another city entirely. But his sister, under the autocratic thumb of their grandmother, scarcely ever left their out-of-the-way quarter except to go to market, to Mass at Saint-Laurent, or to spend the occasional fortnight at the cottage with their parents.

"Amuse myself?"

"You know, go to the theater or the opera, or a concert. Some real music, better than ours." A favorite evening diversion at home was an amateur family recital, where Charles played the violin and Madeleine the harpsichord, and sometimes Jeannette could be persuaded, blushing and giggling, to sing a sentimental air or two. "Or to one of those public balls. Those sound wonderful."

"Go to a public ball by myself?"

"You could take me. I'd love to go to one."

"Grand'mère would have something to say about that!"

Madeleine shrugged. "I know. So find yourself a girl. I think having a mistress would do you a world of good."

He felt himself blushing. A mistress?

Surely I'm not old enough for a *mistress*?

"You shouldn't know about such things." He frowned and tried to concentrate on the book he'd been staring at for the past hour, though he'd not been able to get past the first paragraph.

"What—mistresses? Oh, come, Charlot, we don't live in a cloister. Listen to me. When you're not—not attending to your duties, you just sit here in your room and study and read your books and . . . well, you think too much. You're alone too much of the time and you probably can't help thinking about what they make you do. You ought to go out and have a little fun."

Charles snapped the book shut and shoved it aside. "You think I deserve to have *fun*."

"Everybody deserves to have some fun now and then," Madeleine said demurely.

"Madeleine!" he exclaimed, wheeling about to face her. "Do you have a . . . a *lover*? Who is he? Does he know who you are—I mean, whose daughter you are?" he added, when she smiled and a tinge of pink rose in her cheeks.

"Of course he does. I wouldn't be so foolish as to take up with someone who wouldn't ever marry me. And I do intend to marry and get away from Grand'mère, before I'm as old as she is."

"Who is he?" he repeated.

"That's none of your business. And don't get all huffy—all that ever happened was that he kissed me, *once*, and I enjoyed it. And if you breathe a word of this to anyone, especially Grand'mère, I'll never speak to you again."

"Cross my heart." He made the gesture. Madeleine's amour had to be one of the assistants. Olivier, the stableboy? Too young and most definitely too dirty. Jérôme? Far too old. Pierre, the executioner of Melun's son and heir, a solemn young man with a secure future ahead of him? Perhaps—though at twenty-six or twenty-seven, just a little old for a fourteen-year-old girl . . . no, of course, it had to be Auguste, the new aide Marthe had hired six months before, a strapping youth of nineteen. He opened his mouth to ask her, but decided it was better not to pry. "Look—I'll tell you a secret, if you promise not to go blabbing it."

"I promise."

"Uncle Gabriel—well, Uncle Gabriel thinks I should go out and amuse myself, too. But not at the opera."

She stared at him a moment, puzzled, then burst into giggles. "Don't tell me—you mean a—a house of . . . well, a *maison de plaisir*?"

"Yes."

"Have you been?"

"Not yet." The back of his neck grew hot with embarrassment at the thought of his frequent, vivid dreams about alluring, unattainable girls. "But he says he'll take me when I've turned sixteen."

"You'll be sixteen next month!"

Charles nodded. He wasn't altogether ignorant, of course; he hadn't passed all his time with only his schoolbooks. He had spent much of his solitary leisure, during the past year, covertly reading notorious novels of a sort that were sold only in the publishers' back rooms, works people delicately called "books to be read with one hand." They were the same kind of illegal books, with the same sort of lurid, illegal pictures, as some of those he frequently saw going up in flames in the public square. But the smirking bookseller at the stall on the Pont-Neuf had assured him that everybody owned a few: Just keep them out of sight, young monsieur, and away from young ladies.

"Uncle says it's a very high-class establishment, respectable and discreet—"

"Like us. Respectable and discreet."

"—and that I should learn about such things in a clean, decent, and anonymous atmosphere."

"That does sound like Uncle," Madeleine said. "A little bit pompous. But he wants what's best for you, I suppose." She giggled again. "It sounds as if he knows that place better than he ought to."

"I think he does. He tells me that they don't know who he is, of course, that he just calls himself the Chevalier de Longval when he visits, and I can do the same."

"Naughty Uncle Gabriel."

"I wonder if our aunt knows what he's up to when he comes to Paris?"

"If she does, I suppose she just puts up with it. Grand'mère says," she added, with a severe glance at him, "that men are like that." She paused a moment, gazing at him.

"Are you feeling better now?"

"A little."

He did not mention that he had lain awake for a long time the previous three nights, still hearing the screams.

6

It seemed, over the past two years, Charles mused as he tied a careful knot in his lace cravat, that he'd become two separate and quite different people, or perhaps even three. In the mornings he was the deputy master executioner, the unsmiling young man in the blood-red coat, symbol of his office, who daily oversaw the corporal punishment of petty criminals and the ritual destruction of works that attacked Church or king—or, from time to time, directed a hanging or breaking to keep the public ever aware of the terrifying power of the law.

In the afternoons, though, he was the scholar who voraciously read through Jean-Baptiste's library and experimented with herbs and tinctures in the laboratory, or when Jean-Baptiste was at home and felt himself strong enough to supervise him, dissected a cadaver. For someone who'd been thrown out of two schools as a boy—though for no other fault than that of whose son he was—he had had an excellent education from his tutor and music master. Together with the anatomy, medicine, natural history, and herbcraft he'd absorbed from his father's books, he could claim also a smattering of Latin, an acquaintance with literature, history, and criminal law, and modest skill at the violin and the cello.

He posed a moment in front of the mirror, preening. In the evenings, as Madeleine had urged him, he could be, thank God, another person entirely, neither hangman nor scholar. At night, he was the Chevalier de Longval, a pretty girl at his side, mingling with people of fashion at cafés, theaters, concerts, and the unruly public masquerade balls—no different from any other rich, healthy, thoughtless youth of seventeen-almost-eighteen enjoying the many pleasures, respectable and not, of the glittering heart of Paris. The life of the scaffold and the pillory, though he loathed it no less than he ever had, was just endurable if at night, whenever he wished, he could become the phantom Longval once again.

He stared critically into the mirror. The cravat was knotted well enough. His thick, light-brown hair was passable, neatly combed back and gathered with a black velvet ribbon. For a proper curling and powdering suitable for a night out he would have to wait until he could call on the coiffeur's just off the Boulevard, near the playhouses; no reputable hairdresser, no matter how well paid, would risk being seen visiting the executioner's house.

Always tall for his age, he had grown to above six feet, towering over the average Parisian. Michaud, a tailor with an excellent establishment in the fashionable faubourg St. Honoré, had fitted him out in as stylish a wardrobe as the town clothes of any well-off young man of good family. The fellow had done a fine job with the new coat and embroidered waistcoat; damn the expense.

He sauntered out of the house, ignoring Marthe's disapproving glare as he passed the parlor. She could disapprove all she liked; he'd fulfilled his part of her devil's bargain, hadn't he? He dutifully carried out his orders in the mornings, and whenever the magistrates commanded him to apply their various barbarities, and the rest of his time—and a portion of his generous salary—was his own, to obliterate the memory of what he had been doing in the morning. It was none of Marthe's business how he disposed of either his time or his allowance. Having secured the family position and income by accepting Jean-Baptiste's office and all the beastlinesses that attended it, he felt himself fully at liberty to spend his share of his pay on fine clothes and a pretty mistress—offsetting the unavoidable horrors with the more pleasurable things life had to offer.

True, he admitted to himself as he hurried along Rue d'Enfer, following the tracks in the well-trodden, frozen mud toward Rue Poissonière where an occasional fiacre was known to pass, Zéphire

was no grand courtesan. She was merely a moderately talented dancer on the make, a sixteen-year-old ballet girl in a third-rate troupe
that played beyond the official city limit of the Boulevard, but she
claimed to be ardently in love with him—or at least with Longval,
for he had, naturally, taken pains to conceal his true identity. Few
self-respecting young women, even the loosest of actresses, would
have had anything to do with the *maître des hautes œuvres*.

But it was a delicious feeling, to lie in bed with her there, warm,
beside him after making love, while she chattered endlessly about
theatrical gossip that he could not have cared less about or murmured amorous nonsense into his ear. After a dozen visits to
Gabriel's respectable and discreet brothel, he had learned as much
as he desired to know about the practical side of lovemaking, and
believed himself to be a more than adequate lover, but the girls
were, to his regret, indifferent to the romantic yearnings of callow
young men. He had longed to fall properly in love and Zéphire had
been the first pretty girl to declare her passion for him.

She met him at the doorway to her tiny garret room in the
theater district well north of the Louvre. "You needn't be in such a
hurry," she said, laughing, as he threw off his hat and overcoat and
began fumbling at the laces to her bodice. "I'm not going anywhere. I'm off tonight, remember?"

"I reserved a box for us at the Italians yesterday," Charles mumbled
as he nuzzled at her ear. "Seven o'clock. Carlin's on tonight and I
want to see the play."

"Theaters are closed." She squirmed away. "All of them, even
ours. No performances. They were all putting up signs when I left
rehearsal."

"Closed? Why?"

"No idea."

He scowled for a moment, disappointed at missing the celebrated Carlo Bertinazzi, the most famous Harlequin of the past half-
century, but quickly regained his good humor. "Then we'll just have
to stay warm here, and pass the time some other way, won't we?"

☞   ☜

"I wonder why the theaters are closed." Charles leaned on one elbow and twined a finger in Zéphire's thick mop of hair. He tugged the feather coverlet, a good thick one that he'd bought her for the sake of comfort in her icy little room, more snugly about them in the January chill and bent to give her an idle kiss on the eyebrow.

She blinked up at him as she nibbled on one of the slices of candied fruit he had brought her. "What does it matter?"

"It might be something important. Bad news."

"Nothing to do with us. Maybe some old minister of state dropped dead at Versailles." She pulled his head down to hers. "Who cares?"

Her lips tasted of sugar and oranges, but curiosity was getting the better of him.

"No, I want to know what's happened." He disengaged himself from her groping little hands and reached for his clothes. "Come on, let's go to a café or a *guinguette*. Not everything can be closed."

But the first café they approached was closed also, its shutters fastened, and so was the workingmen's cabaret that Charles sometimes visited, when he wanted livelier entertainment than the decorous public concerts that were often given at the Tuileries palace. "What's going on?" he demanded of the girl at the counter, when at last they found a café whose doors were open.

"Haven't you heard?" She goggled at him. "Somebody attacked the king!"

"The king's dead!" someone cried, crowding in behind them.

"Dead!" Zéphire echoed him as Charles wheeled about.

"Yes, a man stabbed him to the heart—"

"No, he's not," another man interrupted. "I just came back from Versailles. He's only wounded."

"How badly?" Charles said.

"They're not saying."

"But he might be dying—"

"Someone told me the knife had been poisoned," said a voice in the crowd, through the fog of pipe smoke, "and—"

"Did they catch the assassin?"

"I heard he got away—"

"They caught him," said the man who came from Versailles. "He didn't even try to run, they say."

"The monster!" spluttered another. "We should none of us be here when His Majesty's life is in danger, God preserve him." He thrust a few coins at the counter girl and strode out of the café.

They caught him, Charles repeated to himself, and stopped where he stood. He recalled his book of classical myths; he must have looked no less petrified than the men who had gazed upon the ghastly face of the Gorgon.

"I'm for the cathedral," said a man, making the sign of the cross and impatiently dodging around him when Charles did not budge. "The archbishop'll be leading prayers. All of us ought to be praying for him."

Zéphire glanced at Charles. "Shouldn't we go to a church? We ought to go and pray for the king."

"Yes. Yes, of course."

He followed her out of the café and down the narrow, snow-dusted alley to the nearest church. It was packed with people, most of them on their knees on the cold stone floor and fingering beads or mumbling prayers while a priest chanted the Litany of the Saints for the king's survival and acolytes swung censers. Zéphire found an open spot by a column and promptly knelt and crossed herself.

They caught him, Charles said to himself again, staring unseeing at the crucifix on the high altar, wreathed in incense fumes.

They caught him, and he will be punished.

"He's received the last rites, I heard," someone muttered to a companion nearby. "He knows he's dying . . ."

"Chevalier!" Zéphire whispered. "You should be praying!"

He knelt beside her and mechanically slashed a cross, forehead breast left shoulder right shoulder, with a trembling hand, but his mind was not on the Latin. He glanced at Zéphire, absorbed in her own prayers. She had no idea, of course, why a murderous attack on the king should be immensely more consequential to him and his family than to the other loyal subjects surrounding them. But whether Louis lived or died, the king's magistrates would make an example of the assassin, of a man so unimaginably wicked as to attack the king's sacred person.

Marthe had insisted that, as part of his education, he study famous criminal cases of the past. It was impossible to forget the accounts of the horrific punishment meted out to Ravaillac, who had assassinated King Henri IV in 1610, and to other regicides before him. Something to do with burning sulfur and melted lead, and four horses to end it all . . .

He shivered in the stony chill, despite the bodies pressing in around them. It would have been better for the man, whoever he was, if he'd never been born.

7

Louis XV had cried out to his attendants, as his frenzied, would-be assassin flailed at him with the absurdly small knife, "Seize him, but do him no harm!"

He recovered in a week from the shallow cut along his ribs; the icy January air, the thickness of two fur coats, and, he was sure, God's grace had saved him from any worse. Returning to his usual round of amusements, he spared an hour or two here and there for a Mass in which to dutifully thank the Lord for his deliverance.

Once the king's attention was elsewhere, the high court sent a handful of *questionnaires* to the Bastille to break the assassin's ankles, slowly, in order to get the names of accomplices out of him, and debated how best to dispose of him.

The punishment of a regicide, or even a failed regicide, came along only once in a century or two. One of the magistrates of the Parlement thought it prudent to send the Sansons a warning of what they should expect in the court's sentence, so they would have time to prepare for the extraordinary execution. A messenger arrived at Rue d'Enfer with the letter and the rough draft of the sentence while the judges were still deliberating in the Great Chamber of the Palais de Justice.

The Court declares Robert-François Damiens duly convicted of the crime of lèse-majesté divine and human, for the very wicked, very abominable, and very detestable parricide perpetrated on the King's person; and therefore condemns the said Damiens to penance before the principal church of Paris, whither he shall be taken in a cart, wearing only a shirt and holding a taper of the weight of two pounds . . .

If the king was the father of his people, the regicide was many more times a parricide—twenty-five million times a parricide, Charles thought, if you wanted to drag that out to its brutal conclusion.

He had not been inside the prosecutor-general's office since the day, three years before, when Marthe had presented him to Joly de Fleury. He glanced about with surreptitious interest as they approached the massive desk, his uncle leading the way. The gilded, intimidating grandeur looked exactly the same as he remembered.

"You must understand, monsieur," Gabriel was saying, "that here in Paris we have a better class of assistants—that's to say, we get the pick of the men. And none of the assistant executioners in my brother's and nephew's employ will agree to do what the court asks of them for this execution."

The assistants, after all, were respectable men. And the sort of ingenious torture the Parlement had dug up in the archives had doubtless been concocted, Gabriel had grumbled to Charles earlier that day, three or four hundred years before by some medieval cleric-statesman who'd clung too grimly to his vow of chastity and had had to amuse himself in a more perverse fashion. Such imaginative barbarities were only for the most callous, hardened *questionnaires* to administer, the rougher kind of men whom the fastidious and scrupulous Sansons of Paris didn't often care to have anything to do with.

"I believe—" Joly de Fleury began, but Gabriel pushed on.

"Perhaps in your records, monsieur, you have the names of some experienced *questionnaires* who'd be willing—they'd be well paid, of course—to come to town for the day to administer the tortures?"

"*Questionnaires?*" snapped the prosecutor-general. "I don't believe you understand your situation, Sanson!"

"Monsieur?"

"The outrage took place at Versailles. Do you, or do you not, hold the title Executioner to the King's Household?"

Although Charles, standing in for Jean-Baptiste, was officially executioner of both Paris and the small town of Versailles, etiquette decreed that the royal household—a sphere apart, a sphere of almost semi-divine status—could not share even a *bourreau* with the common folk. The office of Executioner to the King's Household still existed, though now a mere sinecure. Owing to some long-ago favor, Gabriel collected a substantial salary from it, while continuing to live and officiate in Reims; everyone knew that the Provost of the Royal Household had passed no sentences since the days of Louis XI, almost three hundred years before.

Until now.

"Certainly I hold the title, monsieur," Gabriel said. "That's why I'm here, because I received a message summoning me to Paris—"

"Are you not aware that the master executioner, as the law's representative and the king's servant, must carry out the sentence himself? The law is quite clear."

Gabriel stared at him, paling.

"Perhaps you did not know," the prosecutor continued, "that the executioner's common valets can't punish a crime as great as an assault on the king's person. That would be considered an insult to the king's majesty. Only the man who holds the royal title can administer the tortures."

Marthe had forewarned Charles to expect something of the sort. He closed his eyes for an instant, bracing himself. Until recently he had believed nothing could be more vile than breaking a man alive on the wheel, but the punishment meted out to regicides—barbarity worthy of the sixteenth century, but surely not of the far more enlightened eighteenth—was atrocious beyond words.

The Court orders that he be taken to the Grève and, on a scaffold erected for that purpose, that his chest, arms, thighs, and calves be burned with pincers; his right hand, holding the knife with which he committed the said crime, burned in sulfur; that boiling oil, melted lead, pitch, and wax mixed with sulfur, be poured in his wounds . . .

As deputy master executioner, it was beneath his official dignity to lay hands on the riffraff who composed the vast majority of the executioner's "patients"; the servants did the work while Charles supervised them and stood proxy for the king and his justice. He had scarcely lifted a finger at an execution or touched a condemned criminal since assuming the title and neither, he suspected, had Gabriel.

Applying torture, moreover, was a different job entirely from that of ordinary hanging and whipping. Respectable executioners had always looked down with distaste on the coarser *questionnaires,* whose trade, everyone agreed, was brutal but—regrettably—necessary for the proper functioning of the law.

What did his stolid, kindly, bourgeois uncle know, from personal experience, about the horrible science of inflicting pain?

"Impossible," Gabriel declared at last. "I could never do it."

"Are you refusing to carry out your duties?" Joly de Fleury demanded. "This sounds like insolence, Sanson, or perhaps cowardice."

"I'm saying that no decent man would do it. Maybe a hundred and fifty years ago, when the times were crueler, but we've come a way since then, monsieur, and we have our standards."

"Your standards!" The prosecutor-general looked Gabriel up and down as if he were some unknown, repulsive creature from the jungles of Asia.

"Our standards, monsieur!" (We executioners are not monsters.) "I'd rather resign my office, even my situation in Reims as well, than do what you're asking. It's not my place to do such barbarous things to a man, not as a good Christian nor even as a sworn servant of the law. They're saying at the Bastille that the man's no spy or conspirator, just touched in the head—and His Majesty didn't even fall ill of his wound," he added as Joly de Fleury began to rise from his seat. "Saints preserve us, all that cruelty for inflicting a mere scratch!"

Charles could not stop himself chiming in—"It's frightful, monsieur!"—and now Joly de Fleury was shooting a glance at the presumptuous schoolboy. Suppose yourself qualified to be master executioner at eighteen, do you, he could imagine the prosecutor-general thinking.

"That's irrelevant." Joly de Fleury glared from Gabriel to Charles and back again. "And it's not your place, either of you, to question the king's magistrates. Do as you're told or forfeit your positions."

"Uncle!" Charles murmured as Gabriel bristled, thinking it was time he spoke up before Gabriel really did resign all his offices, or became completely insubordinate and infuriated the prosecutor-general further. Gabriel swallowed his angry reply and stepped back a pace.

"Your pardon, monsieur. I spoke without thinking."

"And are you now prepared to carry out your duties?" Joly de Fleury said coldly.

"I'll oversee it, yes, if I must. But I'll not do it with my own hands. Never."

"You refuse—"

"That's too much to ask of an honest man. What's more," Gabriel added as the prosecutor-general reddened and leaned toward him across the broad, gilt-trimmed desk, "if you think you'll find a public executioner elsewhere to replace me, a *maître des hautes œuvres*, a master in the profession like me or my brother or even Charles here, who'd be willing to do what you're asking of him today—well, then, you're mistaken, monsieur!"

"Only a *questionnaire*, monsieur," Charles dared to add, "a professional torturer—"

"And a disreputable one, at that," Gabriel interrupted, "the sort we don't often hire—"

"—would agree to carry out a sentence that cruel. And he'd have to be well paid for it."

Joly de Fleury scowled and settled himself back in his chair. Some concessions would have to be made, and royal etiquette was, perhaps, not quite as rigid as it once was; this was the eighteenth century, after all. He paused for a stretch of time precisely calculated to convey official irritation.

"Very well, Sanson: Go ahead and find your *questionnaires* if you must. Your presence and direction at the ceremony will be sufficient."

"I'm most grateful, monsieur," said Gabriel, bowing. Charles could hear the relief in his voice.

"Young Sanson, I expect you to be at your uncle's side, since it's to take place at the Place de Grève," the prosecutor-general added.

"But the crime, monsieur," Charles began in feeble protest, "it happened in Versailles—" He fell silent, realizing that the magistrates must have chosen Paris, with its far vaster population, for the theater of the execution, in order to impress upon everyone the awesome and terrible spectacle of the king's law at work.

"That's no concern of yours, young man. And as executioner of Paris and Versailles, it's your duty to preside."

"But Charles—he's only—" Gabriel sputtered. "Monsieur, it's inhuman; you can't ask a lad of—"

"If he is capable of directing a breaking, he is old enough to be present."

. . . And after that his body be pulled and dismembered by four horses, and the members and body consumed in fire, and the ashes scattered to the winds.

God help you, Charles said to himself; despite your silly pretensions to sophistication, in truth all you are is a kid six weeks past your eighteenth birthday, and you know you're scared to death.

8

"Is this where you've been going every day?" said Madeleine, in the doorway of the stable, the long shadows of evening stretching before her. Charles glanced over his shoulder at her, startled, as he heaved the mare's saddle off and handed it to Olivier, the stable-hand.

"Where?"

"Out riding, I mean."

"Yes."

Madeleine clasped her hands behind her back and approached him, taking small steps, as if he were one of the shy, stray cats she fed with kitchen scraps behind the outdoor privy when Marthe was elsewhere. "You can't keep doing it forever."

He concentrated on unbuckling Rosette's bridle as the boy scurried off with the saddle. "I don't know what you mean."

"Yes, you do. You're running away, or you're trying to. If you had your own way, you'd whip up Rosette and just keep going, never come back." She moved closer, laying a hand on his arm as he removed the bridle and slipped a halter over the mare's head. He ignored her and reached for a horse blanket but she edged in front of him.

"Olivier can do that."

"*What*, for God's sake!" At last he made himself look at her. "What do you want?"

"I want you to talk about it."

He knew at once what *it* was. "I can't."

"You've got to. Olivier, please see to Rosette." She clamped a hand over Charles's wrist and drew him outside, into the last warmth of the day's sunshine. It was impossible, he thought, or sickening, perhaps, that there should still be soft spring weather and jonquils blossoming in the garden when men allowed—decreed—such horrors.

"You look awful. It's been almost a week. Have you slept at all?"

"Not much."

"You ought to take a sleeping mixture. Poppy juice or something. Doesn't Father have mixtures like that?"

"I took some. I took some laudanum that night." *And every night following*, he almost said.

"Didn't it help?"

"It helped. A bit." He turned from her again, so she wouldn't see the tears welling up, the tears at the edge of a vast flood of anger, shame, helplessness that he had fought for days. "I wish I'd taken the whole bottle."

"But that would—"

"Yes. That would've killed me."

"Charlot! It's a sin! It's wicked even to think about such things!"

"Wicked? I'll tell you what's wicked! It—it . . ."

Suddenly, to his acute embarrassment, he began to sob. Madeleine flung her arms about him as he ducked his head away from her.

"Oh, Charlot—go ahead. It's all right. Cry." She had to crane her neck to look up at him. "Cry all you want. But tell me about it."

He shook his head and she seized his shoulders in a firm grip. "Talking about it will help. Don't you remember, when we were little, and we had nightmares, and Mamma would comfort us? We always told her about the nightmare, because then it didn't seem so frightening."

"It's not the same. It . . ." He shuddered. "It was real."

"*Now,* Charles. You've got to talk about it." She took his hand and drew him, unresisting, away from the shadow of the stable and into the muddy yard. Jérôme, who had not been seen much in

the house for the past few days, was sitting by the woodpile behind
the tackroom, silently whittling a hunk of wood into a horse. When
not hanging men or breaking them, he made toys for the various
small Sansons to play with.

Madeleine stood in front of him, looked down at him, not without sympathy. "Jérôme, you were there. On the twenty-eighth."

He glanced up at her and quickly thrust away the flask that had
been waiting at his side, close to hand; Jean-Baptiste did not care
to employ assistants who made a habit of drowning their memories and nightmares in cheap brandy, no matter what sort of shame
consumed them or what sort of foul mood they were in.

"Yes, ma'm'selle."

"Tell me about it, both of you."

"It's not fit for you to hear."

She planted her hands at her waist and stood gazing at him, looking remarkably like Marthe. "I'm an executioner's daughter, Jérôme,
not some naïve little rabbit. We may not talk about where you and
Charles go every morning, but I know perfectly well what you're up
to. And if my brother could bear to witness what you did, then I
can bear to hear about it."

"Yes, ma'm'selle. If you say so." He set down his knife and sat
turning the half-carved horse over and over in his hands, staring at
it.

"Jérôme?"

"It was bad."

"I've no doubt."

"Everything went wrong. Some of it was the fault of that old
fool that M'sieur Gabriel hired. He just made it worse."

"Who?"

Charles kicked at a thick chunk of log and leaned back against
the shed, shoulders bowed, not looking at either of them. "Uncle
found an old *questionnaire* who said his grandfather had been present when they executed Ravaillac. He said he knew how it was
done, so Uncle hired him for the day."

"Maybe he did know," said Jérôme, "or maybe he was just boast-
ing, but the old fool lost his nerve. When your uncle and I got to
the Place de Grève in the morning, we found him asleep on the

scaffold, dead drunk, stinking of brandy. He hadn't done a damn thing he ought to have, hadn't bought supplies, nothing." He turned away and spat on the ground. "Useless old soak."

Charles shuddered. "They still weren't ready when I brought him—Damiens—to the Grève. Nothing was ready."

They had already tortured the madman so much at the Bastille and the Conciergerie, demanding names of accomplices who had probably never existed, that he was unable to stand; the *brode-quins*, the infamous "boot," had crushed his ankles. "He had to sit on the steps with Père Gomart, while Uncle swore at that stupid old man and tried to get him to do anything. So it began a couple of hours later than it should have."

"How?" Madeleine said, when he fell silent. She came to stand beside him and slid an arm about his waist, shielding him as always. "What did you have to do?"

"They—we—had to take his hand off," he said, still without looking at her, "because it was the hand that had struck at the king. Like a parricide. The law says that they have to chop a parricide's hand off before they break him."

"This time, we couldn't just chop it off with an axe and be done with it," Jérôme said, voice subdued. "Damiens's hand had to be burned off."

"Burned off!"

"Yes, ma'm'selle. With a pot of burning sulfur. And M'sieur Gabriel had to do it himself."

"What then?" she said, after a moment of shocked silence.

"Then . . . no. It's not fit for a young lady to hear."

"There were plenty of young ladies watching," Charles said.

Perhaps that had been the worst part, worse even than Damiens's agonized shrieks that went on, and on, without end.

He had grown accustomed to the crowds that came to watch a hanging or a breaking, crowds of rough workmen and slatternly women, for whom an execution—like a religious procession—was merely free, open-air entertainment. Among the rabble were always a few curious bourgeois or aristocrats, watching from the comfort of their carriages, but never many. The latest popular, sentimental novels had brought sensibility and decorous squeamishness into style among the leaders of fashion.

Yet the fashionable had turned out, in their ruffled, curled, and powdered multitudes, rented choice windows for the occasion, to watch them tear a living man's flesh away, rip apart his ravaged body. Perhaps the attraction was merely the chance to say that they, too, had witnessed the execution of the century: like a coronation, probably a once-in-a-lifetime event.

"They watched," he muttered. "They clapped. People in all the windows around the square. Ladies and gentlemen. Girls no older than you and I. All watching. Laughing and talking, as if they were in their boxes and it was a comedy on the stage! And Legris was—was torturing him with red-hot pincers and they—they—we—"

Madeleine turned a fierce, questioning gaze toward Jérôme, who bent his head and stared at the ground.

"We had to pour melted lead and boiling pitch and oil into his wounds, ma'm'selle."

"He couldn't stop screaming."

In the distance, at the back of his mind, Charles could still hear it all, the applause and the jeers and, above them both, the screams that had gone on and on until the tormented creature's voice had hoarsened into a pitiful sob and rattle. And then there had been the smell—the pervasive, hellish reek of sulfur and smoking pitch mingled with the odor of human flesh sizzling at the touch of molten metal. The oily stink had clung to his hair and his skin for days, no matter how he scrubbed himself with the maids' harsh laundry soap.

He'd wanted to scream, too, and sob, and run away like a child. And instead, he was telling Legris and the rest that he would give them a hundred livres each, three months' pay for an hour's ghastly work, if they'd torture the wretch. Because somebody had to.

He paused, took a deep, shuddering breath.

"There were magistrates from the Parlement watching, too. But they couldn't take it. They left, long before it was over."

Jérôme spat again. "Sentencing a man to a filthy punishment they couldn't even bear to watch. Bastards."

"And then we had to tear him apart, tie his limbs to horses and pull him into pieces . . ."

God-damned sanctimonious hypocrites, Jérôme added, and all

that for a little pin-prick that Louis the Not-So-Well-Beloved re-covered from in a week.

"... and he was still alive, I could see him breathing, and—and he ... wouldn't come apart. He held together. They tried three times, and he held together ... the—the flesh wouldn't *tear* ..."

Madeleine clutched Charles's arm, steadying him. "Enough!"

"M'sieur Charles kept his head," Jérôme said. "M'sieur Gabriel, he'd gone to pieces, he was retching and near to fainting—old Père Gomart had already fainted—and M'sieur Charles had to take over."

Madeleine's grip tightened. Charles straightened, as if he felt her strength flowing into him, but could not bear to look at her.

"You did well, lad," said Jérôme. "Your father himself couldn't have done any better."

He glanced up at Jérôme, who had hastily gone back to his whittling, concentrating on the fine grooves in the wooden mane and tail. "I just wanted it to be over."

"And you did right, M'sieur Charles. He saw that it couldn't be done, you see," he added to Madeleine, "the pulling apart, so he told Legris to chop at his sinews."

Cut him up, still breathing, cut up a living man like a carcass at the pork butcher's ...

"But we hadn't a knife, and Legris had to use the axe the wood-cutters had left behind." Jérôme looked over again at Charles. "M'sieur Charles told him just where and how to cut, at the joints, to do it quick and get it over with, so the horses could finish him. Like a proper surgeon, he was."

Like a proper surgeon ... is that all that studying anatomy has brought me? A better knowledge of how to torture and kill a man?

Did I want to learn medicine for that?

Charles ground the heels of his hands into his eyes and sucked in deep breaths of the warm spring air.

"I won't do this. Never again. Never."

"Father," he said, a fortnight later, as they sat together after Sunday dinner in the back garden at Rue d'Enfer, "I—I want to leave France."

"Leave France?" Jean-Baptiste echoed him, puzzled.

"I want to go abroad and study medicine. Magdeburg, Heidelberg, anywhere they'll have me—I don't care. As long as it's a place where I can earn a living as a doctor, and where the name Sanson doesn't mean anything."

His father sighed and was silent for a long moment. The scent from the wisteria arbor, heavy and sweet as a cordial, drifted across to them. "You know I'm not yet fit enough to resume my duties."

"But you're so much better—you'll be well soon, within six months, a year." In the peace of the countryside, Jean-Baptiste had slowly regained the use of his limbs and was coming more often on extended visits to the household in Paris. "Look how much progress you've made. And when you're well, and don't need me any longer as your deputy, I beg you, let me go."

"Who'll serve as my deputy and heir if you're gone?" Jean-Baptiste said, with a glance at the younger boys, kicking a leather ball back and forth through the tattered grass at the far end of the stableyard. "Nico? Martin?"

Nicolas was still only thirteen, but big for his age, and never admitted to nightmares; Martin, his twelve-year-old shadow, seemed no different. Charles shrugged. "You took me to the scaffold when I was no older than Martin. In another year or two . . ."

"And who's to pay for these studies of yours?"

"Let me go, with enough to pay for my passage, and I'll work my way through. I'll take anything offered me—I'll work in the charity hospital or the plague house if I have to—if it'll help me to become a healer instead of a killer."

Jean-Baptiste flinched.

"Please, Father."

He dropped to his knees beside his father's chair. "Please, understand. You know I don't think of you as a monster, and I never would. But what we did—to Damiens—it was monstrous, and I had a hand in it. You didn't see it—you don't know what it was like. Ask Uncle if you don't believe me." The affair had so horrified Gabriel that, upon returning to Reims, he had resigned all his offices and titles and shut himself away in his house, leaving his chief assistant and his twelve-year-old son to take over his duties.

"If I thought I should ever have to take part in something like that again, I'd throw myself in the river now and be done with it."

Jean-Baptiste squeezed his shoulder and let his hand linger there for a moment as he stared at Madeleine's bed of tulips, pink and yellow and crimson in the sunshine. It was an unexpected intimacy from a man who had grown ever more somber and distant as the years passed. Jean-Baptiste had spent so much of his life building about him an armor, a shell that would shield him from his profession, that Charles suspected he no longer knew how to pierce that armor.

"I never had a choice," Jean-Baptiste said at last. "My mother made sure of that. And I'd like my son to be able to choose his own future. But do you truly want to forsake your family, your home, your country, everything you know?"

Charles stared at the tulip bed himself and imagined never seeing it again, never again visiting the airy cottage at Brie, lively with the squeals and laughter of his little brothers; never again walking through the familiar corridors of his home.

Madeleine's tulips . . . why had she felt it necessary to plant crimson flowers, the color of blood?

"If it meant I could start afresh, that I would never have to stand on a scaffold again, then I'd make that sacrifice."

His father glanced at him, nodded, and said nothing.

"And if I did well," Charles added impulsively, "got up a good practice, then I could send for you, all of you."

The Sansons would be able to leave the profession behind them. Wouldn't that be worth leaving France forever?

"Do you imagine," Jean-Baptiste said at last, "that folk in Saxony or Bavaria feel any more broad-minded or tolerant toward our brothers in the profession than the French do?"

"What do you mean?"

"You might go to a medical school abroad as merely a young Frenchman who wanted to acquire the latest knowledge from German doctors and scholars. But the prejudice against our kind is everywhere—I've no doubt about that. Should it ever get out that you were the son of a French executioner, do you think that the doctors at any of those foreign universities—or anyone who crosses your path—will treat you any more kindly or generously than our fellow Parisians do?"

Charles sighed. "Father, I have to try. I have to take that chance."

"You're still a boy," Jean-Baptiste said, "and you have the luxury of unlimited dreams. It won't be as easy as you think." He fell silent for a moment. "But I owe you the chance to try."

"What's this nonsense about your going abroad?"

Marthe swept into the little salon where Charles was practicing scales on his violin. "What do you think you're going to do with yourself?"

He twisted about to face her, stunned. Jean-Baptiste had spoken to her of the matter. Though he was nearing forty and had fathered fifteen children, nine of them still living—with a sixteenth, predictably, on the way—Jean-Baptiste was still as much under Marthe's thumb as if he were the small boy whom she had made executioner of Paris.

"I'm going to study medicine, Grand'mère." Miraculously, his voice was level. "You know I always wanted to be a doctor."

"Yes, and I always wanted to be queen, or to fly like a bird! But wanting something doesn't make it so. Your father and grandfather did well enough with their physicking and their herbal remedies; why not be satisfied with that?"

"Because even if Father and I earned a fortune from selling herbal salves," Charles told her as he laid the violin aside, "and cured a dozen patients a day, I would still be what I am."

Still the hangman, he repeated to himself, obliged to do a job I hate, and to follow orders that are often cruel and unjust; people here will point at me and stare at me all my life.

She gazed at him, a tiny frown gathering between her fine, arched brows. "What of it?"

"I don't want that life."

"That's not your choice to make!"

"I can seek my own happiness, can't I? As soon as Father's well, within a year or two, I'm going to go far enough away from here so nobody knows who I am, or what I was, or what my family is."

"Are you saying you're ashamed of your family?"

He immediately recognized the dangerous glint in her eye.

"No! Never! But I'm ashamed of what I was ordered to do in March. Someday they'll call us barbarians, all of us, for allowing that to happen."

"You followed your orders, did your duty—nothing more. Your office is an honorable one. For four generations, duty and honor have been what this family lives by. Don't ever forget that!"

"Then why do we let people call Father the *bourreau*?" he demanded. "How can you bear to hear street brats yell that word at your own son and grandson? What's so honorable about that?"

"What do we care about words? A word never cut flesh or broke bone."

"No? Words still hurt, Grand'mère." They throb and fester like fevered, unmended wounds.

"Though if Jean-Baptiste wishes," she continued, "he could bring an action for slander against anyone who called him a *bourreau*. It's been done before."

He laughed, without humor, and she moved a step closer to him, shaking a bony finger in his face.

"Listen to me, boy: The executioner's task may be painful, but he's as vital to law and order as any police official. He has no need to be ashamed of his position, or to wrestle with his conscience. Leave that to the magistrates who pass the sentences! You're the king's servant and you'll do as you're told, with honor and pride."

"I would rather live my own life, and pass the title along to someone who could find more honor and pride in it than I do."

She colored and raised her hand as if to slap him, as she had slapped him when Jean-Baptiste first fell ill. He held his ground and gazed at her; he now stood nearly a head taller than she.

"We'll have no more nonsense about your leaving this household," she said at last. "Look at you. You and your fine clothes and your box at the theater and your cheap actresses. Oh, don't think I can't guess how you're spending your nights! I know you like tomcatting and throwing your money about."

"What if I do?"

"Do you really suppose you'd give up a good situation, a royal appointment with a fine salary, to play at doctoring out in foreign parts and live on scraps? Or that you're going to traipse around Europe like some pampered lordling on his grand tour, while the rest of us go without?"

"Of course not—"

"You're still responsible for twenty souls for as long as Jean-Baptiste can't walk farther than the garden gate. How dare you decide to take yourself off, without a thought for your duty—"

How weary I am, he thought, at only eighteen, of that hounding word *duty*!

"—to the family that's raised you, clothed you, fed you? You have obligations, Charles-Henri Sanson, and you'll stick to them!" For emphasis she held up the thick letter she carried and shook it in his face before thrusting it at him, with a grunt.

"This arrived a quarter hour ago."

He opened it, recognizing the form and the great wax seal at the bottom of the page. It was an order for the *maître des hautes œuvres* to cause a gibbet to be erected at the Place de Grève, for the hanging on the morrow of Antoine Grospierre, condemned to death for theft and assault.

"You'll do your duty, of course," said Marthe, with a glance at the seal. "Even if it's distasteful. Because it's your duty to the king, and to God, and not least of all to your family, to fulfill your responsibilities. God made you what you are, and it's not your place to abdicate it.

"You'll realize someday," she added as she reached for the door, "that the executioner can't abdicate; any more than the king can."

The hanging was the first execution ordered since that of Damiens. It was Charles's thirty-eighth hanging; he always jotted down brief, impassive notes of the executions he witnessed, as if to remind himself of what he was and what he was determined to escape.

He found, and felt oddly resigned to the fact, that he could watch without emotion, with little more than detached pity for the wretch about to be cast out of the world, the young man who stood trembling atop the ladder, hands bound behind him, the noose around his neck.

Grospierre began to blubber in terror as the sound of the crowd singing the *Salve Regina*, customary at all executions, faded away.

"*O clemens, O pia, O dulcis Virgo Maria.*"

Until the priest and the spectators sang the Amen a reprieve might still arrive, but that, Charles knew, was usually a forlorn hope.

"*. . . Amen.*"

He nodded to Jérôme, who gave the cord in his hand a hard tug and kicked the ladder away. The rope went taut and the man at the end of it writhed and jerked. Auguste, straddling the gallows, swung himself down from the arm of the gibbet and leaped onto Grospierre, his feet landing expertly in the cradle formed by the man's bound hands. Ten feet away in the breathless silence, Charles heard the man's neck snap, just a soft dull *pop* like knuckles cracking, under the sudden weight.

Six weeks ago he had seen the worst that men could do to a fellow being. He stared at the dangling, lifeless body, as urine began to stain the man's coarse trousers; a simple hanging seemed kindly in comparison.

But please, God, please, don't let me become callous, indifferent, don't let me become an unfeeling brute . . .

When it was over, and the meager crowd dispersed, he left the men to lower the corpse and dismantle the gallows. He stripped off his ceremonial red coat with the gibbet embroidered on the back in black thread and strode swiftly away, losing himself among the passersby. It was a long walk to Zéphire's room by the far end of Rue de Richelieu, past the palace and extensive gardens belonging to the Orléans branch of the royal family, but he was thankful for the chance to be alone and to clear his head of dark thoughts with some brisk exercise.

Zéphire deserved a present. He had not visited her since before Damiens's execution; he had not had the stomach, with visions of that horror still raw in his mind, to indulge in something as shallow as frisking with an empty-headed dancer who, without a doubt, would chatter inanely of the notorious spectacle that all Paris was talking about still. Pausing at a little dry-goods shop, he bought a length of wide, fine lace that, the shopkeeper assured him, would be enough to trim a lady's gown, and continued northward.

Of course, she might be out, he reminded himself as he climbed the five flights of stairs to her room. He had sent her no message warning her of his arrival—no messages at all, in fact, he recalled with a guilty pang, during the past four weeks.

Zéphire was at home. At home with company, Charles realized as he was about to knock at the door. A few squeals and moans rose above the creaking of the bed's rope springs, together with an indistinct baritone grunt.

He considered bursting in, like a cuckold in a tedious comedy, but after an instant smiled bitterly instead and turned away. Zéphire, in the end, had not meant very much to him—and how could he have explained his lack of attention to her without revealing who he was? She had been an amusing companion, and entertaining in bed, but he could scarcely fault her for finding another protector after a month of utter neglect.

He trudged home through the clamorous, indifferent streets and gave the lace to Madeleine, who, though delighted, was not deceived.

"And who did you actually buy this for?" She ran it through her fingers and let it drape across her hands like a frothy waterfall. "Don't misunderstand—it's lovely, and you're sweet to give it to me, but you intended it for someone else, didn't you?"

"A girl. Just a cheap little dancer. I won't be seeing her any more."

"I told you before, you ought to find a girl who you can talk to, not some silly featherhead who's no more than a good tumble—and who's always on the lookout for a richer protector."

"How on earth do you know about such things? Nice girls shouldn't—"

"I may be a nice girl," she said, draping the lace across her bodice and surveying herself in the mirror, "but I'm not a nun." She turned from the mirror, pleased, and rummaged in her clothes chest. "Listen, Charlot. You need to talk about your—what you do—to someone who can comfort you. You think too much. You can't keep it all in and brood over it and expect to keep your sanity."

Charles smiled, still astonished he could smile from time to time, and dropped onto her bed while she went on rooting in the chest. "I have you to talk to, sister. You know me best. Why would I need anyone else?"

"Because I won't always be here to listen to you and cheer you up. Haven't you ever thought about that?" She pulled out her sewing basket and her green flowered Sunday gown and began pinning the lace along the edge of the overskirt.

"Where would you go?"

"I might get married, blockhead."

"You'd still be nearby."

"I might not be. I might end up marrying someone who lives a week's journey away."

"You can't do that!"

"Yes," she said, through a mouthful of pins, "I can. In fact, it's likely I will, you know."

"But you *can't*. I—I mean, I don't want you to."

Madeleine turned and gave him the superior, pitying, sisterly look that he had grown accustomed to seeing on her face ever since they had entered their teens. "You've never stopped to think about it, have you."

"Think about what?"

"There are only so many people who'd marry us. Only other executioners, or their sons and daughters. You know our mamma and our stepmother were both *questionnaires'* daughters. When I marry, God willing"—she turned to the wooden crucifix hanging on the wall and swiftly crossed herself, for luck—"it'll be someone in the profession, of course, and what are the chances that the man I marry will live in Paris, or near Paris?"

She was right; he'd scarcely thought about it. His sister's reassuring strength had become an accepted, comforting fact of his day-to-day existence, one he could not imagine living without.

"Were you expecting I'd marry Jérôme, perhaps, just so I'd go on living in the same house with you?" She folded her arms, still giving him the look, though her tone was kind. "I've already refused one offer, did Father tell you? Oh, he was just after the money; I wouldn't have had him, no matter what. I didn't care a fig for him and I'm not ready to marry just yet—but mostly I thought that I'd better stay here, and keep an eye on you, a while longer. But it'll happen someday. Or do you want me to be an old maid?"

"Of course not." He had always assumed that Madeleine, a healthy, pretty girl with a handsome dowry, would receive more than one offer of marriage, but the reality of it had never quite sunk in.

"Find a girl you can talk to," she repeated. "Find one who'll marry you, if possible."

"Marry! I don't want to get married yet. I'm eighteen. Do you think I want to be like Father, marry at sixteen and produce nine or ten children before I'm thirty?"

"He wasn't sixteen!"

"Yes, he was."

"But our mother was twenty-two."

"Twenty-three," he corrected her. "Hasn't Grand'-mère ever mentioned it?"

"Not a word."

"Father and Grand'-mère don't talk about it, but he and our mother married in 1735. Perhaps there was a scandal and they were in a bit of a hurry, perhaps she thought she was pregnant; I don't know. Perhaps there was a miscarriage or a stillborn baby that no one talks about. Or maybe they were simply caught in a compromising position and got married to still any rumors. But they were married in 1735—two months after he turned sixteen."

She stared at him. For once in his life, he had actually baffled her. "How do you know that?"

"Ask anyone when they were wed. Ask Father. Or Grand'-mère."

"Heaven help me. If he doesn't talk about it, I'm not going to bring it up."

"I know who you can ask," he said. "Monsieur de Lally's still in Paris—didn't Father mention that he's been invited to dine tomorrow?" The Comte de Lally, a gruff, hard-bitten, decorated soldier of fifty, field marshal and veteran of some of Louis XV's greatest battles, had long been a friend of Jean-Baptiste's.

"Yes, why?"

Charles almost grinned. "He was at Father's and Mother's wedding. He'd remember."

ço ௮

Sunday dinner at Rue d'Enfer was often a convivial affair for the Sansons. Despite the cloud that hung over the executioner's household, a few broad-minded people outside the profession, including a handful of aristocrats, had grown friendly with Jean-Baptiste over the years, and frequently were guests at his table. After dinner was over and they retreated to the garden to enjoy the warm spring sunshine and the birds raising a riot of twitters and chirps in the blossoming pear trees, Charles drew the Comte de Lally to one side.

"Monsieur, my sister would like to ask a favor of you."

"And how can I be of service to you, mademoiselle?" Lally inquired, with a crisp military bow, superb in his full dress uniform. "You've grown so pretty, you're the image of your poor mother, you know."

Madeleine dimpled, with a quick, pleased glance downward at the new lace on her best gown. "Charles tells me you were at our parents' wedding, monsieur."

"That I was—at the banquet, at least."

"When was it? Do you recall, exactly?"

"It was in the summer, mademoiselle. Late June of 1735. I was just a junior officer then."

Charles exchanged a glance and a raised eyebrow with his sister, who blushed. "You're sure, monsieur?"

"Oh, I know I'm not mistaken, because 'thirty-five was when I was in Paris on leave with two of my comrades, and it was the very day I first met your father."

"You met Father for the first time on his wedding day? But what were you doing at the wedding, monsieur, if you had never—"

Charles snickered; he knew the story already. "He gate-crashed the banquet."

Madeleine stared and Lally beckoned her over to a bench, shooing a stray hen out of the way. "Hasn't your father told you? Now, your brother is exaggerating a bit. We didn't come in uninvited. But Montarly and Rolland and I were on leave, as I said, amusing ourselves in every way you can imagine that young officers would, and one night we went to a cabaret in the faubourg Poissonière that someone had recommended to us. Then we managed to get lost afterward, on the way back to quarters, in an unfamiliar part of Paris. It was late and chilly and raining like the devil. So we looked for someplace to take shelter, but it wasn't a lively district and we couldn't find any taverns or inns. And all the houses seemed to be shuttered and locked up tight for the night. Except for one house." He gestured behind him. "This house.

"It was lit up like the château at Versailles itself, and we could hear music from inside and see dancers through the windows. 'Well,' we agreed, 'we won't be waking up a sleeping household if we ask them for shelter from the rain,' so we rang the bell. Your father answered the door—he was dressed in his best, in a fine brocade waistcoat, and looked like a young prince. We introduced ourselves and explained our situation, and he told us that it was his wedding day, and he'd be honored to receive such gentlemen, officers in the king's army, in his house and at his table. 'But,' he added, 'I fear that the company you wish to join here is not, perhaps, worthy of you.'

"'Never mind that,' said I, and pulled off my cloak. He looked like a respectable young man, and so did his guests, what I could see of them. Bourgeois, of course, but certainly prosperous—they hadn't stinted on the banquet or the candles or the musicians, and plenty of servants in livery were going about, pouring out wine—good wine, as I soon found out. So my companions and I went along inside, without even asking our host's name. We'd caught sight of some pretty young ladies in the salon and none of us delayed in asking them to dance a gigue.

"My friends and I enjoyed ourselves so much at the party that we stayed long after the rain had stopped. But finally, at half past four in the morning, the guests began to leave, and we thought we'd better take ourselves off, too—though not before asking directions from our host, and thanking him, and—oh, yes—asking his name."

"Oh, my," Madeleine exclaimed. Lally let out a bark of laughter.

"Yes, he must have been looking forward to it, knowing that the joke was on us. 'I am Charles-Jean-Baptiste Sanson, messieurs,' he told us, 'the public executioner of Paris and Versailles.'

"Well, that shut the three of us up pretty fast! And before we could say a word, he went on, still smiling, and polite as you please: 'Moreover, most of the guests present tonight are my relatives, and of the same profession as I.' Imagine—we'd been making merry with a whole houseful of *bourreaux*, including even the servants in their fine livery, turned out in their Sunday best!

"Montarly and Rolland were mortified, and wanted to get out of such a house and shake the dust from their feet without delay. But I never did like the business of judging a man by no more than his looks or his name—there are far too many damned fools and scoundrels hiding behind ancient names and fancy titles, in the army and out of it, and I'm not afraid to say it. I didn't see, and I still don't see, why simply engaging in an honest trade and follow-ing his orders, with a title from the king, should make an other-wise decent man an outcast, or make his daughter or sister unfit to dance with." He bowed to Madeleine. "Well, I told my friends they were finicking fools for being so particular without knowing the man and his character, and introduced myself to your father, in my turn, for he seemed like a perfectly pleasant lad. So he and I grew to know each other, in time, and have remained friends ever since."

Madeleine smiled and seemed ready to ask Lally more questions, but excused herself as Marthe beckoned her away. Lally rose and turned to Charles.

"How are you managing, young Charles? You've been acting as your father's deputy, haven't you?"

Charles nodded. "Yes, monsieur. I've managed well enough."

"You had to oversee that filthy business back in March?"

"Yes, monsieur. With my uncle." Dear Lord, he thought, don't let him start talking about it.

"I can't begin to imagine what it must have been like," Lally said, strolling to his side. "Trust a pack of lawyers and pen-scratchers to come up with something that disgraceful! But perhaps—as a soldier—I can understand your position better than others can."

"Monsieur?"

"Well, when his country's at war, a soldier's first and most dreadful duty is to kill the enemy in order to defend his king and his homeland, isn't it?"

"Yes, of course." At war—oh, yes, the war. Though Lally had been ordered off with the army and navy to fight in the war with England that had been flaring up here and there on the Continent, in the New World, and in India, delays and unfavorable winds had kept the fleet at home for some months. The fleet would be leaving for India any day now, Lally had told them during the soup; the winds were finally changing. He wouldn't be visiting his old friend Jean-Baptiste for a long time. But the war, not being fought on French soil, all seemed very vague and far away, and much less important than Charles's own private concerns.

"I don't see that your duty is much different from mine, lad. The executioner puts evildoers to death in order to defend honest folk. Why," Lally added, "if truth be told, your duties could even be considered more moral than mine. You put only criminals to death, while a soldier has to kill honest men who are merely defending their own king and country."

Charles frowned; he had never before thought of the family profession in such a fashion.

"But I still hate it. I'd much rather be a doctor."

"Few of us like it, lad, nor should we. Killing the enemy is a soldier's duty; it should never be a pleasure. Look here: When your father hires a new assistant, say, does he choose a man who declares that he enjoys killing or torturing, gets amusement out of it?"

"No."

"Wouldn't such a man be the ideal hangman's lackey?"

"No—never."

"Sure of that?"

"Yes. Father won't hire men like that, nor will my uncle."

"Why?"

"Well . . . they say that that sort can be dangerous, and sometimes they exceed their orders. And since they help about the house and stables and wait at table and so on, when they're not—not working with me or Father . . . he once said he wouldn't dare allow someone like that in the house." You didn't want such men and their twisted desires anywhere near your wife or your seventeen-year-old daughter.

"Exactly, lad. It's the same among soldiers. We shouldn't take any pleasure in killing our fellow men, for whatever reason."

We soldiers, he went on, we fight because we have to, and we shoot at the enemy to defend our ground and our own lives. The scum who actually like the killing—any officer worth his salt keeps a watch on those, if we see them in the ranks, because men of that kind will usually prove to be more trouble than they're worth. They've no true allegiance to anything or anyone but themselves. For whatever design, God failed to give them a conscience, and they're the ones who'll turn around, after the battle, and murder or rape the people on their own side, for their own pleasure or profit.

Lally grasped Charles's shoulder and looked him in the eye. "A good soldier doesn't enjoy killing the enemy, nor should he. You could say that the only good soldier is the man who dreads carrying out a soldier's chief duty. Understand?"

"I—I think so."

"Try to think of yourself as a good soldier, obeying your orders in the great battle of law against crime. Always do your duty and you'll have nothing to be ashamed of before any man."

"Yes, monsieur."

Duty and honor, monsieur? I've heard that before.

He would not have said so, but he found he could not agree entirely with Lally. Unlike the executioner's victims—*patients*—enemy soldiers at least had weapons in their hands and the chance to fight back and preserve their own existence. They were not, like a man waiting to be hanged, watching their deaths looming inexorably before them, approaching like a leaden, swift-moving summer storm, all the time knowing while the seconds ticked by that they would die precisely at such and such an hour.

And what if the executioner's orders were unjust? What if it was likely that the condemned man or woman was innocent of the crime?

Where was his duty then?

It suddenly occurred to him that *law* and *justice* did not always mean the same thing.

He was sure Lally meant to be kind; though his everlasting rough heartiness could be daunting. He almost staggered as Lally thumped him on the back—the clout was intended as an encouraging pat, he supposed.

Lally was off to Cherbourg and the fleet in the next day or two. "Do you think, young Charles," he added, "that I *want* to sail halfway around the world to some damned, hot, dusty heathen land in order to fight the cursed British? But it's my duty to my king—and, to be sure, a duty to the Irish among my ancestors to take on the English—and I'll do it whether I like it or not. Even if it means being seasick for six months."

I wish I could travel to India, see the world, Charles thought, but said nothing. Someday he would. He was still a free man, no matter what anyone might say to him, and no law could prevent him from quitting Paris, in time.

He glanced over at Jean-Baptiste, who was speaking with Père Gomart, thirteen-year-old Nicolas beside him. Nico, though a bright boy, showed few signs of possessing an active imagination and was probably better suited for the role of executioner than Charles would ever be.

In a few years, when Nico or Martin is sixteen or seventeen . . . in a few years I can get out and study medicine, be what I was meant to be.

II

Sanson Green

1757-1765

*L'amour plaît plus que le mariage, par la raison
que les romans sont plus amusants que l'histoire.*

(Love is more pleasing than marriage, for the same
reason that novels are more amusing than history.)

—*Des Femmes, de l'Amour,
du Mariage et de la Galanterie*

9

When you live deep in the country, even sleepy old Brie-Comte-Robert seems like the center of the world. Jacques and I lived for the day, every Thursday, when we went to market there with a few of the farmhands. They took fruit and cheeses and such from the orchards and farms my father claimed to work, and sold them in the town square, but the truth was that we always spent more for necessary provisions and supplies than we ever took in.

Still, market day was a break in the monotony. We'd run off for an hour or two, sometimes, and explore the town, or exchange boasts with the rough local boys who hung about the fountain, lifting apples from the market barrows, throwing stones at stray dogs, and making faces at the country bumpkins in their homespun blouses. As we got older, Jacques wanted to watch the girls who came trailing behind their mothers to market, exchanging winks and smiles when mamma wasn't watching, but I thought that that was pretty dull, so sometimes I'd sneak off without him.

One of the locals, a big boy named Paul, always acted as if he didn't know whether to kiss our asses because we were nobility and might be somebody someday, while he was as common as dirt; or to beat us up because we were nobility and mincing, stuck-up nancies. Not that we were wearing silks and lace like court nobility, of course. Honestly, in our mended breeches and scuffed old leather town shoes—we wore wooden shoes like the peasants when we were at home, when there was no one about to see—Jacques and I didn't look much different from Paul and the rest.

"Hey, little chevalier," he said to me one Thursday in the summer, a little before I turned twelve. "Come on. Got something to show you."

When Paul said he had something to show you, it could be anything from a maggoty dead dog in the gutter to a naked woman washing herself behind shutters that hadn't been closed properly. But it was usually interesting, so I slipped away when Jacques was busy—he was watching in particular for one girl, one he thought he'd fallen in love with—and I went along with Paul and the pack of boys that loafed around the market square together. He led us right out of the town, half a mile at least along the dusty, well-worn wagon tracks beyond the gates, to a stone cottage that you could just see from the highroad, through the trees.

"What's out here?" I demanded at last, stopping to catch my breath.

"You know what a *bourreau* is?" said Paul.

"Sure. He's the public hangman. Everybody knows that."

"Well, the *bourreau* of Paris owns this house. Everybody in town knows *that*." The other boys snickered, elbowed each other at the bumpkin's ignorance.

"So?"

"He's here. Want to see him?"

I shrugged and tried not to look too excited. That would be something to tell the village boys back at Férolles, that I'd dared to take a peek at a hangman—the *bourreau* of Paris, no less, which made him almost sort of a terrifying cannibal or a fairy-tale monster, like the Cyclops in antique Greece, which I'd read a little about in the least boring of Father's old books.

Paul led us off the road, around the property at the back of the house, through some trees and thickets until we reached a high stone wall. "Here," he told us. "If you climb up, you can see the garden."

"How do you know he's here?" one of the other boys said, with a suspicious glance at the wall.

"'Cause my papa's repairing his roof. He said he wanted extra to work on the *bourreau*'s house, and they paid it. He's here, all right."

I shinnied up the wall. On the other side was a stretch of lawn, with some flowerbeds beyond. The *bourreau* liked flowers?

A couple of little boys were playing ball on the grass, and a skinny gray-haired man was sitting on a bench by a cherry tree, watching them. Actually, except for the gray hair, he seemed younger than Father, but he looked ill, and he was leaning on a cane.

"Where's the *bourreau*?" I whispered to Paul, who had climbed up next to me.

"That's him." He made an old pagan sign in the air, two fingers against evil.

"The man with the cane?"

Even before I'd dipped into Father's book about the old Greeks, I'd always imagined a *bourreau* should be sort of an ogre, fierce-looking, seven feet tall. But this man didn't look even a little frightening.

"That's him," Paul insisted. "Sanson."

"That wasn't worth coming all the way out here," another boy grumbled, on my other side.

"That's all *you* know. He's the *bourreau* of Paris, stupid! The most important one of all."

"More important than the Hérissons?" I said. Michel, the cowherd, had pointed one of the Hérissons out to me a couple of months before in the market square. The whole family—fathers, brothers, uncles, grandfathers, you didn't know which was which—were our own local *bourreaux*, the *bourreaux* of Melun, the nearest town big enough to rate its own law court and prison and executioner. He hadn't seemed like much of a ogre, I'd had to admit; actually he'd been youngish and middling height and looked a lot like Father's notary, like a respectable bourgeois, and he was talking with a pretty girl just like anyone else.

"*Lots* more important."

"But this one's an old grandfather. What's so scary about *him*?"

"He's the *bourreau* of Paris—the hangman for the bigwigs at the king's high court! That's what my papa told me. And he says I shouldn't ever go near him, 'cause it's bad luck if he touches you or even sets eyes on you and it might stop the hens from laying!"

Our whispers must have grown louder, for one of the little boys ignored the leather ball as it rolled past him, and turned as if he was listening. Then we heard footsteps, crunching through the brush. Paul made another sign in the air, a ruder one, and we scrambled down as fast as we could, but not before I caught a glimpse of a tall boy and girl, about the same age as my brother, just a few strides away. We stared at each other for a moment and then the boy shouted, "Leave us in peace, can't you?" and reached for the nearest bit of dead branch to throw our way. "Go on, get out of here!"

The girl—I thought she just might have been the same girl I'd seen with young Hérisson last autumn, and now I understood why she'd dared to go near him—she put a hand on the boy's arm, saying something to him, and they both threw us a dirty look before turning away and going back to the lawn.

You can't blame them for wanting to be let alone. I suppose the local boys were always daring each other to go out and sneak a look at the *bourreau* and his family, and anybody would get tired of rowdy kids spying over the wall, pointing and shouting ugly names.

We took off and pelted back to the highroad, but not before Paul had grabbed up a few stones. He shouted, "Filthy *bourreau*, go back to Paris!" and flung them at the wall, without really trying to hit anything on the other side. The rest of us threw a couple of pebbles at it, too, mostly because Paul seemed to expect us to. Then we ran and didn't stop running until we passed the town gates.

10

"I heard just now, in the city, that the Comte de Charolais has died," Pierre Hérisson said as Marthe began to serve dessert. Jean-Baptiste and Charles both turned in their chairs at the dining table, startled, to look at him. "Wasn't he a friend of yours, Monsieur Sanson?"

"I wouldn't say a *friend*, precisely," Jean-Baptiste said, "but we were acquainted, and he's dined at this table, seated where you are now, more often than once. His town house is on Rue des Poissonniers, only half a mile away, so we are—I should say were—practically neighbors. I'm sorry to hear your news." The count, Charles recalled, had famously done Jean-Baptiste some great services in the past, interceding with the king when the ministers had neglected to pay the executioner's salary.

"I heard he had a terrible reputation," Hérisson said. "They say he—well, I shouldn't speak of it before the ladies."

"I was present once when he came to dine," piped up Père Gomart, beside him, "and I confess that he did not seem as wicked as rumor had him."

Marthe sniffed from her seat at the foot of the table, opposite Jean-Baptiste. "Appearances can be deceiving, *mon père*! He had an aristocrat's fine manners, and he could be charming when he wanted to be, no doubt about that. But I expect he, like a few others, dined with my son just so he could boast about having broken bread at our table."

"Isn't there a story," Hérisson began, "about how he carelessly shot a man dead?"

"He explained it to me when we first met," said Jean-Baptiste. "And I believed him. But the story has been circulating for a long time; perhaps it's been exaggerated as it spread throughout the provinces."

Hérisson, though he had served as assistant to Jean-Baptiste in Paris a few years before, had now taken up his family's title of executioner of Melun and lived three leagues south of the cottage at Brie-Comte-Robert, a day's journey from the city. He smiled at the mild gibe at provincials, but was not to be dissuaded. "How did you meet a great lord like him in the first place, monsieur?"

"He came to us," said Marthe, before Jean-Baptiste could reply. "A dozen or fifteen years ago, it was. He came here, in his carriage, bold as you please, to learn the truth behind some foolish rumor he'd heard at court."

"He stepped out of his carriage," said Jean-Baptiste, "saw me taking the sun on the bench beside the front door, and, without even raising his hat to me, asked me if I was the *bourreau* of Paris. I replied that I had the honor to be the *maître des hautes œuvres*. Then he demanded to know if it was true that I, like Junius Brutus, was a man of such rigid morals that I had secretly condemned and executed my own eldest son for committing a terrible crime."

"Gracious God," Père Gomart exclaimed, fanning himself with his napkin, for the day was hot. "What nonsense!"

"Indeed. After all, I was only about twenty-six at the time. But I expect that a preposterous rumor of that sort had been circulating about 'the *bourreau*' since my grandfather's day, or even since the Guillaumes, who held our office before him. But I asked him in return, that even if the tale were true, was I likely to reveal such a grave secret to the first idle and insolent courtier who questioned me?"

Charles exchanged smiles with Madeleine beside him. He could imagine Jean-Baptiste giving the count a frigid stare.

"That annoyed him, as it was meant to, and he colored and said, 'Do you know to whom you're speaking, *bourreau*? I am the Comte de Charolais, a cousin of the king.' "

"Typical damned aristocrat," said Hérisson. "Thinks he's God Almighty . . ."

"I recalled an equally ugly rumor," Jean-Baptiste continued, "one involving Monsieur de Charolais, and I fear I couldn't resist returning his impertinence. 'I'm sure, at least,' I said, 'that I shall never have to exercise my official functions in connection with you, monsieur le comte. For I hear that His Majesty has promised to pardon any man who might kill you with just cause, just as you took the life of an innocent man and considered it of little importance.'"

"So he did shoot a man without compunction?" said Hérisson.

"He turned pale with anger, but controlled his temper, and explained to me, coldly enough, that the tale was above twenty years old, had become distorted in the telling, and had always been a matter of mistaken identity: His brother, known to be mentally deranged, had one day taken a pot shot at a roofer atop a house, in order to show off his aim, and had killed the wretch. One of the count's servants, a very honest young man—Monsieur Chesneau, it was," he added, with a glance at the rest of the family, "he confirmed the story. So I apologized for my rudeness and led Monsieur de Charolais into the garden and showed him Charles, here."

"I remember that!" Madeleine said, as Charles's thoughts strayed to Chesneau, the count's armorer and an occasional visitor, a friendly youth with scarred face and arms—the result of a rifle he was testing having exploded in his hands some years before. The count had hurried the wounded man to Jean-Baptiste, who not only saved his life but, with careful treatment and herbal compresses, prevented him from being too severely disfigured. Chesneau, a clever mechanic with a passion for making, repairing, and caring for fine firearms, would now have to find another wealthy employer, though Charles doubted he would have much difficulty in that.

". . . We were making mud pies, I think," Madeleine continued, "and Father came in to the garden with a strange man and pointed at Charlot. He said . . . something about Charlot being *dead*, and I couldn't understand it at all . . ."

"I said to him, 'You see, monsieur, your concerns about the

tragic death of my son and heir are quite unfounded.'"

Madeleine laughed. "Yes! So that's what it was about. It was so peculiar that I've never forgotten it."

"I should add that Charles was six or seven and had not, to my knowledge, committed any capital crimes."

Charles smiled. Jean-Baptiste rarely made anything approaching a joke; perhaps the quiet country life at Brie had changed him for the better, even now when he had returned to something resembling his former life in Paris. He did seem in a particularly good humor that day.

"Is something troubling you, Père Gomart?" Marthe deliberately changed the subject. Jean-Baptiste, Jeannette, and even Marthe usually strove to maintain their dogged illusion of an ordinary bourgeois household. The family profession was rarely mentioned in the house, and never at table or before guests not in the business—Père Gomart, as the prison confessor who accompanied condemned men to the scaffold, was an exception. The priest started and turned his mild gaze to her.

"I was preoccupied . . . forgive me. It's a private matter," he admitted, "and I shouldn't be worrying you with it. Though—yes, yes, I should welcome a woman's advice, especially from a lady as distinguished as you, madame."

"Indeed, Father?"

"I have a young niece newly come to Paris, and she's causing me a great deal of worry. She's only sixteen and very beautiful, you see, and she's found it far too easy to exploit her charms in order to get whatever she wants. She received some education in a convent, but now she works as a shopgirl at the Maison Labille."

"The Maison Labille?" Hérisson said.

"One of the most expensive gentlemen's outfitters in Paris," Charles said. He had once ordered a few cravats there, but the inflated prices were, for the most part, beyond his reach. He smiled to himself. Père Gomart's niece, if she was a pretty girl of easy morals, had procured herself a job at the right place; she might easily find a wealthy protector at such an establishment.

"The poor girl is illegitimate," Père Gomart continued, a faint blush rising to his cheeks, "and I fear such a loose atmosphere, together with the unfortunate influence of her birth, will over-shadow the moral precepts the sisters taught her. I suspect Jeanne's ambition—for she has ambitions far beyond her station—will lead her into a life of dissipation and ungodliness, madame. Perhaps you can advise me how I might protect her?"

"Does she live with you, monsieur?" Marthe inquired.

"No, she most categorically refused my offer to give her a home. She rents a garret on Rue du Bac with a friend, another shopgirl."

"Ha! You may as well save your breath, Father. She needs no protecting. When a girl's sixteen, on her own, ambitious, and a beauty into the bargain, you might stop a whirlwind with your bare hands before you'd keep her from having her own way. Give in to the inevitable and let her do as she likes; I expect she's already sold—and for a good price, too—what a respectable man looks for in a bride." She returned her attention to her dish of baked apples and cream, with the air of a magistrate who had pronounced judgment, as Père Gomart retreated diffidently into his wine glass.

Jean-Baptiste cleared his throat in the pause that followed. "Well, my friends, now that my mother has spoken of brides, this would seem to be the appropriate moment for the announcement I'm about to make." He waited a moment, as all heads turned toward him, and continued.

"I'm delighted to tell you all that Monsieur Hérisson"—he nod-ded to his guest—"asked me yesterday for my daughter's hand, and I gladly gave him my consent."

Charles stared.

"Madeleine?" he said in a low voice, as the rest of the company showered congratulations upon the future bridegroom. He glanced across the table and back. "You—you're going to marry Hérisson?"

She nodded. "In October."

"But he's *old*!"

"He's thirty-three."

"And you're twenty."

"Well?"

"Well, he's . . . older. Thirteen years older—a widower—"

"I knew this was how you'd react," she whispered back, impa-tient, "which is why I didn't tell you. I like him quite a lot and I don't care how old he is. Pierre's responsible, and decent, and— and comfortably off, and more to the point, he's one of us."

Charles shrugged and shook his head and she sighed. "Charlot, we haven't so many options that I can be too finicky about a husband, and he's a good man—Father thinks highly of him. You'd be friends if you were closer in age, or if you'd had the chance to know each other better."

"What about Auguste?" he said, thinking of his sister's lengthy teenaged flirtation with his aide.

She gave him the usual superior look. "I only ever flirted with Auguste to distract everybody's attention, because Pierre was still working for you then and I didn't want Father or Grand'-mère—or you—to get suspicious and sack him. Auguste's good-looking, but he's still only an assistant, after all, and he's about as clever as a bale of hay."

Jeannette and Marthe converged upon her and she pressed his hand. "We'll talk later."

"You'll go to live in Melun." Charles aimed a halfhearted kick at a squawking hen that quickly flapped out of the way, and threw himself onto the garden bench, scowling at the marigolds and flowering sage that bordered the vegetable plot. Madeleine nudged him over and sat beside him.

"It's not so far away."

"It's a whole day's journey!"

"We can visit each other easily enough at Brie. I'll make the time."

"How often—one Sunday, once a month? Less?"

Madeleine stared at him for a moment. "You're actually sulking. Don't you want me to be happy?"

"Of course I do. But . . . but I don't want you to go away."

"Oh, Charlot."

'You're the only friend I've got. I need you here."

"There's Nico, or Martin . . ."

"Not for long." Nicolas was going to Soissons in four months to work for their cousin, René Zelle. "And Martin's just a kid. I love him but we haven't anything in common. You know he never opens a book."

You're my best friend, he wanted to shout, you know that, you're my best friend in the world, we've shared everything all our lives, and I don't want to lose you. He twisted about and met his sister's eyes.

"You said yourself that it was hard to find a husband because of who your father is. Don't you think the same thing's true of me? How is the public executioner supposed to make any friends?"

"Father made friends," Madeleine pointed out. "Père Gomart, Monsieur de Lally, Monsieur de Charolais, God rest him—"

Oh, yes, he said silently, Father's grand "friends"—people from the outside world who come to dinner now and then, congratulating themselves on their broad-mindedness in being polite to the *bourreau* and treating him like a human being, and who might not snub us in front of strangers if they met us on the street.

"They're not close friends, the way you and I are." Not confidants, not friends and siblings, inseparable since they were in diapers. "Father hasn't any friends of that sort, except for our uncle. Why do you think Uncle Gabriel visits so often? Because he probably hasn't any friends outside the profession, either."

"But at least they have families. Wives who understand, because their fathers and brothers are in the same fix. You should get married, too."

"I'm not ready to get married. Who would I marry?"

"I'm sure there are plenty of candidates. You're a good catch, Charlot, with the Paris title—aristocracy among executioners."

Charles could not help a brief, bitter laugh. Madeleine elbowed him.

"It's true. And it doesn't hurt that you're prosperous and have a good education and nice manners, and that you're very, very handsome."

"Flatterer."

She stuck out her tongue and pulled a horrible face at him. "We're a good-looking family."

"Well, I don't want to get married and tied down just yet,

because I still intend to get out of here and study medicine some-where. Nico can have Paris if he wants it. And I don't intend to marry some . . . some provincial hangman's daughter," he added, thinking irresistibly of broad-faced, big-bosomed, muscular country girls, rustics a generation or two up from the peasantry, scarcely suitable brides for Sansons.

"Can it be," Madeleine said with a giggle, "that, deep down, you're a snob? People like us aren't good enough for you?"

"Perhaps. Because I'm not going to be an executioner 'like us' for much longer. As soon as Nico or Martin is a little older—"

"You've been saying that ever since you were sixteen."

"I still mean it."

He stifled a familiar flicker of doubt. During the past three years, he had reluctantly begun to wonder whether or not Marthe had been right when she had told him that he was unlikely to give up his well-salaried position in order to "play at doctoring."

Did he, indeed, enjoy the safety and comforts of a secure income too much to take that first audacious step into the unknown, to risk abandoning those comforts for the precarious prospect of a new life?

"It's the uncertainty I'd fear," Madeleine said, echoing his thoughts. "If it were I . . . well, I don't know if I'd have the courage to do it. To give up what I knew I had."

"Even though it's payment for blood?"

"Even then." She was silent for a moment. "Even though you detest it, and of course you ought to detest it like any decent man, you're used to it—to the job—by now, you see. I suppose the ques-tion is: At this point in your life, after half a dozen years of doing the offices"—the family's customary euphemism slid off her tongue as easily as it did from Charles's or Jean-Baptiste's—"do you still dread your duties more than you dread uncertainty?"

He sighed and hunched forward, elbows on knees. "I . . . I don't know any more."

But I still could be a good doctor, he said to himself. If things were different. If I'd ever been given the chance.

11

Jeanne Bécu pushed herself up on one elbow, swallowed down the last of the wine in the nearest glass, and with a leisurely finger began to trace little patterns across Charles's bare chest. "I'm sorry I spilled wine on your shirt. That was clumsy of me."

"Never mind." He stroked her satiny cheek. His companion had proved to be far more experienced and skilful than he had expected, especially from a priest's niece, illegitimate or not. The previous hour had passed like an extraordinarily vivid episode from one of the salacious novels he kept well hidden in a drawer beneath his clean linen.

"I could wash it for you."

"I'd rather you washed me."

"In a bathtub?" She giggled. "A *big* bathtub, with plenty of hot water, and scented oil?"

"All that water, up six flights of stairs? Do you even have a proper fireplace here? Or a tub, for that matter?"

"No and no. We go to the bathhouse like everybody else. But it's fun to imagine, isn't it?"

The thought of it sent a flicker of desire through him, though he had supposed he couldn't possibly summon another ounce of energy. He rolled over and pinned her beneath him, framing her face in his hands, kissing her lips, her throat, working his way toward her perfect little breasts, but she squirmed away.

"That's enough now, love."

"Not for me."

"My, you are a stallion, aren't you?" She giggled again. "Are you sure you really came here in my uncle's name, to rescue me from a life of wickedness?"

"Well . . . in a way."

"You don't look like a priest to me, Monsieur . . . what was your name?"

"Longval. Charles de Longval."

"How on earth do you know Uncle?"

"He—Père Gomart is a friend to my family, and he's often spoken of you."

Père Gomart hadn't exaggerated his niece's charms. Charles's first glimpse of Jeanne Bécu, barely seventeen years old, with her melting blue eyes and cloud of golden-red curls, had been the most ravishing sight he had ever seen.

He ran a finger down her throat to her breast and toyed with the nipple. "You see, he's described you in such terms—though you're far more beautiful than I imagined—that I knew I had to meet you."

"Did he say I was pretty?" She preened a little, enchantingly. "Poor Uncle. He believes I'm going to go straight to Hell, and every week he visits Toinette and me and tries to persuade me to mend my wicked ways. Well, he should talk."

"I beg your pardon?"

"Oh, my mother told me he had plenty of fun himself, before he entered holy orders. You know, I call him uncle, but I'm convinced as anything that he's actually my father. So he needn't be so self-righteous. I don't hurt anyone by having a good time, do I?"

"I should think not."

On the contrary, he said to himself.

"And I don't think I'm interested in being respectable," Jeanne added, "in marrying the grocer and settling down for the rest of my life. That would be an awful bore, and I was meant for more exciting things than that. So of course when you mentioned Uncle's name, I supposed you were a missionary he'd sent to me . . ."

"Well, I had good intentions, but you distracted me." Charles reached for her but she sat up in the bed and clambered over him, reaching for the shabby chemise he had impetuously pulled off her and flung aside an hour before.

"No more, love. Toinette'll be back soon, with supper from the caterer's."

"And after supper?" Lively images danced before his eyes as Jeanne slipped her chemise over her head, shivering in the chill of the unheated garret room. He had never had two girls at once and wondered if Jeanne's friend Antoinette, who shared the tiny parlor and bedchamber with her, was equally enthusiastic.

"After supper you must go home. I'm tired, and Toinette won't join in, if that's what you're thinking. We're just friends, and she doesn't believe in interfering with my business."

"May I come back tomorrow?"

She turned and looked him over as he rolled to his side, the sheets flung askew across him. "Oh, la," she said, her gaze seeming to caress him, "why not?"

Charles knew full well that he was not the only man sharing Jeanne's bed, but he found he could not help himself. Jeanne was like poppy to an opium eater, each encounter feeding his desire all the more. His passion for her let him forget his other life, his true life; in Jeanne's arms he was no longer Charles Sanson, despised executioner, the law's instrument, deputy Master of High Works, but Longval—wealthy, debonair, carefree. He now carried out his distasteful duties each morning always knowing Jeanne awaited him across the city, far from the pillory and the Place de Grève, with her enchanting blue eyes and dainty figure and her soft, tender, clever hands.

He tried his best, as the weeks passed and spring approached, to believe that Jeanne adored him as passionately as he adored her. Though his share of his salary did not permit him to set her up in a private apartment as all self-respecting mistresses required, he bought her trinkets and two new gowns, and regaled her with tasty little suppers sent up from the *traiteur* down the road. She

was an incurable coquette, nonetheless; if she had a luxurious establishment of her own, she often hinted, her heart would belong only
to her protector, but until that day—well, a girl had her way to
make, didn't she?

He rarely saw Antoinette, Jeanne's friend and roommate, except
from time to time at supper, for she seemed to vanish as soon as
he appeared at their door. "Jeanne should have her privacy, and
her opportunity to reel in her prize catch," she told him in early
spring, when he asked her why, for he liked her well enough.

With delicacy and discretion, she added, a handsome, wealthy
admirer might become a permanent patron. Who am I, Antoinette
Vitry, to stand in her way?

Charles knew, in his heart of hearts, that he could not keep
Jeanne forever. As ambitious mistresses of bachelors did, she had
begun, he suspected, to daydream of the opportunities open to
her: moving on to a grander and wealthier protector, or keeping
tight hold, with marriage vows, of the prize she already had. And
how could he tell her that the obstacle to their marriage was not
her station in life, but his own?

12

One sunny afternoon, he encountered Antoinette on the staircase to the apartment. "Just leaving again, mademoiselle?" he chaffed her, smiling. "Shouldn't you be at the Maison Labille?"

"I haven't worked there for weeks, monsieur. I've become friends with an actor—a prosperous one. That's much more amusing than slaving at a shop."

And more profitable, he guessed. Her new yellow gown was, while not an expensive one, surely finer than the two modest dresses, suitable for a shopgirl, that he had seen her wearing previously.

"And," she added, "I can go to the Italian comedy any time I like now, for nothing."

"Careful: Actors make unreliable husbands."

She smiled. "I don't want to *marry* him. He's forty-five at least, and married already. But he's funny and charming and kind, and I enjoy his company, and he'll take care of me for a while."

Jeanne's perfect, porcelain beauty, flirtatious charm, and skill at the art of making love had so besotted Charles for the past months that he realized he had scarcely noticed Antoinette. She was not even pretty, according to the tastes of the day, though he would have called her striking; she was thin and dark, lacking the fair, delicate coloring and softly rounded face and figure of the simpering shepherdesses that adorned every cheap print sold in the engravers' stalls. With her black hair, angular features, and elfin hazel eyes, she was what some discerning folk called a *"jolie laide,"* a plain woman of beauty, whose wit and character made up for what she might lack in conventional comeliness.

It was not so surprising, really, that she had found herself an admirer. Perhaps she had, in truth, done better than had Jeanne; Antoinette knew that her lover was an actor, a shadow on the stage, while Jeanne believed her illusion was real.

"So what about you, Chevalier?" she continued. "When are you going to make up your mind?"

"Make up my mind?"

"Well, you can marry Jeanne, as she'd like you to, and make a titled lady and an honest woman out of her; or you can set her up as your mistress in a proper sort of apartment, not this rat-hole; or you can keep on as you've been doing, sharing her with a couple of others until she discards you and moves on; or you can walk away and be free of her."

"I can't marry her."

"Married already?"

"No. But it's impossible—she would never—" Charles bit back his words before he betrayed himself. Antoinette shrugged.

"I'm only suggesting you ought to think it over, before she breaks your heart. She will, you know. Once she realizes you can't or won't give her what she wants."

"What's that?"

"Oh, carriages, jewels, estates, titles, half the kingdom! Jeanne is convinced you're a duke in disguise, gone slumming in Paris, and she means to have you one way or another. But you aren't, are you, Chevalier?"

"No. No, I'm no duke. I—"

Suddenly he wanted desperately to share his secret, to do away with all the pretense, but fear of humiliation held him back. He smiled at her, awkward, and went on up the sixth flight of stairs to Jeanne's apartment.

To his surprise, three weeks after their last encounter it was Antoinette, rather than Jeanne, who met him at the door to the garret on Rue du Bac. "What, not on your way to the theater?" he began, remembering her talk of an actor, but she raised a hand to silence him.

"Jeanne's ill. Better not disturb her."

"Ill?" Jeanne had enjoyed robust, glowing health all the time he had known her. "What's the matter? Have you had a doctor in?"

"Just let her be, Chevalier!" she snapped. "She'll be all right. Let her regain her strength."

"I know a little medicine myself," he insisted. "Let me see her."

"Chevalier—"

"Let me see her!" He pushed past Antoinette and hurried to the bedchamber. Jeanne lay asleep in the big bed and her breathing was soft and regular, but she was terribly pale, almost as pale as the sheets.

He took up her wrist to feel her pulse and her eyes fluttered open. For an instant she gazed at him. Then she shrank back as a faint pink tinge flooded into her cheeks.

"Jeanne, dearest," he began. "Toinette tells me—"

"Get away from me!" she shrieked, and snatched away her hand. "Don't you touch me!"

Charles stared at her.

"Get out of here!" She burst into noisy tears. "Don't come near me—you're *disgusting*! Keep away from me!"

She knows.

He drew a deep breath and turned away.

"I truly am sorry to have deceived you, Jeanne." He did not— could not—look at her. "But I do love you—"

"*Love*—how can you love anyone? *You*—it's revolting! To think I wanted to *marry* you! You've ruined me, you bastard, you've ruined me!"

She dissolved into even louder sobs and buried her face in the pillows, wailing "You've ruined me, you've ruined me!"

He knew he would only distress her more by staying. He left the room.

"Well, are you happy now?"

Antoinette followed him from the doorway where she had stood, arms folded. He took a step toward her, then checked himself.

"What's made her ill? It's not just a case of hysteria?"

"I'd think it would be obvious she's lost a lot of blood."

"She . . ." He began to understand. "She was pregnant? And she lost—"

"Don't be a fool, Chevalier. She didn't miscarry. She went to an old witch-woman somewhere and got rid of it. As soon as she realized you might be the father."

He glanced up sharply at that, but saw no revulsion in her countenance, only a cool pity.

"You know—"

"Who you are? Yes."

Jeanne had told her, no doubt, between sobs of rage. But Antoinette seemed to cherish fewer prejudices about him. At least she had no qualms about merely speaking with him at arm's length.

"I don't understand," he said at last. "Why does she say I've ruined her? She was no virgin when we met."

"You're surprisingly naïve, aren't you, for someone in your job?"

Perhaps, Monsieur So-Called Longval, Charles said to himself, you know more about dead men and women than about living ones.

"It's not about that kind of reputation," Antoinette continued. "Look: Jeanne's set her sights high. She knows that her future depends upon her being a kept woman, and she wants to be the grandest of grand courtesans, mistress to princes. But who'll have her now? A prince or an archbishop, who can have anyone he wants, would have second thoughts about her, if he knew that the *bourreau*, of all men in the world, had plowed that field before him."

Charles winced at the word *bourreau* and she gave him a brief, wry smile. "Forgive me. I wouldn't call you that. But that's what others will say and think. Let her be," she added when he opened his mouth to reply. "Come back in a day or two, when I've calmed her down."

He fled the house and tramped aimlessly through the streets of the faubourg St. Germain, unable to shake off the look of horror Jeanne had given him. The passersby swarmed around him on their private errands, oblivious and indifferent, but everywhere he imagined people shrinking from his touch, pointing, shuddering.

Don't you touch me! Don't come near me—you're disgusting!

Look there, that's the *bourreau*, keep away from him, it's bad luck to step into his shadow.

Love—how can you love anyone?

He could no longer bear the anthill of faces all about him. Pausing on an impulse by a livery stable at the edge of the district, he hired a saddle horse for the afternoon and went for a long hard ride, crossing the Seine and circling the city, through the fields and farms that lay on the outskirts.

At last the late afternoon shadows stretched out beside him. It was warm for June and his throat was parched with the road dust by the time he cantered through the village that clung to the wind-milled slopes of Mont-Martre, beneath the ancient church that crowned the high hill. Seeing a public well in the square, he slowed the gelding to a walk and approached the young woman hard at work cranking the windlass.

"I'll help you with that, if you might spare me a dipper or two of water."

"You're welcome to a drink, monsieur." She held the gourd out to him, with a swift curtsy. He drank and then, dismounting, reached for the windlass. "Oh, no, you needn't. I'm done, anyway."

"At least let me help you carry the water."

She gave in, with a shy smile. Charles took a bucket in one hand and the horse's bridle in the other. Together they strolled the rest of the way through the village past modest farmhouses where hens scratched in the dooryards and sows and their piglets lolled bliss-fully in the sunshine. Mont-Martre, he recalled, where not pocked by gypsum quarries and studded with windmills, was inhabited by small farmers, peasantry who tended vineyards on the slopes or raised vegetables for the Paris markets.

The young woman led him to one of the farmhouses along the highroad, where a thickset man was taking his ease in the shade beneath an arbor. He sprang to his feet and doffed his shabby broad-brimmed hat as he saw them approach.

"This gentleman offered to help me with the water, Papa," the young woman said, as the man looked curiously at Charles.

"That's kind of you, monsieur, kind of you indeed. Though

Marie-Anne's a good strong girl, aren't you?" Marie-Anne smiled. "My daughter, monsieur. Would you care to stop and rest a while," her father continued, "and take a swallow of wine with me?"

Charles accepted the invitation, grateful for any distraction from the thoughts of Jeanne that still bedeviled him. The father went inside as Charles tied up the horse, and returned with a wineskin and a pair of battered pewter cups. "My name is Jugier, monsieur, Jacques Jugier at your service."

"Longval."

"What brings you to Mont-Martre, then, Monsieur de Longval?" Jugier inquired, as he poured the wine. "The hunting?"

"Hunting?"

"Oh, not right hereabouts, but we see gentlemen pass through on their way to the forests at Saint-Denis." He jerked his head northward. "Good shooting out that way."

Charles rarely went shooting, being more interested in the sophisticated amusements Paris had to offer, but Marthe often said his grandfather had been fond of the chase. A few weeks or months of hunting, solitary tramps through the woodlands and meadows, might be preferable to revisiting all the theaters, pleasure gardens, public balls, and other such frivolous urban amusements that he knew would remind him of Jeanne for a long time to come.

He drew a long breath, taking in the comfortable, simple scents of kitchen garden and barnyard, of herbs, vegetables, and animal musk. Suddenly the artificial, dissipated pleasures of Paris seemed oddly distasteful.

"Perhaps I'll return and try my luck in the forests sometime."

Mont-Martre wine, he recalled as he tried a swallow, was not highly regarded except for its medicinal and diuretic qualities: People still repeated the old joke, "Mont-Martre wine—drink a pint and piss a quart." Jugier's wine was predictably dreadful, but Charles smiled politely and, after a quarter hour, took his leave. Marie-Anne and a younger sister stole out of the farmhouse to bob curtsies to him, blushing and smiling that such an aristocratic young gentleman would deign to pass the time with their family.

♥   ♥

He returned the next day to Jeanne and Antoinette's rooms, after a sleepless night, but Antoinette would not let him past the door.

"Jeanne never wants to see you again. She fears she'll never find a wealthy protector now and she hates you for it. Do you blame her?"

"Then let me be her protector. Let me take care of her forever. I—I want to marry her," he blurted out, thinking guiltily of Père Gomart and his fears for his so-called niece's earthly reputation and heavenly salvation. "As my wife—"

"Do you honestly believe Jeanne would settle for being the wife of the executioner?"

He could not help but think of the hundreds—probably thousands—of haggard, pox-scarred, desperate public women who haunted the shadows of every alley and riverbank. "It's better than becoming a common whore on the streets, and—and starving in the gutter or dying of syphilis or consumption before she's twenty! I'm well off—I can give her security. I love her. I want her to be happy."

Antoinette sighed. "You just don't understand, do you? You won't make her happy by marrying her."

"But I can offer her—"

"Chevalier, come out of your fantasy for a moment. Jeanne's a complete nobody, the illegitimate daughter of a poor seamstress, and she wants to be a princess. She's far too ambitious to marry the sort of petty merchant or notary who'd be so besotted by her looks and her considerable bedroom skills that he'd overlook her birth and her lack of fortune—and her reputation. She can't become a princess by marrying a prince, but she always had the chance to live like a princess by becoming his mistress—or at least she thought she did until she took up with you."

Charles, she wouldn't entertain the thought of marrying you even if you were a respectable professional gentleman like a doctor or notary; why would she marry you when you are what you are?

"But if a liaison with me has spoiled her chances," he began when Antoinette was done with her lecture, "she ought to be glad—"

"Well, yes, I expect so. But try to convince Jeanne that she'd be better off as your wife. No one ever said she had any great powers of reason."

He pinched the bridge of his nose between thumb and forefinger, rubbed his eyes. All his elaborate, wishful daydreams that Jeanne might be his forever were fading like snow on a spring day.

"Toinette," he said at length, "why should anyone else discover who Jeanne's old lovers may have been?"

"People always find out. Men like to boast about who had a woman first."

"But if the name of the Chevalier de Longval should arise in society, it would mean nothing. No one knows me—I mean, no one knows who 'Longval' is. Only a few other members of my family know it's an alias we use, and we . . . we keep to ourselves. And I've never told a soul about her. I loved her far too much to allow my brothers or anyone else to crack jokes about the tawdry mistress I was hiding somewhere."

She was my private treasure . . .

Antoinette eyed him, appraised him. "No one else knows you and she were lovers? Not the old priest, not any of your family? You can swear to that?"

"No one. I swear to you on my life that I won't now, and never will, betray her. Let it be our secret. I give you, and her, my word of honor that no one will ever learn of our liaison from me or from anybody I know. If the hangman's word is worth anything, that is."

"Your word's good enough for me. But it's Jeanne whom you'll have to convince."

Jeanne was still huddled in the big bed, though her color was better. At her first glimpse of Charles, she shrank back and cried "Don't you dare let him come in here!" but Antoinette stopped, folded her arms, and scowled at her like a disapproving nurserymaid.

"You ought to listen to what he has to say."

"No! Take him away! Get him out of my sight!"

"Be quiet," Antoinette told her, "and do listen to reason for just a moment."

Charles stepped forward, absurdly recalling his schoolboy days, as if beckoned to the head of the room to recite in Latin. "Jeanne—

dearest—*chérie*—I beg you to forgive me."

His voice was trembling, he realized, and drew a quick breath and composed himself.

"If I'd known that loving you would lead to such catastrophe for you, I would have torn myself away somehow, before you ever learned who I was. But I swear to you, as a man of honor—"

"You? *Honor?*"

Jeanne slumped back on her pillows and averted her gaze from him as she dabbed at her eyes with a sodden handkerchief.

"Yes—on my honor as a gentleman. I swear to you that no one but the three of us here has known of our liaison, and no one else ever will."

He glanced up toward the battered crucifix that hung over the head of her bed and strode toward her, ignoring her gasp of protest. He took the crucifix from its hook and clutched at it with both hands, like a man drowning.

"All I ask from you is your forgiveness, Jeanne."

And why, a rebellious little voice within him insisted, should I have to ask anyone's pardon for being something I can't help?

"I—I promise you, on my honor and on the holy Cross, that I'll never stand in the way of your ambitions, or seek to take advantage of any good fortune that may come to you. I swear to you that I'll never reveal our secret and that you will never see me again as long as you live."

Jeanne gazed at him for an instant before turning her face to the wall once more and sobbing. Charles left the crucifix on her night table and tiptoed out.

13

At dinner at Rue d'Enfer on the following Friday Père Gomart mentioned, in passing, that his niece had refused to see him at his last visit, and expressed his usual worries about her dissolute life.

A fortnight passed, at the end of which Père Gomart repeated sadly that his cherished but troublesome niece seemed to have chosen to break ties with him. The next day, having himself received no word of Jeanne, Charles returned once more to Rue du Bac.

"Breaking your promise so soon, Chevalier?" Antoinette inquired, as she answered the door.

"I didn't come to see her. I only wanted to ask you how she was."

"She's much better."

"Please take this, for whatever she needs," he began, reaching into his pocket for a few silver écus, half his month's allowance.

"Keep it. She's gone."

"Gone?" he echoed her, uncomprehending.

"Jeanne went out on Tuesday and didn't come back."

The next day Antoinette had had a letter from her, ill-spelled, tear-splotched, thanking her for her friendship and for all her various kindnesses. Jeanne would be lodging elsewhere, but she gave no address. A carter collected Jeanne's trunk.

"I didn't ask him where he was taking it," Antoinette added. "I felt that that was no one's business but Jeanne's."

Though Charles had told himself a dozen times a day that she could never be his again, it was not until that moment that he realized he had truly lost her. He must have looked as if someone had plunged a bayonet into his guts, he thought, for Antoinette touched his hand and said, in a warmer tone of voice, "I was about to leave for the theater. Come walk with me."

As if he were a young child, she led him across the Seine and found them a seat below the bridge, just above the gravel beach, in the sunshine. "I'm sorry," she said as he sank onto the crude bench and hid his face in his hands. "I'm sorry Jeanne reacted as she did. It was uncalled-for—and unkind of her."

"Why should I be surprised?"

He did not look up at her. He should have been used to such scorn, he knew, for he'd seen people shrink away from his touch since he was ten years old, since they'd thrown him out of two different schools—oh, they'd asked him to leave, so delicately, so politely, "we fear that your family connections are unsuitable . . ." But it came to the same thing—when they learned who his father was, it seemed young Charles de Longval, young Longval of the commendable thirst for knowledge and the excellent marks and quiet disposition and polished manners, wasn't fit to share a schoolroom with the sons of gentlemen.

"I'm sorry," she repeated. "But she didn't love you. She never did."

"She cared for me!"

"I think she was fond of you, as fond as she can be of anyone. But I don't believe she really knows what love is."

He glared at Antoinette. "That's a shabby thing to say."

"It's the truth. I'm fond of her myself, but I know what she is." She bent and tore up a flowering weed that had twined itself through the nearby stonework, and idly wound it through her fingers.

Jeanne's a decent person, really, she said. She's generous when she can afford to be, and kindhearted in a childish, careless sort of way. But she's never truly loved anyone in her life but herself, never made sacrifices for a soul. Don't you think, if she really loved you, *you*, Chevalier, Monsieur Sanson, that it wouldn't have mattered to her who you are?

He kept on staring down at the water-smoothed pebbles at his feet. "I suppose I always knew . . . I knew I'd never be able to keep her. But—but for her to rebuff me like that," he added, "as if I were a—a leper, or some monstrous criminal—" He could bear no more and sprang to his feet, flushed and trembling, blinking away tears of rage.

"Christ in heaven! I'm no criminal! I've nothing to be ashamed of! I'm a good Christian, a gentleman, the king's servant—an officer of the law, the equal of any of them—I only follow the orders the judges give me. Why should *I* be pointed at, hissed at, despised?"

Antoinette rose. "Chevalier—"

Before Charles realized what was happening, she slipped her hands about his face, pulling his head down to hers, and stifled his outburst with a hard kiss on the mouth.

"There," she said, when at last she drew away from him. "Not everyone despises you."

"Toinette?"

"If you hadn't been so infatuated with Jeanne, I might have spoken up earlier."

"You should have." He was still dazed.

"Don't delude yourself."

She gave him a quick, sardonic smile and continued, still smiling a little, though she avoided his gaze.

"Look at me. I'll never be a famous beauty. How could I compare with her? When we both believed you were a rich nobleman, I thought, 'Well, let her have her chance'; because you barely noticed my existence. She outshone me as if I were a candle in the sunshine. But then when we knew who you really were—"

"How—how did Jeanne learn . . . ?" By sheer ill luck, no doubt.

Antoinette said nothing for a moment, then raised her head and looked at him, meeting his eyes. A warm breeze from the west whispered along the riverbank, scouring away the stink of the murky water and surrounding them with the scents of dust and green trees from the Tuileries gardens.

"I told her."

Charles stared at her. For a moment he could not breathe, cry out, say a word, and all the cries and uproar of all the streets of Paris seemed to ring in his ears.

"*You*—told her?"

"Yes." She drew a breath. "I won't lie to you. I'd crossed your path, three weeks before, when you were taking someone to do penance at the cathedral. You didn't see me, but I recognized you." She paused, but he said nothing, in his outrage could not have stammered another word. "You're a public figure, Chevalier—whether you want to be or not. You must have known it would have to happen sooner or later."

"And you told Jeanne?" he cried, finding his voice at last. "Deliberately? You *told* her? Why, in God's name? Out of spite? Because you were jealous of her beauty and couldn't bear to see her climb the ladder ahead of you?"

A hot blush crept into her cheeks and he realized he had spoken over-harshly as she nodded.

"I suppose I was. A little. But it was for your sake, really. I might never have said anything to her if she hadn't told me that she was pregnant. 'It's probably Longval's,' she said, 'though it doesn't really matter whose it is, because it's just what I need, in order to persuade him to marry me. He's so naïve and besotted, he'd believe anything I told him.'"

Antoinette paused and glanced up at him, but he had not the faintest idea how to respond.

"She still believed she'd get a title and a château by marrying you. But I knew the truth, and I was sure she cared for you no more than she cared for any of her lovers. It was a test, you see. If she'd really loved you, it wouldn't have mattered to her.

"So I told Jeanne who it was she'd been sleeping with, who might be the father of her child. She wouldn't believe me, of course, not until I dragged her to the Halles the next morning and showed her—there you were, beside the big pillory, telling your servants what had to be done—and . . . well, you saw what happened. First she slapped me for destroying her fantasies, and then she burst into tears, and then she ran off to go to the abortionist. She couldn't even bear the thought of carrying a child that might be yours."

She brushed herself off and straightened her skirts. "I have to go to the theater now. If you want to see me again, you know where to find me."

He could think of nothing more to say. Antoinette turned and left him, climbing to the embankment and striding along it toward the high, arched passageway that led beneath the Grand Gallery of the Louvre. Just as she disappeared behind a heavy four-horse coach lumbering along the quay he recovered his voice and cried her name, but she was too far away to hear him and an instant later she was gone.

14

Hunting alone in the meadows and woodlands around Saint-Denis, two hours from Paris, soothed his bruised heart very well. As old Jugier had told him, the forests were well stocked with game. Though only the gentry and aristocracy were allowed the privilege of the hunt, Sanson the Second (or possibly the First) must have insisted upon his genteel Longval pedigree, for the Sansons had always enjoyed the right to go shooting—discreetly—in the royal preserves.

Jean-Baptiste had recovered enough, after seven years, to return to his duties at the scaffold and pillory, though often Charles still took his place. Soon the habitués of the scaffold, those connoisseurs who never missed an execution, took to calling them "Old Sanson" and "Young Charlot" in order to distinguish between them.

If I ever have a son, Charles thought grimly after hearing "Young Charlot" for the dozenth time on the lips of drunken strangers, *I'll break the family tradition and name him something other than Charles.* "Charlot" was what Madeleine called him, and her absence from the household on Rue d'Enfer still felt like the gap where a tooth had been recently drawn, unfamiliar and painful.

When he had a few days of leisure in fine weather, usually he chose to decamp for Saint-Denis, riding Rosette along the Beauvais road that skirted Mont-Martre. He soon saw Jugier again, outside his cottage, and was invited to take another glass of the sour local vintage whenever he rode by.

"And the devil of these bad harvests, monsieur," Jugier confided to him one afternoon, during a inevitable conversation on the state of the weather and the crops, "is we've nothing to give the girls for their dowries but the odd sheet or two we could scrape together." Various misfortunes had plagued his small farm and Charles suspected that the Jugiers might not be averse to accepting a few "loans" from a prosperous acquaintance.

"Babette," Madame Jugier added, "she was the prettiest, she wedded Rollin the blacksmith last year, but they'd been sweethearts since they were little ones together. Take my poor Marie-Anne, now—she's a good girl—woman, I should say, for she's twenty-eight already—hardworking, a good cook, and she'd make some man a fine wife, but she has no fortune and they don't come courting her. Though she's never one to complain about having no sweethearts."

He glanced over at Marie-Anne, who was scattering grain for the chickens and geese. She was no dainty beauty like Jeanne, but she had a pretty smile and glowed with robust good health. Surely some prosperous farmer would want to take her, even at her age and with no more dowry than a few household linens.

"Doesn't mademoiselle wish to marry?"

"Every woman wants a husband, doesn't she, monsieur? But the hard truth is, not all of them are going to find one. She's talked now and then about nunneries. I'm guessing she might take vows."

"And she's a good, generous child," Jugier added. "She's the eldest, you know. Six months ago she told me she'd decided that any goods I could spare for a dowry should go to her sister. 'It looks like I'm to be an old maid,' she says to me, 'but Thérèse is young enough still to find a husband. Let her have her chance.'"

Charles wondered where he had heard those words before and recalled that Antoinette had said much the same thing at their last meeting: "*I thought, 'Well, let her have her chance'; because you barely noticed my existence.*"

He turned the conversation to other matters and shortly took his leave of them and untied Rosette from the fence post, with a brief "good day, mademoiselle," to Marie-Anne as he passed her.

"Monsieur?" She tossed away the last handful of grain to the clucking hens and approached him. "Monsieur de Longval, they were talking about me, weren't they? I heard them say my name."

He nodded and went on tightening the saddle girth, but she unexpectedly moved closer to him, bringing a faint, not unpleasant whiff of hay and fresh earth with her. "My father was complaining like he always does, I suppose, how he can't get me wed and off his hands."

He paused, curious, wondering what business this was of his. "Something of the sort."

"Well, he doesn't say the whole of it. The local lads, they won't have me because I'm secondhand goods, and who wants that when there's no dowry with it?"

"Mademoiselle?" he said, startled. "Why are you tell—"

"I was promised," she persisted, as if determined to tell him everything, no matter what, "to one of the local boys, six years ago it was. We were going to be wed when we'd both saved up a bit . . . but sometimes you can't wait, and you go to the altar after you've already been husband and wife to each other. But then we had a cold summer and my father's crops failed, and everything went wrong, and for a couple of years we hadn't a sou left over for me to put in my stocking. So Jean-Pierre said we'd have to wait a while longer, till I had something to bring to the wedding, and then after a spell he thought he could do better, and married the grocer's daughter instead. And everybody knew about us, of course. I suppose my father knows, though he won't say so. But that's why I won't be having a wedding, now or ever."

"Forgive me, mademoiselle, but why are you telling me this?"

"'Cause I'm lonely."

She went on, speaking rapidly, as if she could prevent him from protesting or interrupting by the sheer rush of words: The way things were, she'd never be anything but an old maid. She was twenty-eight already, and maybe she'd go to the holy sisters and take vows if she wasn't needed here after her brother wedded his girl, but first she wanted to live a bit. She wasn't ugly, or lame, or sickly, or half-witted; there was nothing wrong with her but that she had no fortune and she'd given up her reputation too quickly to a man who didn't wed her.

She paused for breath and Charles gave her an encouraging smile. "No, indeed."

"I just want to have a little fun before I get old. That's all. I want to be able to tell myself someday, when I'm an old biddy alone between a pair of cold sheets, that I did have a handsome young lover once, beyond the selfish bastard who threw me over for six silver spoons and a bedstead with a feather mattress." She smiled awkwardly and ducked her head, avoiding his eyes. "There—you can do as you wish now, or forget we ever spoke."

The sun-browned, buxom, homespun-clad woman before him was so unlike Jeanne, or even Antoinette, that Charles could not help a quick, wry burst of laughter. Any woman was to be had for the taking, evidently, except the one he wanted, and the one he perhaps-wanted.

She glanced up at him, hurt, and backed away, but he seized her wrist.

"Forgive me. I wasn't laughing at you, but—but at myself, and my circumstances. Mademoiselle—Marie-Anne—I appreciate your offer, and I can't say I'm not tempted, but I'd be taking advantage of you."

"Because you're a rich chevalier and I'm just a peasant?" She grinned, an honest, open, cheerful grin, not the coy little smile of the polished Parisian flirt. "*I* asked *you*, monsieur. You didn't go seducing me, like the wicked lord in the play I saw once. I spoke up because I fancy you, and I think you'd be decent to me. We'd go into it with no ideas of anything more between us than . . . than a bit of sport.

"See here," she added, "if I took up with the hired hand, who's a well-made man, the whole village would be talking about it in a week, and snickering into their sleeves whenever I went into the square. But you're a stranger here, only passing through now and then, and nobody knows you to gossip about you. And that's the way I want it."

The thought of that blunt peasant girl, he realized, a woman as simple and wholesome as fresh milk or sweet ripe apples, seemed vastly appealing, an antidote to Jeanne's well-rehearsed, irresistible coquetry. He brushed his fingertips across her cheek.

"I like you, Marie-Anne, I won't deny it; but this must be your choice, for I won't have anyone say I forced you into sin. Think it over again. I'm going to Saint-Denis now, to hunt, and I'll return in two or three days. All right?"

Marie-Anne grasped his hand. "All right."

He mounted and shook the reins, glancing over his shoulder as the mare fell into a trot. Marie-Anne stood unmoving, hugging herself as if a chill breeze were blowing, staring after him.

He plunged into the quiet of the woodlands and for two solitary days endeavored not to think of women at all, neither of Jeanne who had spurned him, nor of Antoinette who had betrayed him, nor of Marie-Anne who had offered him a certain solace. When he returned to Mont-Martre, he found her lugging a pail of water to the house, just as when he first had met her.

"Good day, Monsieur Longval, did you have good luck hunting?"

"Good enough: a pheasant and a couple of rabbits. Perhaps," he added, on the spur of the moment, "you'd like a rabbit for the pot? I hear you're a good cook, Marie-Anne."

She smiled. "That's kind of you. But you needn't go giving us presents. That's not the way it is."

"I didn't mean it so."

"I'm not a loose woman; you ought to understand that. I won't have you giving me gifts, as if you were paying me—and I won't ask for anything, ever. I just want a bit of tenderness. But if you'll have me, then—then here I am."

She was handsome, in her countrified way, with a sturdy, well-rounded figure, thick dark hair, and a laughing mouth. He scarcely knew her well enough to think he could love her, but for the moment, he realized, "a bit of tenderness" was all he, too, desired.

"Monsieur?" she said, when he did not reply.

He slid his arm about her waist and drew her nearer. "First of all, you can't go on calling me 'Monsieur.' My name is Charles."

15

Ruined.

I suppose that was what killed my father. That, and the wine, and loneliness, and despair. I was sixteen and a half. He left my brother and me a worthless, mortgaged estate, eight dozen books, a few pieces of furniture that didn't match, six pairs of sheets—all with holes in them—and a mountain of debts.

Now I wasn't even a *hobereau*, what they call a shabby country gentleman with nothing much more than a coat of arms, a tumble-down house that might pass for a château if you didn't look too close, and a scrap of land to call his own. I was just a penniless, landless orphan with blue blood and the no-account title of chevalier, which weren't going to pay for a meal or get me anywhere that mattered. I hadn't any education beyond what the curé had taught us; all I'd read were bits from a few of my father's books, but most of them were dull going.

The one thing I did know was that I was noble, because our parents had drilled that into us from when we were little: Even if you must go without luxuries, and walk the grounds in wooden sabots like the peasants, you must always remember that you are a gentleman, of the noble family of Lefebvre de La Barre. I knew my brother was someday going to become one of the royal Body Guards, because that was what people with old titles and no money did. I also knew that once all the debts were paid, we'd have nothing beyond the clothes we wore.

Father Jouffroy saw my father buried next to my mother in the chapel, and found us a guardian, a lawyer in Paris, to sign papers for us and sell the château and lands. Then—it was like a miracle, a gift from God—just a couple of weeks later, even before La Barre was sold out from under us, he told us that our cousin, Madame Feydeau de Brou, the abbess of the convent of Willancourt in Abbeville, had offered us a home with her. (We were that ignorant, we didn't even know where Abbeville was, except that it was somewhere "up north.")

So in April, with the curé's blessing, we set off in a market farmer's wagon for Paris, where lawyer Guibert sent a servant to meet us and gave us supper and beds for the night. I'd have liked to have seen a little of Paris beyond a lot of crowded, noisy streets, but probably he just wanted to do his duty and get rid of us, for early the next morning the same servant took us to the coaching station and saw us off on the stagecoach northwest to the county of Ponthieu.

Coming from Férolles and Brie-Comte-Robert, and having seen barely anything of Paris, we thought Abbeville was a great city. At least it was much bigger and busier than sleepy old Brie, which had its little market and its crumbling castle and not much else. Abbeville, on the other hand, was a big river town, almost twenty thousand people, they told us. It had grand houses and churches and broad squares and a fortress with barracks full of soldiers, and carriages and carts rattled about everywhere in the streets, which were swarming with peddlers, boatmen, dock workers, cloth workers from the manufactory. Jacques and I clung to each other like peasant kids on market day, caught somewhere between ecstasy and terror.

A gardener from the abbey found us soon enough at the coaching inn and drove us across the town to meet our cousin. Father Jouffroy had told us we had to be on our very best behavior before her, because she was somebody important, almost as important as a bishop, being an abbess of a convent and all. I'd never seen an abbess before. From what the curé had said, I imagined some grim old lady wearing a starched veil and a great heavy silver cross, who was determined to shut us up in the church with our rosaries and prayer books and turn us into monks. I nearly fainted with relief when she turned out to be about forty, with plenty of wit and good humor, and as pretty as a middle-aged woman in frumpy nun robes can be.

"Well, let's have a look at you," she ordered us, when the old doorkeeper nun, who was as sour-faced as I'd dreaded our cousin would be, had left us alone with her in her parlor. We straightened up, licking our lips and swallowing. Our second-hand clothes and shoes, old and nothing special to begin with, were a mess: badly mended, ill-fitting, and travel-stained. To Madame Feydeau we must have looked like a pair of Red Indians from the far-off wilds of New France. God knows I was an ignorant little whelp, though my brother was a bit more civilized; he could remember our home the way it used to be, before Mother died, before the rot set in.

"It's Jacques and François, is that right?"

"Yes, madame," my brother mumbled.

"Speak up, boys, no need to be frightened. How old are you, François, thirteen? Fourteen?"

"Sixteen, madame."

"You're a bit undersized," she said, surprised.

I didn't know what to say to that, and said nothing. I've always been skinny and small-boned. Back in Brie-Comte-Robert, Paul and the other toughs used to sneer that my lord the chevalier was so dainty, he ought to go play with the little girls. But Madame Feydeau was almost right, in a way; I suppose I might as well have been nine or ten, for all the education and refinement I'd had at home at La Barre.

"We'd better feed you properly," she added, with a smile. "Have you eaten?"

"We had some bread and cheese on the stagecoach, around noon," Jacques said, "and a meat pie between us."

"Good Lord," our cousin exclaimed, "what manner of accent is that?"

Jacques and I looked at each other. We didn't know what she meant by accent; we talked the way our friends talked, that was all.

Of course our friends had been the village boys at Férolles, farmers' kids, peasants, and aside from a bit of La Barre pride and a little frayed lace at our cuffs on our Sunday shirts, you couldn't have told us apart.

"I can see," she added firmly, "that you two will want some polishing."

She lodged us in the guest quarters by the abbey courtyard, the house used for lodgers who couldn't, in decency, sleep within the walls. Their priest lived there, and also an old fellow who my cousin felt sorry for, Beauvarlet, a former merchant who had ruined himself somehow. He was friendly enough at first, but pretty soon I decided he was just an asslicker, showing off his piety to impress people and get favors from the abbess, and covering the walls of his room with crucifixes and holy pictures.

We couldn't go calling somebody as important as the abbess of Willancourt "Cousin Marguerite," and "madame abbess" or "Madame Feydeau" seemed too formal for a relative we'd see almost every day. Eventually we settled for just calling her Madame, like a princess.

We took dinner and supper alone with her for the first couple of days. I don't think my table manners impressed her. But she wasn't the type to nag and carp. When she wanted something done, it got done.

"I declare, you two are the most ill-educated pair of bumpkins I've ever met," she told us, on our third evening in Abbeville. "Like a couple of stableboys. But you're not stupid," she added, when we looked at her like hound pups expecting a whipping. "All you need is proper instruction. What was your poor father thinking of, letting you run wild?"

"He didn't pay much attention to us, after Mother died," I said. "And he couldn't afford schools, or tutors."

"Well, both of you need an education suitable for a gentleman, before you're fit to join society. That's music, dancing, fencing—I suppose neither of you knows how to use a sword?"

We shook our heads. Father had made a bit of an attempt to teach us the basics of swordplay, years ago, but he'd soon lost interest. We could gut and skin a rabbit or squirrel in no time flat, on the other hand, but it looked as if that skill wasn't going to be as useful among the citified gentry of Abbeville.

"You'll have to work on improving your speech, so you don't sound like peasants every time you open your mouths. I'll oversee your table manners myself. Oh, and you'd better practice your penmanship, I suppose, and try reading some of the latest books so you can manage a cultivated conversation. You do know how to read and write, I hope?"

I gave her a furious glance at that, because we weren't *that* backward, but she was smiling. "Never mind, François," she continued. "I wouldn't be so hard on you if I didn't believe I could turn you into gentlemen, fit to be seen at court, when you're old enough to join the king's guards."

"But we haven't any money, madame," Jacques said. "None at all. We haven't got much more to our name than a change of clothes. We can't afford to pay music masters and fencing masters and such."

She held up a hand. She had pretty hands and she was always showing them off with graceful little movements like that. "Leave that to me, Jacques. Mercy, how often does an old maiden like me become this lucky?"

"Lucky?"

"God has unexpectedly allowed me—*me*, a bride of Christ—the happiness of being mother to a pair of fine, handsome boys, my dear. Why, you're my family now, of course. I'm happy to pay for whatever you need, including the cultivation you lack. And even to provide you with pocket money," she added with a wink, "because I know young men want to go out on the town from time to time and enjoy themselves . . . but when I loose you into local society, in a few months if you prove not to be dullards, then I expect you to repay me by not embarrassing me. Do we have a bargain?"

"Yes, madame," we chorused.

As if I was going to try anything that might spoil our amazing luck. I'd been rescued from beggary, against all the odds, and I swore I was going to become a gentleman worthy of my name.

16

His trysts with Marie-Anne, Charles often thought, were rather like the rustic farces that shabby acting troupes played in pantomime in the unlicensed theaters beyond the Boulevard, in which heroic peasant lovers pursued saucy milkmaids while avoiding the eye of a scowling father. Marie-Anne made no promises to him during their clandestine meetings in the hayloft over Jugier's cow shed, and he made none to her.

He did not discover any great passion for her, though he did discover, after a few months of intimacy, that he had grown fond of her. He found her restful; she continued to ask nothing of him but what they furtively shared in the hay above her father's scrawny livestock. She spoke little of herself when afterward they lay panting together on an old horse blanket, watching the swallows swooping beneath the roof, and the kittens prowling among the rafters and the hay bales. The sweet scent of dry grass all around them was soothing, despite the less agreeable odor of cattle and pigs below, and the manure heap not far away.

Marie-Anne's talk was of comical local gossip, or her family's doings, and often she and Charles laughed at the bawdy jokes she learned from the farmhands. The difference in their ages had somehow smoothed out the difference in their stations; if Charles, as Marie-Anne believed him to be, was a wealthy gentleman of rank and she a mere farmer's daughter, then at least she, six years his elder, held some sort of superiority of life experience over him.

From time to time, as he headed home to Rue d'Enfer, he found himself imagining a simple country life at the family cottage at Brie-Comte-Robert, tending a garden full of roses and tulips, raising chickens for the market, exchanging those earthy jokes and a glass of red wine with rustic neighbors. A moment later he would grin at his own sentimentality; he was not really cut out for a rural existence. In the end, he knew well enough that he preferred the more sophisticated pleasures of the city.

He had kept company with Marie-Anne for more than a year, shutting out ever-present memories of the scaffold with what he had come to regard as a bucolic idyll, when Madeleine paid one of her rare visits to Paris, in order to show off her eight-month-old daughter.

"So," she said when she had left the rest of the family clustered cooing around the cradle below, and she and Charles were alone together in the little bedroom they once had shared. "You're still here and the same as ever. I thought you might be abroad at some university by now, studying for your medical degree."

He twisted about, unwilling to meet her eyes. "Matters didn't work out as I thought they might."

"Nico's eighteen and already out of the house, Martin's seventeen—imagine it! Our little brothers! They're all growing up."

"I know."

"I expect Martin's assisting you."

"And?"

"So why isn't he already taking your place, as you used to keep saying one of them would?"

"Well . . . I met a girl. Not long after your wedding."

"As I've been telling you you should? Somebody you can open your heart to?"

"No. It went wrong." He turned to the window, gazing out at the leafless trees beyond the stables. "I was a fool. I was obsessed with her. I—I missed you, you know."

It's all your fault, really, he wanted to say, though he knew he was close to wallowing in self-pity. *All your fault, for sailing off to Melun when I needed you here to set me right.* "I missed you and I desperately wanted the company, someone who could take your place. So I couldn't have gone abroad and left Jeanne behind."

"But?"

"I pretended to myself that she could be as much of a friend—a support—to me as you are. But she wasn't, of course. I never dared tell her who I was. And then she found out another way, about me, and took it badly, and . . . it ended."

"And you were so devastated that ever since then, you've been more or less sleepwalking, going through the motions."

He glanced at her. "You're no less perceptive than you ever were, are you? How does Hérisson like it, that you probably know him better than he knows himself?"

"Oh, I can manage Pierre well enough. He's an earnest soul." She smiled and came to stand next to him at the window. "It's you I'm worried about. I don't want you to turn into an automaton, a half-dead machine. Either go abroad and get away from this life, or stay here where you know you have a place, but find something that will occupy you, something you're passionate about, like Father and his laboratory. Or get married and start a family—children do make a difference, I'm finding out, with Pierre's little boy, who's adorable, and now our own baby. You need to find something that will make you happy, Charlot."

"Where is it written that the *bourreau* deserves to be happy?"

She gave him the old, familiar look. "You're a good, decent person, Charles, no matter what your orders oblige you to do, and you deserve your chance to snatch a little happiness. And don't you ever say that word again about yourself. Do you have a mistress now?"

"In a way."

Was Marie-Anne his mistress? Yes, if you wanted to be particular about it. She'd have turned scarlet with mortification if he'd ever used the word with her, though. Mistresses were grasping courtesans; mistresses expected compensation for their favors, no less than street whores, though they dressed it up as "maintenance," didn't they—gowns and trinkets and apartments and carriages. And Marie-Anne had never accepted a thing from him but, once or twice, after much urging, a plump rabbit for the family stew pot. Better use just "lover," or *petite amie*," "little friend," as Bastien, his newest assistant, would vulgarly put it.

"You mean, a girl you're keeping company with. But I suppose she doesn't know who you are," Madeleine continued as Charles nodded, "and you're not telling her all you need to tell her."

"Yes, Madame Snoop, if you must know."

"Tell her who you are."

"God, no! I don't want to see that look on her face—the way Jeanne looked at me that day."

"She'll find out sooner or later, and then where will you be?"

"No, she won't. She's in an outlying village; she doesn't come in to Paris. I doubt the name Sanson would mean anything to her."

Madeleine sighed. "I'll tell you something. You know Mamma's rule, that none of us should ever talk about Father's profession at home unless it can't be avoided, and then only in private."

"Well?"

"Well, in *my* house—Pierre's house—I don't have that rule. Of course we need to curb our tongues in front of the children, until they get a little older, but Pierre and his brother and I talk freely about it among ourselves, when we need to. Maybe Mamma's embarrassed to speak of it with her own husband—pretends to herself that he's an ordinary civil servant—but I'm not."

Charles looked at her. She resembled Marthe, in both handsome looks and unflinching character, more than she would have cared to know. "You're rarely embarrassed to speak about anything."

"That's right. I'm the executioner of Paris's daughter and the executioner of Melun's wife and I don't see why I should deny it in my own home, with my own husband, when I know perfectly well what he does to earn his pay. He talks about business with me, expenses and hiring and so on, if he needs to. And after an execution, if it upsets him, Pierre knows that he can come home and talk to me about it, get it off his chest. Just the way it helped you to talk about Damiens. You can't just keep on bottling it up, or you'll go mad."

"Or . . ." he began, at last expressing the fear that had haunted him for some years now, as he found himself growing more and more accustomed to the daily duties, however grim they might be, "or turn into an unfeeling monster . . ."

"No, I don't think you would. That's your trouble. You feel things too much, and you think too much, to ever turn into an unfeeling monster. You know," she added, turning and perching on the bed, as she had done when they were children, "I spent a lot more time than you did with Grand'mère when we were growing up, and she told me stories while we were knitting or sewing. Once she realized that I was just as tough-minded as she was, and not afraid to talk about the family business, she began telling me about her husbands, Grand-père and Monsieur Prudhomme and the other one—"

They'd all forgotten his name, Charles realized. Who could remember all of Grandmother's three or four long-deceased husbands when Marthe's personality had elbowed their memories aside?

"—and what sort of men they were, and which famous criminals they'd executed, and how they'd behaved honorably in some incident or other."

"So?" Charles said, wondering where on earth she was going with this.

"Well, I don't remember a lot of it, but I did get the impression that our grandfather was—I can't express it any other way—that he was the perfect executioner—"

God save us, he wanted to say, how should one be a perfect executioner, then, but she continued.

"He did his job as he was ordered, and was matter-of-fact about his profession. He'd been brought up to it, and knew he could never be anything else, so I suppose he accepted it as God's will, that he was meant to be who he was. Just like Father, he studied medical books and tried to help the poor people in the quarter when they were ill, to make up for his other work. So he was content with it, and led a respectable, happy, domestic life—"

"Until he died of a fever at forty-five."

"That's not the point. He was at peace with his situation all his life. He didn't love his work, but he didn't hate it, either. To him, it was just his job and his duty and God's will. Probably he stopped thinking about it."

"So you think that I ought to be like him?"

She shook her head. "No, I don't. No, indeed. You can't help being yourself, and you think and feel much more than our grandfather probably ever did. I expect he had no imagination at all. But

I do think, if you've given up the idea of going abroad, that you're simply going to have to accept what you are, be at peace with it, as he was. Find some solace elsewhere, in order to keep on in your position for years and remain sane. I mean it, Charlot."

"Solace? I've got solace, of a sort."

"I don't mean keeping mistresses and flinging your money about. That's just distraction, empty amusement. Find an occupation that really means something to you, that you can take genuine pride in. What about music? Do you still play the violin?"

"Most evenings."

"You're a good player. Our uncle—"

"I'm not anywhere near as good as he was." Chrétien Zelle, Jean-Baptiste's sister's husband, had been an accomplished harpsichord player, often giving public concerts, his audience willingly overlooking the fact that he was a retired *aide-bourreau* and the father of the *maître des hautes œuvres* of Soissons.

"But he obviously found an avocation that took his mind off his job."

"I like playing, and it's something to occupy my evenings at home, but I'm scarcely talented enough to give concerts, and I never will be."

Besides, he thought, Uncle Zelle didn't hold an official title, he wasn't conspicuous—imagine what sort of audience the Master of High Works of the City of Paris were to have, if he dared to give a public concert.

You've still got medicine, like Father, Madeleine persisted. Have you been keeping up with the laboratory, and with your reading?

Charles sighed. He had to admit he had been slack about it. Distractions . . .

"Loose women aren't the answer, Charlot. Your real passion is. I expect you already know as much as any doctor, anyway—why do you cling to the notion that to be a proper healer, you have to sit in an anatomy theater, listening to some pompous professor talk about something you've already done a dozen times with Father? If you haven't the courage to go abroad—"

"I'm not afraid of leaving!"

"Aren't you?" She faced him, her sharp dark eyes capturing his, and after an instant he lowered his gaze. "It's not so easy to leave everything you know and start afresh with nothing. Not many people could do it. But if you haven't the courage and drive to go abroad and leave everything behind you, still nothing's preventing you, is it, from taking over Father's practice, and helping people who need a doctor and can't afford one. It's not all-or-nothing, you know. You can still be a healer without running off to a foreign university and breaking with your whole family.

"You always said you wanted to heal people, not kill them. Well, grow up. Perhaps you can't escape the office Grand'mère shoved you into; but you could make up for taking lives by saving some other lives, instead of just moping about it. Not everything's all about *you*."

Charles stared at her for a moment, openmouthed. At last he dropped onto the bed beside her, buried his face in his hands, and began to laugh.

"*Parbleu*," he managed to say between whoops of laughter, "how the devil does Hérisson tolerate you?"

She gave him the refined, distilled version of the sisterly look, the pitying gaze that women evidently reserved for thickheaded, callow brothers who were finally beginning to behave like adults. "Pierre adores me. And he knows I'm usually right. You've known me all your life, so you should know it, too. Well? Am I right?"

"Yes, of course you are." He glanced out the window again. The outbuilding that housed Jean-Baptiste's laboratory was just visible at a corner of the stableyard, beyond the garden. He hadn't been inside it for weeks. Neglecting his responsibilities to the neighborhood, Madeleine would say next: He ought to accept and be thankful for what he could have, and what he could do, in spite of what he was. "Of course you're right."

He was silent for a moment, his smile fading. At last he turned to Madeleine again.

"Do you get the news from Paris often, in Melun?"

"A fair amount, though it's a few days old."

"Have you heard that Monsieur de Lally's back in France?"

"I only knew what Father mentioned in a letter: that the British army had captured him in India. The newspapers never give you many details."

They had held Lally prisoner in England, he told her, repeating all he had lately learned at the Palais de Justice, where the clerks knew everything. Then people at court, at the snake pit of Versailles, began to accuse him of being in the pay of the British, because he'd lost so much territory with two disastrous battles; and the British gave him leave to stay in England after the war, if he wished, to avoid the accusations of high treason.

"*Treason*? Monsieur de Lally? You're joking."

"It's monstrous. He insisted on coming back to France, three months ago, to clear his name. If that's not the sign of an honorable man, and one who has nothing on his conscience, I don't know what is."

"Then he should be able to—"

"It's not that simple. I hear plenty of rumors, you know, at the courts. They say he has enemies, a great many enemies, who wish him ill."

"But why?"

"Well, you know his manner. Underneath, he's the best of men, but he's gruff and high-handed and doesn't tolerate fools—"

"And I expect there are plenty of fools in the army," Madeleine interrupted him, "now that any idiot with a noble title and enough money can become an officer!"

"Yes. I'm sure Monsieur de Lally incensed quite a few people, made it easy for them to hold a grudge. But because he was too busy serving his king for forty years on the battlefield to surround himself with influential friends at court," Charles added, parroting words overheard from an indignant counselor who had clearly planted both feet in the Comte de Lally's camp, "and because his family was Irish rather than French, it's likely he'll be the scapegoat for all our losses in this stupid war. There's going to be a special commission that will investigate everything he did in India; it looks as if they won't be satisfied until the Parlement tries him for high treason—and finds him guilty."

Madeleine laid her hand on his. "So that's what's been eating at you."

"Yes."

"His rank . . . it entitles him . . ."

Their father had never had to behead anyone, in all the years he'd been doing the offices; she knew it as well as Charles did.

"Wouldn't it just be my foul luck, that the first person I might have to butcher with my own hands would be a man I knew, a man who'd been kind to me?"

17

Looking back, I think I must have been a bit of a disappointment to Madame. Jacques was all right; he was four years older than I, nearly of age, grown up. He had some sense. But I—well, I was a silly teenaged kid who'd had to do without for a long time, and then suddenly found myself with fine clothes on my back and a handful of gold and silver in my pocket.

I'd grown up in the back of beyond, in that drafty château where the roof leaked, the furniture didn't match, and the moth-eaten old tapestries were in rags. So of course I thought Madame's parlor, all done up in cream and sky-blue paneling with little bits of gilded fruit peeping out here and there, was like a hall at Versailles. She was an aristocrat and had the income and status from her position to live like one: She received nobles and gentry from all the greatest houses of the province, and gave dinner parties nearly every week and went visiting in her carriage, like a duchess. Instead of being just the two penniless whelps of the old drunk in the dilapidated château, Jacques and I counted for something again; we were the cousins—the cosseted cousins, with a noble name and the right to call ourselves chevaliers—of the lady abbess. More than that, now we had a future to look forward to, a future beyond scratching a bare living from played-out soil.

Not that it was all jolly. We counted for something, but that didn't mean the town took us to their hearts straight away. Abbeville is traditional, to say the least. More like stodgy. They don't like strangers there. Everybody seems to know everybody else, at least in genteel society, and if you're a new face everybody'll stare at you until you start to think that maybe your nose has fallen off.

And the *religion*! *Mordieu*! You'd think the town was inhabited only by old tonsured mumblers in cassocks, with calluses on their knees from praying. Everywhere you look, you'll see shrines, wooden saints in niches, holy pictures painted on the walls along the streets, and a church around every corner—Saint-Vulfran, near the marketplace, is about three hundred years old and the biggest, fanciest church I'd ever seen, much bigger than anything even in Brie, with a front to it that's just mad with carvings of angels and monsters and grotesques, and it isn't even a cathedral. What a to-do about a lot of superstition and fairy tales!

You have to watch your mouth all the time in Abbeville: You could get a week in jail and public penance on the steps of Saint-Vulfran for a bit of boisterous blasphemy like a stray *"Foutre-Dieu!"* in public. Someone repeated a story to me about one young fellow who got a little drunk and smacked his fist at a mural on the wall, a picture of Christ, and some workman saw him do it and straight away broke his head for him.

Even the filthiest beggar in town, or the vilest *bourreau*, has a bee in his bonnet about the state of his soul, and everybody else's, too. When my friends and I went once to watch them hanging a thief in the Place du Marché, we could see he wasn't the least bit sorry for what he'd done, just angry and sullen that he'd been caught, and he wouldn't kiss the crucifix and ask God's pardon for his crimes. So the *bourreau* strung him up, let him dangle a moment, sent a couple of aides to grab him and hold him up, and let him drop again. Then he repeated the performance five or six times before finishing the wretch off, to make him repent. And the monk who had come along to pray for the thief's soul let the hangman do it.

Although it's not all stodgy piety in Abbeville. At least those old medieval stonemasons had a sense of humor. Not long after I'd met him, my friend Bertrand Gaillard d'Étallonde and I were out for a walk through the middle of town and he handed me a spy-glass and told me to look high up on the side wall of Saint-Vulfran. I looked where he pointed, and tucked away in an angle, you can see a carved stone devil that's got its knees up around its ears and is grabbing its arse so that it's showing its—well, showing its big, gaping fundament to the world, maybe passing a fart. Not a very refined sculpture for the wall of a church. It made us both laugh till we nearly had fits. Then a priest came by and gave us a good shaking and a lecture on unseemly behavior around God's house.

Maybe that's why some people, especially the starchy, up-and-coming bourgeois, didn't like Madame so much; they took their religion seriously, and a lot of them thought the local aristocrats weren't such devoted Catholics as they might have been. Madame was a great lady, and worldlier than they believed an abbess ought to be. Though I guess she was more pious than some of the bishops I read about. Étallonde secretly lent me some illegal books that'll tell you all the dirt about the bishops and cardinals who keep mistresses and don't even know their catechism, who are just younger sons from great families, less interested in serving God than in enjoying the fat incomes of their lands and abbeys. Madame was young enough to enjoy herself, and still handsome, a bit of a coquette, so people thought she put on airs, with her carriage and her dinner parties, and the way she flirted with all the gentlemen.

Some of the gossips even whispered that she'd broken her vows and wasn't virtuous. Everybody knew she had a special friend, Du-maisniel, the seigneur of Belleval, who was a big noise in Abbeville—in all of Ponthieu, in fact. Belleval knew everybody worth knowing and had a fine house in the best part of town and a pile of money to keep it up. Everyone who was anyone in Abbeville had Monsieur de Belleval at the top of his list of dinner guests, because he had a quick wit and plenty of style and always went out of his way to charm the ladies. They said he'd been a real skirt-chaser all his life and that, if he ever tried, he probably could talk even the chilliest virgin saint into bed with him.

I don't know exactly what was going on between our cousin and Monsieur de Belleval before Jacques and I came to Abbeville, whether it was a real affair or just a harmless flirtation. People who didn't approve of one or the other of them said the worst, of course, and I could see for myself that Belleval was always hanging around Madame like a kid making eyes at a saucy chambermaid, though he was old, must have been fifty or sixty. Jacques and I talked about it once; he thought that Madame hadn't given in to Belleval and that what we heard around town was just vicious gossip. If Madame was Belleval's mistress, Jacques said, Belleval would have gotten tired of her company a lot sooner. Maybe she was the one thing he wanted that he couldn't have.

Belleval's youngest son Pierre was all right, like the other fellows of my own age who I met in Abbeville—people of "our sort," as Madame would say—especially Bertrand Gaillard d'Étallonde. Like the Bellevals, the Gaillards had plenty of money. Bertrand d'Étallonde liked to throw it about, treating us to wine and so on, while his father (who was the chief magistrate of the high court, Monsieur Gaillard de Boëncourt), seemed willing to ignore and smooth over any scrapes he got himself into. It must be a treat to be that rich and that powerful.

When you're of the gentry in a city the size of Abbeville, pretty soon you know everybody else of "your sort." I made friends soon enough and didn't want to let Madame down by behaving like some grubby *hobereau* in front of them and their snooty families, so I did try to learn all the things that she said would polish us. Four months after we'd arrived, once Jacques and I had improved our speech and our table manners enough to satisfy her, she let us join one of her dinner parties for the first time. We'd profit from the example of the gentry, she said, so long as we kept quiet and behaved ourselves and watched how polite town society conducted itself.

I braced myself for a dull time, but at least the food was tasty and there was a lot of it. Madame had put her friend Père Bosquier, a monk who was a scholar from the university in Paris, on one side of me at table; he was friendly and pretended not to notice when I forgot myself and nearly licked my knife, although he talked mostly about a lot of books I'd never heard of. But she'd seated a pretty girl at my other side. I dared to open my mouth long enough to talk with her a bit. Her name was Marguerite Becquin and she was the daughter of the *lieutenant criminel* of Abbeville, the chief of police and a most important personage, Madame said. Between us, Jacques and I tried to amuse Marguerite during what was otherwise a pretty boring dinner. She and I were about the same age and I think she took a shine to me, though she kept glancing over at Pierre de Belleval's brother Charles, who was five years older than I was, and a lot taller.

Madame asked me later what I'd thought of Mademoiselle Becquin. I grinned and said I hadn't found anything about her to dislike and Madame patted my cheek.

"Cultivate her, François. She's a sweet girl and, what's more, she's Monsieur Becquin de Vercourt's only child, which means she'll have a fine fortune someday. She'd be an excellent match for you or your brother."

That was a nice thought, but I knew of plenty of other fellows our age in Abbeville she could choose from, fellows from rich, noble families like the Bellevals. "She probably thinks I'm a peasant," I said.

"Never fear, you're coming along splendidly," said Madame. "No gaffes yesterday." (She hadn't noticed my slip-up with the knife.) "You did me proud, both of you. Both Père Bosquier and Monsieur de Belleval remarked to me how polite and well-bred you were. Keep it up. And you could do worse, you know," she added, "than to model yourselves after Monsieur de Belleval."

Oh, very well, then. I didn't want to look like an ignorant farm boy in front of Marguerite Becquin de Vercourt. I tried to copy him as much as a penniless kid who'd grown up in the middle of nowhere could copy a gentleman with estates, a grand town house, and money to spare. Belleval had been a fine swordsman in his youth, Madame said, so I worked hard at learning swordplay. I went almost every day to Monsieur Naturé's fencing school for a bout or two with Pierre, who was also, I guess, trying to make as much of a splash in society as his father.

Belleval was an accomplished musician and dancer, according to Madame, so we had music lessons. Music was all right; I found I wasn't bad at the violin. We even had a dancing master in twice a week, though I thought court dancing—minuets and gavottes and such—was pretty sissified. Give me the lively dances the peasants used to do at weddings back home, any time.

Not that Pierre and Bertrand and I danced minuets and gavottes together much, of course. Mostly we were raising a racket in the streets, Pierre and I showing off our fencing with some quick bouts among friends, or playing pranks on the pompous bigwigs in their stuffy mansions. And don't forget passing around naughty books with even naughtier pictures in them from one of us to another, and hanging about the taverns by the river and getting drunk, or chasing girls, trying to get the barmaids to lift their skirts for us. Dirty jokes, a lot of wine, a lot of laughs. Just high spirits, feeling our oats, as they say.

Typical young men with too much time on their hands and too much money in their pockets, right?

But we really didn't mean any harm.

18

Madeleine and Pierre Hérisson visited Paris again at Christmas. As a special surprise for his sister and brother-in-law before they returned to Melun after the new year's celebrations, Charles rented a box at the Comédie-Italienne, where Carlin, the troupe's famous Harlequin, was appearing in a new play that everyone said was his funniest yet. The long, costly war, which people were already calling the Seven Years' War, had been over for months and fashionable Paris seemed eager to resume its customary blithe extravagance.

Carlin, Madeleine agreed, was a genius at his craft. His springy body might have been made of that strange substance from the New World, rubber, and the actor's round, mobile comedian's face was so animated that, despite the black eye-mask he wore, anyone seated in the lower ranks of boxes could make out every exaggerated emotion that crossed it. Charles had not laughed so much in months.

During the interlude between the third and fourth acts, Madeleine remained in the box with Hérisson while Charles strolled about, exchanging glances with the pretty flower sellers who hovered at the doors to the theater. He could not help gazing sentimentally at the spot where he had stolen a kiss from Jeanne when he'd taken her to the comedy. Already two years had passed, he realized with a jolt, since he had last seen her.

The musical interlude ended and the people milling about him began to return to their boxes. A step behind him as their chatter faded; a familiar voice said, "Chevalier?"

It was Antoinette. Her ruffled, hooped silk gown was finer than any he had ever seen her wear on Rue du Bac, and her hair was formally dressed and powdered in the neat, close-to-the-head style favored that season, rather than carelessly tucked beneath a simple linen cap, but otherwise she had changed little. He detected the same ironic gleam in her hazel eyes as before.

"It *is* you," she said. "How do you do, then?"

"Quite well, thank you." They eyed each other for a moment. "You're looking well."

"I could say the same of you."

"Do you . . . you don't still live on Rue du Bac?"

"No, I moved to much better lodgings a year ago."

He could think of nothing to say and she continued. "Do you come here frequently, to the Italians? I've not seen you here before."

"I don't go out often, these days, not to the theater."

"I'm here most nights when Carlin is playing. He was especially good tonight, wasn't he? You'd think he was twenty, the way he takes those pratfalls."

Charles was about to agree, before he remembered that she had once told him she had taken up with an actor. "Do you know Carlin? Is your . . . actor friend . . . in the company?"

Antoinette laughed. "You needn't be so discreet. 'Lover' will do. But he isn't in the company, he *is* the company."

"You don't—it's not Carlin himself?"

"Don't you believe me good enough for a man as famous as that?"

"That's not what I meant. I was merely surprised." He spoke carelessly, but an unexpected, uninvited twinge of jealousy prickled. How well could the despised executioner, of all men on earth, measure beside a luminary as adored and celebrated as Carlo Bertinazzi?

"What news have you had of Jeanne?" he added, for something to say.

"She writes to me now and then. She's doing well. An apartment of her own, and plenty of new gowns, from a rich and titled admirer. She's been working her way upward through the ranks of the minor nobility."

"You needn't make it sound so coarse."

She gazed at him, eyebrows raised. "How else is one to say it? I see you're still feeling protective of her."

"Why should I not?"

"Well, she doesn't feel the same way about you. Why don't you give up, Chevalier?"

"Give what up?"

"For heaven's sake! Your adolescent infatuation with a woman who wishes you'd never been born."

She swept off, silk flounces rustling. Charles stood gasping in outrage before recovering himself and striding after her.

"None of it would have happened if you—"

"The devil it wouldn't," she retorted, without turning, as she reached for the door handle to Box 2. "You know she would have found out sooner or later. Perhaps from someone not as discreet as I."

"Oh, I'm sure you're very discreet. Are you now going to liven up your evening," he continued, abruptly ill-tempered, "by telling—telling whomever you're sharing that box with—that I'm sitting a few paces away?"

Antoinette glared at him. "That's unjust and you know it. I don't break my word and I don't reveal confidences. Your identity's as safe with me as if I were your confessor." Before he could retort, she slipped inside the box and slammed the velvet-lined door shut with a muffled thump.

Charles stalked back to Box 14 and tried to give heed to the play and to Carlin's antics. He could not, however, resist peering around the dividing wall for a glimpse of Antoinette, six boxes over to the left. She was alone in the box and doing the same as he, he realized, and they both hastily turned away to fix their attention upon the stage.

"Whatever is the matter with you?" Madeleine demanded, after the play ended and the actors were taking their bows. Charles scowled and fidgeted as Carlin reappeared from the wings yet again, to tumultuous applause.

"You were in a perfectly good temper when we arrived. What happened?"

"Oh, I saw a girl I once knew, someone I'd parted with on bad terms."

"Not the girl who wouldn't have anything more to do with you!"

"No, no . . . it was her friend, the girl who told Jeanne who I was."

"It's hard," Hérisson chimed in, "but we all ought to be used to that by now, to people shying away from us."

"She didn't tell Jeanne about me because she . . . because she was repulsed by me . . ." He stopped and thought about it for a moment, scowling once more. "She told me she did it because she wanted me for herself."

Madeleine gave him the familiar, superior look.

"She did you a favor, Charlot."

". . . But I was so miserable about losing Jeanne that I couldn't forgive Toinette for what she'd done."

"Go make it up to her."

"What?"

"Go make it up."

"She already has a lover—in whose company she wouldn't be ashamed to be seen, unlike *mine*." He glared even more ferociously at the great Carlin, the posturing mountebank, damn him, conceited and cocksure, baggy white comedian's costume flapping and swishing as he made his elaborate bows below them.

Madeleine sighed.

"She wanted you for herself. Well? She wanted you for herself, when she already knew who you were."

"I—I suppose she cared for me."

"And do you care for her?"

"I scarcely know her."

Madeleine gave him another dose of the sisterly look and he turned to stare over the railing, avoiding her gaze. "Well, then, I do like her. Even though she . . . I like her very much."

"Is she one of us?" Hérisson inquired.

"No. That is . . . I've no idea. She—no, surely not."

"But she knew who you were, Sanson, and didn't care. That does mean something."

"Don't be such a idiot," said Madeleine. "Swallow your pride and patch up your quarrel. Good Lord, Charlot," she continued, "you know few people are broad-minded enough to look past the trade and see the man. Don't throw away your chances."

"And what about her present lover?"

"He might become less important to her, if she knew you cared a fig for her! Saints above! I think men, or at least brothers, are hopeless at understanding anything." She flung open the door to their box, pushed Charles out into the corridor, and snatched up Hérisson's umbrella. "Go find her, before I knock some sense into you. Go *on*."

He blundered his way toward Box 2, through the chattering theatergoers. Despite his fears that Antoinette would be surrounded by fawning admirers, he found she was still alone in the box, leaning on the rail and gazing out at the curtained stage.

"Toinette?"

"Chevalier?"

He blurted out the first words that occurred to him, fearing he might lose his nerve if she should speak first.

"Toinette—I've been a fool—"

She did not smile. "Have you?"

"It couldn't be, I told myself; it couldn't be . . ." A drop of sweat trickled down his forehead. He impatiently dashed it away, sucked in a deep breath, and began again.

"I—I've gone for years, now, with people shying away from me, cursing me, as if I were some monster. I couldn't believe anyone could actually care for me, just care for *me*, not for what I could give her, not when she knew who I was and when she wasn't—like me. But the way you behaved, jabbing at me, as if you were daring me to come too close. Because you had to look on while I made a silly ass of myself over a woman who would never be in love with me." He paused. She continued to look at him, unsmiling and silent.

"I never took the time to think you might care, care in a way that Jeanne never would. If you had ever said anything to me, while I was still so infatuated with her, I'd have thought you only wanted my patronage for yourself. But I see now . . ." He lurched forward and seized her hands. "Toinette. It was *you*, ever since that day at the riverside."

"Are you saying that you think you could care for me after all?"

He swallowed hard. "You know how I was that day. I was too self-absorbed and wretched to know it. But I do—I think I could love you if you could love me. You—God only knows why and how, but you do care a little for me, don't you?"

She continued to gaze at him, her face still and unreadable. Then without warning she smiled, with a sheepish little laugh, and squeezed his hand.

"What took you so long, Chevalier?"

19

I didn't mean to be in the Place du Marché that day, the sixth of September. We were just out swaggering through the streets on our way to the fencing school, Bertrand d'Étallonde and I—rough-housing, whistling at girls, the usual horseplay—along with some of the other fellows, Pierre de Belleval, and Louis Douville, whose father had been mayor of Abbeville until recently, and Marcel de Moisnel, Pierre's orphan cousin who'd lately come to live with the Bellevals, tagging along as always.

We'd forgotten, if we'd ever heard it, that there was going to be a big event that day. First we heard a to-do at the end of the street, and then all at once people were streaming out of doors, leaning out of windows, as if it was a festival day with a holy procession. It was a kind of festival, all right: a parade with soldiers and drummers and mounted dragoons. But the drummers were doing that slow, solemn drumroll—*rat-tat-tat-tat, tat, tat*—over and over again—that tells you right away that whatever's happening isn't supposed to be jolly.

"What's going on?" I asked Étallonde.

"It's the execution," he said, trying to be careless about it. "Joseph de Valines."

I'd heard of the Valines case, of course—who hadn't?—but Étallonde's father was Gaillard de Boëncourt himself, president or chief magistrate of the high court of Abbeville, very high and mighty indeed, so Étallonde knew about everything at the law courts as soon as it happened. I'd never met Joseph de Valines, but I knew he was my age, just eighteen or so, maybe even younger.

People who'd known him said he was a likeable enough fellow at first meeting, although some added that he was spoiled and vicious, with a nasty sense of humor, when he wasn't trying to make a good impression on you. But he wasn't riffraff; he was a landowner, seigneur of the village of Valines, petty nobility like me and Jacques, genteel enough to fit in with Madame's crowd, though just barely.

His parents, both of them pretty elderly, had died of a strange fever the year before, one right after the other. Of course whenever there's a suspicious death and a question of a comfortable inheritance, people start to talk. Right away people began to say the old folks had been vomiting nonstop until they died, and it was like no fever anyone had ever heard of, and that their son had poisoned them—and had tried to poison his uncle, too, later on, just for the thrill of it. Maybe Valines really did poison his parents; but I don't know that they ever found actual proof of that, beyond what they got out of him when they tortured him with the *brodequins*. I guess you'll admit to anything when they're smashing your legs between boards with a wedge and a mallet.

"They're going to break him today at the market square," Étallonde continued. "My father told me."

"Break him?" I said. "On the wheel? But he's a gentleman."

He shrugged. "He's a parricide. Poisoned his father and his mother, too. They break you alive for that, no matter who you are, unless you're first cousin to the king or something."

I swallowed hard, wondering what people think when they know that in an hour or so they're going to be tortured to death.

Bertrand d'Étallonde was all for following the crowd and seeing the show. Pierre de Belleval backed him up, as usual, although the rest of us weren't so eager. Don't get me wrong; the two of them were good fellows, but Étallonde was bored that day and wanted a thrill. He was rich, good-looking, and used to getting what he wanted, and Pierre, being old Belleval's youngest son, always had his eye on the main chance. Pierre wouldn't take unfair advantage of you, but he was always sharpening his skills at sucking up to people who could help him get ahead someday, secure him a good position.

I felt a little funny, myself, about going on to the Place du Marché. I'd seen a few criminals hanged, of course, but I hadn't yet had the chance to see anyone broken, and I wasn't sure I wanted to. In the end, though, Étallonde got his own way; he usually did. So we joined the crowd and followed.

They'd dressed Valines in a long, coarse shirt and hung a noose around his neck. He wasn't in a cart, with a priest beside him, the way they take people to the gallows. They'd made him walk, even though he was limping from the pain. He looked awful, like an old man, after months in prison, and torture, and misery. Somebody was supporting him, helping him on, and another man was behind him, holding the end of the rope, as if he was a dog. Three others carried a lit brazier, an iron bar, and the biggest candle you ever saw, thick around as your wrist and two feet tall.

At the back of the procession came the magistrates in their official robes, riding in a few carriages. Étallonde's father, President Gaillard, looked as if he'd rather be anywhere else, but Monsieur Duval de Soicourt, the mayor and criminal assessor—that's a sort of examining magistrate who sends cases to the courts—he was looking pleased with himself. As if he was smug that they'd got another conviction.

But then we didn't expect much else of Duval, since none of Madame's set could stomach him. Recently he'd grabbed the mayorship from Louis Douville's father, while he'd also been filling the job of *lieutenant criminel* as well as criminal assessor after Becquin, the old lieutenant and pretty Marguerite's father, suddenly died. Now and then Duval's name came up at dinner parties, and Monsieur de Belleval or President Gaillard would smile in that aristocratic way of theirs and repeat that he might be mayor now along with everything else, but he was still just a vulgar, jumped-up, pettifogging little lawyer, a poor relation to the Becquins, who would do anything to get ahead. The social climbing was obvious enough; Duval fawned over anybody with a title who might receive him, but not many did unless they couldn't get out of it.

Étallonde's father also claimed Duval didn't have many scruples and that he already had young Hecquet de Roquemont, the new prosecutor for the district, completely under his thumb. President Gaillard had said once, at one of Madame's dinners after he'd had a few glasses of wine under his belt, that they really didn't have much evidence—beyond a motive—against Joseph de Valines. And maybe, he added, Duval had sent Valines off to trial to be prosecuted and tortured just so he could mark down another victory in the tribunal's accounts. It would make Duval look good, after all—help to earn him a seat on the magistrates' bench and even a title of his own someday.

I'd like to be able to say the crowd that was heading for the breaking was so huge that it just carried all of us along, like a river in flood, whether we wanted to go or not. But actually we could have shoved through at any time and made tracks out of there, and we didn't.

If any one of us, besides Bertrand d'Étallonde, had been alone, probably we'd have cleared out pretty soon, but none of us wanted to let the others think he was a sissy and couldn't take it. So we followed the procession to Saint-Vulfran, where Valines did his penance on the church steps, and then on to the market square, which is just a few dozen steps farther on, and we watched. You don't often get to see a man broken alive on the wheel.

A hanging is over pretty fast, once all the singing and praying is done. A breaking isn't. It took them an hour to kill Valines, and that was before they burned his body on the bonfire—because if you're extra wicked, Étallonde told me, the final part of your sentence is to have your body burned to ashes and your charred bones ground to powder and dumped in the river, so there's not a single trace of you left, nothing to bury in consecrated ground. Then, when the Last Judgment comes, you'll be denied resurrection of the flesh, since there's nothing to resurrect, and your soul will go wandering for all eternity. Punishment in both this world and the next, you might say.

I don't really know how I stood it. But we watched, as they broke his bones, and Valines screamed and groaned and wept to God for mercy, and the crowd yelled out the count with each whack of the iron bar. And we kept watching. It was like coming across a carriage accident where somebody's been trampled or crushed and there's blood all over the cobbles—you find you're sickened by the sight, but you can't look away.

Once or twice I sneaked a glance at the magistrates, sitting in their carriages. Étallonde's father had turned away, with a handkerchief pressed over his mouth—maybe he felt like puking—but I'd swear Duval de Soicourt was enjoying himself. He had a funny sort of look on his face, and he kept licking his lips. What's more, his left hand was on his carriage door, but his right wasn't anywhere to be seen. I never did see it during that whole hour. I'd bet anything, from the way he looked, that his hand was inside his breeches.

The breaking went on, and the screaming, and we watched, half fascinated and half horrified, blinking and turning away when we could, pretending that the stiff breeze was blowing our hair into our eyes. Then we'd exchange furtive glances, checking up on each other, seeing who would flinch first. It was Moisnel, of course; but he was only fifteen then, just a kid.

He stuck it out until the breaking was over and they lowered Valines onto the bonfire and lit it. That was bad enough, because we who were nearby could tell that Valines was still alive, barely, when they threw him on the fire. His lips were moving, but he didn't have strength enough left to groan.

And then, as the flames grew hotter and drove everyone back, when the fire had settled in, we started to smell it, burning flesh, and the very worst part was that it smelled—well, it smelled pretty good, just like a roast pig turning on a spit, until you remembered what it was. That was the moment when Moisnel went white as a sheet and dodged away and started retching. Pierre began to rag him for being soft; but Louis Douville told Pierre to lay off, because we were all in the way of losing our appetites, or worse.

I hope to heaven Valines died of his wounds and his pain before the flames reached him. For days afterward I couldn't get the smell of a man burning out of my mind, but what I really couldn't forget was the sight of his lips still moving as he went into the fire. Probably he was just praying: "Please, God, let me die now, let me die, let this be over, let me die . . ."

That's what you wish for: *Let this be over, let me die* . . .

20

"You never saw such a wretched actress," Antoinette said, as she and Charles lazed together in her bed one rainy afternoon, amusing themselves by reading one of Molière's lesser plays aloud to each other. "I found out soon enough that I was better offstage than on. I was simply dreadful."

"Surely not." He brushed his lips across her hair. During the past year, he had discovered depths in Antoinette that he had never expected to find. Within the haven of her cheerful apartment, far away from the Place de Grève, the world seemed bright as dew on a fresh spring morning.

Antoinette was the illegitimate daughter of a country nobleman and one of his chambermaids. Just as she and Charles were both forever condemned to stand a little apart from the rest of the world, so had they, for the most part, educated themselves outside formal schooling. Her passion for reading and hunger for knowledge were so like his own that he adored her all the more. Art, music, dramatic art, history, political thought, natural philosophy— all were like food and drink to her as she devoured the books he lent her.

"Oh, believe it," she continued, looking up from the book they held. "I couldn't recite the simplest speech in front of an audience without tripping over my tongue, and I wasn't funny and outrageous enough to play comic mutes. So instead I worked for a while in the boulevard theaters as a costume mistress, and then I sold gentlemen's cravats at the Maison Labille, where I met Jeanne. But I kept up with my friends in the theater; that's how I met Carlin."

Charles glared at the book. The great Carlin—the one cloud in his sunny horizon. No matter how he pleaded, grumbled, or cajoled, Antoinette would not give up Bertinazzi.

He and another gentleman and I have a satisfactory arrangement, she had told Charles, when he entreated her for the third time to be his alone. They pay for this apartment, and for all my wants, and in return they get companionship and discretion, which Carlin especially needs, because his wife is a jealous shrew. He's not particularly jealous himself—which is remarkable, I think, for an Italian—and he knows I'm not really in love with him. But I'm fond of him, just as he's fond of me, and I've no wish to give either of my gentlemen up.

"You might let *me* keep you," Charles insisted. "I don't care for the idea of making love to you on a bed that other men paid for."

"That's just your pride talking," she told him, and slid her arms about his neck. "I don't want anything from you except your own self. Business and love ought to be kept separate. Carlin is a business arrangement, like a marriage between a poor nobleman's daughter and a rich merchant—they each get something out of the bargain—and he knows it. But you, Charles Sanson, are the one I love, with all my heart, without reservation. After all," she added, with an impish smile, "Carlin is fifty and my other friend at least sixty—you need have no fear, my darling, that you can't measure up."

At length, he had agreed that he would call upon her on certain days of the week, and Carlin and the unnamed and invisible gentleman on the others; and that they would endeavor to behave like rational and civilized men (ha!) if ever, by chance, they should meet.

"Let's not talk about Carlin," Charles said, and snapped shut the book of plays.

"What's the matter? You're cross."

"Oh, just foolishness."

"Well?" Her tone of voice reminded him irresistibly of Madeleine. She twisted to her side, supporting herself on an elbow, and gazed down at him. "Something upsetting? Talk to me."

"Just foolishness," he repeated. He glanced over at the arm-chair between the two tall windows, on which he had flung his clothes earlier that afternoon. "My new blue coat."

"What's the matter with your coat? It's a nice coat, and it fits you beautifully. Though," Antoinette added, eyeing him and sliding her hand beneath the sheets to stroke his thigh, "I think I prefer you when you're *not* wearing it—or anything else . . ."

"Yes," he went on, ignoring her teasing fingers and only half hearing her, "it's a very nice coat. But somebody must have seen us at the concert last week—probably some self-important magistrate from the Parlement."

Normally, he paid his official morning visits to the Palais de Justice or, more often, to the Châtelet clad in the scarlet coat that he was obliged to wear at the scaffold. The blue dress coat, on the other hand, cut in the latest style, was for the evenings, when sometimes Antoinette and he went dancing or took a box at the theater, though Charles flatly refused to patronize the Comédie-Italienne when Carlin was playing.

Fortunately, he was usually able to preserve his anonymity when they enjoyed the amusements of Paris; the people most likely to recognize him, the usual habitués of the scaffold—the laboring classes—were a world away from the stylish folk with whom he mingled at theaters and public balls. To them, if they had ever ventured out to such low entertainment as an execution, the *bourreau* might seem a half-remembered face, an image in a cloudy memory, but surely could have nothing to do with the self-assured young man of fashion glimpsed across a glittering promenade or ballroom.

"Somebody—probably a judge or a lawyer—recognized me, at any rate," Charles continued. "He seems to have complained to the prosecutor-general himself that a rascal of a *bourreau* was daring to pose as a gentleman."

"I don't understand," Antoinette said, yawning. She snuggled closer to him. "You *are* a gentleman. What does that have to do with your coat?"

"Well, yesterday Joly de Fleury summoned me to his offices and reprimanded me for overstepping my station in life. Since blue is the color of nobility, I, of all people, apparently have no right to wear a blue coat and hat."

She laughed. "Lots of people wear blue!"

But they aren't, he brooded, *filthy executioners who presume to rub shoulders with genteel society while wearing blue brocade, pretending they're as good as anyone else.*

"Only a nobleman, it seems," he said at last, "is truly entitled to wear formal dress of blue, and put his servants in blue livery, and so on. 'Blue blood' and all that nonsense."

"Well, you're not exactly a peasant yourself, Chevalier."

"I'm not exactly a chevalier either. My great-great-grandfather was the steward of a lord's estate and a gentleman, that's all. Not an aristocratic landowner, though my grandmother would like everyone to think so."

"Still, how did such a man end as an executioner?"

It was his younger son, he explained. Sanson the First, like many second sons, began as an army officer, but—without knowing, at first, who she was—he was foolish enough to fall in love with the daughter of Pierre Jouënne, the master executioner of Rouen, and get her with child. Then her father threatened to kill her if the lieutenant didn't marry her, and his regiment wouldn't have him back after he'd married into such a family. So he had to become an assistant to his father-in-law or starve. The Paris title became vacant some years later; he saw his opportunity to rise to the top within the profession he'd unwillingly entered, and bought it; his children went as a matter of course into the profession.

"And here I am today, Charles-Henri Sanson, *Maître des Hautes Œuvres*, by the grace of God and the king—and God help me—deputy master executioner of Paris and Versailles."

"I'd think that such an ancestry would still be genteel enough to allow you to wear blue brocade, for heaven's sake. How petty. Show the prosecutor-general some family papers."

"I won't give him the pleasure of seeing me grovel." He felt unaccountably mutinous at the thought of having to justify himself. "My grandmother's right; no royal office, even ours, is anything to be ashamed of. If he doesn't like me wearing blue, he can take his damned blue and—"

He broke off as Antoinette laughed again and kissed him on the mouth, silencing him.

"Charles, Charles, order a new coat, and keep the blue for family parties. Surely there are enough weddings and christenings at which you can show it off."

"Yes; I'll have an even finer one made. That'll show them. What color, then?"

"How about dark red—almost wine color? That would suit you."

"Not red."

"No—no, of course not. Green? A rich emerald green would be lovely."

Green. Yes. Deep green brocade, the best Michaud's shop had to offer, with an embroidered gala waistcoat to match—

"Will you take my advice? Tell your tailor you don't want wide skirts to the coat. You're so tall, a narrower cut would suit you."

"Why not?"

—and the bigoted snobs of the Parlement could damned well watch him wear it.

At last he bade her a fond goodbye and reluctantly slipped out and downstairs to the now-familiar foyer. Antoinette's apartment had once been three rooms in the second floor of a vast private mansion on Rue Saint-Thomas-du-Louvre, one of several once-grand houses along the narrow alleys of the ancient quarter that huddled between the Tuileries and the vast square bulk of the Louvre. Since the court had decamped for Versailles, eighty years before, and the two abandoned palaces had been partitioned and given over to royal pensioners, the district had, here and there, grown shabby and raffish. One street away—though "street" was too kind a word, for two carriages could not pass each other on the broadest of them—seedy Rue Fromenteau, lined with cheap hotels, swarmed with streetwalkers and shady adventurers.

A stranger passed him on the polished stone staircase, a tall man of late middle age with a finely chiseled, ascetic face. His black suit and hat were simply cut and unadorned and he wore only the small dress sword that any gentleman of means, including Charles himself, wore in public. Charles doffed his hat politely, upon encountering a stranger of (presumably) his own class, and the other reciprocated before continuing up the stair. Despite the stranger's evident efforts at anonymity, Charles knew he would not soon forget the piercing, chilly gaze that lit upon him for a moment.

Curious, he lingered as the man in black reached the landing, glanced about him, and started toward Antoinette's door. At the last minute he caught sight of Charles watching him and they exchanged a second frigid glance before Antoinette's maid curtsied and stood aside.

So that's Carlin's rival, he mused, as he left the house. A carriage was just quitting the courtyard, a modest dark-green coach with drawn blinds, bearing no coat of arms on the door. Who could the stranger be, he wondered, that he was so eager to remain anonymous?

He idly put the question to Antoinette at their next excursion, a stroll through the nearby gardens of the Tuileries, which were still royal property but were open to all who were well-dressed and respectable. He received only an enigmatic smile as they ambled among hedges and flowerbeds.

"You mustn't ask me about him. All you need to know is that he's my other business arrangement, and has nothing to do with you and me."

"And what does Carlin say to that?" Charles inquired.

"Carlin doesn't call as often as he used to"—(oho, he doesn't, does he?)—"I daresay we're both growing just a little tired of each other's company, after three years. This gentleman will do nicely instead. He asks, above all, for discretion, and that I can give him."

That, Charles knew well. Everyone of Antoinette's acquaintance knew of him only as the Chevalier de Longval. To her small circle of friends he was merely a young country nobleman of modest means and simple tastes who kept a lodging in Paris. If Antoinette was discreet enough to preserve the identity of the public executioner, she would be equally closemouthed about her second "business arrangement."

And how are you proceeding with your consulting room, Antoinette inquired, adroitly changing the subject and strolling toward a marble bench by the fountain.

"Well enough, thank you."

"Saved any lives yet?"

"I couldn't say." He dusted off the bench and took a seat beside her. "But since the word's got out that I've joined my father in practicing medicine, as well as sharing the daily offices, quite a few people have sought us out. I've fixed some dislocated shoulders; set a broken arm; given out enough willow bark tea to ease a good many fevers; sold a few dozen pots of Father's magical salve; and I hope I've cured several grateful souls of the clap."

He laughed. "One of them . . . he raised his hat to me on the street yesterday when I was out for a walk near Saint-Eustache. I didn't remember him and thought he'd mistaken me for somebody else. But he knew who I was, to be sure, and wanted to thank me again for curing him. He even asked me to have a drink with him. 'After what you did for me,' he told me, 'I'll never again think uncharitable thoughts about *bourreaux*.'

"We actually became chatty over a jug of wine. He's a journeyman printer, and though he hasn't had much schooling, his work allows him to read a good deal, of course, and he seems remarkably well read. He's even read that new book by Voltaire—the one they banned—and we talked it over a bit."

"The *Philosophical Dictionary*?" Antoinette interrupted. "You'll lend it to me when you get hold of a copy, won't you? I'm dying to read it."

"Of course. When I'm not burning it in the Place de Grève, that is," he added in a lower tone.

"Why do they even bother?"

"Bother?"

"The book censors can't possibly keep control of all the political books that people are publishing these days—and all the muck that they smuggle in from abroad."

Charles smiled and leaned back, staring into the nearby hedge, where a dozen sparrows quarreled over a crust of bread. "It does seem like a losing battle."

"Perhaps you could filch a copy of the *Dictionnaire* for me from the bonfire when no one's looking," she suggested, laughing. "I won't mind if it's a little singed."

"Well, to make a long story short," he continued, "this fellow

Moreau finally told me that our paths had crossed already, even before he'd come to me to be cured of the clap. He claimed that, last year, he'd carried on an affair with your cook."

"With Louise?"

"'You and I crossed paths once or twice at the house,' he told me, 'when you were going in the front by the foyer, and I was leaving through the kitchens at the ground floor. Louise told me who you were, and I thought the lady'—that's you," Charles added, with a sly glance at Antoinette, "'I thought the lady had funny tastes in gentlemen—not only the lead actor of the Comédie-Italienne, but also the lead actor of the Place de Grève!' "

Antoinette laughed. "Evidently, despite all our efforts to be discreet, nothing can be kept secret for long from the servants."

"He wasn't so far off the mark."

He considered it a moment. *I suppose I really am just as much an actor on my own stage as Carlin is, cavorting about in his eyemask and baggy smock—except that the sideshow horrors are real, the blood's no red rag, and the stage is littered, not with stuffed dummies, but with corpses . . .*

"Each in his own way, we provide diversion for the masses, don't we."

"Diversion for the masses?" she echoed him. "Do I detect a note of bitterness? What have you to be bitter about?"

"I didn't mean to be." He drew her to him and kissed her, for an instant becoming just one more of the lovers who haunted the shady alleys of the gardens, just a young man in love like any other.

"In truth," he added, gazing at her, "I've found I have all I could ever want."

21

The first dust-up that told me Abbeville wasn't exactly a haven of good will and kindness, after all, was the matter of Marguerite Becquin and our friends the Bellevals.

Madame had told me more than once that Marguerite was an heiress, a rich one, and of course a prize for every bachelor in town. Her guardian was our old chum Duval de Soicourt, the criminal assessor. He was some kind of distant cousin to the Becquins, I heard, and when old Becquin died, he'd grabbed control of Marguerite at the same time as he'd taken over Becquin's duties as *lieutenant criminel*. As I've said before, nobody in our set liked Duval and his nasty little backstreet-law-office manners much—Étallonde referred to him as "Old Beakface" most of the time, because of his great hook of a nose, and his father usually let him get away with it. And when I thought of Duval at Valines' execution, smirking, probably groping in his culotte, as a man died screaming, I felt a little sick to my stomach.

Rumors had started to go about, too, that he'd been dipping into the Becquin fortune. And from the way I'd seen Marguerite glancing once or twice at Duval when Madame and I paid our condolence calls to her—as if Duval had been a pile of dog mess in the middle of the Aubusson carpet—it was pretty clear she didn't think much of her new guardian. So, late one night in the autumn of '64, barely a week after her formal mourning was over, Marguerite unexpectedly arrived at the abbey gates with two valises, a hatbox, her yappy little lapdog, and her maid, and asked for shelter.

"Any place where that man can't get to me!" she said, when Madame had ushered her inside. "He wants to marry me to his son, so he'll have me under his thumb forever, and I'd rather die!"

Duval the younger was a decent enough fellow, just returned from a tour of duty at Versailles in the king's musketeers, worth a lot more than his father. But he was at least thirty, while Marguerite was sixteen. And if I'd been Marguerite, I wouldn't have wanted to be related by marriage to Duval de Soicourt, either, or to let him get his claws anywhere near my money.

Madame assured Marguerite that she had a home and friends at the abbey for as long as she needed them. And the next day, when Duval came looking for her in order to take her home again, Madame oh-so-politely threw him out and rounded up all of Marguerite's other relations to discuss the situation.

Marguerite Becquin was a handsome girl and had plenty of spirit and I liked her a lot, so I spun a few fantasies about asking Madame to arrange a marriage, and getting a pretty wife and a nice fortune all at one go. But I guess Marguerite had had someone else in mind from the beginning, long before I'd ever shown up in Abbeville, because two months after the family conference, she married Pierre de Belleval's brother Charles in a grand ceremony at Saint-Vulfran. And Duval de Soicourt was left with a public snub sticking in his scraggy throat.

So after all the fuss about Marguerite Becquin was over and the dust had settled, it was nearly Christmas, with the usual lively New Year's celebrations just around the corner, and we were all a bit lit up. After a long night at our favorite wine shop down by the wharves, my friends and I weren't ready to head for our beds yet, so we thought we'd take the long way home and see what mischief we could cook up on what was otherwise a dull night.

At half past two in the morning on a Friday, we couldn't think of a lot of mischief to do, except for waking people up. So we pulled a few bell chains at the smaller houses on the way to the district of Saint-Gilles where the grand mansions are, just for the sake of seeing somebody come to the door—probably expecting some life-or-death message waiting for them—and then we'd run off, whooping, as they yelled at us. After a few tries it occurred to us that it would be funnier if, before taking off, we'd take a moment to make the good loud farting noise you get when you put the heels of your hands over your mouth and blow hard. That infuriated people even more, so I suppose we counted it as a success.

We kept on, that way, for a few streets more, until we'd passed the Gaillards' *hôtel particulier*. Bertrand d'Étallonde still wasn't ready to go home yet, although the rest—Pierre and young Moisnel, and Métigny—had dropped away, one by one, as we passed their houses. Since pulling the bell chains in that neighborhood would only get servants out of bed, and who cared about annoying some servant or other, Étallonde thought—he was pretty drunk, of course—that it would be a fine idea to break a few windowpanes, just to hear them smash. "Anybody who lives around here," he said, wobbling a bit and waving his arm, "can afford a few pieces of glass. Let's take some starch out of old Belleval's collar!"

We broke a couple of windows and made tracks before anyone could catch us, although Étallonde declared that President Gaillard would fix it if somebody did finger us for the prank. Another street or two and another few windowpanes farther along, he stopped suddenly.

"Hey, La Barre! You know whose house this is?"

I barely knew what street we were on, much less which house was which. "No, whose?"

"Old Beakface's."

"Huh?"

"Wake up! Duval de Soicourt's."

"Well, if anybody deserves a broken window or two, it's that—that turd in a silk coat," I said, and before I knew it I'd lobbed a piece of cobble at the nearest windowpane. It went through with a satisfying crash and we both whooped. Étallonde grabbed a loose stone for himself and heaved it through another bit of glass.

"Wait—wait," he said to me, grabbing me by the shoulder, as I got ready to trumpet a fart-sound in case anyone came to the windows, and then run for it. "Beakface thinks he's God Almighty; he ought to get more than just waking up to a broken windowpane in the morning. Let's ring the bell."

"So we wake up his maître d'hôtel and get yelled at. So what?"

"We could wake *him* up."

"How?"

"Aw, leave that to me." He strode up to the front door, pulled the bell chain a few times, good and hard, and glanced back over his shoulder at me, grinning. A couple of minutes later a footman answered the door, sleepy-eyed and in his shirt. I could see, from where I was hanging back in a shadowed doorway, that he was ready to curse somebody out until he realized that Étallonde was standing at the top of the steps, hat on his chest, holding himself still and respectable in spite of everything he'd drunk, and looking innocent as milk.

"Is this the house of Monsieur Duval de Soicourt, the criminal assessor?" I heard him say. The footman nodded yes and Étallonde went on:

"Please wake your master and tell him that a courier is here with an important message for him, to be delivered into his hands only."

For a moment I wondered about Étallonde's nerve, pretending to be a messenger when the servant might have recognized him, but of course we didn't exactly frequent Duval's house with social calls. At least it looked like the servant didn't know Bertrand from Adam. The man nodded again and shut the door.

"Come on, now's our chance," Étallonde said to me, stifling fits of laughter, as he hurried back down the steps. "Let's give him a real treat."

"Isn't a couple of farts enough?" I said. The wine I'd drunk was starting to get to me and I was ready to stumble home and fall into my own bed.

"No, Beakface deserves something special, more than just a fart, don't you think?"

"Well, like what?"

"Like . . ." He thought a moment, with a hiccup and a giggle. "Hey, you know that devil up on the side of Saint-Vulfran?"

"What about it?" There was another bare-arsed medieval sculpture that we used to snicker at—though it wasn't nearly as splendid as the other—up on the wall of Saint-Gilles, which we'd just passed; no doubt that was what had made Étallonde think of it.

"Well, the bits we can see up there—that's about all of myself that I'd want to show to Duval de Soicourt."

Finally I understood and started to unbutton my culotte, even though it was cold enough that night to freeze your balls off, and Étallonde laughed harder than ever.

✎   ✎

The next day, of course, Madame heard about it and hauled me onto the carpet, so to speak.

"And what, in the name of all the saints, do you think you meant by last night's mischief?" she demanded.

"We were just having fun," I mumbled. "Maybe we'd had too much to drink . . ."

Well, of course we'd had too much to drink. I had a splitting headache and, when I looked back at it, I wondered what, in the end, had been so particularly funny about breaking other people's windows. Though it had seemed hilarious at the time.

" 'Fun,' " she echoed me. "Childish antics that would make a drunken bargeman blush for shame!"

"Yes, madame," I repeated. I was starting to feel pretty ashamed of myself, now that I could think straight again.

"Do try to remember who you are, François. You're a Lefebvre of La Barre, and the ward of the abbess of Willancourt, and the relative of a president of the Paris Parlement, and you might keep it in mind before you go making an utter ass of yourself!"

"Yes, madame. I'm sorry, madame."

"Apologies can take you only so far." She took up a letter from her desk and brandished it at me. "Do you know what this is?"

I shook my head, then regretted it as my skull throbbed again.

"It's from Monsieur Duval de Soicourt."

Oh, Lord, now I'm in for it, I said to myself.

"'Rest assured, madame,'" she read aloud, "'I intend to prose cute this matter to the fullest extent of His Majesty's law, which your ward has so blatantly and maliciously defied by this wanton assault upon the property of the criminal assessor of Abbeville.'" She slapped down the letter. "What on *earth* did you hellions manage to perpetrate last night?"

"We . . . we chucked some stones and broke a few windowpanes. We weren't thinking—"

"No, you never do think, do you? Sweet heaven, François, you're like a child of six. What am I going to do with you?"

I hung my head. "I'm sorry, Madame. I'll pay for the windows. Take it out of my allowance."

"I certainly shall. And President Gaillard de Boëncourt will hear from me, too, about his son paying for his share of the damage." She sighed, tapping one slender finger against her lips. "What other ungodly mischief did you do?" she added. "Duval continues with something about 'moral turpitude' and 'offensive misbehavior that is an outrage to public decency.' Please tell me he's exaggerating."

I could feel myself blushing. "Well . . ."

"Well?"

"Étallonde thought it would be funny to pull people's bell chains."

"To annoy them, or at least their servants, by turning them out of bed at three in the morning."

"I . . . I suppose so."

"Without any thought as to how unkind such silly pranks would be, especially to a hardworking domestic who needs his sleep?"

"Yes, madame. But we were drunk," I added lamely.

"That's no excuse. No one ordered you to guzzle wine until you couldn't think straight, did they now?"

"No, madame."

"Well, go on. The two of you were disgustingly drunk and you thought you'd pull a few bell chains, just for the fun of making nuisances of yourselves."

"Yes, madame. And when somebody came to the door, we'd—we'd run away."

I didn't think I needed to supply extra information about making vulgar noises.

Madame muttered "mm-hm" and I thought that would be the end of it, but she smacked her hand down on Duval's letter again and continued to stare at me as if she could see right through to my entrails.

"That's not all of it, is it? What haven't you told me?"

Very well, then. Might as well have it out.

"When we got to Duval's house, we were bored with just waking people up. All they did was yell at us and then slam the doors. So after we broke the windowpanes, we—we thought it would be a good laugh to get Duval himself up out of bed. Étallonde told the footman he had an urgent message. And when Duval came to fetch it, we . . ."

"Well?" she said when I stopped, my face flaming again.

"We . . . pulled down our culottes and waggled our bare arses at him."

"You *what*?"

"We showed him our arses," I repeated miserably. "Nearly froze, too. Then we ran off. But I guess he got a look at our faces somehow . . . or guessed who we were . . ."

I'd been staring at the floor, my cheeks (the cheeks on my face, that is) still burning. When I heard Madame make a little choked sound, I was truly afraid she was going to be so angry with my foolishness that she'd throw me out and tell me never to come back, that I was on my own, that she was through with me and my witless, obnoxious antics. But I finally dared to look up at her and found, instead, that her face was red and her shoulders were shaking, not with anger, but with laughter she was trying to suppress with one hand over her mouth, and not making a very successful job of it.

"Oh, François," she managed finally, "you will be the death of me! What am I going to *do* with you?"

"You're not angry?" I stammered.

"Yes, of course I'm angry. Very angry. But—" And then she broke down in a fit of unladylike giggles.

"Oh, go on with you, you devil's spawn of a boy!"

That could have been the end of it, but no. If we hadn't guessed it before, we soon found out that Monsieur Nicolas-Pierre Duval de Soicourt, criminal assessor and mayor of Abbeville, had no sense of humor. And that he didn't believe in repeating indulgently, "boys will be boys," as President Gaillard did whenever he heard about some new bit of tomfoolery of Étallonde's. Everybody else whose windows we'd broken was content to accept new glazing plus a handsome apology in person from the two of us, and a little extra silver to sweeten things; Duval was the only one who ended up raising a stink about it.

No, Duval chose to throw his weight around; he wrote to the prosecutor-general and the Paris Parlement, of all things, the highest court in the land, and complained that Bertrand d'Étallonde and I were seditionists, part of an infamous criminal conspiracy, rebelling against the king's sacred law by smashing two of the criminal assessor's parlor windowpanes!

Luckily for me, Madame had a few cards of her own to play. As soon as she heard about Duval's little tantrum, she wrote some letters to Paris herself, to Monsieur Lefebvre d'Ormesson, who's some kind of second or third cousin and who just happened to be a member of the Parlement, or maybe he was even president. Even though we haven't a sou, we Lefebvres of La Barre do have some useful relatives. Monsieur d'Ormesson pooh-poohed the affair, twisted a few arms, and hushed the whole thing up. And that should have been the end of what was only a couple of drunken teenaged boys having too good a time.

It's too bad you can't look ahead and see what's coming, see how a lot of little things can add up to one big calamity, like pebbles rolling down a hill that start a landslide. Too bad that the whole Belleval family just about laughed in Duval's face over Charles landing Marguerite Becquin (and her fortune). Too bad that Madame thought Duval was too vulgar for her soirées and only invited him when she invited everyone who counted for anything in the town, times when it would have been too obvious he hadn't been included.

Too bad, when Étallonde and Louis Douville and I got a bit tipsy and boisterous and played pranks on people, that we didn't consider that Duval had no patience with brainless kids, and that he probably hated us because we were related to so many people who'd snubbed him and cut him. Too bad that Duval and Monsieur Douville de Maillefeu, the ex-mayor whose job Duval had nabbed, my friend Louis's father, had been quarreling for years over some old privilege or contract.

Too bad that Duval wanted to be a titled magistrate and top dog in Abbeville, and he would have done anything, sold his soul, maybe, to bring Gaillard de Boëncourt down and take his place in the president's chair at the high court.

You like to believe, when you're eight or twelve or fifteen, that mature adults are superior beings, that they're better and smarter than you are, that they've grown out of the spite and resentment and jealousy you can't help when you're a kid. Wouldn't you think adults could behave themselves better?

22

It had been merely another hanging.

All had gone smoothly; or so Charles had thought at first. The woman, pretty and not long out of girlhood—a habitual thief to whom the police courts had accorded no more leniency—had played her part, making her final confession to the priest who was still doing his best to save souls at the foot of the scaffold. She'd climbed the ladder, docile, defeated, without fighting Auguste's firm grip, merely shivering in the icy winter breeze, for women went to the gallows clad only in their shifts. And had waited at the summit to be launched into the hereafter, hands bound behind her, shoulders bowed, eyes closed.

> *Eia ergo, Advocata nostra,*
> *Mos tuos misericordes oculos . . .*

Her lips trembled in prayer as they sang the *Salve Regina* all around her.

"O clemens, O pia, O dulcis Virgo Maria . . . Amen."

No use in prolonging her misery. Charles promptly nodded to Jérôme and, with a tug of a cord, he pulled her off the ladder and kicked it away. For an instant she hung above them, jerking like a marionette, before Bastien, waiting above, swung himself from the crossbeam and landed on her shoulders to add the sudden wrench and weight that would break her neck. The crowd had fallen silent as it always did and Charles half listened for the inevitable dull *pop*, the sound of bones cracking apart in a fashion that Nature had never intended, that meant all was over.

He heard nothing. She continued to writhe at the end of the rope. Jérôme and he exchanged a swift incredulous glance; Bastien, a compact, muscular young fellow of about Charles's own age, had never before failed in his task.

The woman was still twisting uncontrollably, kicking, straining, back arching, and the crowd had begun to exclaim and point.

Charles turned to Bastien, clinging pick-a-back to the wretched creature, his expression one of utter confusion. "Again! Go!"

He dropped nimbly to the platform, to turn and scramble like a monkey up the rear ladder to the top of the post, twelve feet above them. How many times had Bastien climbed that ladder, crawled the length of that fatal crossbeam? He sped across it in the space of a breath, positioned himself, swung himself down once more to land neatly on her bound hands, arms about her neck, heaving her chin upward.

And still her neck would not snap.

For a moment Charles stood paralyzed with horror. What, in truth, could he do?

Without waiting for orders, Jérôme sprang at her and seized her ankles, letting his full weight swing beneath her. How could the mass of two grown men could not finish her off, put an end to her agonized thrashing? And yet still she jerked and twisted, eyes bulging, mouth gaping in a silent cry. The priest hastily crossed himself and looked away, trembling.

Charles pressed the back of his hand to his mouth as a cold bead of sweat crept down his back. If Auguste, he found himself thinking, had expertly garrotted her with a cord as they sometimes did in a breaking when their orders allowed it, surely her agony would have been over far sooner.

Jérôme dropped away, cursing, as urine began to drip from beneath her shift. "No use," he panted. "Sweet Jesus, have mercy." A few men in the crowd booed and suddenly the air was thick with pebbles, mud, and half-frozen lumps of horse manure.

The crowds, the men always agreed, were peculiar; they would jeer and shriek with fierce joy at every agonizing blow of a break-ing, yet if the execution was a hanging, expected to be swift and clean, they inevitably erupted with outrage when—as it rarely did—the process went wrong. They could do nothing but dodge the mis-siles as best they could and wait for her to shudder to stillness.

Even a botched hanging, Charles knew, must inevitably come to only one conclusion. At last, after an endless quarter hour, it was over and the woman hung limp and still from the gallows. The spectators drifted away, muttering and casting narrow-eyed glan-ces over their shoulders at the executioners.

"What in the seven hells went wrong?" Jérôme demanded, of no one in particular.

"Her *neck*," Bastien said, landing with a grunt on the platform. "Her neck wouldn't snap. Thick and stiff as a board. God forgive me, M'sieur Charles, I couldn't get her neck to snap, no matter what I did."

Charles pressed his shoulder. "You did your best. You did nothing wrong."

Auguste, he found, was bent over the edge of the scaffold, shak-ing and deathly pale. He rose, wiping his mouth.

"I told her . . . I promised her it would be *quick*," he said, avoiding Charles's eyes, and crossed himself. "I always tell them that, them who're about to be hanged, that it'll be quick and won't hurt much; they want to hear that. I promised her it would all be over in a minute. Holy Mother of God."

"God willed it." That was Bastien, who was inclined to be super-stitious. "He must have meant for it to happen, a punishment. She must have been very wicked."

"Strong, I'd say," Jérôme said to Charles in an undertone, plant-ing fists on hips and scowling at the dangling corpse. "Too strong for her own good . . . and maybe I placed the ropes wrong, though I'm sure I set them as I always do, as God is my witness."

"You did nothing different?" Charles said. "The ropes, the lad-der, all as usual?"

"As God is my witness," he repeated. "I don't know what went wrong, M'sieur Charles."

Charles swallowed away his nausea and glanced once more at

the corpse, gently swinging in the chill breeze from the nearby river. "You're not to blame, Jérôme. Go ahead, take her down."

He went straight to Antoinette's apartment that evening when they had finished with their work at the Place de Grève. Antoinette, sensing his grim mood and remaining determinedly cheerful, chattered through supper of *La Nouvelle Héloïse* ("weepy drivel, my love— Rousseau's political works are much superior") and the *Dictionnaire Philosophique*. Voltaire's notorious book had appeared the summer before in a small, easily portable—and concealable—edition and had been immediately banned by the censors for its stinging and, naturally, hugely entertaining criticism of the vices and foibles of France's absolute monarchy and the corruption rife in the Gallican Church. Charles ate little and said less until they had finished their meal and the maid had cleared the salon of supper dishes.

"What's fretting you?" Antoinette said, as she handed him back the *Dictionnaire Philosophique* and poured him out a demitasse of coffee. "Or should I not ask?"

He thrust the book aside and, without looking at her, described the hanging, knowing that she would not shrink away. Antoinette grimaced in distaste, but said nothing at first. She considered the matter a moment while she stirred her own coffee.

"I'm sorry for the poor woman," she said at last, "but even that death must have been quicker and kinder than most natural ones. If I were forced to choose between being hanged and, say, taking days or weeks to die of hunger, or the smallpox, or childbed fever, I know which I'd pick. Are you sure, Charles dear, that you're not sorrier for yourself than you are for her?"

What on earth did she mean by that, he wondered, as he glowered at the fire crackling in the hearth.

"Despite all," she went on, after a moment's silence, "you still can't accept the fact that, through no fault of your own, you're a man different and apart, and will be until you die. I know your dearest wish is to be an ordinary man like any other; but why not make the best of what you are, instead of tormenting yourself about what you want to be and never will be?"

"This has nothing to do with me. I'm talking about a miserable thief who stole a few old clothes and died in agony for it—"

"Of course it's to do with you. There wasn't any question of her guilt, I suppose? Well, you didn't know that woman," she continued as Charles shrugged and shook his head, "and you'd consider yourself far too genteel to ever look at someone like her as anything more than riffraff. You simply wish you hadn't had to be present when they strung her up."

"Is that a crime?"

Antoinette sighed. "Good Lord, Charles. Sometimes I think you're over-queasy about something you've never had to do. You've never actually put anyone to death yourself, have you?"

"Not since Damiens."

"Even then, you merely told someone else how to hack the poor creature apart. Yet you take it so hard, though you scarcely lift a finger on the scaffold. What about your men, who do the work? How do you imagine *they* feel?"

He shrugged again. Perhaps, he realized, he had unconsciously assumed that his servants, not being gentlemen, were far less sensitive about such matters.

"What do you suppose that man who fumbled the hanging is thinking right now?" Antoinette added. "I hope he has a wife or a sweetheart to comfort him." She snatched away his empty cup. "Think of him, for a change. You've never once had to soil your own hands with an execution."

"No, I haven't, I confess it; but that's not to say I never will. If the condemned prisoner is a nobleman—"

"Oh, pooh, how often does that happen?"

"It may happen much sooner than you think!"

Antoinette paused, the coffeepot balanced over his cup. "I don't understand."

"Haven't you heard what's happening to the Comte de Lally?"

She frowned. Despite her insatiable appetite for books, she took little interest in current political matters—politics, she often declared, was for the imbeciles and vipers at court. "I suppose so . . . something about India, wasn't it? Well? Who is he?"

A decorated officer, a marshal of France, who was sent to India to keep the British at bay and hold our possessions there, he said patiently, recalling the follies of the best-forgotten Seven Years' War, which already seemed like one of the Sun King's wars, a relic from another age. And instead he'd lost France's greatest Asiatic territories, though you wouldn't find half a dozen people together who'd agree why—a talent for battle, but none for negotiation; contempt for the heathen Hindus; more contempt yet for the bunglers among his own officers, inspiring no loyalty; sheer ill luck.

The general who lost Madras and Pondichéry to the English in 'sixty-one, my love. The battle at—some strange, unpronounceable Asiatic name—Wandiwash, that was it. Maybe you heard of it.

"Why should he concern you, particularly?" she inquired. "It sounds like yet another bit of ghastly politics to me."

"I know him."

"You *know* him?"

"He was a friend to our family. He and my father were friends before I was born."

She laughed. "You're full of surprises. How did *that* come about?"

He related the story of Lally's unexpected intrusion at Jean-Baptiste's wedding banquet. "Monsieur de Lally held my father in high regard," he concluded. "He often used to dine with us. I was just eighteen when he sailed for India at the beginning of the war, but I remember him well; he was very friendly with me.

"He's a good man, Toinette, and the bravest officer who ever served his king. But even I could tell you that he's a soldier first of all, not the least bit a diplomat, and they sent the wrong man for the job. Everything went wrong for him in India, and now he's in the Bastille while they investigate this so-called treason. *Treason,* my God, for a man who earned the Cross of St. Louis for valor on the battlefield! If they sentence him to death . . ."

". . . The master executioner will have to behead him," she finished for him. "I see. But if your father's so frail—"

"Of course he is." Jean-Baptiste was only forty-five but looked far older, with the prematurely white head and cane of a grandpapa. "If they do try Lally and sentence him to death . . . my father can barely lift that sword now. I'll have to do it myself."

"Do you even know how to use the sword?"

Charles grimaced. "Father taught me, years ago, before he fell ill, and I grew pretty adept at it, but I'm out of practice."

He had hoped it was something he'd never be called upon to do. Naturally. You nurtured such hopes and called them beliefs.

"It can't be easy, beheading a man with a sword," Antoinette mused. "In England the honorable execution was the block and axe, which must be easier for the headsman; but even so, I've read about some accidents . . ."

"I wish it were so simple." He recalled Jean-Baptiste's words from years ago: *Chopping with an axe on a block—a clumsy method.* "All that's required of an English headsman is steady nerves."

But they hadn't beheaded anyone in England in nearly twenty or thirty years, and since then an English earl had been hanged for murdering his own steward, just a few years ago; they both remembered reading about it in the newspaper amid the snips and scraps of the foreign news.

"The English are so sensible and progressive," Antoinette said. "Why shouldn't the Parlement change the law and just hang aristocrats like everyone else?"

"Hang a nobleman?" he echoed her. "How degrading. It would put them on a level with common criminals."

She smiled, indulgent. "Listen to yourself. You're such a snob, my love. If a nobleman commits a crime, what makes him any better than that woman who was hanged today?"

"This is a political matter," he protested. "Lally's no felon. He's not even guilty. And it's not as if he's accused of housebreaking. He's still a high-born gentleman—"

"And why should a high-born gentleman deserve a different and easier mode of execution than does a thief?"

Charles scowled. A hard little knot of worry had begun to form in his belly as soon as he had learned of the extent of Lally's misfortunes from the most gossipy of the clerks at the Palais de Justice. He had returned to practicing once again with Jean-Baptiste's heavy wooden sword as soon as rumors of Lally's forthcoming trial before the Parlement reached him. Soon, despite his constant prayers that he would never need to do so, he would have to take the sword of justice—*justice?*—out of its crate and accustom himself to its different weight and suppleness.

To behead a man or woman with a sword, Charles, Jean-Baptiste had repeated, *you must whirl it about, over your head, before striking. It must gather enough momentum to slice through the patient's neck as he kneels before you. The patient must hold himself absolutely still, and you, at the same time, must be completely sure of your aim . . .*

"Beheading with a sword is not always an easier death," Charles said, unsmiling. "Not if the headsman has little experience."

"No, I grant you that. So why can't the parlements be persuaded that it's not always as simple and 'honorable' a manner of death as they'd like to think?"

It requires strength, control, and a keen eye . . . Only practice will make you skilled at it . . .

"Though I read once," Antoinette added, "that a French executioner beheaded a queen of England with a sword, about two hundred years ago. They brought him from Calais. The book said he took her head off in an instant."

"What?" He was only half listening; for Antoinette, it was merely an intriguing theoretical problem, not a terrifying possibility.

"Beheading with a sword—it's been done plenty of times."

"Yes, of course, but I've never done it, or even seen it done." He did not mention that his great-grandfather, he who had once fainted on the scaffold, had had to behead the notorious Madame Tiquet, who had attempted to rid herself of her husband, in just the same fashion in 1699. Perhaps inexpert, perhaps flustered by the lady's beauty and self-possession, Great-Grandfather Charles Sanson the First had scandalously bungled the job.

Charles set down his demitasse untasted and Antoinette reached for it, but he waved her away. "What if it goes wrong? What if I botch it as badly as Bastien did today?"

"You mustn't dwell on that."

"I can practice all I like, but despite all I've seen and done in the past ten years, I'm not sure—Toinette, I'm not sure I'll be able to put a man to death with my own hands . . ."

23

So how did it begin?

The truth is, it began long ago. Generations ago. Or maybe it really began the first time that somebody with a title—or his conceited teenaged son—snubbed Duval de Soicourt for being a slick, narrow-minded, petty lawyer with more ambition than manners. But for me it began on the night of the eighth of August, 1765, a month before I turned twenty.

I scarcely even remember that night. I'd spent it at home, because I'd woken up that morning with a queasy stomach and a really brutal headache from the night before. So I'd taken it easy and passed the day reading, and playing chess with Madame in her parlor. Then I'd gone back to my room, practiced playing my violin for a bit, and turned in for the night.

The night before, though, the night of the seventh . . . we'd gone out, my friends and I, the whole lot of us, and I'd come home blind drunk. So my recollection's a little blurry. But I do remember we'd been arguing (again) about Voltaire and his new book on how preposterous religion could be, and Étallonde agreed that most people were such hypocrites, the ones who looked so pious at Mass and then went out to screw their fellow man any way they could. It was a favorite topic; though mostly because we thought attending daily Mass, the price I paid for living in cushy quarters as a guest in a convent, I suppose, was a real waste of time—time that could have been spent doing much more amusing things than going up and down on your knees in a drafty church and worshiping bits of bread and gabbling a lot of Latin that you didn't understand.

Étallonde said something to us when we broke up that night, something like, "I'll give the starchy old prunes something to think about!" But I didn't pay much attention, because I needed to throw up. So I'd gone and puked in an alley, and then I'd slouched off home and fallen into bed.

In the afternoon of the ninth, when the news must have been buzzing all around town, Madame called Jacques and me into her parlor and gave us the gimlet-eyed look that she was capable of when she knew we hadn't been on our best behavior.

"Well? How much do you two know about the damage to the shrine on the bridge?"

"Damage?" I said. What was she talking about? I didn't know anything about the shrine.

"Did either of you have anything to do with this? Did you think this might be indulged as just another of your adolescent larks?"

"I don't understand," I managed to say. "What's going on?"

She gave me a suspicious look, but went ahead and told us. If you cross the Pont-Neuf, the main bridge of Abbeville, you can't miss the big shrine in the middle of the span, a wooden crucifix, painted white, that's almost life-size. Sometime during that past night, it looked like somebody had hacked away at Jesus with a sword or a sturdy knife, and left him with gashes in the legs and arms, one arm nearly broken off, and a stab right through the chest. Abbeville being Abbeville, they're attached to their crucified Christ, and everybody was up in arms about it.

"So?" Madame said.

I repeated that I didn't know anything.

"God's truth?"

"Yes, madame."

"And do either of you know how it might have happened?"

"No, madame." Jacques was set to join the Guards, too grownup to be carousing with teenaged kids—although we all knew about that scrape during the past January, when he and Louis Douville had brawled with one of Duval de Soicourt's underlings at the Château des Comtes, the town's barracks, fortress, and prison. That, of course, hadn't made Duval feel any kindlier toward our family, especially after the humiliation he'd received at Madame's hands over Marguerite Becquin.

"François?" Madame said, looking me in the eye.

"Well . . . Bertrand Gaillard d'Étallonde said something the other night before I left them . . . but I never saw him *do* anything."

"That one!" she exclaimed. "Spoiled rotten, and his father helps him wriggle out of every mess he gets himself into. He's a bad influence on you, François. Now," she continued, "you keep your mouths shut, both of you, and lie low for a while. And if anyone in authority asks you about this, François, you're to tell him whatever it is you heard young Gaillard d'Étallonde say. And you say nothing else! Not a word."

"I don't understand," I began. I couldn't see why she seemed so grim and earnest about it. Sure, carving up the shrine was a pointless, offensive thing to do—but, after all, it's only a piece of wood.

"My dear simpleton, this outrage to the shrine is exactly the sort of odious prank that a handful of drunken, boisterous, puerile young men—young men who swagger about with swords—might commit. Everyone in town is going to be looking toward you and your friends. The good Lord knows you've earned quite a reputation."

I blushed, because I really did want her to be proud of me, and I'd never meant to hurt anybody, but I hadn't exactly lived up to her expectations. "What do you want me to do?"

She tried to glare at me, but she couldn't keep it up. Instead she smiled and patted my cheek. "Just keep quiet and out of sight for a few weeks. Don't worry—I imagine this will soon blow over."

That damned wayside cross . . . I wonder what really happened.

Maybe it really was Étallonde who did it, showing off, and he was drunk enough to think that carving up a holy figure was just a big laugh. But it wasn't I.

Or maybe it wasn't anybody. Maybe some late-going passing wagon full of firewood or paving stones gave a lurch on the bridge and gouged the wood and knocked off Christ's arm without the driver ever giving a backward glance. Or maybe it was a fractious mule. Funny, that, if Jesus lost his arm to a mule's kick. Or maybe some souse, blind drunk, thought he was climbing a tree and grabbing a branch. Snap, off comes the arm. Hard luck, Jesus.

Maybe Madame believed the matter would die down soon enough. But the townspeople didn't look at it that way. After a fortnight they were still bellowing "Christ has been murdered in Abbeville!" or some such pious rubbish.

And who do you think was in charge of finding the fiends who'd committed the crime?

Why, the examining magistrate, of course: none other than our precious criminal assessor, Duval de Soicourt.

So what do you do when you're the last word in a criminal inquiry, and you've got a few private scores to settle? Well, if you're Duval de Soicourt, you find witnesses who'll be happy to swear, with a little prompting, that the people you hate the most were mixed up in it. And Duval had a particular bone to pick with Bertrand d'Étallonde and me, beyond all the petty feuding between our families, because of that little escapade with his windows and our bare bottoms the previous Christmas.

Monsieur Linguet, the lawyer, who dug up all the dirt when he was gathering evidence to help me, told me Duval never actually produced any names during four days of questioning about the damaged crucifix. Lots of witnesses, yes, but none of them could give him much beyond, *I saw some sinister strangers crossing the bridge three weeks ago . . . Don't know their names . . . Gypsies, they were, maybe . . . Looked like the sort of dodgy folk who'd do such a wicked thing . . . Might recognize them again, might not.*

And then what do you think should happen?

Why, Monsieur Naturé, the master at arms who owns the fencing school where I practice, turned up with a tale that seemed to have been burdening his conscience. Not that he'd seen me profaning the shrine, oh, no, since that would have been a complete lie, but that, back in June, he'd seen me—and Étallonde, and Marcel de Moisnel—showing disrespect to the annual procession of the Holy Sacrament: We hadn't taken our hats off, nor had we knelt, as it passed.

I'll say right now that I barely even remember that, but it's true, as far as it's worth. I kept my hat on, and stayed on my own two feet, when the procession went by, thirty yards away. Thirty yards away, and it was raining. I'll bet anyone in his right mind, even though the Host was passing at the head of a line of monks, would have preferred not to go down on one knee in the mud.

But isn't it funny that Naturé should wait a couple of months before reporting that little breach of piety? If it had bothered him so much, why didn't he go straight to the authorities and denounce me as an unbeliever back in June?

And isn't it funny that Étallonde and Moisnel and I just happened to be kids from the three families Duval de Soicourt hated most?

So when Duval started hinting that anyone wicked enough to insult a holy procession would also be capable of sacrilege and desecration of a shrine, Madame wrote some more letters to Monsieur d'Ormesson in Paris, and Monsieur d'Ormesson said he'd look into it. The whole thing should have been over in a fortnight. But we'd underestimated Duval's rancor, I guess. And we didn't expect people we'd thought were our friends to betray us.

It's easy enough, now, to figure out why old Belleval told lies about me. His son Pierre was part of our crowd, and Duval nursed a fierce grudge against the Bellevals after Marguerite Becquin's marriage into the family. And Moisnel was Belleval's cousin and ward. So Belleval, the old fox, must have decided that the best way of keeping suspicion away from your own family is to shift the blame onto somebody else, somebody—like a penniless orphan from a different part of the country—somebody like me—who doesn't really matter.

Besides, he'd hankered after Madame for ages, without getting anywhere. He was just plain jealous of Jacques and me, and sulky like self-important people are when they don't feel they're getting enough attention paid them. You could see it, the way he looked at us. Our cousin's attention had been turned to us, to "her boys," for the past three years, and Belleval, the fine gentleman who till then could have had any woman he wanted, was the loser for it.

I don't know why Beauvarlet, the bankrupt merchant, Madame's charity case, had it in for me, except that at heart he was just an oily, self-righteous toady, with his holy pictures all over the walls— cheap, ugly stuff—and he'd seen me snickering more often than once at his vulgar saints and crucifixes. Maybe it was pure spite, because we lived in the same house at the abbey, courtesy of Madame, and our being around just rubbed it in, that Jacques and I were young and cocky, with a future ahead of us, and he was a sour old failure. Whatever the reason, he sneaked off to the criminal assessor's office and repeated every rumor he'd ever heard, and every coarse, careless word I'd ever said in front of him, and then the old snoop finished by telling Duval I kept banned books in my room.

And if you think Duval de Soicourt didn't take advantage of every hint and half truth Belleval and Beauvarlet handed him, then you really don't know Duval.

The nearest I can figure it out, why people got so upset about a couple of cuts to a crucifix that was soon mended, is that the priests claim that if you wound an image of God or Christ, then you're wounding God himself. Now it seems to me, if God is as all-powerful as they insist, then how can a mere human being wound him, especially through nothing more than a stick of wood?

I've had time to think about it for a while now, and I guess it doesn't really have anything to do with God. What it comes down to is, if you deny God, or insult him, or question anything the priests say, or do the tiniest thing that might show you're thinking for yourself, then you're pretty much saying God and religion aren't everything.

And since the king is king, they say, by divine right, by the grace of God, then if enough people decide religion is rubbish, it follows that maybe the king has no special right from God, or from anyone, to be king. A dangerous idea, that. So it's in the king's interest to make sure everybody swallows every crumb of the clap-trap the priests tell them, and to torture them and kill them if they won't.

Just politics, and power.

Isn't that what it's really all about?

24

In September Monseigneur de la Motte, the bishop, came to town from his cathedral at Amiens and called for a penitential Mass at Saint-Vulfran. They said it was in order to help Abbeville cool off after the outrage, but actually there's nothing like a grand, breast-beating public ceremony to get emotions heated up all over again. And when a big noise like the bishop did public penance in the name of all his flock at the hacked-up shrine, prostrating himself bare-foot with a rope around his neck and a lit candle in his hand, like a jailbird going to the gallows, it was enough to get the pious into a mighty rage. Find the blasphemers who murdered God, and loose the wrath of God onto them!

I'll skip a lot of it. By now you can guess what was brewing. But I was dense and thoughtless enough, still behaving and thinking like a silly kid, that I didn't suspect half of what was going on around me—remember, I only turned twenty a couple of days after the bishop's visit. I even kept on taking fencing lessons from Étienne Naturé for a few more weeks, everything just as usual.

It wasn't till the end of September that I finally realized how serious things were, when Madame suggested, gently, but with a worried look in her eye that I'd never seen before, that it would be better if I got out of town for a while.

She was the one with some sense. She'd had her ear to the ground and had heard the rumors coming out of the law courts about

Duval's plans to find somebody, anybody, to punish for the sacrilege—preferably somebody he bore a grudge against anyway. She'd already been laying her plans, in case things got ticklish for me; they were expecting me at the abbey of Longvilliers, not far from Boulogne, just a day's ride away. I was to lie low there, or, if I chose, I could take the first ship out for England, until she could find a friend at court who would pull strings for me.

I didn't like to run, but Madame insisted, so I packed a couple of shirts, took some gold that she gave me and a good horse from the abbey stable, and set out on the Montreuil road. Maybe I was wondering, in spite of all her assurances, if that was the last chance I'd have to ride in the countryside. I took my time, like a traveler seeing the sights, as if I wanted to drink in the sight and smell of the valleys and the autumn mists and the clean rain-washed skies before they snatched it all away from me.

But I suppose, by taking off, I just gave Duval an excuse to act.

His muscle appeared the morning after I'd arrived at Longvilliers, along with an officer of the Boulogne gendarmerie, very firm and very polite. So back we went to Abbeville, and to the Château des Comtes, where they weren't so polite. Then I went the next morning, after spending the night getting acquainted with a few rats in a damp cell, to have a little chat with Hecquet de Roquemont, the prosecutor, and with Duval de Soicourt.

Moisnel was there, too, it turned out, and we huddled together on a bench in an anteroom. The poor kid looked scared to death. He was only just sixteen, after all.

"Where's Bertrand Gaillard d'Étallonde?" I dared to ask Lieutenant Merlin, the officer who'd escorted us in.

"Seems he got out while he could," he said. "He's probably in Holland by now."

"Is—is it that bad?" Moisnel said.

Merlin stepped closer to us and lowered his voice. "It's worse than you think. Listen, you lads: You take care what you say. Tell the truth, whatever the prosecutor asks you—but don't give them anything more than they ask for. No reason to make it easy for them."

He led me into a room where Duval de Soicourt and Hecquet

and a couple of clerks were waiting. Duval pointed me to a stool and began to march back and forth in front of me, hands clasped behind his back, and head hunched low between his shoulders like the pictures of carrion birds in Madame's book about Africa.

"On the day of the Feast of the Holy Sacrament," he said, "did you wear a hat?"

"A hat?" I repeated, and stared. What did *that* have to do with anything? And why the devil was he going on about something that had happened more than three months before, long before the shrine was damaged, something that was past and forgotten?

"I suppose so . . . why wouldn't I have?"

"Who were you with?"

"My friends . . . Étallonde and Moisnel," I said, when I'd searched my memory.

"The others, were they also wearing hats? Did you see the procession of the Capucin monks? Was it your intention to insult Divinity by not uncovering in sight of the procession?"

I'll admit that usually, between hangovers, I couldn't remember much of what I'd been doing the previous night, much less months ago. I scarcely recalled anything about the Feast of the Holy Sacrament back in June, but I tried my best to explain.

"I was a little late for dinner. I'd hurried up to get ahead of the procession. I didn't stop, or kneel, or take off my hat—but that wasn't in order to insult anyone—or—or anything—it was just because I was in a hurry to get back to the abbey."

It went on like this, one stupid question after another. Nothing about the sacrilege to the shrine on the bridge, but more and more about that damned procession, and about what my friends and I used to say in private about religion—all the coarse jokes we used to make in order to look oh-so-clever and shock our relatives and make the girls blush and giggle. Whatever else you say about Duval, he's a smart, sly lawyer. He knows how to twist your words until the most innocent phrase becomes something they can hang you with. *Did you do this? Isn't it true that—?*

Isn't it true that you called the Holy Virgin a whore? Didn't you once, on going to your knees, make the sign of the Cross and say "In the name of the holy asshole"?

Maybe I did do something silly and infantile like that in front of my friends, just for a laugh. But it was in fun. Cheekiness, not malice. Just something stupid that boys do.

"When you're tipsy," I started to explain—though I had a strong suspicion that Duval had never been tipsy in his life, or at least not tipsy in front of his friends, because he couldn't possibly have had any—"when you're just talking with your friends to pass the time, you—you say a lot of things you don't really mean, and in the morning you don't remember saying them . . ."

"Did you, or did you not, once desire to buy a plaster figure of Christ from the Sieur Beauvarlet, in order to take and desecrate the image of Our Lord?"

What in the name of all the saints was he talking about? I thought back, and finally remembered what he must have meant, but he pushed on.

"If it wasn't you, who was it who accompanied you that day into Beauvarlet's private chamber at the abbey of Willancourt?"

"Gaillard d'Étallonde," I said. Étallonde was my best friend, but now that he'd left town, I didn't worry about telling the little I knew. "I remember now. He wanted to buy the plaster crucifix from Monsieur Beauvarlet because he thought it was so ugly. He said, 'If I owned anything as ugly as that, I'd smash it,' but it was just a joke. He didn't mean it as sacrilege."

Duval nodded, scowling, and then he said, "Isn't it true that you've given scandalous books to other young men, and that you've gone down on your knees to pay homage before your tabernacle of immoral and disgusting writings? Books such as *The Abbey Gatekeeper*, *The Nun in Her Nightgown*, *Conjugal Love*, and so on?"

He knew all the racy titles on my shelf—though of course they weren't on a shelf, where any servant could see them, but safe at the bottom of the chest where I kept my out-of-season clothes. Had Duval and his men already searched my room? Better be honest about it, I thought.

"I did pass around some books to my friends." Then I supposed that maybe they would think better of me if they knew that now and then I read something other than pornography, and that not all my books had naughty pictures in them.

"But I also have some serious books, monsieur, ones I prefer: Voltaire's *Dictionnaire Philosophique*, and a few by Helvétius . . ."

Faith, what a witless fool I was. Digging my own grave with a couple of words! What's a little insipid pornography, compared with works by notorious philosophers who question religion and criticize the state?

What kind of idiot was I, not to realize that, in Abbeville, Voltaire might just as well have been the Antichrist?

Duval paused for a moment, and you could almost see the wheels turning inside his head. Piecing the evidence together like bits of a shattered dinner plate, whether or not it added up to a plate or to a chocolate-pot instead, something else entirely, but just as useful.

He said suddenly: "Where were you on the eighth of August last, between eleven and midnight?"

"At home with madame the abbess," I said, more confident. He was finally getting to the matter of the damaged shrine, and I knew I was on safe ground there. "She'll vouch for me."

"You didn't cross the Pont-Neuf, in the company of several other young men?"

"No, monsieur. I know I didn't, because I didn't go out at all that night."

"If it wasn't you, then who mutilated the Christ of the Pont-Neuf on the night of August eighth?" He leaned in over me, his Adam's apple bobbing. *"Who did it?"*

Until then I hadn't really believed we could be in serious trouble. We were nobility, after all—petty nobility, it's true, but still with titles, and the privileges that came with them, and influential relatives, that ordinary people didn't have. But at that instant I realized that being a chevalier didn't count for as much as I'd thought it would, not with Duval de Soicourt, criminal assessor of Abbeville, and a chill lance of fear stabbed right through me.

"It might have been Gaillard d'Étallonde," I said, and prayed he was on a ship heading for Holland. "I know he'd had his hunting knife sharpened; it could have done the damage."

But it went on, question after question, and then Duval turned to a completely different subject, a cross in the cemetery that they'd found a couple of days later smeared with shit, and asked questions about that, too. I hadn't been there. That evening I'd gone back to the abbey with my chum Nicolas de Métigny. On the way, because we were a bit drunk, as usual, we'd raised a little hell and pulled a few bell chains, just to make nuisances of ourselves once again, but we hadn't gone near the cemetery.

I was telling the truth, so help me God, but by that time I was so scared and mixed up that I must have looked guilty as sin.

The last thing I noticed, before the guard led me back to my cell, was a triumphant smirk that Duval tried to hide, and couldn't.

It all became a nightmare, an endless stream of voices and faces and lies. What else can I say about the next few days, except that Duval bullied poor Moisnel until he cracked, until the kid was so terrified he was ready to say anything they wanted to hear?

The only news that cheered me up for five minutes, after they'd formally decreed me under arrest, came when Madame visited me in prison. She said she'd told that fawning old toady Beauvarlet that he was a monster of ingratitude, and she'd thrown him out of his cozy lodgings at the abbey.

25

Like most executioners throughout France, the Sanson family lived at the edge of the city, where their unwelcome presence would not trouble many nearby householders. Few folk, Charles imagined, would relish looking out their windows into his stableyard to see their neighbor whirling a three-foot-long blade at a man-sized dummy.

The Comte de Lally remained in the Bastille and the Parlement continued to wrangle over his case. Charles offered a prayer of thanks to heaven for the reprieve, for he had dreaded most of all that Lally should be tried and—God forbid!—condemned before he had grown proficient with the sword of justice, and continued to practice.

He had not spent much of his leisure at home since Antoinette and he had become lovers. On those days when Jean-Baptiste supervised the business of punishment at the Place de Grève or at the pillory in the marketplace, and when Antoinette's attention was occupied with Carlin or the mysterious gentleman in black, Charles went hunting after passing an hour or two with Marie-Anne in Mont-Martre. The house on Rue d'Enfer had grown dull since Madeleine's marriage and after two of his three eldest brothers had gone off to apprenticeships as *aides-bourreaux* with various provincial cousins. The youngest of his nine surviving siblings were still children, scarcely the companions whom a smart young man-about-town would desire in his pursuit of diversion.

Marthe had long since guessed he was keeping a mistress elsewhere in the city. For some time she had badgered him to take a wife and settle down to comfortable respectability. As the only real purpose in his marrying seemed to be the production of more little Sansons to populate the scaffolds of France, Charles did not feel duty-bound to obey her.

Jean-Baptiste, whose two agreeable marriages had long compensated him for the strain of his profession, also stressed the joys of matrimony to him. "When I look at you and your brothers and sisters, all my fine sons and my pretty daughters," he told Charles one autumn day, "I thank the good Lord that I've been so blessed. And then I think how He saw fit to give me more children to brighten my old age"—he had recovered sufficiently from his apoplexy to sire yet another son and daughter within the past half-dozen years—"and I wonder how a man like me has deserved such good fortune."

Honestly, Charles thought, I'd rather have no children at all. Why would I take joy in raising a family of my own, when the title of executioner is the only lasting legacy I can leave my sons?

Jean-Baptiste punched him on the shoulder, lightly enough, for his arms were still weak. "Find yourself a good girl and marry her, Charles. I know just the girl, nineteen, well-dowered, and pretty as a rose—Émilie, one of the Desmorest girls—"

Charles knew her, had met her last year at somebody's wedding or somebody's christening or somebody's funeral—one or more of the Paris Sansons inevitably put in a dutiful appearance at all such tribal gatherings within a day's journey, for they owed it to their own kind to stick together. Indeed quite pretty, he recalled: pretty, domestic, bland, probably not a thought in her head beyond the next week's menus.

"I'm sure she's a lovely girl," he said, as diplomatically as he could, "but I've no wish to bring a bride to a household that Grand'mère still considers her own. At some point, she'll choose to step down and leave the running of the house to someone else, and then . . ."

Jean-Baptiste smiled. He smiled more readily than he once had, now that they shared their duties at the scaffold. "Perhaps. Though you may wait a long time."

"I've not really thought of marriage yet."

"You're twenty-six. I—"

"I know; you were married at sixteen, and a father at nineteen. But I'm not ready to settle down." And why, he thought as he seized the poker and prodded at the fire, would I want to take up with some other girl, now that I'm happier than I ever thought I could be, with Toinette?

And why not Toinette?

He recalled a half-serious notion he had had once, that Antoinette, who had never shrunk from discussing his profession, might make an ideal executioner's wife. Why should he not marry her, and all at once make a respectable woman of her and keep his father happy?

Antoinette was polished, vastly intelligent, practical, and, most important of all, unafraid of what her lover did to earn his living. He smiled to himself as he considered that she might even, in a rougher age, have made a creditable *bourrelle* herself—for the feminine form of the word did exist and it was rumored that a few female executioners had, indeed, plied the trade in centuries past, widows or daughters clinging to a well-paid hereditary title by carrying out their duties disguised in male attire.

Why, he wondered as he set down the poker, had he never before considered marrying her? Men married their mistresses, from time to time; even the Sun King himself, sixty or seventy years ago, had married his mistress, in his old age. Of course Antoinette was a courtesan and of low birth, despite the spice of noble blood in her veins; she was not of the class from which a gentleman should consider selecting a wife.

He smiled again, at his own pretensions. Like it or not, despite his efforts to appear the gentleman and be like other men, he was still the public executioner and did not have the luxury of picking and choosing a bride from among the gentry, or even from the upper bourgeoisie.

No, it was Antoinette's reputation, rather than her birth, against which the family would erupt in outrage. But, by God and the devil, he would brave the inevitable storm. He was of legal age, and the head of the household in all but name; Jean-Baptiste still spent stretches of time at the country cottage and Charles, rather than his father, tended to most matters that required the attention of the master of the house. Though officially he still needed his father's formal permission to marry, legal recourses were at hand for those adults whose parents denied permission out of mere selfishness—or snobbery.

Yes, it was the perfect answer to his dilemma. And moreover, once Antoinette was his wife, she would no longer entertain her wealthy, aging patrons. They could go hang themselves, for all he cared, and for an instant he guiltily entertained a fleeting and malicious image of a harlequin, baggy white costume drooping about him, dangling from a rope. She would, at last, be his alone.

"Father . . ."

"Charles?"

"If you're so eager for me to marry, then I'll propose a solution to you. There's a woman I'd happily marry, a wonderful woman—a woman I adore."

Jean-Baptiste sat fidgeting with a penknife for a moment before he looked up and met Charles's gaze.

"You love this woman, do you?"

"More than anything. She . . . she's my support, my courage."

"She's your mistress."

"Yes. We've been keeping company for two years now."

"You truly wish to marry a woman of that kind of reputation, and bring her into our family?"

"I don't care about her reputation. She's no vulgar demimondaine or empty-headed actress; she profits by discretion. She won't embarrass us."

"Well, not so many of us are as lucky as I was, marrying for love," Jean-Baptiste said, unexpectedly wistful. "I loved your mother . . . she was an extraordinary young woman, so perceptive and intelligent, far too good for me."

Charles said automatically, "Surely not," though he found himself perplexed by the usually taciturn Jean-Baptiste's sudden candor.

"I'm sorry you and Madeleine never knew her," Jean-Baptiste continued. "You're very like her, Charles . . . perhaps too much like."

"Too much like?"

"Old Tronson, her father, was a *questionnaire*, you know, and she could never bear to hear or speak of what her father and bro-ther—and her husband—did to earn their bread. Too much imagin-ation, you see. Like you, she'd feel on her own flesh every horror they were obliged to mete out. Who knows why God chose to make you resemble her, and make your sister more like my mother?"

"I think Madeleine inherited the best traits from both you and Mother, and even from Grandmother. She's always been the clear-eyed one, shaking sense into me. Antoinette, my mistress," Charles added carefully, eyeing Jean-Baptiste, "shares many of her traits. With Madeleine so far away now, Toinette's the one I turn to when I must speak of . . . unspeakable things . . . and can share them with no one else."

"We have little enough, besides those we love, to give us joy," Jean-Baptiste said at last, after a long silence. "You should marry the woman who will make you happy."

"I have your permission?"

"I won't stand in your way. Though I wish you luck with your grandmother," Jean-Baptiste added as Charles gave a stifled whoop.

"I'm not asking for Grand'mère's permission." He bent and impulsively kissed his father on both cheeks. "Thank you, Father. Thank you. You won't be sorry!"

Jean-Baptiste added that Marthe might be in the kitchen, over-seeing dinner preparations. Charles found her berating a clumsy scullery maid for breaking a saucer.

"Grand'mère," he said, after persuading her to let the poor child alone, "I've decided to get married."

"High time, too." A gleam of triumph flickered in her old eyes. She was at least seventy-five by then, he guessed, if not eighty, though she would never admit her age even to her own sons. "Who is it? Louise Férey? Or that girl of Desmorest's, what's her name, Émilie?"

"Neither. You don't know her; she's not one of us."

"Who is she, then?"

"Her father was the seigneur of the village and estate of Saulcy, in Champagne."

"Not a legitimate daughter, I suppose," she snapped. "You want to marry a bastard, do you? The love child of some country squire, some *hobereau* nobody's ever heard of?"

"I love her, Grand'mère. We love each other."

"Bah! You young people with your sentimental notions. Marriage should be approached with a level head. What sort of advantage is there in marrying somebody's dowerless bastard? She can't have any fortune to speak of."

"I expect she has plenty of property," he declared, without thinking. No doubt Antoinette's various "gentlemen" had, over the past few years, provided her with more than just the rent and furnishings for her small but comfortable apartment. "Jewelry, furniture, probably capital. She may even own some land, for all I know."

"And where did some *hobereau*'s little by-blow get hold of a fortune like that?"

He could think of nothing to tell her but the truth and, while he debated how best to phrase his reply, she pounced.

"She's your mistress, isn't she? A public woman!" She thumped her cane on the floor. "Everything she owns was given her by her paramours! And you want to marry this whore?"

"Antoinette is not a whore!"

"No? Then I'd like to know what you think she is!"

Charles drew a deep breath and counted to a dozen before replying. He had steeled himself to expect the worst. No matter that Antoinette loved him, that she expected nothing from him but his love, that she entertained her other patrons decorously and discreetly—to an adamantly respectable matriarch like Marthe, a whore was a whore whether she walked the streets by the wharves or, like the late Marquise de Pompadour, was kept by the king himself.

"Antoinette and I love each other. She has never taken anything from me. She refuses my gifts."

"But not other men's gifts, that's plain!"

"And how is such a woman, with no money of her own and no name to build on, expected otherwise to live? She can't go on as a shopgirl or a dressmaker all her life. And Toinette is far too intelligent to be content with such work—"

"She's no less a whore!" Marthe blazed. "How dare you even consider bringing a woman like that into our family! Do you want to humiliate us in front of—"

"For God's sake," he shouted, "be silent, for once in your life!"

She stopped in mid-sentence and stared at him, a cherry-colored blush of rage mottling her papery cheeks.

"You may have ruled this house with an iron fist for the past forty years, Grand'mère, but, by God, I've had enough of it. You forced both my father and me into this monstrous profession, and you denied me the freedom to escape it. You may browbeat my father into obedience to your every wish, but you'll not rule me any longer!"

She opened her mouth to retort but he plunged on before she could speak.

"If I choose to marry Toinette, I tell you so not because I need your permission, but because I seek your blessing. And if your blessing isn't forthcoming, I'll damned well marry her without it. I'm above twenty-five and I no longer answer to anyone in what I may, or may not, do to please myself and order my life. Moreover, I'm bringing Toinette back to this house, and if you don't wish to live under the same roof with her, then I'm sure you'll be comfortable in the cottage at Brie. Do I make myself clear?"

Her face had paled from crimson to ashen in rage and astonishment and her hand trembled on her cane. "Quite clear." She turned and hobbled away, her back rigid. As she seized the door handle she paused and glanced back at him. "Good to see you've got some spirit in you, at least."

Charles heaved a great sigh and found he was sweating.

He dressed himself with care the next day, after returning home from the pillory at the Halles, where the men had whipped and branded three pickpockets to discourage them from future misbehavior. His fine dark-green dress coat, he thought, thrusting memories of the flogging aside, would do nicely; perhaps, after he had asked Antoinette to marry him, he would take her out to the opera (the bills had announced that something comic by Gluck was on that night), and order in an intimate little supper afterwards, to celebrate their engagement.

He shouldered on the coat and glanced in the mirror, straightening his collar and lace cravat. It would be amusing to see how many other patrons in the private boxes at the opera house had chosen to wear "Sanson green." That autumn, half the beaux of Paris, it seemed, were wearing Charles's particular deep shade of forest green, for one of his tailor's other clients, a handsome and stylish young marquis, had noticed his half-finished new coat at the workshop, admired its cut and color, and requested one like it. Far from being disconcerted when he discovered the identity of the mysterious customer at Michaud's, the marquis—who was one of those who set the tone for people of fashion—had evidently decided that aping this audacious *bourreau*'s style was delightfully daring, the tiniest bit decadent, and just the thing for the new season.

Antoinette's pretty maid answered Charles's ring and then, upon recognizing him, stepped back with a little gasp from the door.

"What's the matter, Sophie?" Nothing could dampen his spirits at that moment.

"Oh, well, monsieur, we—we weren't expecting you today. And a gentleman—"

"You were expecting some other gentleman? Well, never mind. I want to see her." He brushed past her and into the salon, where Antoinette, laced into a becoming yellow day gown, was idly playing her clavichord and humming a popular air. She glanced at him with a puzzled smile.

"*Chéri*, what are you doing here? You know I'm always occupied on Wednesdays."

"He can go to the devil. Tell him to go away. Toinette—I want to ask you something: something terribly important."

"What's that?" Her smile faded a trifle.

"You know how I adore you. I want to do the right thing by you. Because I love you. Toinette—" He felt like a stage lover, going down on one knee to her, but he could scarcely ask her such an important question while carelessly leaning over the clavichord.

"Toinette, I want to marry you."

To his perplexity, she did not at once dissolve into a delighted smile and a joyous assent.

"I expected you would tell me that sooner or later," she said at last. "You're so invariably decent, Charles; I might have known. Eventually you would want to do the honorable thing."

"It's nothing to do with 'the honorable thing,'" he insisted, rising and brushing a few specks of dust from the skirts of the green coat. "I love you. I want you to be my wife."

"You want a courtesan for a wife? You ought to think long and hard about that."

"I have. And I don't care what you are and what you've done, and with whom you've kept company. I care about *you*, not your reputation. What's past should be past."

"Don't dismiss it so cavalierly. People might say all kinds of cruel things about our children, especially our daughters. People would whisper that their mother was a harlot, and that they might take after her. Do you want that for your children? When they'd already be at such a disadvantage, as children of the executioner?"

"Nobody will say that about our children, or about you, while I'm able to defend you!" He paused and smiled, amused at his own vehemence. "Why all these fears? We'll confront them when the time comes, if the time comes."

She said nothing and he leaned closer in to her, lifting her hand to his lips. "Say yes. One little word."

"Charles—"

"Don't look so solemn, sweetheart. This ought to be a joyous occasion. Why, one would think you didn't want to marry me."

"Charles, you mustn't take this the wrong way, but I don't."

"Don't what?"

"I don't want to marry anyone."

"But—every woman wants a household and—and a family of her own—"

"I have a household of my own already, my darling, as you can see. I have a comfortable home—and I'm not sure I want any children at all. What else would I enjoy as your wife, that I don't already enjoy? And I don't want to *be* a wife."

All he seemed to be able to say was "But . . ." like a halfwit.

"A housewife, that is," she added hastily. "I like my life just as it is, and when I'm too old for this sort of thing and I grow fat and hideous, I expect I'll have saved a tidy sum to invest and keep me comfortable into my old age."

Charles stared at her, all his fantasies crashing down about him as they had on the day Jeanne vanished forever.

"Are you saying," he faltered at last, "that you don't love me any more?"

"No! No, of course not!"

"Then how can you—"

"Charles, you know I adore you! But I don't want to become a housekeeper and a deadly respectable bourgeoise, and raise a dozen children, like your stepmother, and look over the household accounts every Saturday. I simply want us to go on as we've done for all the time we've been together."

"With Mondays, Wednesdays, and Saturdays reserved for somebody else?"

She flushed and looked away. "You men and your pride. You know you're the only man I love."

"Then be my wife, and let me really be the only man you love. I'm through with sharing you; I want you all to myself."

"For heaven's sake, Charles," she said, just a little crossly, "you know perfectly well I have nothing more than a business relationship with my other gentlemen. Tell me: If I owned a dressmaker's shop and created gowns for rich women, instead of providing a little occasional amusement for rich men, would you view my business differently?"

He had always admired her intellect, her logical mind, but today of all days she was being obstinately logical, and it was maddening.

"You ought not to view it differently," Antoinette went on, "because it's not different. And I rather enjoy it; I like my gentlemen, and I like the gifts they bring me, and most of all I like my independence."

He rubbed his nose, baffled. How, how could she possibly choose perpetual spinsterhood and the sinful life of a courtesan over honorable, sacred marriage with a man who cherished her?

"But . . . don't you want to put things right before God? What

we've done—I love you so much, but it's a sin, it's fornication . . .
you're a good Catholic . . ."

"Perhaps it's a dreadful heresy, but what I do with you doesn't
hurt anyone else, and I don't see why making love with one I love
should be considered a sin. And I also don't quite understand how
saying a few words in front of a priest ought to wipe away a couple
of years of fornication, if it *is* a sin in God's eyes to love someone
without a formal blessing."

Charles was about to persevere with his pleas, if for no other
reason than that he did not wish to admit his mistress wouldn't
have him for a husband, when he suspected the reason for her
obstinacy.

"No. That's not it at all, is it?" He backed away a pace, feeling
his cheeks grow hot with wounded pride. "Of course. It's I, myself.
Who I am."

"You?"

"It's too much to ask, that you should marry *me*. Because even
someone like you can still consider herself a step above the hangman! You, the gentleman's bastard, don't want to be the hangman's
wife. You don't care to lower yourself as far as all that. Why should
I have expected otherwise?"

"That's complete nonsense. Don't be ridiculous."

"Is it?"

He recalled all the snubs and sneers he had ever endured, from
high and low alike. *Bourreau*—

"Oh, it's one thing to take the executioner to your bed—it's
exciting, isn't it—like those people who think it deliciously macabre
to copy my clothes—do you find it some kind of sordid thrill to
make love to a man who must kill and torture people for pay?"

If she was going to prick his confident little bubble of self-
congratulation and be so obstinately logical about it, he would be
as mulish and self-pitying as he wanted to be. He wheeled about,
coming up short by the clavichord, and, scarcely knowing what he
was doing, slapped his hand down on the little instrument's key-
board, a brief, harsh chord punctuating his words.

"But it's another thing entirely to marry him. The way you've
talked about my—the profession—with me—I should have guessed.

It's some perverted fancy of yours. You don't mind in the least what I *do*, but you—even you, a bastard, a public woman—you'll sleep with an *actor*, a capering excommunicate mountebank, but you think yourself too good to marry a pariah like the hangman— to join your life and your name with his in Christian marriage, and live under the same roof with him and his tainted family—*that*'s too loathsome for you to contemplate. My God, you're no different from the rest!"

Antoinette seized his hands and pressed them between hers. "Charles, *chéri*, I don't know why you're so overwrought, but please, *please* believe that your profession was the farthest thing from my mind. I adore you—you know that—but I simply don't wish—"

If she had had the chance to continue, Charles realized later, they might have made up their quarrel within the next quarter hour. Instead, the double doors that led to her foyer flew open without warning.

"Mademoiselle, I do not relish being kept waiting by your serving woman!"

It was the nameless gentleman in black, eyes like flint beneath bushy gray brows. Antoinette turned to him and Charles saw her first pale, then blush, as she sank into a deep curtsy. And Antoinette, who had decidedly acid views on aristocratic privilege and calcified social etiquette, didn't curtsy to just anybody.

"Forgive me, monseigneur. I was occupied—"

"You may leave us," the stranger said, glancing at Charles, as if ordering away a footman.

"I beg your pardon," Charles said, eyeing him, "but my business here isn't concluded."

"I say it is. Good day to you."

"This is none of your affair, monsieur. The lady and I were discussing matters of the most private nature, and I don't take kindly to being dismissed."

"Chevalier," Antoinette said, glancing from Charles to the gentleman in black, "you ought to go now. Please. Remember, I was expecting monsieur."

"I don't care if you were expecting the king himself. We're going to have this out—"

"Charles!"

"I suppose," said the man in black, striding past them with a humorless smile and a swift, condescending glance at him, "if we were characters in a poor play, you would be the inevitable youth of high breeding, sterling character, and little fortune, who possesses mademoiselle's heart; and to whom she gives what the rest of us pay for. But it's of little importance to me who you are. Out, young man. Now."

Charles flushed again and seized Antoinette's arm. "Damn it, Toinette, this is why I want you to marry me! Not just this," he added, grasping at words, "you know there are plenty of other reasons—but I don't see why he should come between us—he and however many others, when I'm capable of giving you anything you might wish for—when you could be my wife instead of a pr—a kept woman—"

"This isn't the time!" she told him in a fierce whisper. "Tomorrow. *Go.*"

The stranger turned, impatient, from where he was staring out the window at the long, high silhouette of the Tuileries palace in the near distance, and fixed Charles with his chilly glare once again. "Young man, will you do as mademoiselle asks and remove yourself, or do I have to send for my lackeys to throw you out?"

After having built up a fine head of resentment against the world in general, Charles was damned if he was going to let this arrogant patrician, whoever he was, dismiss him so casually.

"Monsieur, I have as much right to be here as you do. If you'd care to meet me tomorrow in the Bois de Boulogne, or the park of the Luxembourg, near the Observatory, we can settle our differences in an honorable fashion—"

To his astonishment, the stranger gave a short, sharp bark of laughter. "You wouldn't be so quick to challenge me if you knew my name. I regret I can't accommodate you. Let's part on civil terms; I have no quarrel with you, save that you're wasting my time, and you should have none with me."

Charles stared at him, baffled. For one frightful moment he wondered if his distinguished, middle-aged adversary was, in fact, the king incognito, and if his previous words had been ill-chosen in the extreme. Then he recalled the fine oil portrait that hung in Joly de Fleury's chambers at the Palais de Justice, and the colored print above the fireplace in his own salon at home, and decided, with relief, that the stranger did not look in the least like the king.

At last the fervent appeal in Antoinette's eyes persuaded him that he would do himself no good by remaining. Face burning, he turned about, muttered "Good day" between his teeth, and stalked out.

26

As always, Charles sought consolation in hunting and in an hour with Marie-Anne. The morning after his quarrel with Antoinette, he saddled Rosette, packed his hunting rifle and fowling piece, and took off for Saint-Denis.

No one was in sight when he approached the familiar farmhouse at Mont-Martre, but Marie-Anne had been looking out the window, for she came running as Rosette cantered along the muddy road and into the barnyard. "It's been almost a month!" she exclaimed, looking him over as he dismounted, and squeezing his hands. "Nothing's amiss with you? You don't ride by near as often as you used to."

He had never told her about Antoinette, nor had he told Antoinette about Marie-Anne; women, his uncle Gabriel had advised him long ago, were best kept in a state of blissful ignorance when it was a question of other women.

"Of course I'm all right. It's merely—some matters at home. Business. Don't you worry about it."

"I miss you. It all seems empty when you're not here and I don't know when I'll see you next."

With a guilty pang he realized that, despite their tacit agreement that theirs was to be only a liaison of friendly convenience, Marie-Anne seemed to feel toward him a tenderer emotion than friendship. He was as fond of her as he had ever been, but he did not love her as he loved Antoinette.

"I would never go off and leave you without a word. I hope I'm more honorable than that."

"Some men would. I'm not getting any younger."

"A good woman is like a good wine, and improves with age. Do you think you're an old hag at thirty-two? I assure you, you're not."

At last she laughed and they retreated to the barn and the snug corner they had arranged for themselves in the hayloft. After they had made love and were drowsily sharing a cup of wine—from a flask Charles had brought with him, not Jugier's vinegary brew—Marie-Anne stirred and squirmed about until she could gaze down at him.

"Charles, I have to tell you something."

"What is it?"

"Well . . . you don't visit so often as you used to, and every time you leave, I wonder if I'll see you again."

"I told you, I wouldn't use you so."

Oh, Lord, she wasn't going to become sentimental and weepy, was she? He plucked a loose straw from his hair and hoped she would not make a scene.

"No, you're too decent, God knows. But still I miss you when you're not here. I know there wasn't supposed to be more between us than a bit of sport, but I can't help it."

"I'm sorry." He could think of nothing else to say.

"So I decided."

"Decided what?"

"I'll end this, before you go away for good, and break my heart. It won't hurt as bad if it's on my own terms."

"What on earth do you mean?" He rolled to his side and faced her.

"I'm going to take vows. It's all arranged. I'm going to the convent at Saint-Denis."

"You want to be a religious, then?"

"I can do a lot of good that way. Nursing at the Hôtel-Dieu, or helping the poor, and it's all in God's service. I'll be content enough."

Charles had little firsthand knowledge of religious life, for none of his relatives—none he knew of, at least—had entered the Church as priest, monk, or nun. Perhaps the Church wouldn't have them, tainted with the heritage of *bourreaux*?

"Marie-Anne, I wouldn't try to change your mind, but do you really believe it will suit you?"

"Why not?" She gazed up into the rafters, anything to avoid looking at him while she outlined the rest of her life in a handful of plain sentences.

"It can't be much different from what I have here, can it? If I stay here on the farm, nothing will change, ever, except someday you'll leave me and I'll be alone again and still an old maid. Seems to me I'd be just as well off with the sisters, better off maybe, doing some good on this earth and offering prayers to God, and then they take care of you when you get old. Quiet, peaceful, no surprises. It's not a bad life, that."

He flopped down again on his back and stared up into the rafters himself, following a starling that had blundered in and was squawking about, trying to find the sky. "No, I suppose it's not. There's much to be said for a quiet life."

"So this spring, after the planting's done and the baby's come, I'll—"

"*Baby?*"

He twisted about to face her. She gasped and turned away.

"I didn't mean—oh, Lord help me, it just spilled out. I didn't mean for you to know."

"Baby?" he said again. "What baby?" They had always been careful about such matters, with dainty little sea sponges soaked in vinegar, a reliable method he had observed both Jeanne and Antoinette using and had suggested to Marie-Anne, but everyone knew pregnancy could rarely be avoided forever. "You're with child? You're sure?"

She nodded, her cheeks crimson. "Yes."

"Mine?"

"Yes, of course it's yours! Who else?"

Oh, put your foot in it, Charles, he said to himself. She's a good girl, a good Catholic, if she's telling the truth then she's fornicated with only two men in her life, she doesn't throw herself at every man who passes, and that was a thoughtless and offensive thing to say. He fumbled for words.

"You should have told me."

"You never needed to know."

"That I got you into trouble? Of course I needed to know."

"If it was one of the village lads, maybe my father would've raised a stink until he married me; but you're a gentleman and there's nothing Papa could have done. So I didn't want to stir up a quarrel."

"You ought to have told me before this," he repeated.

"And what would you have done about it, except hand me some gold and disappear?" She paused, rubbed her eyes, and continued. "I'm going to have the baby, and then, if it lives, take it to the orphanage; and then go straight to the sisters to take my vows, and that'll be the end of it. I wouldn't take your money, anyway."

Charles sat up, horrid possibilities flashing before him as he remembered Jeanne's deathly pallor. Jeanne had survived a visit to an abortionist, but many did not. "Promise me you won't try to rid yourself of the baby. Promise me you won't go to an herb-woman or a wise woman or whatever you call them—"

"Of course I wouldn't!"

"It's far too dangerous. Women die from that—"

"After sinning with you this long, do you think I want to risk my soul even more by doing something that wicked?"

"Promise me. Swear to me that you won't." He tugged her upright and cupped her face between his hands. "I . . . well, I don't want to see any harm come to you."

"Even if I was wicked enough to think of going to one of those old women, I wouldn't. I want to have this child, though I can't keep it. Because it would be *your* child. Don't you understand? Because I love you. I can't help it." She twisted away again, tears sliding down her cheeks.

"Marie-Anne . . ." The ghost of an idea took form in his mind.

"There," she added a moment later, drying her eyes on her apron, "I've said my piece. I didn't mean for you ever to know, but now you do know. Well, the baby'll be taken care of, and I'll be with the holy sisters, so you needn't have any worries about either one of us, and that's the end of it. Now you can go away and never feel you have to come back."

He suspected Marie-Anne did not know the harsh facts that

Parisians knew, if they troubled to find out, about the public orphanages and the slovenly peasant wet-nurses who were paid a pittance to feed abandoned newborns; four out of five of the babies died. ("The baby'll be taken care of"? That's all you know, kind-hearted, well-meaning, naïve Marie-Anne.) Did he really want to keep on with his manner of living as if nothing had changed, knowing that his child had probably died in some squalid hovel before it was six months old?

"Have you told anyone?"

"No. I was thinking out what to do."

"How far along are you?"

"Two months, maybe, or three." She wouldn't look at him. "I've been missing my courses, which usually come along regular as Sunday, and I'm sick now and then in the mornings; but there's nothing to see yet."

"You've time." He paused a moment, reflecting. Fatherhood was a new and rather frightening prospect.

He abandoned his hunting trip and returned to Rue d'Enfer, where he found a letter awaiting him from the local post. Recognizing the handwriting, he tore it open.

My dearest love,

I am desolate that we should have parted yesterday on such bad terms. Will you not let me explain everything? I dare not tell you in this letter the name of the gentleman with whom you exchanged some words, for letters can be opened; but rest assured he is a gentleman of high rank and great influence. Better he should be a friend rather than an enemy to us.

Please visit me on Sunday afternoon. I shall await you with impatience, for you know I shall love you always.

Your loving
Toinette.

Mon Dieu, he thought, what now?

Women!

Antoinette greeted him in her pale blue-and-gray salon as if their quarrel had never taken place, and rang for refreshments. "Well?" Charles said, once Louise, the cook, had served them coffee and sweet cream-cheese pastries and retreated to the kitchen. "What dark secret have you to tell me, then? Who on earth is this man, that I should fear his influence?"

"First you must promise me you'll never breathe a word of what I tell you here. He insists on complete secrecy, and I'm revealing his identity to you only because I wish you to understand that you mustn't antagonize him. I mean it, Charles. Swear it."

"I swear it." He made the sign of the cross, impatient, wondering why she felt such precautions should be indispensable. "Well?"

She lowered her voice, as if fearing she would be overheard. "Monseigneur de Beaumont, the archbishop."

He blinked. The *what*?

"Er—archbishop?"

"Christophe de Beaumont."

Definitely the archbishop.

Surely no other woman had ever been able to boast, if she were so inclined—which of course Antoinette was not—that she was sharing her bed alternately with the archbishop of Paris, the leading light of the Comédie-Italienne, and the public executioner?

"I met him through one of his secretaries, whose mistress is an actress in Carlin's troupe. Now do you see why he wishes to remain anonymous, and why you mustn't make an enemy of him?"

Good Lord, he thought. The archbishop of Paris was as well known for his intransigence as he was for his intense piety and his generosity to the poor. A kindly man, to be sure, so long as his will was not opposed.

"You see, it just wouldn't have worked, Charles. Imagine the *maître des hautes œuvres* and the archbishop of Paris crossing swords at dawn in the Bois de Boulogne."

He could not help laughing at the preposterous image—including that of Beaumont, sword in hand while wearing his archbishop's miter and full canonicals—that her words conjured up. Antoinette joined him, whooping with mirth, until the maid thrust her head into the room to see if anyone was unwell.

"Dear me," he said at last, with a wild, quickly suppressed flash of curiosity at what sort of lover Beaumont might be, "I suppose even archbishops must heed the demands of the flesh now and then. But at least *he* won't be asking you to marry him . . ."

"No."

"Toinette—"

"*No*, Charles. Let's not argue about that again. I hope you've abandoned your ridiculous notion that I would reject you because of who you are. I simply don't want to get married, to anyone. I want to be my own mistress, not somebody's wife."

"Toinette, I have to marry, sooner or later. My family will nag me until I settle down."

"But that's just it, my sweet; I'd be completely incompetent— and wretched—at 'settling down' and being the sort of wife your family would expect me to be."

"So if I don't marry you, I must marry someone."

"Have you someone in mind?" She pushed the pastries closer to him.

"Yes, in fact I have."

"An executioner's daughter?"

"No. She doesn't yet know who I am."

"You've not already asked her to marry you!"

"No, no, no."

"Perhaps you ought to tell her before the wedding," she suggested, a wicked smile hovering at the corners of her mouth.

He frowned. The conversation was not proceeding as he had imagined it would.

"I assumed you would be angry."

"Angry? Why?"

"Jealous, then."

"Why should I be jealous? Charles, for the tenth time, just because I don't want to marry you, it doesn't mean I don't love you! And I know very well you love me. So why should I be jealous of the bride you may take?"

"Because . . . because she and I have been lovers, now and

then, since before you and I kept company."

She blinked in surprise, but remained unperturbed. "Do you love this woman?"

"I'm quite fond of her," he admitted. "Of course she hasn't your wit or polish. But she's a good, loving, decent woman; I know that much. She deserves an attentive husband."

And a father for her child. He owed her that.

Antoinette smiled. "Dearest, I've no need to be jealous of someone you *respect*. Go ahead and marry her, if you must. I imagine she'll be an excellent wife to you. But you and I can be just as happy together as before."

"That—that's not right." He sprang to his feet and paced across the room. Antoinette watched him, still smiling. "I do care about her. I can't just marry her and then sail off and go back to my mistress, and leave her at home to keep house."

"Why not? The nobility do it all the time."

"And we all know what paragons of rectitude the nobility are!"

"Chevalier, you're so easily shocked. Beneath your affectations of gentility, I believe you'll always be a complete bourgeois."

"Am I too dull and respectable for you, then?"

"I only mean you can't help being restrained by bourgeois morality," she said, her smile fading, "and just as I said before, you're so invariably decent. You can't help believing, in your heart of hearts, that you should always be faithful to a wife whom you care for, even though you married her merely as an expedient."

"That's a fine speech, coming from a woman who sees nothing wrong in abetting a priest in breaking his vow of chastity."

"Oh, Charles, that's really too much. Show me one priest who hasn't given in to temptation at one time or another. You know how corrupt the Church is." Everybody who had read Voltaire's notorious *Dictionnaire Philosophique*, or any other banned work that lambasted the Gallican Church, knew that plenty of the bishops were utterly debauched and irreligious into the bargain, complete embarrassments. "At least Beaumont," Antoinette added, "seems to be sincere in his faith."

"But there's no reason why you should be the one who—who—"

"With whom he breaks his vow? Well, if I hadn't caught his eye, it would be someone else, you know, so it might as well be me. He won't be reformed by Antoinette Vitry virtuously announcing that she'll no longer tempt him into sin every Wednesday."

Charles turned back and gazed at her, feeling suddenly as though he had never truly known her. Though they had shared so many interests and pleasures, they were different on that fundamental level, that craving for a foundation of propriety and morality that he, his family, and all executioners could cling to in their struggle—that vain struggle—to be treated like other men.

"I'm sorry," he said at last, with an effort. "Because I do love you. But it—can't be. You said once that if Jeanne had loved me, it wouldn't have mattered who I was; she would have made sacrifices to remain with me. But if you truly loved me, you would make those sacrifices, too."

"It's not the same, my love. Not at all. I *want* to remain with you; I simply want my independence as well."

"But I can't accept that. I can't bring myself to wed Marie-Anne, as she deserves, and then promptly betray her by returning to someone else. Can you understand that? You can't contemplate making a sacrifice of your own, of marrying me and giving up this—this career of yours?"

Antoinette was silent. After a moment, she rose, approached him, and reached up to stroke his cheek.

"My love, why must it always be the woman who should make sacrifices?"

She returned to her armchair and rang the bell. "Sophie, you may clear now," she said, when the maid arrived.

He muttered "Goodbye, Toinette," under his breath and strode out, past Sophie who stared at him, open-mouthed, as he flung open the door to the landing and hurried down the stone staircase.

He rode out to Mont-Martre the next day. It was a mild day for November, the sunshine casting a gentle warmth. He found Marie-Anne and her sister Thérèse in the kitchen garden by the farm-house, digging the last of the summer's planting into the soil, hair straggling from beneath their plain linen mobcaps and their faces begrimed. Charles withdrew to the broad rough bench beneath the grape arbor, out of earshot of the oblivious Thérèse, and gestured to Marie-Anne to join him.

"Marie-Anne, you and I have been happy in our times together, haven't we?"

"I've been happy. I hope I've made *you* happy."

"I must tell you something—"

She sighed, already looked resigned to desertion. "You won't be back. Now that you know about the baby."

"No—not at all. I must tell you something about myself. I ought to have told you this long ago, but . . . I was afraid to."

"Afraid?"

"I . . . I'm not what you think I am."

Her quick startled glance said, I don't understand, what about yourself would you want to hide; are you a bankrupt or a whore-monger or a Protestant then, because you can't be a queer, I know that much, surely.

"I'm not a nobleman." Let her down by degrees, that was the best way. First she ought to understand, as poor Jeanne had never learned until too late, that he was not the prince of a fairy-tale kingdom or of anywhere else.

"But you're gentry," she said after a moment. "A gentleman. Anybody could see that."

"Gentry, yes. I and all my family consider ourselves gentlefolk. But I'm not a lord, I'm an officer of the Paris Parlement."

Her mouth opened a little at that, at the thought of such a lofty assembly, the high and mighty magistrates of the high court, as far above her and her folk as archangels were above mortal men.

"My formal title, which I share with my father, is 'Executor of High Works,'" he continued as she gazed at him, somewhere between astonished and puzzled. "*Maître des Hautes Œuvres*. Do you know what that is?"

"A judge?"

"No. I . . . I serve the judges. The executor—or the master—of high works is the official who carries out the magistrates' sentences." He paused for a quick breath. She couldn't seem to put it together—

a shortcoming, no doubt, of a sheltered rural life. Damn it, he was going to have to spell it all out for her, every ugly word.

"He's the master executioner. The public hangman."

For an instant he saw a flicker of horror or panic in her eyes, though she did not shrink back from him.

"You're the—*you're* the *bourr*—"

"I much prefer to be called 'executioner.'"

"Oh?"

"I know how most folk regard us," he added, after a moment's frightful silence. "Do you want me to leave? If you can't bear the thought of being in my presence, say so, and you'll never see me again."

She shivered, as if a sharp breeze had crossed her, but quickly recovered. "You must be the son of the old *bou*—executioner, then—Old Sanson—aren't you?"

"Yes."

As if against her will, her glance strayed downward, then toward Charles. He followed her gaze: she was staring at his hands.

"There's no blood on them, Marie-Anne. I'm no ogre. We're not monsters. I—I don't take any pleasure in what I'm obliged to do."

She turned away from him and in the silence Thérèse's distant, tuneless humming, as she rhythmically spaded and turned over the pale earth of the kitchen garden, seemed unnaturally loud. He waited. Just as he began to think that Marie-Anne had chosen to treat him as if he did not exist, she spoke again.

"It's all right." She paused; then, with an effort, looked up at him.

"If you—if you'd told me all this before I got to know you, maybe it would have been different. I'd have believed all the horrid things they say about *bourr*—about people like you, and why nobody goes near them and why folk make the horns"—her hand swiftly, unconsciously formed the ancient two-pronged gesture against evil as she spoke—"when they pass their houses and all. But when you know someone for years, know he's a kind lover, share things with him—give yourself to him like I've done with you—then you can't just go and believe the worst about him in the wink of an eye. I know you're not a—a—what strangers would say you were."

They fell silent again. "You're still going to take religious vows, are you?" he asked her at last.

"Yes."

"But if a suitor were to ask for your hand before then, would you accept him?"

She shrugged. "Depends who he was, of course. Even with a baby coming, I'd much rather be a nun than just wed the first man who might ask me. And he'd have to be fair desperate, wouldn't he, to marry an old maid over thirty with no dowry and no reputation and a baby on the way."

"I'm not looking for a dowry." He plunged ahead before second thoughts, and her forthright words, could get the better of him. "Marry me."

"Beg your pardon?"

"I asked you to marry me."

Perhaps, despite his resistance to the idea in the past, he had nevertheless reached an age to be "fair desperate" for a companion and domesticity.

"*Marry* you?"

Clearly the idea that he might propose marriage had never crossed her mind. Be my wife, for God's sake, woman. Think of what I'm offering you.

"Why ask *me*?"

"You know why. Because I owe you that."

"But you're a gentleman, and I . . . I'm a peasant. Just a market farmer's daughter. Nobody could force you into it."

"Nobody's forcing me. It's my own choice." You deserve more, Marie-Anne Jugier, he said to himself, than an illegitimate child and a stone-cold cell in a convent. And we already know, don't we, that we're compatible enough between the sheets?

"You and I—we get on well together. Or, now that you know who I am, does the idea of marrying me, becoming part of the executioner's family, horrify you?"

"No, I meant—I mean—oh, dear," she stammered, and scrubbed furiously at her grimy hands with the bottom edge of her apron. "And me dirty like this . . . Oh, Charles, I'm too old. You don't want to wed me."

"Why not? I'm fond of you, and I know you care for me. Or don't you, now that you know the truth? Can you still think of me in the same way, or would my profession be an obstacle?"

She stared down at her lap as a stray breeze blew wisps of dark hair about her face. "No," after a moment's hard thought, "I suppose not. If I could still bed you, now I know who you are and all, then surely I could wed you. You're only doing your duty, as the—the executioner. Wicked folk'll always be about, and someone has to put the fear of God into them."

"Then—"

"But—but no matter how you earn your bread, you're still an educated gentleman, and you talk so genteel; and I'm—well, that doesn't matter up in the hayloft, but it would matter in Paris."

"My life at home's not so aristocratic as all that. You needn't fear that you might embarrass me at a duchess's reception." A self-conscious giggle escaped her and he forged on, encouraged. "Why not marry me? You can't believe I'd find you undesirable, not after everything between us. And I fancy myself a rather good lover."

She did not answer, but flashed him the broad grin he had come to know during the past three years.

"I'm well off, too; you would live in a big house in the city—well, at the edge of the city—with plenty of servants," he told her, mustering all the arguments he could. This was something he wanted, it seemed. "An entirely different life, Marie-Anne. A new gown as often as you like, a box at the theater if you wish it. No more farm work. No harder work than keeping house—than mending, or dusting, or tallying the household books and directing the servants. You would never want for anything."

"But I'm too old for you," she protested. "I'm six years older than you."

"What of it? My mother was seven years older than my father." Evidently the Sansons were making a habit of marrying women half a dozen years older than themselves.

"In ten years I'll be old—when you're still nearly a young man."

Peasants' perceptions of "old," Charles realized, evidently anything over forty, were less sanguine than those of the bourgeoisie, who could expect to live to sixty or seventy, if they were lucky.

Marie-Anne glanced down at her belly for an instant. "'Course we've already made a start at a family, haven't we; but for all that, I might not be able to give you more children. All the women say it's harder when you're above thirty and carrying your first."

"It makes no difference to me whether we have one child or twenty, or none at all. Do you think I want to breed half a dozen little executioners, like my father?"

He stopped, hearing the bitterness in his words, and with a rueful smile reached out to smooth her hair and tuck one errant lock behind her ear. "Marie-Anne, consider this. I've been overseeing executions since I was fifteen. I'm twenty-six and sometimes I feel sixty."

"Fifteen," she echoed him, brown eyes wide with indignation and pity.

"Be my wife, Marie-Anne," he urged her. "Be my wife, and a friend and companion, for I'll always need a friend. Marry me and let me give our child a name."

She leaned her head to one side, with a slight frown. "The sisters at Saint-Denis . . . I did promise . . ."

"I won't presume to say I know God's will, but by bringing you and me together, perhaps He decided you would serve Him better outside the convent. Think about this: A man who was a friend to my family, a man whom my father liked and respected, is right now a prisoner in the Bastille and accused of high treason. Someday I might have to execute him. By my own hand—cut off his head, with a sword. I'll need the comfort and strength a friend like you could give me."

She drew a long breath. "Let me think on it. I . . . Come back tomorrow and I'll have an answer for you."

He returned the next day, before suppertime, and found Jugier and his wife withindoors, warming themselves on a high-backed bench near the kitchen fire. Jugier greeted him jovially and offered him the usual cup of wine or eau-de-vie but he declined both the glass and the chair to which Jugier gestured him.

"Monsieur Jugier." He remained on his feet before the farmer, hat in hand. "I ought to have told you the truth about myself at our first meeting."

He braced himself and told them everything, save that he had been their daughter's lover. When the word "executioner" left his lips, Madame Jugier gasped and Jugier scowled and nearly dropped his pewter cup.

"The *bourreau*? A nice well-spoke young gentleman like you?"

"I confess it; though I'm not ashamed of it."

"Well, I never was one for slipping over to the pillory when I'm at the great market, or I'd have fingered you sooner, maybe. To think a fine fellow like you could be a hangman."

"If you don't find the idea of sharing a glass with the hangman agreeable, let me at least pay you for the wine you've—"

"No, no, let it be," Jugier told him, waving a dismissive hand. "Now if somebody'd asked me yesterday what I would do if I found myself sharing a drink with the *bourreau*, I suppose I'd have said, 'I'd throw the wine in the villain's face.' It's bad luck, people say. Nothing good comes of touching a cursed brute like that, or even going near him. But you're no brute, monsieur; anybody can see you're a proper gentleman, with lordly manners and all. Will you sit down and take a swallow of brandy with us now, then, to wash away differences?"

Jugier whistled and Marie-Anne soon appeared. Returning a moment later with the brandy bottle, she caught Charles's eye as she handed the bottle to her father. Charles rose, as if acknowledging a woman's presence, and followed her to the far end of the kitchen.

"Charles, I thought it over. I'll be your wife."

He pressed her hand as she glanced uneasily at Jugier. "Come, then." Drawing Marie-Anne to his side, he returned to the hearth.

"Monsieur, madame: I hope you'll receive the proposal I now offer you as kindly as you just received me in your home. I want to marry your daughter. As soon as possible."

Jugier goggled at them as if he could scarcely credit what he had heard. "Marry? You want to wed my Marie-Anne?"

"Marry?" his wife echoed him.

"But I told you, she has no dowry, and—and you're a gentleman . . ." He banged his empty cup down on the bench. "*You*? You're the *bourreau*! I won't have any girl of mine wedding a hangman!"

"Papa," Marie-Anne said, "Monsieur Charles is a respectable gentleman. You just said so yourself. You think well enough of him to—"

"There's a world of difference between drinking with a man like that, and allowing him to marry your daughter!" he roared. "I won't have a *bourreau* for a son-in-law!"

"Now cease your shouting, Jugier," his wife admonished him, rising and planting hands on broad hips. "Here's our Marie-Anne asked for at last, and by a rich gentleman, too. Don't you stand in her way."

Charles had prepared himself for Jugier's reaction and promptly put forth his own argument. "Your wife is right; my family is well off. As my wife, Marie-Anne will live more comfortably than she ever could on a market farm. And as your son-in-law, I'd be in a position to advance you some help, should you ever need it . . ."

"Don't you try to bribe me with your filthy money! I wouldn't touch it!"

"Wouldn't you?" said Madame Jugier.

"Of course you would, Papa." Marie-Anne deftly snatched away his brandy bottle and hugged it to her chest. "Don't let pride out of a bottle sour your common sense. Who else would take me, at my age, and with no dowry?"

"So you'll have the first man who asks you," he demanded, glaring at her, "even the *bourreau*?"

"No, I'll have him because I fancy him. Because I love him, Papa. Did you think monsieur's been visiting us all these years just to share our wine?"

Jugier took a step toward her, purpling, as his wife merely smiled, and Marie-Anne faced him with a defiant stare.

"He wasn't the first and you know it, so don't you go shouting that he ruined me. And he's a good man and he'll be a good husband to me. If it was otherwise, I'd be taking vows. And besides," she added, jerking her chin upward, "I'm a grown woman and you can't forbid the wedding."

"Can't I? We'll see about that! I won't have my name tied to the *bourreau!*"

"I fear she's right," Charles said gently. He had consulted one of the lesser jurists at the Palais de Justice about the matter that morning. "A certain legal procedure," he continued, quoting the lawyer and hoping he sounded as impressive as if he were wearing a judge's robe and full wig, "is available to those adults whose parents insist, out of selfishness—or mere prejudice—upon withholding permission for the said adults to enter into honorable marriages. It requires only the approval of the *lieutenant général* of the district, which I—as a high-ranking officer of the Parlement—shall find easy enough to obtain; and some witnesses to swear to my good character, as evidence that mademoiselle intends to make a most respectable and advantageous match."

Jugier stared. Charles found he was enjoying himself.

"I'm fully prepared to call in the prosecutor-general himself, if necessary, as a witness to my character. You see, monsieur, there's little point in your opposing us."

"You grit your teeth and bless the match," Madame Jugier told her husband, "for it'll happen with or without your consent. Oh, don't you worry, girl," she added to Marie-Anne, "he'll come round in the end, when one of the oxen dies or there's a bad harvest."

Jugier glared at them all for a moment before stomping out of the kitchen. "Wed the hangman, then, if you must," he growled over his shoulder, "but don't expect me to dance at your wedding!"

Marie-Anne looked up at Charles, with a smile suddenly bashful. "Well . . . what do we do now?"

III

Amende Honorable

1766

Il y a deux choses auxquelles il faut se faire,
sous peine de trouver la vie insupportable:
ce sont les injures du temps et les injustices des hommes.

(There are two things that one must grow used to,
or suffer the penalty of finding life unbearable:
the ravages of time and the injustices of men.)

—*Suite des Maximes Générales*

27

I found I had a lot of fair-weather friends in Abbeville, people who pretend not to know you when things turn black: maybe because I was still an outsider to them, a foreigner, someone who hadn't been born in the town. But I had one ally, Simon-Nicolas Linguet, a man of letters, now a lawyer, who'd once been Louis Douville's tutor (till he'd got on Duval de Soicourt's bad side, they say). Whatever you say about him, that he's irascible, opinionated, obstinate, and rude, you also have to say this: Once he believes in you, he'll never give up.

"Monsieur Douville de Maillefeu sent me," he said, when the guard had left us alone in my cell. "I know something of the law and he hoped I could advise you. Perhaps you know his son Louis is also in danger of being arrested in this foul affair, and has fled Abbeville?"

If even the former mayor is worried about his family getting tangled up in this, I thought, then Duval must be running the whole show, and maybe we're screwed—it'll be a public whipping for me, or something just as shameful that'll bring disgrace on my name, and Madame's, forever. And I'd always wanted to make Madame proud of me.

"They don't tell me anything."

"No, of course they wouldn't," Linguet echoed me. He jerked one of the two battered chairs away from the table and thumped it into place. "God! What kind of justice is this!"

I stared at him through the murk of the cell, startled, and he calmed a little and sat down opposite me.

"Monsieur de La Barre—Chevalier—have you the faintest idea how your trial is to be conducted?"

I shook my head. What did I know of the law?

"All I can do, as your advocate, is gather evidence in your behalf against these malicious charges. But the law doesn't allow an advocate to defend you before the high court. I'll do my best to present your case in a judicial memorandum to the king and pray for his intercession, of course, if need be, but before the criminal court of Abbeville you'll be naked, so to speak, with no recourse but whatever witnesses are ready to testify in your favor, and your own wits." He stopped, waiting for me to say something, but I just felt stupid and bewildered, as if I'd woken a minute ago from a drunken sleep.

"The entire process," he continued, "is weighted in favor of the prosecution, as if suspicion alone is enough to make a man guilty. It's not spelled out, but our precious legal system is based upon the idea that example is what keeps the populace in line—it doesn't really matter who is guilty or innocent of a crime, so long as someone pays for it and pays dearly, because the instructive sight and account of his punishment will deter others. And you cannot imagine how this principle has eased the way for Monsieur Duval de Soicourt's exercise in rancor."

He shuffled through a satchel full of notes, squinting in the dim light, and told me everything he'd learned about Duval. Faith, how blind and naïve I'd been, never to realize how I'd slipped into Duval's clutches with my heedless behavior over the past three years. But then how could I have imagined, at eighteen or nineteen years old, that my friends and I might become the scapegoats in a nasty provincial feud, and the victims of every injury and humiliation that Duval wasn't able to visit on our elders?

He finished with Duval and then, with a hard look at me, started reading off another list, a list of all the idiotic things I'd done since I'd arrived in Abbeville, all the stories of the stupid, childish, drunken scrapes I'd gotten into or pranks I'd pulled with Étallonde or Métigny or Pierre de Belleval or on my own, which he must have collected from everybody who knew us, and by the end of it I felt pretty ashamed of myself. He stopped finally, and I stared down at the table between us, wishing I could sink into the floor.

"Chevalier, you're a spoiled brat and a fool."

"Yes, monsieur," I said miserably, still not looking at him.

"Calling the Blessed Virgin and the virgin saints harlots, merely to provoke people with your crudity."

"It was just a joke, monsieur—in front of my friends—I didn't mean it—"

"Crossing yourself and genuflecting in front of a stack of pornographic books, as if they were the high altar."

I nodded. I couldn't deny it. It had been funny, at the time.

"Smuggling away the consecrated Host after Mass, and pissing on it?"

"Étallonde did that," I said. "Well, we all thought it was a big laugh . . . just a *joke*—"

He smacked his fist down on the pile of notes, rose out of his chair, and leaned into my face. "These are not *jokes*! Not to most people in this town! Not if someone like the criminal assessor decides to take them seriously!"

I stared at him. *How* seriously?

"I repeat," he went on, settling back in his chair, "you, young man, are a brat and a fool. But I doubt you're much more of a brat and a fool than any other brainless puppy of your age and station—and I'll be damned if that petty provincial bully is going to make a harsh example of anyone for no other crime than that of being a brat and a fool. And it's clear that the one witless prank you're *not* guilty of is the outrage to the shrine, for Madame Feydeau tells me that she, and others, can testify to your whereabouts all that night."

"Yes, monsieur," I managed to say. "I never did that. I swear to you. And I—we only did the—the other things without thinking. We never meant anything by them."

Linguet sighed. "When will you get it into your empty head that your intentions have nothing to do with it—that Duval de Soicourt doesn't care?"

He gave me what advice he could, how I should behave in front of the tribunal and what I should say, and left promising me that he'd keep on doing his best for me and the others. Madame visited me not long afterward. She'd spent most of the past month in Paris, calling in every debt of blood and honor she could. A famous Parisian lawyer, the deputy prosecutor himself, had taken a look at the dossier of my case and told her the high court of Abbeville didn't have enough real evidence against me to whip a cat.

"His exact words," she told me, hugging me. "This will soon be over and we'll have you out of here, my dear—never fear!"

I felt tears on my cheek, but I didn't know if they were hers or mine.

28

"And how did the wedding night pass?" Madeleine inquired, eyes gleaming, when at last Charles appeared in the kitchen to scavenge some breakfast from the cook.

He rubbed his eyes. "Very well. Yes. Very pleasurably." Though it had seemed almost odd to be making love to Marie-Anne on a mattress rather than in a nest of straw, with the warm musky scent of cattle drifting up from below and perhaps a barn cat staring at them from atop a bale of hay, with supercilious, yellow-eyed disinterest in human endeavors and eccentricities.

"You could try to be a little less enthusiastic, you know," she observed tartly. "What's wrong with her?"

"There's nothing wrong with Marie-Anne. What do you think of her?"

"She seems like . . . a pleasant soul. Uncomplicated. An interesting choice, Charlot."

"If you must know—" He snatched up the bowl of white coffee that the cook placed in front of him and retreated to the passage where they would not be overheard. "Our wedding night, while pleasurable enough, was not exactly a revelation. I married Marie-Anne because I felt I owed it to her."

"She was your mistress?"

"She—no. I had a mistress, a proper one. Marie-Anne—"

"Marie-Anne chanced to be a diversion?"

He could feel the sisterly look coming on, no doubt augmented by the moodiness of pregnancy; Madeleine was six or seven months along with her second child, he judged.

"Marie-Anne initiated it, years ago!" He would have said more, but at that moment the bell at the front door jangled. He glanced out from the rear passage to the foyer. No one was hurrying to answer the door; undoubtedly the servants were still clearing up from the lavish and boisterous wedding banquet of the day before.

He answered it himself, to find a youth of eighteen or twenty, in shabby but clean work clothes, hat in hand and gaze averted, waiting on the step.

"Monsieur?"

"Is this . . . is this the house of Sanson . . . the *bourreau?*"

"I'm Sanson, the *executioner*; or is it my father you wish to see?"

The boy blushed crimson. "Monsieur, they say the *b*—the executioner can do all sorts of wonders. They say—they say you can cure people . . ."

Charles looked him over. The violent blush, signifying embarrassment beyond even that of being seen at the executioner's doorstep, usually indicated that the visitor needed a remedy for an ailment he had picked up from a prostitute.

"Go around to the back of the house, and meet me at the shed with the green door. I'll attend to you shortly."

"Do you love her?" Madeleine said, coming up behind him and handing him his coffee bowl as the stranger sprinted for the path to the stableyard.

"I suppose I do, in a way. She means a great deal to me."

"Can you talk to her as frankly as you'd talk to me?"

"I hope so."

"About, say, Monsieur de Lally and—"

"Yes—I know."

"I hope so, too." She paused a moment. "I didn't expect you to go and find a bride outside the profession. Don't misunderstand, Charlot—I like her, I really do, and it's obvious she worships you. But I hope she'll continue to be more to you than the woman who runs your house and bears your children."

"As do I." He sighed and lowered his voice again. "You may as well know now: The first of our children will be along a little sooner than you'd expect."

"Oh," said Madeleine, unsurprised, with a glance downward at her own swelling belly. "Well, that explains a great deal. At least the cousins will be of an age to play together. When's she due?"

"June, she thinks."

"Well, I wish you happiness, of course, but I hope . . . when you come home, someday, after a particularly unpleasant episode, I hope she'll have the stomach to listen to you speak of it. And you know it's going to happen, sooner or later. Probably sooner."

"You sound like Grand'mère." He wanted to laugh it off, but he could not help thinking of Lally, still waiting in the Bastille to defend himself in self-righteous indignation and fury before a court not disposed to be merciful.

She went on tiptoe and kissed him on the cheek. "Grand'mère's a realist, brother. And so must you be."

29

Though they didn't have enough evidence against me to whip a cat, somehow Duval still went forward with it.

In the end it was just Moisnel and I who were in front of the high court of Abbeville on February twenty-seventh. The sieurs Bertrand Gaillard d'Étallonde, Louis Douville, and Pierre Saveuse de Belleval were included in our indictment, but of course none of them were there.

I went into the unheated antechamber, where we were to wait, with Madame's words echoing in my head, and thinking Duval's case against us would be pretty quickly laughed out of court. You could hear it all; the court was sitting right next door. Even after Hecquet had begun his indictment and demanded Moisnel's punishment—a formal reprimand, and probation, and a fine—I thought it wouldn't be so bad.

But nobody was in the mood to dismiss a case of sacrilege and blasphemy as just a few boyish pranks. Hecquet demanded death for Étallonde; after having his hand chopped off.

Death?

That sick grip of fear began to claw at my guts again, but I fought it down by telling myself that they were being so harsh because they couldn't get at Étallonde, and probably never would. It's easy to be harsh when the sentence is only symbolic.

Then I heard my own name. He didn't mention the shrine on the bridge; they knew I had witnesses to where I'd been that night, and they couldn't make that one stick. So instead it was that same old routine about lewd and sacrilegious acts, and singing blasphemous songs, and insulting the Sacrament by not taking off my hat, and offering respect and adoration to infamous and abominable books.

"For reparation of which the said Lefebvre de La Barre must be condemned to perform the *amende honorable* . . ."

Formal penance . . . penance wouldn't be too bad, I thought. Just a bit of ritual humiliation, sackcloth and ashes on the church steps to amuse the crowd: *Blah, blah, blah, I ask pardon of God, the king, and Justice. Amen. Back to work, people, haven't you anything better to do?*

". . . after which he must be beaten with switches—"

Public whipping—maybe no more than I deserved, really . . .

"—and branded with the mark of a felon, then to be chained and taken to the galleys to serve as a convict in perpetuity."

The galleys?

I remembered every horrible story I'd ever heard about the galleys, where they work you and freeze you and starve you until after a couple of years it kills you, and I wondered if I wouldn't be better off dead right away. Then I thought of what they'd demanded for Étallonde, and I couldn't think at all.

They beckoned me inside to the court chamber, beneath a couple of tall windows, where the sky outside was as gray as my mood, and the interrogations began and I was cold all over, cold and sick and shaky. But I was determined not to tremble in front of Duval and his lapdog. I tried my best to remember what Linguet had told me and somehow, somehow, my voice was calm as I answered their questions.

Are you, or are you not, a Christian? Do you deny that you have been heard to question the teachings of the Church?

"If I argued about some bigotry or other, it's because I don't like hypocrites."

Do you deny that you and your friends sang sacrilegious songs?

"D'Étallonde sometimes sang a few verses, but it didn't mean anything. It was only a game, a joke. As for me, maybe I did that once or twice, maybe; but I must have been drunk."

You have admitted that often, with Gaillard d'Étallonde, you discussed religion, in consequence of what you had read in certain diabolical and perverse books?

How could I deny it? All you can do is brazen it out.

"I read those arguments in the *Dictionnaire Philosophique*."

"I see they'll stop at nothing," Linguet said to me, as soon as the guard had shut the door behind him. "This filthy affair has become a matter of politics."

"You know what went on?" I said. I'd seen no friendly faces in the chamber: only judges, and clerks, and enemies. Even the president of the high court himself— Étallonde's father—had been kept out, since his own son was on trial without being there—*in absentia*, Linguet called it, I think. That's only fair; but not when Duval de Soicourt stacked the bench with his own asslickers instead.

"Monsieur Gaillard de Boëncourt found me a room where I could listen. You realize, don't you, Chevalier, that Duval and Hecquet have gone far beyond a matter of private rancor? They're implying now that you and your brainless friends are an active part of the great satanic conspiracy of freethinkers."

"Conspiracy!"

"They've placed you on a level with Voltaire, Diderot, d'Alembert, Helvétius, those who would overthrow the Church and the state through their villainous books—and anyone who dares to publish them or read them, or think for himself. It's a battle of ideas now, between the old and the new, and I fear you're little more than a foot soldier in it."

A foot soldier, I thought. Cannon fodder.

Their lives don't matter, except to themselves.

February twenty-eighth.

They came to my cell just after dawn, while I was still half asleep, and one guard hauled me out of bed while Marcotte, the clerk of the court, placed himself in the middle of the room, rattled his papers, and cleared his throat. The guard told me to stand up.

"Being guilty—"

Guilty.

This is it, I said to myself. Oh, God help me. I'm for the galleys. Hell on earth.

But maybe still Linguet or Madame could find someone to put in a good word for me to the king . . .

"—of the crimes of impiety and blasphemy, the high court condemns François Jean Lefebvre, Chevalier de La Barre, to make public penance before the church of Saint-Vulfran, to which he shall be conducted in a tumbril."

He paused to catch his breath and I tried to take a deep breath, too, but I couldn't. Penance, whipping, branding, the galleys. I felt as if they'd laid heavy weights on my chest.

"And at the said place, he is condemned to have his tongue torn out."

I stared at him, heart pounding like a drumroll. That had never been part of Hecquet's indictment! And they don't cut out criminals' tongues unless—

"This accomplished, he shall be conducted in the same tumbril to the principal square of the city, where he shall have his head severed from his body; and his dead body and head thrown into a bonfire, there to be reduced to ashes and scattered to the wind."

I must be dreaming, I told myself.

"The court orders further that, before the execution, the said Lefebvre de La Barre be put to the torture ordinary and extraordinary in order to have, from his own mouth, the truth of all facts related in these proceedings."

The clerk shuffled the papers, adjusted his spectacles, and gave me a queer little apologetic nod before turning away. I couldn't move.

Death.

Death.

Duval had actually done it, the foul, hateful, heartless bastard. He'd hated my cousin so much that he'd proposed torture and death for me, just to feed his spite, and his tame judges had gone along with it.

They must have gone out, but I didn't hear them. I didn't even hear the door swing open again, but suddenly, blessedly, Linguet grabbed my shoulders and pushed me onto a stool as I began to tremble.

"Chevalier."

Death.

First torture, then my tongue torn out—my head cut off—my body burned to ash, to nothing, never to rest in holy ground—and my soul would go wandering forever, or so all the priests said, even beyond the Day of Judgment, lost for all eternity—

"Chevalier!" he repeated. He thrust a pocket flask at me. "You have to collect yourself. It'll do no good if you collapse, understand?"

I clutched at the flask, though my hands were shaking so much I could barely hold on to it, and took a gulp. It was a decent brandy, not the cheap swill you buy out of a cask from the peddlers at street corners, and it warmed me right through.

"This is atrocious," he said. "An outrage. Not even in Rome, or in a backward, priest-ridden country like Spain, where the Inquisition rules, would boys like you and Moisnel be punished for your idiotic pranks with more than penance and a fortnight in jail."

"Moisnel?" I croaked.

"The same sentence. For a child of sixteen! And also for young Gaillard d'Étallonde, if they should ever find him—I think they included burning alive in his sentence, just to keep things amusing. My God! How we can call ourselves civilized—" He broke off and took hold of my arm.

"You mustn't let this paralyze you. This infamous sentence is the result of blatant prejudice—it stinks of Duval's influence—and it can't possibly be upheld by a disinterested court. The Parlement of Paris must confirm your sentences, and it can overrule this judgment if it chooses to. You and Moisnel—and Gaillard de Boëncourt, too, in his son's name—must appeal. You'll have to go to Paris for that, and it will buy you some time, allow word of this iniquitous affair to get around and inflame decent men's indignation." He smiled; it looked odd on his lean face. "Don't give up so soon, Chevalier. You do have friends."

He took off a little later, after telling me what had to be done next, and I just sat at the table, staring at the stone wall opposite me, where little streaks of damp trickled down and glistened in the half-light from the window.

My tongue torn out, my head cut off, my body burned.

I barely made it to the bucket in the corner in time. I huddled on the cold floor for a while, retching, before I dragged myself up onto the bed. Then I buried my face in the hard pillow and wept silently, swallowing the tears, the way you do when you're little, when you're afraid to let anyone hear you cry.

30

She had turned over her keys to Jeannette decades before, but Marthe had never truly relinquished her grip on the Sanson household. Jeannette, a gentle, soft-spoken woman whose thoughts were turned mostly to childbearing, usually deferred to her in matters of running the house, managing expenses, and supervising the servants. Marie-Anne, however, Charles found to his covert amusement, was not so compliant. Within a month of the wedding, she and Marthe had plunged into an incessant war that could be heard, during its frequent skirmishes, at the far end of the garden.

"Why should I do anything?" Jean-Baptiste said, smiling a little, when Charles mentioned his concerns. "My mother's ruled unopposed here long enough, and your Marie-Anne seems equal to facing her. Let them have it out."

Secretly Charles agreed with him, though a household echoing with female squabbles was scarcely to his taste. He soon grew to recognize the warning signs when, during their midday dinner, Marie-Anne—perhaps goaded by pregnancy and irritability—squared her shoulders and cast Marthe a challenging glare before bringing up the subject of some domestic task or other. Charles quickly adopted the habit, when not otherwise occupied, of long walks in the afternoons.

He returned from one of his walks, and a pause at a modest café to share a glass of wine and the latest gossip on a fine spring day with a grateful former patient whose boy's broken arm he had recently set, to find a letter awaiting him. Recognizing the handwriting—Pierre Hérisson's—he broke the seal, wondering what the news was from Melun. Madeleine's baby was due soon, he recalled; perhaps little Geneviève had a brother or sister by now.

My dear brother (it began),
*   It is with deep regret as the bearer of sad news that I write you this letter.*

Oh, dear God, he said to himself, heart pounding, and forced himself to read on.

It is my most painful duty to tell you that my beloved wife was brought to bed three days ago of a girlchild but, owing to circumstances beyond the midwife's and the physician's control, the birth was a difficult one; she was greatly weakened by loss of blood and at last succumbed. All that could be done to preserve her life was attempted, but it was God's will that both she and the child be taken from us.

*   It must be of consolation to us to know that the curé attended my wife in her last hours and that Madeleine was in a state of grace before she died, and was able to receive Extreme Unction in its fullest form. A Mass was said for her soul and many folk who knew her, within our profession and without it, joined her funeral procession, for she was well loved here for her kindness and charity.*

*   She asked me to convey this message to her family, that her final thoughts were of you all. She begged me to tell you in particular, dear brother in law, of her deep and abiding love for you and of her hopes always for your future happiness.*

*   Rest assured, dear brother, I remain*
*   your friend and obedient servant,*
*   P. Hérisson.*

Charles stood still for a long time, staring at the letter. His sister—impossible. Not Madeleine.

At last he trudged down the passage to Jean-Baptiste's study.

"It's from Hérisson." He placed the letter—his hand was shaking, he saw—on the desk in front of his father. "Madeleine—she . . ."

Jean-Baptiste turned to him, surprised. "Madeleine?"

"Gone—dead—and her child, also."

He tried to say more, but could form no words. With a jolt of panic he imagined losing Marie-Anne in childbirth. How was it that some women, like Jeannette, could birth baby after baby with no ill effects, as a matter of course, like a prize cow—fourteen of them, for heaven's sake—while a first or second pregnancy could so often be a death sentence for others, killing his sister at only twenty-six?

And Marie-Anne—Marie-Anne had never before borne a child.

"Please, God, no," he whispered at last, "no, no, no," before dropping into the armchair and hiding his face in his hands.

31

He hadn't lingered long in his favorite café that afternoon, when he'd gone out for a breath of fresh air and an hour's distraction from not only his duties but also his endless thoughts of Madeleine and his ever-present worries about Marie-Anne. "Though there's no need to worry, even if she is a little long in the tooth for her first," Marthe had assured him for the twentieth time: "I'm pleased to see you made the prudent decision in the end and found yourself a strong wife with good wide hips and plenty of common sense. Do stop fretting about her breeding, Charles, and save your prayers for your sister's soul."

"Can you blame me for worrying?" he'd said, and hurried out.

But the café, though usually a congenial retreat—they seemed not to know, or at least politely pretended not to know, who he was—that day was not to his taste; all the conversation at neighboring tables had been of the clamorous treason trial taking place at that moment in the Grand' Chambre of the Parlement. When someone had begun offering odds on the Comte de Lally's conviction, he had quickly paid his bill and departed.

He arrived at Rue d'Enfer to discover the household in an uproar: Marthe was shouting orders like a captain of artillery while the maidservants rushed about with towels and steaming basins of water. Even Marie-Anne's mother, who had never before visited

the household, was present, arguing with Jeannette. It took him
no more than a moment to recognize the same sort of uproar he
was familiar with from his stepmother's many birthings.

Marie-Anne's child was not due, he recalled, for another six
weeks or so. At last he cornered Jeannette in the passage outside
the bedroom. "Is it—Marie-Anne can't be having the baby?"

"It's too early." She avoided his gaze. "Something's gone wrong,
Charles. You must—well, I fear you'll have to prepare yourself."
She shook him off and hurried away.

"Prepare myself?" he echoed her, unable to keep from thinking
of Madeleine once again. If he were to lose Marie-Anne, too—

Jeannette was gone. He prowled unhappily through the house,
ignored by the breathless, chattering women, at last winding up in
the kitchen. His sister Josèphe—at fourteen, just a trifle too young
to assist with "women's business"—huddled beside him on a bench,
in between giving an occasional stir to the simmering stock on the
hearth, and regaled him with gossip and chamomile tea to keep his
spirits up.

Jeannette found him there three hours later, toward twilight.
He sprang up at the sight of her drawn face.

"Marie-Anne?"

"Marie-Anne's doing well enough—"

"Thank God—"

"She's strong. She'll be herself in no time, never fear."

"The child?"

She shook her head. She had lost six herself, at birth or within
months at the wet-nurse's; you were expected to grow used to the
inevitable death of a certain proportion of your children, he supposed, though he did not think Jeannette ever had.

All he could think, when Jeannette and Marthe finally let him
in to see Marie-Anne and Madame Jugier tactfully slipped out of
the bedroom, was that it seemed dreadfully, painfully like a stage
setting, a scene he remembered all too well from a bad play. He
had not forgotten, never would forget, the sight of the pale, pale
figure of Jeanne Bécu, looking small and lost in her big bed. Though
Jeanne, with her creamy-fair complexion, had looked far paler
than Marie-Anne did now, after losing so much blood.

He would *not* think of how pale Madeleine must have looked, lying in her coffin.

He sat beside the bed, next to Marie-Anne, and laid his hand on her arm. She stirred, her eyes fluttering open, and he saw the glint of tears in them.

"Charles . . . I'm so sorry . . ."

Trying not to think of the bloody sheets and the sad little bundle that Marthe had hurried past him through the house, he patted her hand. "It happens, Marie-Anne."

"It was too early," Marie-Anne whispered. "Too small . . . too small and weak to live." A tear spilled from the corner of her eye and slid down to the pillow. He reached over and brushed it away with a fingertip as she continued.

"It was a little girl, did they tell you?"

"No."

"Your daughter . . . but she came too early. I wanted to—I would have named her Madeleine. I'm sorry, I'm so sorry . . ."

The tears were flowing, now, and her broad, usually cheerful face was distorted with misery. He bent over her and kissed her forehead.

"There will be others."

"I failed you. I couldn't give you a child."

"There will be others," he repeated.

"But—but you only wed me because of this baby, and now . . . now there's no baby after all, no reason any more for you to feel like you had to do the right thing by me, and you're burdened with me, all for nothing."

"Burdened?"

"Better *I'd* died, than the little one—"

"Marie-Anne!" he exclaimed, appalled. "How could you say such a thing?"

"You didn't really want to wed me, I know." She began to sob, making thin, hopeless sounds like those of a wounded dog. "You never would have, but for her."

"Perhaps not," he admitted, "but it's done now, and I wouldn't have it any other way. Listen to me: Can you possibly think I would even consider turning you out of the house, sending you back to your father, because—because some sort of bargain between us had come to its close?"

"I don't know," she managed, between gulps.

"Then you must think very little of me."

Her eyes fluttered wide open again at that and she stared at him. "Oh, no!"

"Do you think that—that—men like me—don't keep their word?"

When our honor is all we have to cling to, he thought once again, in the face of the world's contempt?

"You know I love you, Charles—you know I do! But—but I know you don't think of me the same way I—"

"Marie-Anne, I made a vow, back in January at Saint-Pierre, in front of your family and mine, that I would love, honor, and cherish you. I care very much for you and I don't intend to go back on that promise." He kissed her hand and laid it on the coverlet. "Now rest, get your strength back."

He left her when she had fallen asleep, the trace of a drowsy smile on her lips. Martin met him in the passage, clutching a letter.

Oh, Lord, not now, not yet, this isn't the time, Charles said to himself at the sight of the official seal. What is it, then—a hanging or a breaking?

"It's from the Parlement, not the criminal court," Martin said, as if reading his mind. "The messenger just left. I think—I'm afraid—"

Everywhere he'd dropped in, hoping to hear the latest news at the cheap cafés north of Saint-Eustache, the gossip that afternoon had been of nothing but the trial at the Parlement.

"Monsieur de Lally."

"Sorry."

Wordlessly Charles took the letter and trudged downstairs to the study. It was, as he suspected, a curt warning about the order he had been dreading for months.

The Parlement of Paris . . . trial of Thomas Arthur, comte de Lally and baron de Tollendal . . . likely to be found guilty of high treason . . . decapitated . . . scaffold . . . the Place de Grève . . . eight days' time or less . . .

He dropped into a chair, heartsick and weary, and closed his eyes. Jean-Baptiste joined him ten minutes later, leaning heavily on the cane he still sometimes used when overtired.

"Martin told me." He glanced at the paper, with its great red wax seal, that Charles had dropped on the desk. "That's the order, isn't it. Lally's death warrant."

"No."

"No?"

"Merely a warning," Charles said. His voice sounded lifeless in his ears. "The trial's not over."

"Then—"

"But they're so certain he'll be judged guilty that they've sent us notice to prepare a scaffold before he's even been condemned."

"Christ have mercy," Jean-Baptiste murmured. "A bad day, all around," he added, after a moment's silence. "And so soon after losing Madeleine . . . How else will Providence try us, I wonder?"

"I think you should go back to Brie," Charles began, but Jean-Baptiste shot him a fierce glance.

"Certainly not."

"You'll do him—and yourself—no good by staying here."

God in heaven, Father, he thought, do you really want to be in Paris on the day when your son has to behead your oldest friend?

"You don't understand," Jean-Baptiste said. He settled on the nearest chair. "The day Monsieur de Lally and I met—"

"I know the story, Father. I've heard it more than once: Lally came to your house during your wedding banquet, to get out of the rain, and you've been friends ever since."

"You don't know all the story."

"There's more?"

He wondered fleetingly if his father harbored some dark secret.

"That same night . . . naturally I didn't care to mention it in front of the family, though it was harmless enough, I thought. You see . . . once I'd told Monsieur de Lally who I was, and he'd recovered from his surprise, he admitted he'd always been curious about the executioner's profession. He asked me if I kept my tools—'instruments' was the word he used—there, on my property, and when I said I did, he asked me if he and his friends might see them."

"And?" The story seemed innocuous enough, although the visitors' curiosity had been, perhaps, in slightly poor taste.

"I saw no harm in it," Jean-Baptiste continued, "and I took them all to the shed. Monsieur de Lally's friends were interested, for all that they didn't care much for the executioner's company, and asked me some trifling questions about the wheel and the *brodequins*. Then I showed them the sword of justice, as they requested. As soldiers, they found it more appealing than the rest—though the other two young gentlemen refused to touch it. But Monsieur de Lally lifted it, tried the balance, examined it, and then said to me, 'With a fine sword like this, Monsieur Sanson, I now believe that a man could, indeed, cut off a head in one blow.'"

Charles began to speak, supposing that the anecdote was finished, but Jean-Baptiste hushed him with a gesture.

"I'd been practicing diligently with the sword since I was eleven years old, and I was already quite expert; I imagine I wanted to show off. I was, after all, only sixteen.

"'Of course I could,' I said. 'I could take off a head in the wink of an eye.' And, thinking little of it, I added: 'In fact, if the fate of the Marquis de Cinq-Mars should ever someday hang over you, monsieur, and it becomes my unhappy duty to decapitate you, I pledge my word that, unlike *his* executioner, I won't need two attempts to have your head off!'

"Monsieur de Lally laughed at that and told me that he would hold me to my promise."

"That was . . . strangely prophetic of you," Charles said at last.

"You see, I have to do it myself. I promised him."

Jean-Baptiste, he realized, was deadly serious.

"Father."

"I promised him," Jean-Baptiste repeated. "I promised him a clean blow and a swift death. By my own hand."

"Father, it was decades ago. You were joking together—and probably drunk. He probably doesn't even remember—"

"He'd remember."

"He wouldn't seriously hold you to such a promise—"

"That doesn't matter."

"—he'd know your state of health—"

"I'm not *ill*, Charles. And I'm still the master—"

"I know you're well, now, and that you're able to do the offices." Charles stole a quick glance at his father. Jean-Baptiste had recovered enough that he could walk without difficulty and climb the steps to the scaffold and supervise operations, but greater effort often wearied him. "But you're not as strong as you once were, and this is a task you're not equal to. This one is mine."

God help me, he added privately.

"No, I have to show him I haven't forgotten."

"Father, you grow tired after climbing two flights of stairs—"

"It's my duty."

Oh God, not again, duty and honor, always our everlasting duty and honor.

"It's your duty to carry out your orders," he said, "and to carry them out properly. But you and I both know that you're scarcely able to lift that sword above your head, much less swing it." He reached out and held Jean-Baptiste's hand in his own, feeling it tremble. "You're going to have to let me be your deputy in this, as well."

They were silent a moment together. At last Jean-Baptiste sighed. "You're right. I shouldn't delude myself that I'm capable of such a task."

"Then you'll go back to Brie before—"

"No! Absolutely not. No more arguments. Remember, Charles, you're only my deputy; I still make the decisions." He paused for an instant and added, "I hope you're prepared for this?"

"You've seen me. I've been practicing for months now."

"You're sure of yourself?"

"Yes."

"You must do it cleanly. Monsieur de Lally above all—it mustn't go wrong."

"I can do it, Father," Charles assured him. Had he not been preparing for such a moment for half his life? After months of intensive practice he was confident of his skill with the sword; he could strike the mark most times, and rarely was more than half an inch off.

"I can do it. He won't suffer."

32

We had to go to Paris to have our sentences confirmed by the Parlement, and to make our appeal. The police inspector who escorted
us wasn't a bad sort. He let us talk during the journey. Or rather, I
did the listening, and Moisnel did most of the talking, when I
could understand him through his tears.

"I didn't know what I was saying," he kept insisting. "I was so
scared . . . Monsieur Duval threatened me, he told me they could
burn me alive for what we'd done!"

"What did we do?" I said. "We got tipsy and sang a couple of rude
songs in a tavern. We didn't do anything that half the people in
France—half the people in Christendom—haven't done once or twice
in their lives."

"He told me that singing those songs was blasphemy. He said I'd
have my tongue torn out and my hand cut off before they burned
me at the stake. And then I'd go straight to Hell forever. I'm afraid
of going to Hell . . ."

"You won't go to Hell," I told him. "Don't you remember anything? A priest'll absolve you and you'll go to Purgatory, like everyone else."

Privately I was beginning to think that maybe there was no Purgatory and no Hell after all, that it was all just a fairy tale invented
to keep ignorant people in line; or else that Hell was created by

people who liked holding power over other people, and it was right here on earth. But by then—a little late—I had enough sense not to say it out loud.

Moisnel wouldn't stop crying.

"Then he said if I told them everything we'd done when we were out together, he'd go easier on me. I didn't know what to do! I just said yes every time he ordered me to say yes. I don't even remember what he asked me. I was so scared, I just said yes."

We reached Paris, finally, and then we waited.

Something was going on, it seemed, some important affair that had been simmering for years, since the end of the war—high treason, the jailers said—and the Parlement didn't have time to spare for petty provincial matters and a couple of teenaged orphans. So we waited through March, and April, and into May, and waited some more.

They kept us in the Conciergerie, the prison right next to the law courts. The lodging Madame paid for wasn't too bad—though I'm told the Bastille is better, if you can afford your comforts—but the place was dark and the door frames were low, so you had to stoop when they took you out to the corridor or crack yourself on the head. The jailers, making conversation, told us our cells were where Damiens had been lodged nine years ago, and the bandit Cartouche back in 1721. I guess blasphemers like Moisnel and me were supposed to be just as important and dangerous.

33

"We merely carry out the law, Charles, the magistrates' judgments; the blood is not on our hands alone."

Jean-Baptiste, hoping to strengthen his own resolve as well as Charles's, had repeated that credo to him more often than once.

Charles had always tried to believe him, throughout those dozen years he had already spent as the king's executioner, serving justice and the law—or so he told himself—by punishing the riffraff of Paris for all the offenses, great and small, that the poor, the desperate, the bitter, the hopeless committed in their efforts to keep on living. But the Comte de Lally, decorated fifty-year veteran of France's once-invincible army, had done no more than lose one too many battles—lose a battle and surrender a city when faced with overwhelming odds, as many had done before him. How could the executioner be the avenger of crime's victim and of the innocent, if he was ordered to punish the innocent?

And how many, Charles thought with a sudden shiver that he quickly suppressed, how many of those faceless, wretched, already-forgotten dozens who had already passed before him to their deaths, here at this blood-soaked patch of land in front of the town hall, might have been innocent as well? Could every one of them have truly been a criminal?

Had every one of them merited death?

The sun was hot on his shoulders beneath the heavy scarlet coat. From the height of the scaffold, he watched the procession inch forward through the disorderly streets to the Place de Grève. Jean-Baptiste and the prison confessor, riding with Lally in the tumbril, were speaking to him, comforting him. The magistrates, it seemed, had resolved to heap shame upon their scapegoat for all the French losses of the costly and humiliating Seven Years' War: They had chosen to crush Lally further by sending him to execution not in his own carriage, the custom when an aristocrat rode to the scaffold, but in the executioner's common cart. They had also, Charles saw, ordered him bound and gagged for the journey—a cruel, unprecedented dishonor for a nobleman and a soldier. He could tell, even at a distance, from his father's set, stern face, that Jean-Baptiste was furious.

The cart approached and the enormous, boisterous crowd beyond the paling doubled its clamor, eager, on a warm, cloudless spring afternoon, for a good show—a particular treat, one they might see only once or twice in the course of a lifetime. Charles drew a quick breath. The cart and the magistrates' carriages trailing it creaked to a stop below him.

His first thought, upon catching his first clear glimpse of Lally as Jean-Baptiste helped him down from the cart's tailboard, was how old he looked. His hair, once iron-gray, was now white. Fewer than ten years had passed since Lally had last dined with them at Rue d'Enfer, but in those years the robust, seasoned soldier had become an old man, worn by hardship in foreign lands, defeat, and imprisonment.

"They told me he tried to stab himself yesterday in his cell," Jean-Baptiste muttered to him when he reached the platform, as Lally and Père Gomart paused at the foot of the scaffold. "A mere scratch—but it served as an excuse to bind him. This is disgraceful." He did not continue, but Charles knew what he was thinking: *Is his only friend to be his executioner?*

Jean-Baptiste stepped forward as the priest and the assistants helped Lally to the top of the steps.

"In this place, *I* am the master—not the judges." Swiftly he unbuckled the strap, drew the gag from Lally's mouth, and untied his hands. "Monsieur," as the old man silently rubbed at the angry red furrows on his wrists, "you've been scandalously ill-used. I know the Parlement refused to let you speak at the last, at the Palais de Justice. The people want to hear you. Speak now, if you like."

Lally gazed at him, then at the crowd, and shook his head, a short, convulsive jerk from side to side.

"Thank you, my friend. But I've spoken enough to men. I'm weary; now I want only to speak to God."

He knelt and prayed with Père Gomart. Charles bent his head and made the sign of the cross as he had done many times as a man or woman prepared to die. The priest droned on and he hurriedly crossed himself again as Lally rose.

"Monsieur Sanson, my friend . . . I expect you remember as clearly as I do how, many years ago, we jested together—"

"I never dreamed any such calamity could truly come to pass, monsieur; but I always meant to keep my promise," Jean-Baptiste said, drawing himself up as well as he could. "God willed it otherwise. We've grown old, you and I; I haven't the strength." His gaze, and Lally's, flicked to Charles.

"You know my son; he'll keep his father's promise."

Charles stepped forward. His heart was thudding.

Lally eyed him. "Young Charles. Of course. A man grown. You look much like your father did, you know, when we first met as young men."

The old man's voice was unsteady, Charles thought. Was Lally's heart racing as swiftly as his own?

He bowed, as deeply as he dared to one now labeled a traitor to his king. "Monsieur."

He could think only of Lally's kindness to him during his boyhood, and his gruff but encouraging words after the horrific execution of Damiens, when Charles had been eighteen years old and could see no defense for the actions he had been forced to take, or for his intolerable situation.

Why, if truth be told, your duties could be considered more moral than mine. You put only criminals to death, while a soldier has to kill honest men.

Only criminals?

He hoped Lally had forgotten those long-ago words, but suspected he had not. The old soldier was trembling, surely with anger rather than fear, despite his outward calm.

This is judicial murder, Charles said to himself, and I'm the tool of men who want him dead. A killer in the name of the king and the Parlement.

"Monsieur, forgive me, I pray you."

Lally reached out and grasped his arm. "There's nothing to forgive, young Charles." He hadn't been deceived—the old man was trembling. "You're doing your duty—like a good soldier," he added, meeting Charles's eyes and for a moment holding his gaze. "Just as I've always tried to do mine."

No, of course Lally had not forgotten that conversation of theirs. And now this was his duty—to play assassin to slake the spite of fools and lickspittles.

Lally doffed coat, waistcoat, and cravat and then paused, turning again to Jean-Baptiste. He offered his hand and, after a moment's hesitation, Jean-Baptiste clasped it.

"Now proceed."

"*Salve Regina, mater misericordiae . . .*"

As the watching crowd began to sing, Bastien opened Lally's shirt and pulled it below his shoulders, retied his hands behind him, and guided him to the center of the scaffold, where he sank to his knees, his back to Charles. Swiftly Charles stripped off coat and hat—nothing must hinder his movements—as Père Gomart crept forward with a final blessing, made the sign of the cross over the condemned man, and retreated. Knowing his cue, Charles approached with a handkerchief and bound it about Lally's eyes.

"Lift your chin a little, monsieur," he said softly, adjusting the old man's head with a touch, "and keep still, I pray you."

He stepped back, surveying him. All was as it should be. He gestured to Jérôme, who reached for the sword, still hidden beneath the layer of straw.

"*O dulcis Virgo Maria . . . Amen.*"

God grant me true aim . . .

The sword, though it was lighter than the wooden sword with which Charles practiced almost daily, seemed much heavier than it ever had in the stableyard. A thread of sweat coursed its way down his forehead to his cheek. He fixed his whole being on the old man's neck, where a black satin ribbon gathered up his long white hair into a club.

A loud, harsh voice—Lally's own:

"Strike, boy!"

Charles half turned away from the kneeling man, raised the sword above his head and right shoulder, whirled it once.

It descended, faster, faster, but too late he saw the ribbon fluttering in the sudden breeze, obscuring his aim, and at the same time Lally trembled with the sharp, sudden intake of a breath, and desperately he tried to jerk the blade up and away from him, but the momentum was too great and it plunged on, as if possessed.

The crowd gave a great simultaneous gasp as Lally fell heavily on his side. A scarlet stain blossomed in the straw below him.

He was grievously wounded, not dead, and Charles knew at once that he had failed.

Lally fought to right himself, to drag himself to his knees once more as the blood streamed—spurted—from the gaping wounds in his head and cheek. He did not utter a sound. The crowd booed and Charles stood frozen, staring at the fine red flecks that bespattered his hands and his cuffs, battling a violent rush of nausea. If, thank Providence, he had not refused dinner that day, he would have been sick where he stood.

Brute—butcher—

He was barely aware of the sword dangling point-down from his trembling hands until Jérôme snatched it from him. He thrust it at one of the other men and pulled Lally down by his hair into the straw.

"Do it!" he barked. "Quick!"

The man heaved the sword up and chopped down twice as if it were an axe, with the dull thud of a butcher's cleaver. The crowd surged toward the scaffold, shouting, throwing stones and filth.

The clumsy, ill-aimed blows were not enough; Lally was still alive.

Someone pushed in front of Charles and thrust Jérôme aside. With a sudden burst of strength, Jean-Baptiste seized the sword, heaved it high, and brought it flashing down, severing Lally's head with one swift, precise blow.

He dropped the sword and turned to Charles, hands shaking and lips white.

"I *promised* him," he said, before swaying heavily into Charles's arms.

Jean-Baptiste had given orders that the corpse of his old friend was not to be claimed in the usual way by the executioners and was to receive a proper Christian burial. As soon as Jérôme drove the cart away, transporting Lally's remains to the nearby cemetery of Saint-Jean-en-Grève, Charles and Martin took Jean-Baptiste home. Charles left his brother to help him inside and escaped to the well in the back garden, where he tore off his stained waistcoat and shirt and spent a quarter hour scrubbing at his hands and arms and face, long after the sticky flecks of blood had disappeared.

Marie-Anne, clutching a clean shirt, found him later on the bench by the tackroom, staring at the ground.

"Are you poorly? What can I do?"

"You shouldn't be on your feet," he said, with a glance at her. For above a week she had been recovering her strength in the customary lying-in after the birthing, the stillbirth no one spoke of; it was only the second time he had seen her out of bed.

"I'm right enough."

He pulled on the shirt, with a muttered word of thanks. "See to my father, then. He's had a bad shock—he shouldn't be left alone."

"Your father'll be better in the morning. Your mamma's with him. He's dreadful upset and he's overtired himself, is all." She paused and he heard her draw a deep breath. "What happened? The servants won't tell me."

"It went wrong." He could not suppress a quick shudder. "Monsieur de Lally. The execution. I bungled it. He, of all people. It went wrong, and it was entirely my fault."

Marie-Anne said nothing, but she sat on the bench beside him and covered his hand with hers. He jerked it away and she stared at him, bewildered.

"There was blood on it. *His* blood."

Brute, butcher, *bourreau* . . . truly a man not fit to be near decent folk.

"How could it have been your fault?" she said at last. "I—I know how you've been practicing with that sword of yours."

"It was my fault." He refrained from describing the execution; he doubted she had the stomach for it.

The minutes stretched on as he continued to stare at the hoof-prints and wheel tracks in the packed earth. At last she reached for his hand again and clasped it in both of hers. "I don't know what else to say."

He did not reply. He had found he shied from talking with her as he could have with Antoinette or Madeleine, about anything and everything, even the most gruesome scenes he might witness, his deepest fears and nightmares.

They listened to the distant bell of Saint-Laurent strike eight.

"Will you be wanting supper?"

"No."

She murmured something about being sure the rest of the household was fed and tiptoed away.

He had never missed Antoinette's presence, or Madeleine's, so sorely as he did at that moment. Once he could have unburdened himself to either of them as if she were a priest in the confessional, and she would have listened, unflinching, at last saying what he needed to hear. But Madeleine was gone forever and he had turned his back on Antoinette, and instead he had, to comfort him, a wife whose honest simplicity he did not wish to tarnish by talk of violent, bloody death.

He sprang up, hurried inside, seized his dark green everyday waistcoat and coat, and fled the house.

A dozen frightful notions tormented him as he strode southward through the spring twilight toward the Louvre. If only Antoinette had written to him—he had heard nothing from her. She might have fallen ill, died of a fever or an infection or the smallpox months before, and he would have known nothing—though surely Providence could not, it could not possibly be so cruel as to take Antoinette, too, as it had taken Madeleine—

"Monsieur?" said the maid who answered the bell, when at last he reached Antoinette's apartment, trembling with weariness from more than the mile and a half he had swiftly covered. It was not Sophie but a woman he did not recognize.

"Is—does Mademoiselle Vitry still live here?" he asked her, fearing the worst. If Antoinette had died—

"Yes, monsieur."

"Thank God—" he began, weak with relief, and collected himself. "Is mademoiselle at home?"

"No, monsieur, she's away at Sèvres today. Who should I tell her has called, monsieur?"

He looked blankly at her for a moment. "Nobody. Say nothing. Nobody at all."

Three nights later, when at last he fell asleep without taking a furtive dose of laudanum to blot out memory, he relived the horror again, saw Lally kneeling before him, saw the sword descending as he struggled to control it, saw him fall, covered in blood. And then the corpse before him, pale and cold, was not Lally's but Antoinette's, her eyes staring straight into his—no, not Antoinette after all, it was Madeleine, of course—and he had killed her.

"No," he shouted, but could manage no more than a hoarse whisper. "No. I didn't. Not you."

It's your fault, his sister's dead lips seemed to say. Your fault; you botched it, and you killed me.

Before his eyes, the great pool of blood spread about her head like a halo from the gash in her neck.

Your fault.

"No," he screamed again, "Madeleine, no," but he had no voice. Then she said his name, repeating it until it thundered in his ears.

"Charles . . . Charles . . . Charles . . ."

He awoke with a shudder. It was dark as the inside of a tomb, for there was no moon, but he felt movement beside him and the touch of a hand as Marie-Anne leaned over him.

"Charles! Wake up. It's only a nightmare."

He gasped with relief and reached for her. She bent and kissed his forehead and he pulled her down to him. He had not made love to her for weeks, since her late pregnancy and labor, but at that instant he felt no desire for her, found he simply ached for the solace that the sheer warmth of her body could bring him. She cradled his head against her shoulder for a while, softly rocking him.

"Maybe a cup of warm milk would do you good. I could go down and stoke the kitchen fire. Wouldn't take a moment."

"Don't leave me."

"It's what my mamma always used to give us when we couldn't sleep. It does help. Maybe with a splash of eau-de-vie in it—"

"I don't want anything. Just—stay with me."

"It would calm you, love," she began. "Lie quiet for a moment—"

"My God!" He struggled upright. "Do you imagine warm milk and brandy are all I need right now?"

He could scarcely see her in the dark, but imagined her gazing at him, eyes wide with hurt like those of an unjustly scolded child. She had her own sorrows and horrors to contend with, a dead infant and, with it, the lurking terror of finding oneself no better than superfluous; and at that moment he did not care.

"What I *need*," he said, shaking with misery and fury, "is someone who can comprehend what happened, and how I failed everyone, how I failed my father, and my family, and especially how horribly I failed a man who'd been good to me once. Utter, disastrous failure—"

"Charles . . ."

He jerked away from her, wanting to scream and rage at her at the top of his voice: God in heaven! Through sheer evil chance, I'm made to do one thing only in this world, and I failed miserably at it. And she can't understand that. No one, except another like me, can understand it. Madeleine understood—and You, Lord, You took her from us—from *me*—

"Marie-Anne, can you possibly imagine what it's like to take a helpless man's life? To stand over him, with a sword in your hands, and cut his head off?"

"Sweet—"

He cut her short, indifferent to her dismay, voice harsh. "Let me tell you what it's like, to take the life of a man who's been unjustly accused and sentenced, a defenseless old man who was courageous and honorable, a man who'd been kind to me.

"*They* killed him, because he made mistakes, and lost a battle, and gave up some heathen city on the other side of the world. But I was the one who had to do their dirty work for them. And I failed—I couldn't even do it properly. Four blows to cut his head off."

He felt her twist away. He seized her arms in a hard grip and held her in front of him. "Listen to me! Four blows—five—the first, it hit him in the face, it laid open his cheek, cut his ear . . . because I was clumsy. I promised my father Lally wouldn't suffer, but he suffered abominably, because I was clumsy. Then they tried to chop at his neck, over and over, as if he were a goose on a butcher's block. And at last my father had to finish it. Did they tell you that was why we brought him home in the state he was in? Because he did it himself. He had to take the sword and cut off his friend's head, because I failed, like the utter, damned coward I am, to do it properly!"

"Stop it!" Marie-Anne cried. "For the love of God, stop it!"

"You knew whom you were marrying." At that moment he hated her, hated her rustic naïveté, hated her for not being Antoinette, hated her for surviving the ordeal that had killed Madeleine. "You knew what I am, and what I have to do. I told you every ugly truth about myself and my family's profession. I kept nothing from you."

"But, Charles, you're a good man in spite of that, and I want to be a good wife to you. And—and I want to comfort you when you need it."

"*Comfort* me! The least you could do is bear to listen to me at a time like this, the way my sister would have, and it seems you can't even do that!"

She raised her voice above his.

"Yes! I want to comfort you by—by—by giving you a home you can go to, that'll let you forget all those awful things. A home and family like everybody else's. But I don't want to hear about it, what you do. I can't. It's too horrible. I thought I could, for you, I wanted to, because I'd do anything for you—but I just *can't*." She wrenched herself from his grip and huddled against the wall, drawing the coverlet about her.

He touched her shoulder, instantly contrite. "I'm sorry, Marie-Anne—I'm so sorry. None of this was your fault. Please forgive me."

"I did want to do what's right by you." She gulped back tears.

"I wonder if I did you a great wrong by asking you to marry me," he said, after a moment's silence. "Perhaps you would have been happier at the convent. Perhaps I ought to have married a girl from a family like my own, who understood what our lives were like."

"I *want* to be your wife. Don't mistake me. I love you, I do, truly, I always have, no matter who you were, and I want us to be happy together. But—please—don't talk to me about—*that*. Let our home be like a church, what they call a sanc—sanctus—"

"A sanctuary?"

"Yes—a sanctuary, where bad things don't come—a place where your work never comes, not ever. A place you can retreat to."

He pressed fingertips against aching eyes. "If it will make you happy."

"And when we have more children . . . oh, I do want to give you children! Children are what make a home. A proper family. You'll see."

He settled himself beside her, without replying. Though he was as fond of children as anyone else, he could not help thinking that any child of his would be born cursed. He shivered, despite the warmth of the spring night, and Marie-Anne pressed herself against him, clutching him to her, until at last he drifted away again to an exhausted, uneasy sleep.

The next afternoon he rode to Rue Saint-Thomas-du-Louvre and again rang the bell at Antoinette's door.

Antoinette rose as he entered and gazed at him, her hands clasped in the folds of her wide, flounced skirt. "Chevalier." She gestured at the nearest chair. "Won't you sit down? Take some coffee?"

"I won't stay. I only wanted to assure myself that you were well."

"I'm in excellent health. And you? How is your wife?"

"Marie-Anne and I are both well," he began, hearing a hint of mockery in her tone. He had never told her that Marie-Anne was pregnant and he clamped his lips down before he said ". . . but she lost the baby."

"We're well," he repeated. "Thank you for asking."

"I understand you had a little trouble the other day." Antoinette turned away and retrieved the demitasse that she had set down when he entered. "It must have been distressing for you."

"Where did you hear that?"

"It's in all the newspapers." She sipped her coffee, eyeing him above the rim of the tiny cup. "The execution of the Comte de Lally didn't go off well, it seems. They're saying the *bourreau* didn't know his job."

"It was . . . an unfortunate accident. It won't happen again."

"And did you find solace in the bosom of your family—or, should I say, at the bosom of your wife?"

"I prefer not to trouble her with such matters."

"Very wise."

"I can let myself out. I'll bid you good day now. I only wanted to assure myself . . ." He stopped, realizing he was repeating himself. "Good day, Toinette."

He was nearly through the door when she spoke again.

"Charles."

He paused, without looking back at her. "Mademoiselle?"

Her voice altered, softened. "If you—if you should someday need a friend, you know you'll always find me here."

34

I'd learned pretty fast, during my stay in the Château des Comtes at Abbeville, that jailers come in two kinds: the friendly ones, who are rough but decent enough, and maybe feel sorry for you, and treat you with little kindnesses when they can; and the nasty ones. The nasty ones are the sort of people who enjoy watching other people squirm. They reminded me a lot of Duval de Soicourt.

The jailers at the Conciergerie weren't any different. The decent ones brought me some hot water and soap to shave with once in a while, and gossiped a bit about what was happening outside in Paris and at the courts, and were honest and didn't pocket the money Madame had sent me to order in a few good meals for myself. The nasty ones, meanwhile, amused themselves by dropping sinister hints and talking about the torture sessions and executions they'd seen, usually when they knew I could overhear them.

"We had a real show at the Place de Grève the other day, Chevalier," Daubin said to me one day as he brought in my dinner on the caterer's tray. He was one of the nasty ones and I wouldn't have been surprised if someone had told me he'd secretly pissed in my wine, just for laughs. "Did you hear about the Comte de Lally?"

All I knew about Lally was that he'd lately been a prisoner somewhere in the Conciergerie, too, because he'd handed over India to the

British and lost the war for us, or some such, and he was probably the reason the Parlement was taking so long to hear my appeal; but he'd been in the Bastille for a few years before that, long before all the mess at Abbeville ever started. "What about him?" I said.

"Oh, the Parlement condemned him to death, all right. Come to think of it," he added, "now that's over, maybe the magistrates'll have time to tend to your case. But I wouldn't be too eager about it. Lally's head had a hard time parting company with his body."

I couldn't help a quick glance at him and he smirked. "Young Charlot, the *bourreau*—he botched it. Inexperienced, y'know. Four or five chops it took, to take the old man's head off!" He set down the tray and sauntered off to the door, with a look back at me. "How good are the *bourreaux* in your part of the world?"

I must have shivered, though it was a warm spring day, and he gave me a hateful grin as he left. "Better hope you win your appeal, Chevalier."

The Grand' Chambre of the Parlement was like an oven on the fourth of June. The magistrates must have been sweating like horses beneath their robes and their wigs. I'm sure I stank; ever since we'd arrived in Paris I'd been at the mercy of the laundress sister of one of the jailers, who lugged in my linen as often as it pleased her and no more. For myself, I'd been washing as best I could in a can of hot water that arrived two or three times a week and didn't hold much more than a shaving basin.

The clerk of the court asked me the same old questions I'd heard and answered a dozen times in Abbeville. What can you say when you're all alone, in a big, high-ceilinged chamber full of old men glaring at you, old men with hostile faces, thin-lipped old men who don't even care that more than one of your ancestors and your relatives had sat as judges in that same chamber, even in the president's chair? All you can do is deny as much as you dare, and speak the truth when you can't avoid it. I was scared and shaky, as you might expect, and fumbled and stammered, and I don't think I made a very good impression on them.

They asked Moisnel some questions, and it was all over in twenty-five minutes.

So much for the king's justice.

When they took me back to the Montgomery Tower after a couple of hours, the jailer pulled out his keys, said "Sorry, monsieur, orders," slapped a leg iron around my ankle, and chained me to the wall. That was when it hit me that I wasn't just "the prisoner" any longer but a convicted felon, and that the Parlement must have rejected the appeal.

"Fifteen," said Linguet, when he'd finally succeeded in getting permission to see me. He'd followed us to Paris, still nipping like a terrier, on our behalf, at the magistrates' heels. "Fifteen of the twenty-five counselors voted to uphold your sentence."

I tried to look up at him, but it was like swimming through deep water; I couldn't seem to get my limbs to move. The leg iron clanked with every step I took and I hated the sound of it. "What—what about Moisnel?"

"Some final spark of humanity must have persuaded them it's wrong to execute children. They overruled the Abbeville judges and sentenced him only to penance."

I was glad for poor Moisnel, but I had other things on my mind.

"So I'm finished."

"Not yet; there's still the king. You reckon without public opinion, Chevalier. I still have a voice and a pen, and the king can overrule the Parlement if he wishes."

"Voltaire," I said, grasping at straws. "He spoke up for that man they broke in Toulouse. He made them admit he'd been innocent. Couldn't he—"

Linguet actually smiled, though it was sour enough. "Voltaire? Author of the banned book that was the final nail in your coffin? Better Lucifer himself should defend you."

Of course; I never take the time to think things through. What good would it do to have Voltaire sticking up for me, when the truth was, it was really he who was on trial?

"Besides," Linguet continued, "Calas, the man in Toulouse, was accorded a posthumous pardon, and that wouldn't help you much."

I rubbed my eyes. By then I didn't feel so much terrified as just exhausted. "What about my cousin—Madame Feydeau? Or Monsieur d'Ormesson?"

"D'Ormesson," he echoed me, with a shake of his head. "He's promised to appeal to the king, but . . . you see, Chevalier, circumstance has worked against you here in Paris. Maupeou, who's the president of the Parlement now, has a grudge against him—"

Oh, *him*, the one in the high seat; no wonder he'd looked so pleased, smirking like a wicked old ape beneath his wig, not even trying to hide it, when they were reading off the charges.

"—and your sentence suits him well. I wouldn't be surprised if he advises the king to reject d'Ormesson's petition for clemency, out of sheer malice. And then the political climate . . . Since the king issued an edict of eviction against the Jesuits, Beaumont—the archbishop—has been raising a holy stink about it, and the Parlement is attempting to placate the Church by rejecting your appeal. And most of the counselors are simply rigid, complacent old men afraid of change, determined to silence the least whisper of dissent. You're serving as an excellent scapegoat for all concerned."

He sighed and pulled off his own wig to scratch his head before going on. "Even Voltaire, I fear, would prefer to have you a dead martyr to the new philosophy than a living prisoner. The unjust, heartrending death of an innocent youth would rouse more indignation among the public, you see. And raising a racket for the sake of posthumous vindication is easier, and safer, than taking the side of a condemned criminal."

I listened and felt all my hope draining away, like water sinking into a dry field. Linguet went on explaining it, but I just don't understand all the legal wrangling, all the vicious maneuvering, all the politics behind the scenes. I shouldn't have to understand it. I'm twenty years old.

I'm twenty years old and—it's time to admit the fact—I don't think I'm ever going to be twenty-one.

35

Jean-Baptiste recovered from the shock of the Comte de Lally's execution after a week's rest, though Charles sensed his dour mood, and silently returned with Jeannette and the two youngest boys to Brie-Comte-Robert. Charles returned to practicing fanatically with the wooden sword at the rear of the stableyard.

Pierre Hérisson, unexpectedly arriving from Melun in mid June, shook him out of his gloom.

"I've never been so glad to see you," Charles confessed to him, once the first flurry of his brother-in-law's arrival was over and Hérisson had lingered until the two of them were alone in the garden. "It was a lucky chance that brought you here just now—"

"Chance?" Hérisson shook his head. "It wasn't chance. It was something very odd—I didn't want to say anything about it in front of the others. Is your wife—is your wife quite well, after all the sad trials the Lord has sent us lately?"

Charles stared. "Marie-Anne? She's as well as can be expected."

"No hysterical fits, no odd behavior? I understand a stillbirth can affect women strangely, some worse than others."

"Certainly not. Why?"

"Because she wrote to my—to Madeleine. Only a fortnight ago. She wrote to Madeleine, saying that you were in a bad way and needed her. I was worried—came as soon I was able."

"She wrote to *Madeleine*?"

Hérisson retrieved a letter from a pocket and handed it to him.

Dear Sister (it read),

    I doubt that you have heard all the news yet from Paris, but a most painful event has distressed Charles terribly. Your company and the comfort you can give him would do him a great deal of good. Come to Paris posthaste, if you can, I pray you.

                        Marie Sanson, this 16 May 1766.

"That's not Marie-Anne's handwriting," Charles said instantly.

"Is it not? I did think the style was rather formal; and yet it's signed 'Marie Sanson'."

The proper form for a married woman, of course, was to sign herself *Marie Jugier, wife of Sanson*. It was, Charles supposed, the sort of thing Marie-Anne might have written, not knowing any better, having learned to write at a village school without being tutored in the finer points of correspondence, except that—

"Whose writing is it, then?" Hérisson continued.

"It . . . it must be from a friend who wants to remain anonymous."

A friend who could not have known of Madeleine's death, and to whom he had never happened to mention Marie-Anne's surname. Charles refolded the letter, almost smiling. The handwriting was Antoinette's.

Hérisson watched silently as Charles lifted the wooden sword high above his head once again, balanced it above his right shoulder, and slashed it down in a blur of motion to the post. It struck the whitewashed strip and bounced away.

"Good—that's good. Right on the mark."

Charles mopped at his hot face with a grimy linen towel and glowered at the post. "I can do it nine times out of ten. At worst, half an inch high or low."

"I know. I've been watching you do this every day for a fortnight, and Madeleine told me you've been practicing for the past twelve years. I know you can do it. *You* know you can do it."

"Then why did it go wrong?"

"These things happen, Sanson."

"It shouldn't have happened! Especially—not to him. Not to Monsieur de Lally." He flung the towel onto the bench, beside Hérisson, and took up the wooden sword again, scowling at it.

"Sanson, even a hanging can go wrong. It's happened to us all. Hasn't it happened to you?"

He grimaced. "Once—last year."

"But it didn't affect you as much as this did, I think. Or Madeleine would have known about it."

"No . . . it was horrible—but—we could look at it afterward, step by step, try to understand what went wrong." He glanced at Hérisson and his brother-in-law gestured him to continue. "I suppose that's it. My chief aide and I decided that—that it came about because—maybe the nooses weren't set right; maybe the ladder didn't fall quickly enough from under her; maybe her neck was too sturdy and she was simply too strong . . . maybe all of those factors played a part."

"It was beyond your control, what happened."

"Perhaps."

Hérisson draped the towel over the top of the post, where it hung quivering in the gentle breeze. "Look at that. It's distracting, isn't it? You said yourself that the patient's—that Lally's hair ribbon got in the way of your aim. And that he moved just a little at just the wrong instant. And you were upset, worrying about your wife's health and grieving for your child—still grieving for Madeleine, even—how could you not be? Beyond your control."

"Yes."

"Then why do you punish yourself for something that was sheer ill luck?"

"Because it was all on me!"

"I see." Hérisson paused a moment, thinking. "Yes, I can see that. But if you can share the blame with your brother and your aide and the men, then it's not so bad; is that it?"

"You don't know what it's like," Charles said. "You've never used the sword, have you?"

"No, I admit it."

Six weeks had passed since the ninth of May, but the nightmare memory had not yet faded.

"I—it was as if I was naked up there, isolated. For a hanging—you know how it goes. Martin and Jérôme and the men and I—we know our jobs: I supervise, make sure everything's as it ought to be; Jérôme or Auguste sets them up and gets them ready; Jérôme kicks away the ladder and yanks the rope; Martin and Bastien know exactly when and how to swing off the crossbeam and finish them off. We're like a—a machine, well oiled, all the moving parts perfectly calibrated, every part working as it should."

"And once in a while," Hérisson said, "even the machine breaks down—and then we all take equal responsibility for what happened."

"But when it's just you, all alone up there . . . you're no longer part of the machine. Can you understand it? The responsibility—the blame—is all yours. The blood's on *your* hands—your hands that botched it."

Charles raised the wooden sword again. It struck the post an inch outside the white strip and rebounded.

"*Merde alors!*"

He flung the sword aside and threw himself down next to Hérisson. "All you can do is try your damnedest to make certain it never happens again. But I'm not sure that's enough."

"It's not you who passes sentence," Hérisson began, but Charles cut him off.

"Oh, no, no, not that. I've heard that excuse far too often—"

They fell silent as Charles's younger sister Josèphe hurried toward them, lifting her skirts out of the litter of the stableyard. "Someone came with a letter, Charlot, for you." She handed it to him and backed away a step, looking expectant.

"Thanks," Hérisson said, eyeing the thick packet. "Thank you, Josèphe," he repeated, more pointedly, when Josèphe did not move. Though Charles's sister had known for two years now of the family profession, a letter delivered by messenger rather than an ordinary missive from the district post office had not yet come to mean to her what it usually meant to Charles or to his brother-in-law.

"Who's it from?"

"Private business," Charles said. Josèphe, at last grasping his point, sniffed and flounced away. "Well, *really*!"

He turned the packet over in his hands, staring at the seal. "It's from the Parlement. Not the criminal court."

"The Parlement? Have they heard any important cases there since—"

"Not that I know of." Puzzled, he cracked the sealing wax. "'This twenty-fifth June 1766 . . . The Parlement of Paris' . . . and so on, and so on, 'commands the executor of high works to take the tools of his profession and as many assistants as he deems necessary and repair at once to Abbeville'—"

"Abbeville?"

Charles frowned. It was not uncommon for an executioner to be dispatched to another town to carry out a sentence when the incumbent was ill or, perhaps, unskilled in a particular form of punishment. But it was a curious irony that he should be sent to the city in which Sanson the First had been born over a hundred years before to carry out his duties.

"'The Court declares François Jean Lefebvre, Chevalier de La Barre, duly convicted of the crimes of impiety and blasphemy,'" he continued, "'and therefore condemns the said Lefebvre de La Barre to penance before the principal church of Abbeville' . . . all the usual performance . . . 'and then to have his tongue'—oh, God."

"What?" Hérisson said, peering over his shoulder. "What is it?" He took the order as Charles's hands dropped to his lap.

"—'and then to have his tongue torn out by the roots'—saints above!—'after which he shall be decapitated—and his head and body burned—'"

Decapitated, Charles said to himself. Sweet God in heaven.

So the Parlement thought they'd send *me*? Someone thought the bungler should try again?

A bitter laugh escaped him. "Perhaps they've really got it in for this La Barre, whoever he may be—perhaps it's their underhanded way of making the sentence a little harsher, sending *me* to finish him off . . . They know what happened in May."

"Listen to me, brother," Hérisson said. He seized Charles's arm, fingers digging into his flesh. "Do you remember what Madeleine once said to you, years ago? That not everything's all about you?"

Charles stared at him, astounded, and Hérisson nodded. "Yes, she told me about that conversation. You know she was always concerned about your welfare."

Charles drew a long breath, clearing his head. "Sorry."—That was childish, wasn't it?—"But—God help me . . ."

"This isn't about you, Sanson," Hérisson repeated. "This is about this man La Barre. It doesn't matter, in the end, who the patient is or what he's done. But it does matter, always, that we carry out our orders like professionals, because we *are* professionals, and we owe it to them—and to ourselves. Do you understand?

"You can't get out of it," he continued when Charles said nothing, "none of us can—but you *can* perform your duty with the skill you know you have—make it quick and clean and painless for him—and take a certain kind of pride—yes, pride!" he added when Charles muttered a curse under his breath, "in a task—however upsetting it is for you—in a duty carried out and a task well done."

He released him and sat back as Charles stared at the ground.

"If only you knew," Charles said at last, "how weary I am of that word, *duty* . . ."

When he said nothing more, Hérisson took him by the elbow again and turned him about.

"Underneath everything, you know that what happened to the Comte de Lally was an appalling piece of bad luck, and that you can do the job. You *know* it, Sanson. You know you can do it, and you *will* do it."

I must . . .

It's what I was destined for, isn't it?

Duty and honor, Charles, duty and honor.

"You wouldn't care to come along to Abbeville, would you, to back me up?"

Hérisson shook his head. "I wish I could. But I've been away from home too long as it is. Never quite sure my brother's managing properly in my absence. Now," he added, sounding uncannily like Marthe, "you'd better find your chief aide and start making plans."

36

Some people did their best for me. Even the Bishop of Amiens, who'd got people so worked up by celebrating that penitential Mass at the shrine in Abbeville, even the bishop saw that the whole mess was really about politics, not religion, and tried to put in a good word for me, though maybe a little too late. Along with the bishop, my cousin Monsieur d'Ormesson was trying to reach the king's ear, Linguet told me during his second visit to the Conciergerie, but as he'd foreseen, something—or somebody—blocked d'Ormesson at every turn.

"President Maupeou's counter-argument to the king is simple," Linguet said. "If Damiens was executed for the crime of human *lèse-majesté*—high treason—then you, Chevalier, are even more guilty than Damiens, being convicted of divine *lèse-majesté*. The king is a good Catholic. He—the *king*—kneels and uncovers, just like any other man, like the lowest beggar in the street, before religious processions. Why, he asks, should he pardon someone who insults God; who committed a crime even more abominable than that of Damiens?"

"Singing some raunchy songs and not taking my hat off?" I said. At that point, the horrible absurdity of it all had become almost funny. "And owning a couple of illegal books? That's supposed to be worse than trying to murder the king?"

Linguet didn't answer. He sat without speaking for a moment, chin on clenched fists. Finally he jerked to his feet and paced across the cell.

"Chevalier—I don't know how to tell you this."

I could guess what he was leading up to: For some reason—which I probably wouldn't understand—now, at last, I was well and truly screwed. But somehow I couldn't feel much. I was so tired, so weary of it all. I just looked up at him and gestured him to continue.

"Since your case is now officially resolved and done with, the Parlement wants to gag me." He sighed and clawed at his wig, without looking at me. "It's forbidden me to write or publish any petition in your favor. And Monsieur d'Ormesson refuses to support me against the Parlement, for fear of scandal that might damage his own reputation; I'm not well liked there. I suppose he still wants to believe he has a chance of getting a royal pardon for you through his own efforts."

I digested that. An excellent scapegoat indeed, I thought, remembering what he had told me the last time we'd met. They'd stop at nothing, all of them, to have me dead: to keep a grip on their power, to feed a grudge, to slap down everyone who dared to put a toe out of line, to tell those troublesome philosophers "Shut up or you'll be next." To force away the new world of new ideas rushing too fast toward them, to strangle the future in its cradle.

"You tried your best," I said. My eyes stung and I looked away.

He squeezed my shoulder and left me, assuring me he'd never stop fighting for me and for the others, no matter what, no matter who tried to get in his way.

I didn't see him again, for we left Paris that night. Every day I'd spent in the Conciergerie after the Parlement confirmed my sentence had been a gift, but I could guess that going back to Abbeville meant it was all over.

Inspector Muron had Moisnel and me in separate coaches this time, so we couldn't comfort each other as we jounced through the night over those terrible back roads—our route was kept secret, avoiding the highroads, probably for fear someone would try to rescue me. I guess Muron didn't mean to be cruel; he was only following his orders.

In Abbeville, back in the château, they put me not far from Mois-nel. Though they'd chained us, at least we could exchange a few words. He was still scared to death.

It's only public penance, I kept telling him. A couple of hours, a bit of abasement, and it's over.

I wanted to shout at him, yell, "Look, what have you got to cry about? It's not you who's going to be tortured, who's going to have his tongue cut out, who's going to be beheaded in the marketplace." But I didn't. It wouldn't have made me feel any better.

37

As soon as the postchaise was under way, jolting and swaying through lush fields and forests beneath a blazing summer sun, Jérôme leaned forward, elbows on knees.

"M'sieur Charles."

"What's on your mind?"

Jérôme had been glum and silent for some days, ever since Charles had told the men of the unexpected summons to Abbeville, the sentence, and what they would need to transport, first of all the sword of justice and the spare in their well-padded crate. Cart horses, a tumbril, ropes; the boards, straps, wedges, and mallet that made up the *brodequins*—all "the tools of his profession."

"I don't like this," Jérôme said.

"Neither do I." Bloody nightmare visions of Lally's execution still wavered before him.

"No, monsieur, I know. But I wanted to speak to you of one thing in particular. This cutting out of the tongue, that's to be my job, I suppose?"

"Yes." Jérôme was well past fifty now, experienced in all the varied barbarities the law demanded of them; Charles knew he could depend on Jérôme, as he always did, to carry out such a distasteful task. His own duty was to behead the patient, nothing more.

"Well, it's a crime. A crime they ordered it, I mean. That's for incorrigibles," Jérôme insisted, "for habitual criminals and outlaws, for the sort of swine with a record long as your arm, with a brand already on him, who rapes a nun in a church and then pisses on the altar."

"Well?"

"Have you heard about this affair, m'sieur? What it's all about?"

"Very little. Something about blasphemy, isn't it?"

A case of blasphemy or sacrilege was commonly punished by the public humiliation of penance—the *amende honorable*—and packing the culprit off to jail for a few weeks of bread and water and prayer in which to repent his wickedness. What sort of monstrous sinner was this La Barre, Charles wondered, and what had he done to warrant this particularly brutal sentence?

"Some of the guards were talking about it the last time we were at the Conciergerie—the fellow was appealing his sentence before the Parlement, but he lost. It's a local matter that went bad, it seems. A case of private spite among the gentry, gone public at the prosecutor's hands. Did you know that, m'sieur?"

Charles glanced at him, suddenly uneasy. "No."

"What I hear, the fellow didn't do anything to deserve this. A few pranks, some ill-chosen words, barrack-room songs, owning the wrong books, nonsense that we've all been guilty of at one time or another when we were younger—he's young, they say—"

Perhaps *you* played some pranks when you were in your teens, Jérôme, and sang some crude songs that your father would have whipped you for knowing, Charles thought, with a brief, guilty memory of the smutty books he had once hidden beneath his linen. Not all of us had such freedom when we were fifteen.

"—but tearing his tongue out and cutting his head off for a bit of drunken foolishness! It's an outrageous thing to ask of an honest man."

"Are you saying you won't follow your orders?"

Jérôme scowled. "I'll do it if I must; I've done it before. Filthy job. But you ought to know I protest against it."

"I shouldn't worry about it if I were you. This La Barre has noble blood, he's titled *chevalier*; no doubt the court will mitigate the sentence at the last minute." *Or the king may even pardon him,* Charles added silently; *only the chevalier himself would be more relieved than I'd be at such royal clemency.*

"The crowds don't like that, m'sieur. They want the show, and the bloodier the better. If the magistrates do reduce the sentence, it'll be in secret. That's to say, well, maybe your father's told you that it's not hard to sham something like that; they keep the crowd well back, you know. A lamb's tongue and a sponge and a bladder of blood a couple of days old from the butcher's is all you need."

"It sounds as if you've done that before, too."

Charles had once overseen the public breaking of a corpse, a man whose sentence had been commuted and who had been swiftly and secretly hanged, an hour before, in the dungeons of the Châtelet. The crowds at the Grève had cheered as loudly as ever while his men smashed the lifeless body.

"Did it a few times, in your father's day. Keeps the crowd happy— like when we break a man who's actually been strangled after the second blow," Jérôme added, echoing Charles's thought. "But what I wanted to say was, if they don't look like reducing his sentence, I wish you'd speak up about it if you were able. In the name of mercy. Tell them we're honest men, *maître*, and we have our pride, and nothing good can come of a sentence as cruel as this."

Charles nodded. "I'll speak of it to the prosecutor, if I can. And once we've found our lodgings," he added, "why don't you keep watch for a likely butcher shop."

38

When they sent Père Bosquier in to visit with me on the last day of June, he wouldn't speak of it, but I knew, we both knew, it would be soon.

I'm glad he's the one they chose to be my confessor. I'd talked with him a few times before, at Belleval's and at dinner with Madame; he's a gentleman and a scholar, they say, and he's a decent human being, not one of these fanatics.

"My son," he asked at one point, "are you a true Christian?"

Well, I'd like to think I am, if you strip away all the fraud and the hypocritical charlatans and the silly trappings of the Church. I'd like to believe in a God who loves everyone, even heretics and unbelievers and pagans, because some of the books I've read—illegal ones, of course—say that's what a true Christian should do, instead of trying his best to slaughter them. It's the Church that is no longer truly Christian.

I didn't say that, though. I didn't want to offend him, when he was trying to be kind, but I wasn't about to beg for forgiveness. That's what they want, of course, the kings and priests: It's not enough to kill you, they also want you to knuckle under and admit that they're right, and that God gives them the right to rule you, and that you're the shit under their feet because you dared to do or say something that questioned their supremacy.

I just smiled and told him I'd be glad of his company. I don't want to die alone, surrounded by enemies.

"Do you know where madame the abbess is?" I asked him, finally. "She hasn't been to see me."

"I believe she's still in Paris, with your brother."

He didn't elaborate on that, but I understood; Madame was still doing her best to save me, going with Jacques from door to door of anyone who might be able to bring the least bit of pressure on the king or the courts. They'd only been able to visit me once in the Conciergerie. I closed my eyes for a moment as I realized I'd probably never get to say goodbye to them.

"Father, will you tell them both that I love them, and thank Madame for everything she's done for me? And—and tell her, also, I'm sorry I was so much trouble, so childish." I clenched my fists and drew a deep breath. Maybe a good death can begin to make up for an ill-spent life.

"But I'm not a child, and I'm going to behave like a man now. She won't be ashamed of me, I promise. Tell her that."

"I believe you," he said, turning back to me as Tirmont, the turnkey, opened the door for him. "You are a true gentleman, Chevalier."

Tirmont wasn't a bad sort. He'd done what he could for me, some small kindnesses: dry firewood, an extra blanket during the winter, a scrap of news now and then, a few rags to wrap around the leg iron that chained me to the wall, to keep it from bruising me. After Père Bosquier had gone, he paused in the doorway and scowled at the floor.

"Have they told you, Chevalier? When it's to be?"

"It's soon, isn't it?"

He kept on staring at the floor and I realized that "soon" was going to be much sooner than I'd thought.

"Tomorrow?"

"Yes, monsieur." He wouldn't look up. Suddenly he burst out: "It's a disgrace. It's that prick Duval's doing, all of us here knows it." He glanced at me, sideways, like a dog that's been kicked by its

master. "Monsieur, I hear they're sending a *bourreau* from Paris—
the master executioner himself—to—to take care of it. He'll know
his job."

I suppose he imagined that news like that would comfort me a
little. But I'd spent the last three months in Paris myself and I'd
already heard in the Conciergerie from that smirking bastard Daubin,
in gory detail, just how the beheading of the Comte de Lally hadn't
gone smoothly at all.

And now that same *bourreau* was going to improve his aim with
me?

I'll admit, I was terrified, though I was more frightened of pain—
of the torture they'd planned for me and of a sadly bungled execution—than of death itself. The priests say a lot about dying, about
Purgatory and Hell; but I don't think I believe them any more.

Maybe death is just peace, sweet sleep after the hell that living
can become. I think I'd welcome that.

Tearing my tongue out—oh God, Supreme Being, whoever you
are, if you're there at all, and if you give a damn about me, give me
courage. Don't let me shame my family. Let me stand the pain for
a while, just a little while, and let them be quick with the rest of it.

I can stand it, if it goes quickly.

I'm a gentleman, of the noble house of La Barre, and I'll bear
it, because I must. I can bear the pain, and then—then I'll die like a
gentleman, without flinching, and then I can sleep.

God, how tired I am. I'd like to go to sleep, without nightmares.

I can bear it, for the sake of my name. I can bear it.

See, I'm not afraid after all. Though I never had much of a chance
to live, at least I'll show the bastards I know how to die.

39

"The execution is set for tomorrow at midday," Duval de Soicourt said. "This is a thorough scoundrel you have to punish, monsieur. You should be proud to avenge Our Lord, who was so grievously outraged by this ruffian."

Charles eyed him. The criminal assessor of Abbeville was a tall, lanky man with a low forehead and hooked nose, not made handsomer by his unbecoming enthusiasm about the imminent execution.

"Monsieur," he ventured when Duval was done, "about this decree of the tribunal ordering the condemned man's tongue to be torn out . . ."

"What of it?"

There was great symbolic value in such a sentence, of course; the wicked tongue that uttered blasphemies must be ripped away before the final sentence was carried out.

"Surely, monsieur, considering the patient's birth, and the relatively trivial nature of the crime—"

"Trivial? Do you consider sacrilege to be a trivial crime?"

"Surely it's a matter of degree," Charles said, startled. "If the culprit has no previous criminal record . . . I'd expected the court would relent at the last moment, and secretly annul the order—even commute the sentence to a term of imprisonment. My assistants would be prepared to—"

"You thought wrong. Perhaps they do things differently in Paris,

Monsieur Sanson; but this is Abbeville. That foul-mouthed whelp will get only what he deserves."

Jérôme was right; some bitter personal animosity lay beneath the criminal assessor's officious air. Charles rapidly concluded his business at the town hall and asked the way to the nearest church to hear Mass. Taking the Sacrament after an hour's prayer for the condemned man's soul had always helped, in the past, to ease his mind.

Returning afterward to the modest house that had been placed at his disposal, he found a turnkey from the Château des Comtes, the city fortress, awaiting him with a message. The chevalier wished to meet the *bourreau* from Paris, the note said. The concierge of the prison hoped monsieur might, unless he thought it inappropriate, comply with the chevalier's request.

Charles debated the matter. In Paris, some of those condemned to be hanged or broken, despite their bluster, had collapsed in hysterics or in a faint at their first sight of the executioner—for his father and he, it seemed, were as well known to the criminal classes as any leading light of the theater or the opera. He wanted no trembling wretch cowering before him at the supreme moment, weeping in terror and spoiling his aim. Yes, it would be useful to know, beforehand, how the chevalier would carry himself on the scaffold. God help them both, if La Barre proved to be as agitated as Lally!

"Did you know, monsieur," the turnkey added, trotting along beside him on the way to the château, "that when the chevalier's request reached Monsieur Duval de Soicourt, Duval tossed it aside and said, 'Tell La Barre that tomorrow he'll see far too much of this *bourreau.*'" He spat on the ground. "But one of the magistrates persuaded him it would do no harm. Everybody here in Abbeville— at least us at the court and the château, who know Duval—everybody knows that Duval's behind all of this mess."

Some local resentment had tainted the criminal case, it was plain. And it was equally plain, Charles thought, that he had been called from Paris to consummate another judicial murder.

The prisoner was lodged in a small, damp, dark cell and chained to the wall. He was standing as near as his fetter allowed to the narrow window, gazing out at the soft muted blue of the evening twilight, when Charles entered.

His eyes adjusted to the bad light. Merciful God, he thought, what sort of cruel joke is this.

Jérôme had mentioned that the condemned man was young, but Charles realized that, knowing no better, he had unconsciously pictured to himself a hardened, vice-ridden, cynical libertine of thirty. No one had told him that La Barre was considerably younger than his own twenty-seven years, no more than a boy, with the soft, beardless face of a child—but a tired, tormented child, a child who had seen and suffered too much.

La Barre turned and fixed him with a long, appraising gaze, the calm gaze of one much older, or grown old in the space of a few months.

"I beg your pardon for disturbing you, monsieur. They told me you only arrived from Paris today."

"Yes, monsieur."

What did you say to someone whose head you were shortly going to take off?

"I won't keep you; I expect you want to rest after the journey."

And I'd like you to be well refreshed and your hand steady tomorrow, Charles suspected the boy was thinking.

In twelve years of presiding at the scaffold, he had seen many attempts at feigning bravado in the face of death, but true tranquility was rare. The hollows beneath the boy's eyes were smudged purple as an old bruise; his sleep, of late, could not have been peaceful. Yet only his pallor betrayed any emotion he felt on the night before he was to die.

"You're—are you the man who beheaded the Comte de Lally in Paris?"

His cravat seemed over-tight. "Yes, monsieur."

"I was in prison there—in the Conciergerie—when it happened. I heard all about it from the jailers. They told me it went wrong— that it must have been horribly painful."

"It . . . was unfortunate, monsieur."

"I'm less afraid—" La Barre continued, with a small, self-conscious shrug of his shoulders, "—I'm less afraid of dying than of being hurt. If I have to lose my head for not taking off my hat, I hope at least I'll die quickly . . . without too much pain . . ."

Charles kept his own composure, but with an effort. "Ultimately I was to blame for the accident at Monsieur de Lally's execution."

"Yes?"

"But his agitation, at the injustice of his sentence, may have contributed to it. He was never a temperate man—he was courageous that day, but not calm . . . always in motion. In his anger, he moved at the last instant."

Fool, he said to himself as soon as he had spoken; fool. The boy before him, he suspected, had more cause even than had Lally to complain of injustice.

"Decapitation is a gentleman's sentence," he continued when La Barre said nothing, "because it's necessary that the patient should—"

"Patient?" the boy broke in, with a flicker of an ironic smile.

"It's the customary term."

"I see."

"The patient—or the client, then,"—never say *victim*, it upsets them, Jean-Baptiste had told him years ago—"the client's courage is as necessary to a successful execution as the headsman's aim." He paused, dismayed, no, sickened, that he should be obliged to explain such matters to a boy, a child.

"I believe everything will go smoothly. Stay calm and courageous and it'll be quick, monsieur. You'll feel nothing, I promise you."

La Barre gazed at him, impassive, gray eyes veiled. At last he nodded, with another brief flash of a smile. "I'll do my part—and you'll be satisfied with me. I won't flinch."

As the boy looked away, Charles made a decision.

"Monsieur de La Barre, I give you my word of honor that you won't suffer at my hands; nor at those of my assistants."

He turned, with a slight puzzled frown. "Monsieur?"

"They've told you of the other part of the sentence, which is to be carried out after you've done your penance?"

"I'm to have my—my tongue cut out. But I can bear it," he swiftly added. "It won't be much longer after that—will it?"

"I promise you," Charles repeated, "word of honor, once the initial questioning here in the prison—which the magistrates always conduct themselves, at close quarters—once the questioning is over, you won't suffer."

He did not dare be more explicit; anyone, including the criminal assessor's spies, might have been listening to their conversation, ready to report and disrupt any generous gesture that might spoil Duval's triumph.

"Tomorrow my chief assistant and my brother Martin will ride with you," he added, moving closer to the boy, voice low. "They know what I expect of them. After you've spoken the *amende honorable*, at the steps of the church, you must do exactly as they tell you. *Exactly*. Do you understand?"

A spark of relief and gratitude lit the boy's eyes as he drew a quick breath. "Yes, I understand."

As Charles called for the jailer, La Barre glanced back at him.

"Monsieur—thank you."

He could think of nothing to say that would not shatter the young man's careful composure, and his own, and so bowed and left him.

40

So this is it, then. Tuesday, the first of July, the last day of my life.

Probably the longest day of my life.

The last day of your life, the moment of your death, is something you simply can't conceive. You can't truly believe it, even when you know they're here for you to begin the whole rigmarole by shaking you awake at five in the morning.

How did it ever come to end like this?

Because I didn't take my hat off in the rain?

Never mind. It was only a pretext. Just as that copy of Voltaire's book was only a pretext. I'm to be sacrificed to the priests because people question them, but mostly because that bastard Duval held a grudge.

Bastards.

"You have to be put to the 'question,'" Lieutenant Merlin says to me, as I finish dressing. (I won't bother with a coat or cravat today; it seems like a waste of time.) And when I say I'd rather be tortured on a good night's sleep and a full stomach, he nods, apologetically, and tells me that the prisoner has to have fasted beforehand. Custom, you know. Good for the soul.

A brace of guards is lurking behind us, just in case I decide to give them trouble and put up a fight, to march me off to a certain room well away from the regular cells. Far away, where nobody can hear the screams.

The room is high-ceilinged and whitewashed, with a couple of oil lamps and windows looking out over the town, not some damp, rat-infested, torchlit dungeon as I'd expected from the horror stories that you read about in English novels. Duval de Soicourt is waiting there, decked out in his official robe and wig, and half a dozen people I don't know. The chief clerk, Marcotte, who I recognize right off after all the jolly hours we've spent together during other interrogations, sits at a little table, his pen ready, waiting to write down every word I say—and maybe every scream.

Outside, it's raining and a steady drip, drip, drip falls onto the windowsill from above.

Yes, I can guess what that is in the corner, that bench affair you're glancing at with such anticipation, Duval, while Marcotte reads off the decree that allows you to torture me and murder me. I've heard about people like you. The nastier dirty books, Étallonde told me once, are all about perverts who like to use whips and chains and such when they're screwing their whores.

Going to step into the shadows and reach inside your robe and diddle yourself while they break my legs? Or is it more fun to stare into my face and savor every instant of sweet agony?

Duval takes his seat on a raised platform, the better to watch, I suppose. "Interrogations before the torture," he says, and Marcotte starts scribbling.

"Culprit: speak the truth or risk damnation. Did you profane the Host and speak vilely of our holy Church?"

What does it matter what I say? Because whatever I did, it was as a stupid schoolboy with an infantile sense of humor. If they truly think Étallonde and Pierre de Belleval and I made all those coarse jokes for any other purpose than amusing ourselves, or getting a rise out of people, if they think we were trying to start a revolution and overturn the Church, then they're just mad.

"Did you profane the Host?"

"No, monsieur." Not with any true intention to insult God. No.

"Did you ever say to anyone, 'I'll shove a crucifix in your face and up your—'?"

I stare right back at him. "I might have once said such a thing; but I don't remember."

"Did you teach the sieur Moisnel the irreligious song beginning with these words: 'The day Saint Cyr was born, there was a great holiday in Paradise,' *et cetera*?"

"I sang it. But I never taught it to Moisnel."

Questions. Stupid questions, I've heard them all before, and they know the answers I'll give them. Questions, one after another.

"Did you profane the Host?" he finally asks again.

"No. I did not."

We exchange stares, eyes locked. Maybe Duval was hoping I'd already be so scared of what's to come that I'd crack up like Moisnel, knuckle under, start crying, say anything he wants to hear?

Like hell I will.

He gestures to the far end of the room. "Apply the torture."

Two men come out of the shadows and one takes hold of my arms from behind.

"Your pardon, monsieur," says the *bourreau*, as if he'd stepped on my toe, as they hustle me across the room and shove me onto the bench, flat on my back. The older one drags my arms above my head, ties my wrists together and buckles them down, and leans his weight on my shoulders. The other, the younger one, straps me down across the thighs, pulls off my shoes and stockings, then straps the oaken planks around my legs, tight. It only takes a moment. "The boot," they call it, the *brodequin*—it's a simple enough invention.

"Proceed."

Duval's voice, of course—

With a whack of his mallet, the *bourreau* jams in the first wooden wedge between the planks and my flesh. *Christ*—but it's not as bad as I'd expected. I can stand it.

"One," says Duval, nearby, and oh yes, I can see it in his eyes, I can tell the bastard is enjoying this. I could spit in his face as he's leaning over me, with his sour breath and his Adam's apple bobbing in his stringy throat, but he's not worth it. I'm not going to lower myself by behaving like a guttersnipe for *him*.

"Did you teach Moisnel an indecent song known as 'Mary Magdalene'?"

"No. I never taught him that song."

More questions. The bourreau drives the wedge in a little farther, and it hurts just the way it's supposed to, but I've got only one answer: "No." I'm not going to name names or give an inch.

"Again."

The *bourreau* forces in another wedge, a bigger one. That one's just as bad as I'd expected, close to the bone. *Merde alors!*

The man above me tightens his grip on my shoulders as I twitch and jerk like a hooked carp. I'm breathing hard but it'll take more than this to make me cry.

"Two," Duval says. "Did you teach Moisnel the song?"

"No."

Questions. Questions.

The *bourreau* drives the wedge in deeper and it hurts like hell; but I'll grit my teeth and keep on saying "No."

Questions. More questions.

"Again."

Again, and this time the pain is God-awful, with one tap of the mallet the third wedge is bruising my shinbones until it feels as if my legs'll snap any minute. I think I'm going to scream.

"Three."

I *won't* scream. Don't give him the pleasure.

"Did you, at the cemetery of Saint-Catherine," he says suddenly, with a gleam in his eye, "move your bowels and leave the ordure at the foot of a crucifix?"

I'd like to face the bastard and make him repeat his filthy questions to me when I'm not being held down by a man twice my weight. I can't help jerking upward and the *bourreau* leaning on my shoulders pushes me back down, fingers digging into my arms.

"Never. You insult me by suggesting it." I manage to suck in a breath and shout as loudly as I can, so they'll all be sure to hear me. "Never!"

"Surely you're protecting someone."

"No."

"I charge you, in the name of the law, name your accomplices."

"I had no *accomplices*—"

What can I tell them? Yes, I was part of a great conspiracy to break up the cross at the bridge, because my accomplices and I intend to expose the Church for the den of hypocrites, thieves, and tyrants that it is. My accomplices? Why, Voltaire, d'Alembert, Rousseau, Diderot, all the others who dare to question the way things are. Of course. We'll begin to batter away at the Church's supremacy, destroy the Gallican Church and bring down Rome, by taking a malicious whack or two at a provincial roadside shrine.

"I—had—no—accomplices—There was no conspiracy!"

"You must speak the truth to us or risk damnation."

"I'm—speaking—the truth," I say, between clenched teeth.

Duval nods and the younger *bourreau* whacks the third wedge in a little farther yet. I can't help a sharp gasp, but, by God, I'm *not* going to scream. Not in front of him.

My shinbones are going to crack any minute . . . God, keep me strong . . .

Don't scream.

"Chevalier," Duval whispers, "this is only the beginning of the pain that can be inflicted." His voice has turned oily, wheedling. "But it will cease as soon as you confess your guilt, and name your accomplices . . ."

"I've told you the truth." I stop, catch my breath somehow. "If I said anything else, it would be only because of the pain."

My eyes are stinging. It's sweat, my own sweat. Someone, I can't tell who, reaches over with a handkerchief, trying to wipe it off, a small kindness—but I twist away. I'm glad of the sting—it's something to take my mind off the throbbing in my legs.

Questions. Questions. Don't give in, François, don't name names.

"*No.*"

I turn my head back to Duval and look the bastard full in the eye. "You want me to confess to what I didn't do. You'll never have proof—*never*—because I didn't do it."

Duval nods at the *bourreau*, who picks up the fourth wedge, a bigger one yet.

"Do you see that fourth wedge? One word from me and it'll be applied. Do you know this is merely the 'question ordinary'? Next is the 'question extraordinary.' Four more wedges, Chevalier, and larger. The fifth or sixth will tear your flesh and break your bones."

"I've *told* you the truth," I almost shriek at him. "There's nothing more to tell you."

(Dear God, let this be over, let me die now . . .)

"Monsieur Duval." It's the stranger who's been hovering, fidgeting with his watch, at the far side of the room, a tall man in a modest black suit. He shoulders his way forward and feels my pulse.

"Monsieur, you must stop this. Further suffering will kill him."

Oh, I don't think so, whoever you are. It hurts like the devil but I can stand more than this. I'd rather not, thank you—but it'll take a lot more than this to kill me.

"Is that your considered opinion?" Duval sounds as if he's not happy about it.

"You've achieved nothing after a full hour of this barbarity, monsieur. Any more, and he may die."

"Make a note," Duval snarls to the clerk, "that Dr. Gatte recommends ending the questioning at the third wedge, to avoid the death of the prisoner."

So he's Dr. Gatte from the hospital—Madame's mentioned his name once or twice—a doctor must know perfectly well that this kind of persuasion, brutal as it is, isn't nearly enough to kill a healthy young man. I'd kiss him, if I could.

The young *bourreau* unbuckles the straps. The planks and wedges clatter to the floor, and if the other man wasn't holding on to me still, I'd slide right off the bench. I'm breathing as if I'd just run a mile uphill, and from thigh to ankle I feel like a beef jelly. The two men heave me up and lay me on a dirty mattress, gently enough, taking care not to grab my legs. They know their job, these people.

At last they all clear out and the tramping in the corridor fades away in the distance. Duval's gone, and if God is kind, I'll die without ever seeing his odious face again.

I'm alone, and I can hear the drip-drip-drip on the windowsill in the silence. And now, finally, I can hide my face in my arms, face down into the mattress that stinks of piss and mildew and fear, and I can sob with the pain.

41

"Well?" said Jérôme in the morning, which dawned cool and wet with a weeping sky, when he and Charles met to take a little breakfast together. Bastien and Martin had been busy all the previous evening, overseeing the construction of the scaffold and the bonfire in the market square, and Bastien had gone off again at first light. "Are you ready then, M'sieur Charles?"

Ready? To cut off a harmless boy's head?

Prepared, perhaps. He would never be *ready*.

He glanced down at the bread on his plate, without appetite. "Is the questioning done?"

"Aye. He took it well, poor lad. No crying, no bargaining; he never gave up anything, though that smug prick of a magistrate put him through hell. Have no fear about him; he's a courageous one."

"Did you find a butcher?"

"Is that how it is, then?"

"You'd better hurry—"

"Already got what I need, in case he closes his shop early to go to the show." Jérôme patted a pouch at his waist.

They exchanged glances and it occurred to Charles that Jérôme had intended to counterfeit the tearing out of the tongue with or without his master's consent, just as he himself had resolved to disobey the magistrates' orders.

After all, we executioners are not monsters.

42

I'm not alone. Père Bosquier hasn't said a word until now, though he must have been here through all of it—it was his hand, I think, that tried to wipe the sweat off my face. "I'm here, my son," he says softly, "if you should need me."

He's a good man, even if he is a priest.

My poor legs ache like the devil; I've got to talk, do something, or go out of my mind. He pulls over a stool for himself, asks a question or two about where I lived before I came to Abbeville, and lets me prattle like a child about my home, about Férolles and Brie and La Barre and how we lived out in the country without two sous to rub together, just for something to say, to kill time. (Kill time? What an expression.) Now and then he puts a word in, trying to bring up the subject of a good deathbed confession, of absolution. I can't resist turning the subject to Father Jouffroy, back at Férolles, and his bad Latin and his dull lessons about saints and catechisms. No wonder I was a poor Catholic. Who'd ever be inspired by all that hot air and claptrap?

But Père Bosquier's kind; he means well and he really is concerned for the state of my soul. I guess I'll say something pious, later on . . . before the end . . . to keep him happy.

Noon, they said. It won't be much longer.

The bell of Saint-Vulfran tolls half past ten in the distance and suddenly I'm starving. I have a little money in my pocket, still, a livre's worth or so that Père Bosquier had slipped me the day before—from Madame, he said, but I think it's his own doing—and what else should I do with it? Save it for my old age?

"Father, I had no breakfast. Please have them bring us some dinner; it's on me."

He calls a turnkey and asks him to bring food, but only for one.

"Won't you dine with me?"

"I've no appetite, I fear."

"Which one of us is going to have his head cut off today, *mon père?*" Somehow I can still smile. "Do me a favor and join me. You'll need your strength for the show as much as I will."

My legs still ache horribly, but with his help I can stagger up, limp to the ink-stained table that the clerk had used, and drop into a chair. No broken bones, just a lot of vicious bruises and skinned flesh and some deep, raw, bloody scrapes that still throb—they made sure not to break anything, because if they'd smashed me up, I couldn't walk or hold myself properly on the scaffold later today, and where would be the fun in that?

It hurt like this when I was fourteen, when my horse, a wretched old nag because we couldn't afford better, once stumbled and threw me in the forest. At another time I'd be dreading how stiff and sore I'm going to be tomorrow morning.

The turnkey finally brings a pullet and two bottles of wine. The pullet is well roasted, hot and juicy, and the wine isn't bad. One bottle is half gone before I realize it. But don't drink too much wine, François; preserve your dignity. This isn't a riverfront tavern and you'll want all your wits about you, later.

Père Bosquier picks at a wing, but he looks a little pale and doesn't take more than a few mouthfuls. I finish my share and start on his. I can't help it—I never did like fasting, during Lent or at any other time, and I guess being tortured is good for the appetite.

"Perhaps you should have some coffee now?" Père Bosquier suggests, gently, once I've polished off the chicken and I'm pouring out the last of the bottle of wine.

"Coffee?"

I'm not fond of coffee, but maybe I did have a little bit too much wine, and coffee gets the blood moving. I shrug. "Why not."

A moment later I can't help laughing, for a heartbeat or two.

"It won't keep me up tonight."

43

At ten a messenger from the town hall brought them word that the hour of the execution had been postponed until five o'clock in the afternoon, in the hope that the weather would change, and to mollify the sympathetic souls who prayed that a royal pardon for La Barre might yet arrive. Charles remembered Duval de Soicourt's air of malicious triumph and suspected they would be disappointed.

He visited the market square and assured himself that the platform was in good order, well covered with straw, and that all was prepared; that Bastien was on guard, keeping watch over the sword of justice and the spare waiting in their crate, that a bucket of water sat at one side to rinse away the inevitable blood, that the bonfire was properly constructed and of seasoned wood. So much firewood you need, he thought, much more than anyone would think, forty livres' worth, to translate a man into ashes.

Bastien sat on the top step, elbows on knees, sucking at his pipe and ignoring the flippancy below. Despite the light persistent rain, a few men, exchanging jests and passing bottles back and forth, had already secured themselves places by the railing that surrounded the scaffold. The best view was there, of course, and moreover there was a chance they'd be spattered by a stray drop or two of blood, which was good luck.

I am simply following my orders, he told himself as he inspected the two swords, sharpened the day before to a razor's edge, and watched as Bastien carefully concealed them beneath a leather cover and a heap of straw. I'm merely an instrument of the law, following the dictates of the law as duty demands—but all the same . . . dear God above, I want nothing to do with this abominable matter.

He returned to his lodging and sent for a hairdresser. In a provincial town like Abbeville, he had not thought it necessary to preside at an execution with his hair powdered and set in side curls, as etiquette commanded in Paris; but after meeting La Barre, he felt he owed the boy that trifling courtesy.

For a moment, while the hairdresser fussed with curling iron and pomade and hairpins and Charles stared into the mirror, hating the face that looked back at him, he considered refusing to carry out the execution.

But refusing won't save him.

The executioners of Rouen and Amiens, Férey and a newcomer he didn't know, had been summoned to assist him. Or, more likely, to get underfoot. He reminded himself to instruct Jérôme to steer the provincials well out of their way once the ceremonial procession to the scaffold was over.

No lack of hands ready to take up the sword and take his place. Duval de Soicourt had undoubtedly chosen to demonstrate to all witnesses, by the numbers of *bourreaux* present, that this was no ordinary execution.

Nothing can save him.

And what of my own conscience?

At least, despite the consequences if he refused to obey his orders, he could know that his own hands were not stained with that boy's blood, in a crime—yes, *crime*—far greater than any La Barre could possibly have committed.

But my refusal won't save him . . . nothing can save him, except the king's pardon, and they say that's a vain hope.

The hairdresser pocketed his fee and departed. Clutching his rosary, Charles knelt and tried to pray, but, though the Latin phrases tumbled from his lips as they had since his childhood, the prayers would not come.

Ave Maria, gratia plena, Dominus tecum. Benedicta tu in mulieribus, et benedictus fructus ventris tui, Iesus . . .

All my life I've been a good son of the Church and a faithful subject of the king. Yet they're all saying, all but that gloating creature Duval who brought him to this, that La Barre has been the victim of appalling injustice from Church and state alike.

And I, by following my orders, will be as tainted by his blood as any of the magistrates who sent him here to his death.

Can I truly be serving the law and avenging the innocent, as Father always told me, when I'm the tool of a regime that's revealed itself to be corrupt, malicious, and brutal?

He fingered his beads, mechanically whispering—*Ave Maria, gratia plena, Dominus tecum*—as the rain pattered down and his thoughts continued to race.

Nothing.

Did you expect an answer, Charles? A sign from heaven to set your mind at rest, to tell you what you do is right and just, salve your conscience as Father's magic salve soothes a cut on your hand?

When you've stood on a public scaffold and seen pain or death most days for a dozen years, you know that miracles are few.

Perhaps you will go to Hell for this, no matter how you choose to act. You are a coward, Charles-Henri Sanson. Would running away, merely to let some other man take your place, make you any less guilty of that boy's death, when a true servant of justice—*real* justice, God's justice—would rise up and clamor, take up arms against tyranny while knowing the struggle was hopeless, to spare him?

Half past three.

Sancta Maria, Mater Dei, ora pro nobis peccatoribus, nunc et in hora mortis nostrae. Amen.

Holy Mary, Mother of God, pray for us sinners, now and at the hour of our death . . .

Four o'clock.

The rain was thinning to a heavy mist. In another hour the sun would shine. No more excuses, no more postponements.

If I were truly courageous, he realized at last, if duty and honor truly meant anything at all to me, I'd die fighting for that boy rather than kill him.

But I have a perfectly natural, perfectly selfish desire to keep on living.

And so—and so I'll do him the only service I can, and perhaps maintain a shred of my self-respect. At least I can offer him compassion and courtesy at the last, and deny his enemies the satisfaction of seeing him suffer or tremble.

If God guided his hand and his aim, he told himself as he rose slowly to his feet and reached for his scarlet coat, he could grant La Barre the sole gift within his power—the immeasurable gift of a quick and easy death.

44

And so the hours slip away, one by one. It's long past noon and I'm still sitting here at this ink-stained table, leaning my head on my arms (God, I'm so tired) while the rain whispers down and Père Bosquier keeps on trying to save my soul; something's gone wrong.

I wonder, does Madame know? Will she and Jacques spend today in a church somewhere in Paris, praying for me?

Damn it, I don't want prayers. I don't think I want to be Voltaire's martyr. I don't want to suffer for the cause of people I've never met. I just want to see my twenty-first birthday.

Maybe they're waiting for a messenger with a pardon. Don't count on it, friends. If you'd seen Duval's face up close, the way I saw it this morning, you'd know he's not going to let me wriggle out of his claws. If a messenger comes, the guards at the barrier will keep him with some lame excuse or other, and by the time he rides up to the town hall, I'll already be dead meat roasting on the cookfire. Oh dear, too late, what a pity.

I can't seem to feel frightened, though. At the last moment, the last hours of the last day of my life, I'm not afraid; I only want to be done with this.

I shouldn't deceive myself. I wouldn't be so calm if I knew they were going to rip out my tongue or break me or burn me alive. Oh, God, let it be quick. Let it be true, what he told me, that they'll fake the business with my tongue—and that the sword is so fast you feel nothing.

Let it be over, let this nightmare end at last.

He's so *young*. He can't be much more than—what, twenty-eight?

He seems like a decent man, and he talks like a gentleman, as refined and polite as any of Madame's friends.

Funny, that I think I might like the man who's going to cut my head off.

It might have been him, Sanson, the boy who yelled at us that day when I was a kid, at the *bourreau*'s cottage outside Brie-Comte-Robert, years ago. He'd have been the right age then, I guess. Funny. I wonder if he'd remember that.

Five o'clock.

The rain's almost let up; it'll be a pleasant evening.

"My son," says Père Bosquier. He's standing at my shoulder; I didn't even hear him approach. Someone's turning a key in the lock. "My son, it's time."

I want to meet them standing. Christ—my legs are stiff; I can scarcely bend my knees. But I grab the table and the back of the chair, and I'm on my feet.

Sanson isn't among them. It's just Lieutenant Merlin and a couple of his guards, who hover in the corridor, and two husky men in plain coats, the same two *bourreaux* who worked on my legs this morning. The older one takes off his hat and steps forward.

"We must dress you, monsieur."

Or rather undress you, monsieur, because they take away my waistcoat, my handkerchief, my ring with the La Barre coat of arms on it, my shoes and stockings that were lying in a corner, even my hair ribbon, so my hair hangs straggling across my shoulders and around my face, like a kitchenmaid's, uncombed and lank with sweat. Nothing left but my open shirt and culotte, and the dried smears of blood on my legs. Bareheaded and barefoot to the scaffold, stripped of everything that tells the world who and what you are, the mark of a penitent.

I am *not* penitent.

The younger one—he's not much older than I am—shakes out the bundle of cloth he's carried under his arm. It looks like a nightshirt. Over it goes, over my shirt and culotte, hanging to my knees.

The penitent's coarse smock. Joseph de Valines wore one like this, too, before they broke him, and a rope around his neck. Will I—

"Sorry, monsieur," says the older man as he slips the noose over my head. "It's the custom." He moves a little closer, adjusting the knot so it hangs slack and won't choke me, and murmurs into my ear.

"Chevalier, I'm going to sham cutting out your tongue. Understand?"

I nod, once.

"If you do as I say, it'll go smooth. Once you've spoken your piece, Martin here will take hold of you. Don't fight him. And don't fight it when I put the pincers in your mouth. I'll slip a sponge in at the same time, a sponge soaked in blood from the butcher's. Got that? All you have to do is bite down and play along. Give them a little agony and spit out some blood. And for mercy's sake don't forget yourself afterwards and start talking like nothing's wrong."

"I understand."

He claps me on the shoulder. "Courage, lad. I wish to God none of this had to happen—but M'sieur Charles swears it'll be quick. Courage, and God keep you."

They get on either side of me, supporting my elbows, without my asking. They know what the *brodequins* can do.

Down in the courtyard—at least the rain's finally stopped—one more treat is waiting for me before I go into the cart: a couple of placards, strung together. INFIDEL, BLASPHEMER, EXECRABLE AND ABOMINABLE SACRILEGE. Another taste of ritual humiliation for the fellow who dares to question their rules.

They hang the placards over my chest and back and lift me into the tumbril, onto a plank, my back to the horse, and Père Bosquier sits beside me and slips a prayer book into my hands. The younger *bourreau*, Martin, perches on a stool at the side, holding a great tall wax taper. The flame wavers in the pale sunshine as we creak forward.

I'm more notorious than I thought; I've never seen the streets so crowded.

Rat-tat-tat-tat, tat, tat. I remember that drumroll. Valines heard it, too, when they led him to his death. *Rat-tat-tat-tat, tat, tat, rat-tat-tat-tat, tat, tat.*

Père Bosquier probably wants me to pray with him, but I just stare straight ahead of me as the château recedes and the crowd around us spills into the road behind the cart, and follows. It's quite a parade; every mounted horseman they could scrape together from the barracks, three dozen at least, and plenty of soldiers on foot. All this just for me. Who'd have thought I'd ever rate this much attention?

Rue Saint-Gilles, Rue des Minimes. They didn't go this way to Saint-Vulfran on the day they broke Valines. Duval de Soicourt must have arranged this long, roundabout route especially for me and for the people who might still give a damn about me, for now we're passing houses I know: Belleval's, Gaillard de Boëncourt's. Inside those walls, behind those windows, are friends—the few friends I have left, anyway—who can't help but hear the cart trundle by, the drumroll, the mob yelling.

Rue Saint-André.

There are some faces I know in the crowd. A girl from the riverfront who I had once or twice—now she's yelling "Blasphemer!" as if she'd never laughed at Étallonde's filthy jokes about lecherous monks. And I can see Métigny, standing on someone's doorstep, head and shoulders above the mob. He's pointing and staring, and doesn't seem too upset about it all.

Rat-tat-tat-tat, tat, tat, rat-tat-tat-tat, tat, tat.

"Courage, Chevalier," Père Bosquier says. "You don't want them to see you weep."

Are my eyes wet? Maybe. But not from fear.

"What makes me saddest today, *mon père*," I reply, after thinking about it, "is to see people who I used to think were my friends."

Rue de la Hucherie.

It's become a fine warm summer's evening, but maybe it would've been better if it were still raining, and cooler. I didn't count on sweating like a horse beneath this cursed smock.

Rat-tat-tat-tat, tat, tat, rat-tat-tat-tat, tat, tat.

The streets are nothing, compared with the crowd in front of Saint-Vulfran. A couple of dozen soldiers are keeping a wide space clear by the steps.

A hitch. Something's gone wrong again. The older *bourreau's* arguing with somebody, one of the magistrates or the guards. About some damned formality, I guess. While I wait for them to get on with it, sitting in the cart, staring out above their heads, and the crowd pushes in around me, pointing, leering. It's not often they get to see a gentleman suffer the same as thieves and perverts and murdering scum. A parade's all very well, but they want the real show to begin.

The quarter hour chimes. Père Bosquier keeps on reciting prayers beside me. But I think of that farting stone demon, high up on the side of the church, just out of sight now, and in spite of everything, remembering how Étallonde and I laughed at it a century or two ago, I can't help just the ghost of a grin.

Thank God I relieved myself not long before the *bourreaux* arrived, or I'd be squirming by now, or maybe piss myself. They'd love that, wouldn't they?

Mordieu, my legs ache. If they'd made me walk here, as they did Valines, I don't think I could have done it.

The quarter hour's chimed twice now, and I'm still waiting for something to happen, anything at all. For the love of God, let's go, let's get *on* with it.

The *bourreau* comes back at last and the pair of them lift me out, help me over to the lowest step of the church in front of the great carved doors. The older one pushes me down, gripping my shoulders so the weight isn't going straight onto my poor knees. Martin thrusts the candle into my hands. Two pounds—it feels more like ten.

"Hold the candle before you, my son," Père Bosquier says, "and repeat after me: 'I repent my most blasphemous and sacrilegious crimes; wickedly and with impiety, I have passed before the Holy Sacrament without kneeling or removing my hat.'"

He pauses, waiting for me, but the words are drying up in my throat.

I can't do this.

"No."

I won't repent crimes I never committed. Everything I did was stupid and childish and offensive, but it should be no crime, and I'll never admit it was a crime.

"My son?"

"I won't . . . I won't soil my mouth with lies."

My voice sounds stronger than I feel. But I won't do it. I can't stop them from torturing me and murdering me, but they're not going to take away the last scrap of dignity I have. I may have been a troublesome, spoiled, good-for-nothing brat, but I do have my pride still, and my honor, here at the end of everything.

"Would you disobey the Church and the law, my son?"

"Father, I can't."

He gazes at me, troubled, while the crowd begins to catcall and shout "Come on, Chevalier, let's get on with it!"

"Trying to keep your tongue in your head for a moment longer?" yells one.

Behind me the older *bourreau* sighs, impatient. Père Bosquier holds up a hand to him, crosses himself, and turns to face the church.

"In the name of this man, I speak for the penitent. I repent my most blasphemous and sacrilegious crimes: Wickedly and with impiety, I have passed before the Holy Sacrament without kneeling or removing my hat; I have uttered blasphemies and rendered respect and adoration to infamous books, and profaned the sign of the Cross and the benedictions of the Church. I have most grievously offended and I beg pardon of God, the king, and Justice."

Thank you, Father, I know you meant well; but I'd rather you hadn't done that. Your saying so doesn't mean it's true.

Oh God—this is the moment. The *bourreau*—he couldn't have been playing a nasty trick on me, could he—telling me what I want to hear so I won't put up a fight?

Martin says "Stay on your knees," then takes the oversized candle and blows it out before depositing it in the cart. Do they use the same candle over and over at every ritual penance until—what a trivial thing to wonder about—before I know it, he's tied my hands behind my back.

"Don't struggle, now," he mutters in my ear, "and you'll be all right."

Fine. Whatever you say.

He grabs me about the chest with one arm, bracing me against him, and pulls my head back with the other, fingers twined in my hair. The older *bourreau* has a pair of pincers in one hand and a knife in his belt. Don't struggle—but Christ, every nerve in my body is telling me to fight like a wildcat. *Don't struggle.*

His fingers prying my mouth open. The taste of salty sweat and rusty iron. And—oh thank God and the *bourreaux* both for their mercy—something soft and wet thrust in my mouth as his hand covers my face. The bitter coppery tang of stale, putrid blood—God, it's vile—but it's not my own blood, not yet.

His hands jerk and the knife is coming up to my face—I can't help staring at it until I'm almost cross-eyed—but he's scarcely touching me, and then his left hand is high up in the air, and something pale and bloody and slimy is caught in the pincers, and the crowd shrieks and cheers.

Don't forget your own role. Oblige them with a scream and a strangled gurgle and groan, and bite on the sponge, and blood dribbles down my chin as I double over. A mouthful splatters crimson onto the cobblestones. Martin squeezes my shoulder as if to say "Good show."

"Don't spit out the sponge yet," he cautions me, as he drags me upright and shoves a crumpled rag into my mouth. I can't help swallowing a bit of the blood, gagging, retching, and for an instant I think I'm going to puke—they'd love that, too—but I force it away.

Martin unties my hands as he helps me toward the cart. As soon as the older *bourreau* has put away his tools and climbed back to the driver's seat, we're on our way again, the crowd following, noisier than ever. It's only a short way now, a few steps, a few turns of the wheels.

I bow my shoulders and hang my head so they can't get a good look at my face. Père Bosquier takes hold of my hand and presses it, hard.

"My son, try to bear the pain for a little while, just a little while. Think of Our Lord's agony on the Cross."

Martin leans over to me with another scrap of cloth, spitting on it to get it damp, just as I've seen women do in the street to mop off their brats' grubby faces. I mumble the bits of sponge and rag into it as he wipes at my mouth and chin, getting off the worst of the blood.

"Bear the pain with fortitude," Père Bosquier repeats, "and soon you'll be at peace."

He's been kind; it's not fair to deceive him. I lean forward, head still bent.

"They didn't do it." Careful, keep it to a whisper, try not to move your lips. "It was a sham."

The quick, guilty relief that floods his face makes me think there's hope for the Church after all.

That's done. And the rest—the rest is simple, and it'll soon be over.

45

By late afternoon a pale sun struggled through the pearly layer of cloud. At five o'clock Charles climbed to the scaffold in the great market square and waited, hands clasped behind his back, silent in his elegant blood-red coat, three-cornered hat, and high-heeled shoes, with lace at wrists and throat as he wore it in Paris. The local executioner and his two aides hovered behind him, for the sake of ceremony only, having been firmly instructed to keep out of the way.

An actor on his own stage, indeed.

The ever-swelling crowd that had gathered to see the final act of the spectacle stirred and murmured below him, gawking.

"How fine he looks," people whispered, loudly enough for him to hear.

"So young!"

"The master executioner from Paris, they say—at his age?"

"Oh,"—a pink-cheeked girl—"he's handsome, isn't he! What a pity he's a *bourreau*!"

Though outwardly he bore himself with stoic solemnity as he did at every execution—for even the most despicable felon deserved a measure of respect as a human creature at the moment of his ordained death—beneath his composed countenance, his mind was racing still as the quarter hours tolled, one by one. The procession would wind its way slowly through the ancient, tortuous streets of Abbeville, past those frowning houses that shut out the sun, until at last it halted in front of the great church whose twin towers he could see from where he stood.

Was that a muted cheer, a howl of bloodlust not far away? The ritual penance was done, then, and the play-acting of that barbaric gesture of wanton cruelty—the crowds would never know, he hoped, how they'd been duped.

He clasped his hands more tightly behind his back and prayed Jérôme had carried out his task properly.

Only a moment later, it seemed, another sound: drumrolls, horses, soldiers, hoots and jeers. They were approaching.

Though the judges had tried their best to dishonor La Barre, Charles saw nothing humble or penitential about the manner in which he still carried his head, with dignity though without arrogance. The boy's face was smeared with traces of blood; it had bespattered the placard hanging on his chest, and the coarse white shirt.

The tumbril stopped beside the scaffold, and from the tall church tower beyond, the passing bell began to toll, slow and heavy. Martin and the attending confessor had to help the boy up the steps, damp and slippery from the rain.

Charles approached him, meaning to remove the degrading noose and placards, but the boy was too swift for him. He tore them off himself and flung them aside.

"Thank you," he said under his breath, as soon as Charles was near enough to hear him.

Thank God, he can still speak; at least we spared him that.

"Courage, monsieur; it will be quick."

46

Courage, François: it'll soon be over.

I can see it now. Beyond the far side of the scaffold, below me on the cobbles, is a great pile of wood and straw, carefully layered, like the funeral pyres they built for the old pagan Romans. The bonfire awaiting my dead body—the only tomb I'll ever have.

Courage.

Though why I'm going along so meekly with my own destruction, when I never hurt anybody, never killed, or raped, or even robbed—I ought to rage against this, fight to the end of my strength, show the world that I don't accept their sentence, that they have no right to take away my life, even though I know they can overpower me. By letting them play out this charade, by not clawing, biting, screaming denials and protests at every step, I'm consenting to it, admitting they're right and I'm wrong.

But maybe I can be just as defiant in not letting Duval break me. This mob, they want to see me beg for mercy, blubber like a baby. I won't give them what they want. I won't.

Père Bosquier wants me to pray with him. I wish I didn't have to kneel for it—though the pain's not so bad now, except where the straw they've scattered jabs against those raw scrapes on my legs and sets them throbbing again.

(*Pater noster, qui es in caelis, sanctificetur nomen tuum . . .*)

Tomorrow—if there was going to be a tomorrow—I might be feeling halfway better, after all.

He's still reciting the Pater Noster, but I keep thinking of the Ave Maria: *Ora pro nobis peccatoribus, nunc et in hora mortis nostrae.*

At the hour of our death.

Pray for us sinners, now and at the hour of our death . . .

Amen.

The clerk is droning something. A name—Bertrand d'Étallonde's—of course it's his execution today, too, even though he's long gone. "By order of the Présidial of Abbeville . . . condemned to be fixed to a post with iron chains and there burned alive . . ."

A man hangs a placard from the pole that stands at one end of the scaffold. There's a crude drawing on it, a youth chained to a stake, surrounded by flames. It's so hideously, solemnly absurd that I can't help a bit of a smile. They have to have their fun, don't they?

At least Bertrand and Pierre are safe.

"François Jean Lefebvre, Chevalier de La Barre."

The clerk reads out my crimes: sacrilege, blasphemy, possession of infamous books, neglecting to take your hat off in the rain.

I'd never have believed that they could put a gentleman to death for such a trifling thing.

"Courage, my son," Père Bosquier murmurs. I must have spoken aloud. He blesses me with a trembling hand—there's his absolution at last, I knew he wouldn't deny me that.

He helps me to my feet again, while the clerk drones on, and as he gives me an arm up, I can tell he's shaking like a leaf.

For my sake?

I look him straight in the face. He's gone white and his hands are cold and clammy, in spite of the heat. I think his eyes are shining with tears. Do I look as pale as that? I doubt it—I can feel the blood roaring through my veins like a river in the spring flood.

"Father—please—don't cry," I whisper. "Do you think I'm afraid?"

He blinks hard a few times, makes the sign of the cross, surrenders me to Sanson, who lifts away the shirt that's still hanging to my knees. That's better; the breeze is cool. I can draw a long breath, though my mouth is dry. Steady, François.

Steady . . . but I'm not afraid, truly. I'm tired, so very tired, but I'm not scared; not even angry, not any more. Just . . . ready, waiting. Let's get on with it.

He's reaching for—is it now?

Where is it?

"May—may I see your sword?"

47

Charles hesitated. The sword was hidden beneath Bastien's long coat. Despite the boy's fearless bearing, he could not guess how La Barre might react upon seeing his death gleaming before him.

"That's—not to be seen, monsieur."

Martin handed him the scissors and swiftly he cut the boy's long hair to expose his neck, slender as a girl's.

"What good is there in shaving me like an altar boy?" La Barre said abruptly, with the first hint of disdain—or perhaps nerves—that Charles had heard from him.

"For your own sake, Chevalier." After Lally, he had resolved he would never again leave anything to chance.

He doffed his own coat and hat as Martin guided La Barre to the center of the scaffold, amid the heaped straw, and the boy touched his lips to the crucifix the priest offered him. The evening sunshine gleamed in his cropped hair as Charles bound his hands.

"Steady, monsieur. A moment more only."

"Do you see me trembling?"

The boy glanced back an instant before Charles bandaged his eyes with a handkerchief. "Don't fail me, Monsieur Sanson. Just one last kindness. Don't fail me."

Charles made the sign of the cross and gestured to Bastien as Jérôme and Martin helped La Barre to his knees. Bastien silently drew the sword from beneath his coat and passed it to him.

May God forgive me—and guide my hand.

With a brief passionate prayer Charles lifted the sword in both hands and tested the balance.

48

His hands are gentle enough as he binds my wrists and blindfolds me. You'd expect an executioner's hands to be hard, rough, brutal, wouldn't you?

I don't want to close my eyes. The light's still bright through the linen.

That's the last thing I'll ever see.

. . . I won't go away, of course, as they'd like me to, even when I'm no more than ashes on the wind. Probably I'll be more memorable dead than alive. People will remember, and turn me into whatever they need to see.

I suppose Voltaire and that lot'll transform me into some kind of anti-martyr, hounded to death by a tyrannical Church and a corrupt state. Maybe they'll put heroic words in my mouth. But that noble martyr isn't me. I'm only—*me,* François Jean Lefebvre de La Barre, just a rowdy adolescent, a bit of a fool, who found, in a pinch, that he had the balls and the character underneath it all to make an honorable end.

I haven't done so badly, I guess . . .

Someone's gripping my arms—"You must kneel now, m'sieur"— easing me down—faith, I'm sore—prodding me into place, talking to me as he pulls my shirt open and tugs it below my shoulders.

"Keep your back straight, m'sieur—just so; good. Stay upright now, keep still as a statue, and it'll be over before you know it."

This is it, then.

Keep still.

I can hear my own breathing, roaring in my ears, louder than the muffled gabble of the crowd, and my heart is racing at a gallop.

The bell's still tolling my death: *Clang . . . Clang . . . Clang . . .* I can't seem to catch my breath.

A voice nearby—Sanson's, I think.

"Chevalier."

A touch—*don't flinch*—but it's only his fingertips, beneath my chin, nudging it upwards—

"Keep your head erect, so . . . and don't move."

Keep still . . . Sanson, don't fail me . . .

The crowd's shut up.

Everything's so quiet, except for the bell and my own breath, fast and shallow and noisy, and beyond it—something whistling through the air—

It's now

Keep still

It's *cold*—

49

The sword found its mark and scythed cleanly through the boy's neck.

The spectators gasped all together, for an instant were silent, and then applauded, with a few shouts of "Well done!"—as if he had performed a star turn, as if he were Carlin at the Comédie-Italienne, rattling off an especially witty speech.

So much blood. So much blood spilling from that slender young body that lay at his feet in the straw, shuddering with a few last tremors. It had sprayed across his hands again, and glistened along the sword's shining length. Had so much blood gushed from Lally's mangled corpse?

He closed his eyes, swallowing back nausea and breathing hard, before discovering that Jérôme was drawing the sword from his hands.

"M'sieur Charles . . . m'sieur."

. . . gently prying his blood-spattered fingers loose from the grip . . .

"M'sieur Charles, you must show them. You must finish it."

The witnessing magistrates had to see conclusive proof that justice—No, not justice—merely proof that their sentence had been carried out.

Now the boy's body lay unmoving. Bastien knelt beside it, felt for a pulse. An instant later he glanced up at Charles and nodded. *It's done.*

The bleeding head had tumbled away from him. He took a step toward it, bent (for the love of heaven, people, stop your *clapping*), slipped off the blindfold, twined his fingers in the hair to raise it high. The boy's eyes were wide open still.

The blade'll have to be re-ground, m'sieur, Jérôme said as he carefully wiped the sword and returned it to the crate: there's a tiny chip, see, just there.

Charles's orders were to burn the body and severed head to ashes, together with La Barre's copies of the *Dictionnaire Philosophique* and other banned volumes.

Perhaps he should throw in his own copy, the one Antoinette and he had argued over, lighthearted—because everybody knows that the censors and the book police are overwhelmed with the sheer volume of seditious trash being printed these days, because everybody knows that no one really gets in hot water just for owning the wrong books?

The warm summer twilight deepened and the kitchen smell of roasting flesh—for a man was no more than meat, in the final tally, wasn't he—at last overwhelmed the crisp, acrid scent of wood smoke. Martin and Bastien stayed in the market square to keep watch over the bonfire and chase off urchins and old witch-women hoping to steal a relic or two from the embers. Charles left them to it and slunk away to his lodging like a thief in the shadows, avoiding the curious glances. He knelt at the prie-dieu in the corner of his room and tried to pray for the boy's soul and for his own, but the prayers once again caught in his throat.

Again and again the boy's face hovered before him, that calm young face, so prematurely worn. What might that young man have become one day, he wondered bleakly, if a pitiless enemy, a ruthless state, and an unforgiving church hadn't conspired to destroy him, obliterate him?

It was easier, perhaps, to die with dignity than to live successfully. Yet if one died so young, displaying such courage, such character despite all, was that loss not a crime, a tragedy?

And was not he, Charles-Henri Sanson, no matter how he might justify himself, complicit in the crime?

In the stifling silence of his room he could still hear the tiny *crunch*, feel it in his hands: an instant's resistance as the sword struck bone and hacked through.

He shuddered. The smell of flesh and greasy smoke lingered in his senses, in his mouth with the taste of ashes.

He could find no answers in his dark vigil. He quitted Abbeville the next day, scarcely past dawn, alone and mute in a postchaise, leaving Martin and the men to follow when they were done with their tasks: packing away, sweeping up, dismantling the scaffold, crushing blackened bones.

Marie-Anne welcomed him home with smiles and a kiss, but without a word or question about the errand that had taken him from Paris. At last, after a dinner—with no roast meat in it, thank the saints—during which the family chattered and gossiped of the trivialities that made up all their lives, he could bear the banality of it no longer; early the next morning, after another sleepless night, he gathered his hunting kit, saddled his horse, and fled to the silence and solitude of the forests.

Late in the morning, four days later, he returned from Saint-Denis. Marie-Anne smiled up at him placidly from her sewing: had he had a successful journey?

"It was pleasant enough." He kissed the top of her head.

"Did you bring home any game, then?" she added, turning once more to the thread stocking she was darning. "I thought, maybe, for tomorrow's dinner, a couple of nice chickens . . . but I didn't want to buy anything at the market yesterday for fear that you might come home with a brace of pheasants."

"No, no luck this time." He did not add that he had spent the greater part of the past days merely wandering through the woodland, enveloped in black thoughts, his fowling piece still hanging at his back, unloaded.

"I think you're not doing so well at the hunt as you used to," she observed, biting off the thread. "Back before we were wed, most times you'd be heading home with a bird or a rabbit."

"Perhaps my aim is off."

"Never mind." She glanced up at him, unsmiling, and returned her attention to the darn. "I know you like your hunting, wherever it is you go, even if you don't bag anything. You ought to go more often. It's good for you, to get away."

He ought not to have assumed, he realized, a little ill at ease, that merely because Marie-Anne was a woman of uncomplicated character, she would naturally live in happy innocence of where he might spend his hours of leisure. Yet she had chosen, it seemed, to ignore the potential existence of some other woman, just as she had chosen to ignore her husband's profession. He cupped his hand about her neck, her flesh cool beneath his palm, and she leaned against him with a small, contented sigh.

"It shouldn't matter where you take yourself," she added, "or whether you come home with a bit of game or not. Just so long as you come home."

"You know I always will."

They sat together for a time, Marie-Anne humming a little tune under her breath as Charles stared into the fireplace, empty in the hot days of July. He rose as Jean-Baptiste hobbled into the salon.

"You're back, good," Jean-Baptiste said and beckoned him into his study. "Take a look at this."

He passed over a letter bearing the prosecutor-general's seal. Charles glanced through it. Joly de Fleury himself had concluded, it seemed, that the master executioner's bill—for extraordinary services provided outside the city of Paris—was far too high.

"You see, here and here"—Jean-Baptiste stabbed a finger at a copy of the itemized list Charles had hastily and routinely composed before arriving in Abbeville—"he's altered the figures. I recognize it, it's in his own handwriting. For applying the question, instead of the thirty-five livres you requested, they'll pay only ten; for the cost of firewood and oil, constructing the bonfire, and burning the corpse, only fifty instead of ninety; for the *per diem* expenses for you and the others, only seven livres per person per day instead of ten . . ."

Charles gazed at the letter and the bill, but the words seemed meaningless, a black scrawl of gibberish. A few lines swam into focus.

For conducting the said La Barre to make public penance before the principal church, the sum of 20 livres. For, at the said place, cutting out his tongue, the sum of 20 livres. For conducting him to the scaffold, and there cutting off his head, the sum of 100 livres.

He dropped the papers on the desk as he tasted ashes once again in his throat. "I don't really care, Father. It doesn't matter."

"It doesn't *matter*?"

This is business, my son, Charles could imagine him thinking; *our solemn and dreadful profession is still a business, despite all, and you fulfilled your side of the contract; there's such as thing as being paid properly for services rendered.*

"Charles, either you overstepped yourself, or else the prosecutor-general's office is cheating us out of what's rightfully ours. The expenses alone—"

"I don't care," he repeated. He leaned over the desk, bracing himself on his hands, avoiding his father's eyes. "Take what they offer us or badger them until they pay the entire bill; I leave it to you. All I know is that I don't want that money. Not a sou of it."

Jean-Baptiste began to reply but Charles interrupted him. "Pay the men, if you must. Hand it over to the curé. Pay for a Mass for La Barre's soul, and give the rest to the poor, or throw it in the gutter."

Jean-Baptiste frowned at him a moment. "If that's what you wish . . ."

"I wouldn't touch it. I'd feel soiled."

Jean-Baptiste seemed about to say something more, but fell silent. At length he rose from his chair and rested a hand upon Charles's shoulder, in the tender, hesitant way Madeleine—God, how bitterly he missed her now—had used to do.

"I fear . . . it won't be the last time."

He dared at last to turn and meet his father's gaze, and found there a sorrowful sympathy he had never yet seen in him. It had never before occurred to him that Jean-Baptiste might also have felt himsclf, more often than once, the instrument of gross injustice.

"Father?"

"I know. The misgivings, the remorse. I'm sorry for this . . . I'm sorry we're—what we have to be."

"It—I—"

Blinded by tears, he reached for Jean-Baptiste, like a small boy aching for the comfort of his father's arms, but Jean-Baptiste was staring down at his own hands, oblivious. Charles turned and fled to the stableyard, shouting for someone to saddle Rosette.

A mile along the road to Saint-Denis, he reined in the mare. He had left his coat, his saddlebags, and his gun behind in his headlong rush out of the house; and it was, in truth, not solitude he craved. He turned Rosette's head back toward the heart of the city.

Antoinette's maid admitted him without asking his business. Antoinette was curled in an armchair in the parlor, reading in the pool of sunshine that spilled in through a tall window, but she scrambled to her feet as she saw him.

"Toinette . . ."

She neared him and, with the same light, tentative gesture as Jean-Baptiste, pushed the disordered hair out of his eyes. "You look as if the hosts of Hell were after you."

"I *am* a *bourreau*." He no longer cared whether or not the maid overheard him. "No more than a damned butcher."

She said nothing, merely gesturing him to the sofa. He stumbled to it and told her everything of his journey to Abbeville, the words spilling and rushing from him like the overflowing Seine in March.

I'm no more than a butcher, he repeated, a long while later, and turned away from her, in his shame scarcely able even to look at her.

"What choice had you?"

"I could have refused. It was an abomination. Twenty years old . . . an innocent boy hounded to his death, tortured, humiliated . . . and he died with the most courage I've ever seen. I ought to have refused."

"You couldn't have saved him by refusing."

"I told myself that. And I told myself that at least I could do my best to make it quick for him, to ease the pain, the horror, of his death—and it *was* quick, thank God, I kept my promise—but does that diminish my share in the guilt? Is that enough to wash away the blood on my hands?"

"I suppose his blood is on all our hands," she said, after a moment's silence. "Everyone from the king, to the Parlement, to the magistrate who first arrested him; down to people like me who might have read a paragraph about him in the newspaper, said 'it's none of my concern,' and went about their lives." She reached out for his hand and stroked it.

"Blood—don't," he whispered, drawing it away.

Blood on my hands. No wonder the magistrates, a century and more ago, when they bestowed on you the Paris title, used to drop the official documents of your office at your feet rather than risk touching your hands. The old superstitions were right: he was cursed and tainted, no one should ever touch him.

"On all our hands," she repeated. "You were only the last, Charles. We all murdered him, our whole world murdered him, because we let it happen."

She was silent for a while, clasping his hands within her own as he sat with bowed head, staring at the pattern in the pale-blue carpet. At last she rang for the maid and told the woman to go out and fetch a fiacre, before turning back to Charles.

"I know you want to weep for him. And for yourself, because all you can see about you today is a cruel, ugly world full of death. But there's life, too, and hope. Truly." She paused for a moment. "You have a son, Chevalier."

"A s—a son?" he stammered, wondering if he could have heard her properly.

"His name is Louis-Gabriel. He was born in April. He's with a wet-nurse in Sèvres now."

"A son . . . *our* son . . . why didn't you . . ."

"I suspected I was with child not long before you asked me to marry you, and I knew you would want more than ever to make an honest woman of me; and then we had that silly quarrel. When you told me you were going to wed your Marie-Anne, I decided you never needed to know . . . but I was wrong. You do need to know—to know that there's more in the world than cruelty and despair. Will you come with me, now, and see our child?"

He remained mute during the journey through the green and gold countryside to the outskirts of Sèvres, for fear that the driver of the hired chaise would order them out and leave them on the roadside if he knew who was riding in his carriage. But he could not bear to babble of commonplaces and they passed a silent hour, gazing out at the peasants cutting hay in the sun-drenched fields.

He still did not quite believe he had a son until the beaming wet-nurse laid a pink, mewing, gently squirming bundle in his arms. With fifteen younger siblings, living and dead, he was no stranger to babies; he cradled the child, rocking him, fatuously cooing at him. The baby stared at him for an instant and suddenly smiled.

"Look—he's such a happy baby," Antoinette said, beside him. "He loves to smile at everyone."

"Is he really mine, do you think?"

"He has your eyes and your brow."

He did look rather like the two youngest of Jean-Baptiste's brood. Charles rocked the baby in his arms a while longer, as they strolled along the stony lane from the wet-nurse's cottage to the nearby village. In the distance the column of smoke from the porcelain works rose straight into the hot still air.

"You'll let me see him again, won't you?"

"Of course."

"I want him to be always as happy as he is now. I want to see him whenever I can, Toinette, but don't ever tell him what I am. Let me be Longval to him, always."

"If that's what you want."

"He ought to grow up far from me—from the profession—from all that. Let him . . . let him know merely that his papa is a respectable gentleman, an—" He was about to say "an honorable man," and checked himself.

"A man who tries his best to live honorably . . . and that his papa loves him."

"His baptismal certificate says only 'father unknown.'"

Antoinette took the baby from him as they reached the village inn and settled at a table beneath a tree in the innyard, white with the roadside dust of high summer, to take a glass of wine and a plate of bread and cheese and hard sausage. They sat a while in the shade, in a companionable silence broken only by the baby's gurgles, and the distant shouts of children playing, a barking dog, and the occasional angry honk and hiss of a goose.

"Does the world look less ugly to you now?" she asked him as he watched little Louis yawn.

A fantastic impulse seized him, to thrust Antoinette and the child into the first farm wagon that passed them and to tell the driver, *Take us as far from Paris as you can before sunset.* To disappear with his child and his lover, without a word abandon everything and everyone he knew, work his way as an itinerant healer to the Netherlands or the German states or even the New World. To escape the scaffold, never again to have to look into the eyes of the dying, except in trying to save their lives.

He sprang to his feet and paced to the end of the innyard and back, staring down the road as a farmer's cart creaked past, westward toward the coast.

He looked over his shoulder at Antoinette. "Come with me."

"Come with you? Where?"

"Anywhere. Let's run away."

Was it so mad an idea? He could not have done it at fourteen, or even at eighteen; but he was a man grown now, twenty-seven, with some experience in medicine, a man capable of supporting himself and his family. His brothers, too, were grown, could assume the Paris title, the prize he had never wanted; could support the household left behind him. And Marie-Anne—Marie-Anne would forget him, in time. Despite everything, at heart she was practical, and Jean-Baptiste would look out for her.

"Charles," Antoinette said softly, "you can't run away. Not any more."

He sat down beside her again, with a sigh, and offered a finger to the baby's tiny, flailing hand. The little fist closed over it, holding him as tight as the shackles that bound him.

"The world looks—exactly as it always has," he said at last. "Life goes on. Even after such atrocities."

I go on. I do my job, my duty, and it's over, and the world shrugs and goes about its business.

Tears pricked his eyes and he blinked them away as baby Louis gazed up at him with another broad smile.

"That boy in Abbeville is dead, but this tiny creature is alive; and nothing has changed, except perhaps myself, my heart."

"Your heart?"

He spoke haltingly, thinking it out. "All my life I've tried to escape what I am, this profession that an accident of birth thrust on me, escape any way I could." *In pleasure, in chasing women, in hunting, in doctoring, anything to forget what he was obliged to do to keep his place in the world.*

"You told me, once, that I ought to make the best of what I am, instead of tormenting myself by trying always to be an ordinary man, which I can never be. So did my sister, many times. And my grandmother said something similar to me long ago: that the executioner can no more abdicate than the king can."

He paused, watching with a wry, sad smile as the baby spluttered and grasped at his cuff. "Perhaps it's time to accept that."

You're right, all of you; I can't escape. Even when my duty is at odds with my conscience, duty without honor.

"But if I must be a hangman for the rest of my life, if I must be a killer in the name of the king and the law, at least I can try, every day, to ease their suffering as much as I can; to be the best man I can be, despite what I must be."

He brushed his fingertip along the baby's petal-smooth cheek. Fathering a child put matters into perspective.

Suddenly he felt old, old. Had his desire to escape his destiny, all those years, been nothing more than a rebellious, adolescent dream?

I suppose I'll have others, he thought as treble voices rose shrilly from the far side of the inn. *Marie-Anne wants children, certainly. Soon I'll be a good bourgeois papa like my father.*

He sighed again. All Marie-Anne would imagine was the cozy domestic happiness a houseful of children would bring them; he doubted she had thought beyond their bright-eyed, rosy-cheeked, carefree childhood to their future.

I can see my life . . . I can see the rest of my life, stretching out before me, as if it's some other man's: the life of a solid, responsible bourgeois papa, a good servant of the crown who always does his duty and follows his orders . . . and finally retires with a pension from the king and dies quietly in his bed, with a prayer on his lips, surrounded by his grieving family. That's all most people ever hope for, and often never achieve—a home and family, and a comfortable income from a secure situation.

"Charles?"

"Our curé," he said at last, "would say we must all make the best of whatever Providence has doled out to us. I ought to be content."

"That, you will never be, I fear."

"I can try."

He pushed himself to his feet again and wandered to the edge of the yard, staring down the road for a moment at the sinking sun before turning his gaze eastward once more, past the gently rolling green hills toward Paris.

Most authors who undertake the daunting job of writing a novel about a real historical figure do so with a shelf of detailed biographies of that person and his/her family and contemporaries close to hand. Plenty of sources are available for the author who wants to write a novel about, say, Elizabeth I or Leonardo da Vinci; this is not, unfortunately, the case with the Sansons.

Although Charles-Henri Sanson and his family were most definitely real people, and enjoyed a sinister fame in their day, of necessity they kept themselves to themselves, and remarkably few authentic accounts of the eighteenth-century Sansons have survived into the twenty-first century. A novelist faced with such a relatively tiny amount of solid evidence on which to base her characters and plot must, therefore, use whatever material she has, often creating a story from the tiniest of hints in obscure documents, and extrapolate (that is, take a deep breath and consciously invent) the rest.

In writing this novel, I relied heavily on *Sept Générations d'Exécuteurs* [*Seven Generations of Executioners*], the apocryphal history of the Sanson family published by Charles Sanson's grandson, Clément, in 1862. This work, mostly ghostwritten by a hack journalist of the day, is a mélange of genuine documents, family anecdotes, and pure melodramatic fiction, much of it based on material lifted sometimes almost word for word from nineteenth-century history books. Twentieth-century histories of the Sanson family all use the more credible parts of *Sept Générations* as their primary foundation, augmented with the scattered facts that can be found elsewhere in archives and more trustworthy contemporary historical accounts.

Though its sources are dubious, *Sept Générations* is still the most extensive resource available for information about the Sansons.

Wherever possible, when other, more reliable, evidence exists and contradicts a narrative or claim in *Sept Générations*, I have tried to stay true to the more likely historical fact.

The character Antoinette, for example, as I have written her, is fictional, though Charles seems to have had a mistress (apparently a most extraordinary woman) when in his twenties, in the 1760s. Jacques-Louis Ménétra (1738?-1803?), a Parisian glazier and almost exact contemporary of Charles Sanson, was personally, if slightly, acquainted with Charles in his dual capacities as executioner and folk healer, and he mentions Charles several times in the lengthy autobiography-journal he wrote between 1764 and 1802. Though Ménétra is an unreliable diarist—he sometimes recounts well-known "urban legends" of the period as adventures that happened to him personally—one of his odder anecdotes, whether true or not, was irresistible and provided me with the basis for Antoinette and her simultaneous liaisons with three prominent, though wildly dissimilar, personages of eighteenth-century Paris:

> I had a friend whose [fellow] countrywoman worked as a cook for the mistress of Christophe de Beaumont [archbishop of Paris]. She lived behind the Louvre. He took me there one day. The mistress had gone to the theater, we were given a warm reception. . . . [She] told me . . . that [her] mistress kept company with Carlin, Samson, and Christophe de Beaumont. I couldn't help thinking about that motley mix. . . . I wanted to make sure of the truth. I saw them and was completely convinced.

"His profession aside," Ménétra writes in another chapter, after describing how the executioner had cured him of some unpleasant malady, "he was a gentle, friendly, kindly man." Ménétra's positive and surprisingly broad-minded estimation of Charles Sanson, and his cordial relations with him (they occasionally spent an hour chatting over a bottle of wine), are all the more remarkable—and convincing—because Ménétra was, in most other respects, a typical member of the artisan class that normally would have shrunk from the *bourreau* in superstitious horror and disgust.

I have no hard evidence at all to support my theory that Charles Sanson married Marie-Anne Jugier after getting her pregnant. It seems unlikely, though, that the well-off and sophisticated Charles would have married a farmer's daughter with little or no dowry, and six years older than himself, for any other reason, when there would have been plenty of younger, wealthier candidates among other executioners' families. Though *Sept Générations d'Exécuteurs* provides a touching scene, complete with stilted, sentimental dialogue, to explain how the two chastely met and eventually married, I felt it was more probable that Marie-Anne was pregnant, or thought she was, at the time of their wedding. (Shotgun weddings were common in eighteenth-century France: François de La Barre's parents were married two days before their first child was born.)

Every one of the particularly appalling episodes of torture and/or capital punishment described in this novel did take place in France in the eighteenth century, the so-called Age of Enlightenment: from the torture-execution of Robert-François Damiens in 1757, to the routine practice of breaking criminals guilty of especially heinous crimes on the wheel, to the botched beheading of the Comte de Lally, to the politically and religiously motivated scapegoating and judicial murder of François Jean Lefebvre, Chevalier de La Barre, in 1766.

La Barre's story is taken directly from two comprehensive works on the affair by Marc Chassaigne (1920) and Max Gallo (1987). His history, particularly after the famous incident of the damage to the shrine in Abbeville in August 1765, is extraordinarily well documented in official archives, memoirs, and eyewitness accounts—much better, in fact, than that of Charles Sanson.

While I embellished the episode of François and his friend Étallonde mooning Duval de Soicourt after breaking his windows, the actual window-breaking did happen and Duval did, in a fit of pique, write to the prosecutor-general in Paris about it. The rude, bare-buttocked stone carving of the demon, high up in an angle of the church of Saint-Vulfran, may still be seen today.

No historians seem to have remarked upon the ironic coincidence that the estate of La Barre, where François and his brother grew up, was only ten miles from the town outside of which the Sansons owned a country cottage. It is not impossible that, somewhere around Brie-Comte-Robert, as a child François might have accidentally encountered the man who would eventually behead him.

La Barre's friends Étallonde, Douville, Belleval, and Moisnel escaped further punishment and survived to tell their sides of the story to Voltaire, among others. Although poetic justice might demand that La Barre's persecutor, Nicolas-Pierre Duval de Soicourt, would lose his own head during the French Revolution, Duval seems to have died of natural causes in 1771, only five years after the affair of the crucifix.

Laws against impiety and heresy were not abolished in France until 1791, in the second year of the Revolution. François de La Barre's supporters had to wait twenty-seven years to win a measure of justice for the chevalier; he, together with all other French victims of religious intolerance, was officially rehabilitated by the National Convention and his conviction overturned on November 16, 1793.

At least sixty streets throughout France are currently named after La Barre. In 1907, a society of freethinkers erected a monument to his memory in Abbeville, which still stands; two years before, they had raised a statue in Paris, in front of the church of Sacre-Cœur, near the small Rue du Chevalier de La Barre. The statue, like many others of Enlightenment philosophers, scientists, and revolutionary leaders, was melted down in 1941 by the occupying Germans. A new statue was finally raised, on the original pedestal, by the Association le Chevalier de La Barre in 2001.

The 250th anniversary of La Barre's execution—July 1, 2016—approaches and is sure to be commemorated in Abbeville and elsewhere by advocates of secularism, freedom of thought, and human rights.

Acknowledgments

I owe many, many people a debt of gratitude for their help in the writing of this novel, especially Cristina Concepcion, my agent, for all her support and her efforts on my behalf; Mike Amalvit, for his invaluable help in detective work; and Margaret Chrisawn, for critiquing with a historian's eye.

An exceptional thank you must go to my beta readers and wonderful neighbors, Pamela Thrasher and Karen Hasenbein, as well as to Johanna, Berenice, and Walt, of course, for their eternal support and encouragement over the past twenty-plus years.

Reader reviews of books are becoming more important than ever for authors' careers. If you enjoyed this novel, please recommend it to your friends—and please consider leaving a review, or starting a discussion, at Amazon, Goodreads, LibraryThing, or other book forum or history or historical fiction discussion group to get the word out to other readers who might enjoy it as well.

Would your local book club, class, or writers' group like to discuss *The Executioner's Heir* or any of my other novels? Visit my author website—www.susannealleyn.com—for suggestions for discussion topics (no spoilers), or to contact me and schedule a live chat with your group (in the United States, Canada, or the UK), in person or via your speakerphone. I look forward to our conversation.

Thank you in advance,
Susanne Alleyn

A SELECTION OF SOURCES ON EIGHTEENTH-CENTURY FRANCE, FRENCH HISTORY, AND THE SANSON FAMILY

Andrews, Richard Mowery. *Law, Magistracy, and Crime in Old Regime Paris, 1735-1789*. Cambridge, UK: Cambridge University Press, 1994.

Anonymous. *Memoirs of Count Lally*. London: F. Newbery, 1766.

Anonymous. *Procès du Chevalier de La Barre, Décapité à Abbeville, à l'occasion de la mutilation d'un Crucifix*. Hamburg: no publisher given, 1782.

Belleval, marquis de. *Nobiliaire de Ponthieu et de Vimeu*, 2nd edition. Paris: Librairie Bachelin Deflorenne, 1876.

Bernier, Olivier. *Pleasure and Privilege: Life in France, Naples, and America, 1770-90*. New York: Doubleday, 1981.

Chassaigne, Marc. *Le Procès du Chevalier de La Barre*. Paris: Librarie Victor Lecoffre, 1920.

Christophe, Robert. *Les Sanson: Bourreaux de Père en Fils Pendant Deux Siècles*. Paris: Librairie Arthème Fayard, 1960.

Cruppi, Jean. *Linguet: Un Avocat Journaliste au XVIIIe Siècle*. Paris: Librairie Hachette et Cie., 1895.

Darnton, Robert. *The Literary Underground of the Old Regime*. Cambridge, Mass.: Harvard University Press, 1982.

Delarue, Jacques. *Le Métier du Bourreau: Du Moyen Age à aujourd'hui*. Paris: Librairie Arthème Fayard, 1979.

Ducros, Louis. *French Society in the Eighteenth Century*. NY & London: G. P. Putnam's Sons, 1927.

Fierro, Alfred. *Dictionnaire du Paris Disparu: Sites et Monuments*. Paris: Parigramme, 1998.

Gallo, Max. *Que Passe la Justice du Roi: Vie, procès et supplice du chevalier de La Barre*. Paris: Éditions Robert Laffont, 1987.

Garrioch, David. *The Making of Revolutionary Paris*. Berkeley, CA: University of California Press, 2002.

Heron de Villefosse, René. *Le Coeur Battant de Paris*. Paris: Robert Laffont, 1968.

Hillairet, Jacques. *Connaissance de Vieux Paris*. Paris: Éditions Payot & Rivages, 1993 [reprint].

Lacroix, Paul. *France in the Eighteenth Century: Its Institutions, Customs and Costumes*. New York: Frederick Ungar, 1963 [reprint].

Lecherbonnier, Bernard. *Bourreaux de père en fils: Les Sanson, 1688-1847*. Paris: Albin Michel, 1989.

Levy, Barbara. *Legacy of Death*. Englewood Cliffs, NJ: Prentice-Hall, 1973.

Levy, Darline G. *The Ideas and Careers of Simon-Nicolas-Henri Linguet: A Study in Eighteenth-Century French Politics*. Urbana, IL: University of Illinois Press, 1980.

Louandre, François-César. *Histoire d'Abbeville et du Comté de Ponthieu jusqu'en 1789*. Abbeville: A. Alexandre, 1884.

Lough, John. *An Introduction to Eighteenth-Century France*. London: David McKay, 1960.

Ménétra, Jacques-Louis; Arthur Goldhammer, translator. *Journal of My Life*. New York: Columbia University Press, 1986.

Sanson, H.-C. [with d'Olbreuse]. *Sept Générations d'Exécuteurs* [6 volumes]. Paris: Dupray de la Mahérie, 1862-63.

ABOUT THE AUTHOR

Susanne Alleyn has loved history all her life, aided and abetted by her grandmother, Lillie V. Albrecht, an author of historical children's books in the 1950s and 60s. Susanne is the author of the Aristide Ravel historical mystery series, set in revolutionary Paris; *A Far Better Rest*, the reimagining of Dickens's *A Tale of Two Cities*; and of the nonfiction *Medieval Underpants and Other Blunders: A Writer's (and Editor's) Guide to Keeping Historical Fiction Free of Common Anachronisms, Errors, and Myths*. Happy to describe herself as an "insufferable knowitall" about historical trivia (although she lost on *Jeopardy!*), Susanne has been writing about and researching eighteenth-century and revolutionary France for nearly three decades.

She is currently working on the sequel to *The Executioner's Heir*. Read more, or send Susanne e-mail, at www.susannealleyn.com.

Read on to sample the first chapter of Susanne's Aristide Ravel mystery *Palace of Justice*, a novel set in 1793 which features a guest appearance by an older Charles Sanson.

Palace of Justice

1

Paris
October 7, 1793

God help me, Désirée said to herself, as she tried to ignore the dull, persistent ache of her empty stomach, *I cannot even make a living as a whore.*

The fashionable hurried past her, eager to escape the chilly night air, toward the bright lights of the cafés, restaurants, theaters, and brothels of the Palais-Égalité. Along the stately length of the stone arcades, the lamps burned overhead, illuminating the restless swirl of humanity in its never-ending pursuit of amusement.

The women lurking beneath the rows of sculpted lime trees were banished from the light. Patient as the poor who once had formed lines before church doors to receive bread and soup, they waited, unsmiling, their eyes vacant, until some solitary figure from the milling crowd might fade away from the glitter and join them in the shadows.

She had waited hours in the dark, since before the twilight had fallen on a gray, wet October day, and seen the other women come and go, while only one man had approached her.

"You," he had said, out of the darkness, plucking her sleeve. "You've a pretty figure. What's your price?"

She had jerked about, surprised. He was middle-aged, stout, his neat frock coat cut in last year's fashion: a bourgeois from the provinces enjoying a holiday in Paris.

"What's your price?" he repeated.

That, at least, she knew; she had asked some of the other women what the going rate was. Those who had not laughed at her, snickering about amateurs, had been friendly enough. "Th-three sous, and the price of the room."

"If they rent by the hour, then. I'm not looking to spend the whole night with you."

"Yes, citizen." She turned and gestured at the arcades, toward a small hotel that charged lower prices and turned a blind eye to what might go on behind closed doors (as did all hotels in the Palais-Égalité, even after the pleasure gardens had been "officially" purged of prostitutes). The man followed her.

They had nearly reached the hotel when abruptly he thrust his face in hers, squinting in the bright lamplight shining through a café window.

"No wonder you women skulk in the shadows. How old are you?"

"I—twenty-nine." She had shaved five years from her true age, but evidently no one wanted anything over twenty-five or, better, twenty—

"And new to this line of work, from your manner. Well, I'm not paying for mutton dressed as lamb."

She had gazed after his retreating figure for a moment, speechless. At last she had heaved a long sigh, half in regret, half in relief, and fingered the coins in her pocket. Her last two sous—less than the price of a single meal. She had preserved her virtue for another half hour, and soon would virtuously starve.

Of all the misnamed folk in the world, she mused, not for the first time, *I am the most absurd. Désirée . . . but no one desires me, even as a whore.*

"How much?" said a voice, a different voice, close beside her. "Not too much, I hope—you're a little long in the tooth to be charging full price."

"Two sous," she muttered.

"Two sous for you? I don't pay two sous for any trollop who's past sixteen." He ran his hands over her, snickering as he prodded her. "Not much meat on those bones. Half a sou for a quick one in the alley." His hand was on her breast, clutching and kneading at her. "What do you say, little chicken?"

"I say you keep it to yourself until you've paid," she said between clenched teeth, her cheeks burning, as she attempted to push him away, "and don't paw at me in public."

"Don't paw at me in public!" he repeated in a high-pitched voice, with a sneer. "Dear me, how modest we are." His other hand slid down and grabbed at her through her skirt, between her legs. The prodding, grasping fingers fumbled and groped and would not, would *not* let go of her. She wrenched her arm away and slapped him.

"You little bitch!"

Suddenly her ears were ringing, and a sharp pain was creeping along the line of her cheekbone to the back of her skull, and the world was spinning about her. She was sitting—no, lying—on something cold and wet. Struggling up to a sitting position, through a dim haze she saw him dust off his hands and saunter away.

"Bastard," said one woman, a shabby one near her own age, as another laughed drunkenly and swayed off in pursuit of a customer. "All bastards, all of them." She reached down and offered her hand. "Here."

Désirée lurched to her knees, gritting her teeth to swallow back her despair. The skirt of her green gown, her last halfway decent dress, was dripping and smeared with mud.

"Mademoiselle?" said a man's voice beside her. "Are you all right?"

She squeezed her eyes shut for a moment, opened them, and found herself gazing up at a tall, lean man in a shabby overcoat. "Are you all right?" the man repeated, bending toward her. "That was quite a blow he gave you. Better you should sit down—you don't want to faint. Someone might seize his opportunity to rob you."

"Rob me—" she exclaimed, and all at once, to her hideous embarrassment, she burst into violent, gasping sobs. "Oh, dear God, if only there were something in my pocket to steal!"

The stranger shook his head and offered her a hand to help her to her feet. "Come, come, it can't be all that bad—"

"Yes, it *is* that bad!" she screamed, no longer caring who might hear her. "What do you know about it? Look at me! Just a useless woman whom no one wants, not even as a whore, and with two sous to call her own!"

"Here, now," he said, handing her a handkerchief and drawing her aside, away from the other women, "dry your eyes, squeeze out your skirts, and let's get something warm inside you. You've not eaten, I suppose?"

"Eaten . . ." When had she eaten last? "Not since yesterday morning. Some bread."

"Come with me."

Dazed, Désirée followed him. He strode along with the easy step of one who was accustomed to walking, leading her out of the Palais-Égalité to the narrow side streets west of the gardens, at last pausing before a food stall whose owner had not yet hung up his shutters. "Here, some soup will do you good."

She glanced up at him as he pulled out a few crumpled assignats for the soup seller. Her companion was a lean, dark-haired man of forty or so. A broad-brimmed, low-crowned round hat shadowed a long, stern face, which she could just make out in the gloom, though she caught the glitter of eyes in the feeble glimmer from the soup seller's lantern. The man's clothes were less than impressive; he wore an old, well-worn black worsted suit that might have belonged to a lawyer's clerk, and hanging open over that a dark overcoat of indeterminate color, which once had been of good quality before moths and the passage of time had ravaged it.

"You're very kind, citizen," she said, avoiding his gaze. "After what I said to you. Anyone else would have pushed me into the mud again for such insolence."

"Such men are swine. You've not been long in your trade, have you?"

"Only today. I had no more money, and nothing to eat, and the rent is due. And there's no work in Paris, at least nothing I know how to do."

The soup seller put a bowl and spoon before her. She seized the spoon and began wolfing down the soup. Oh, the exquisite feeling of having something in her stomach at last, vegetables, a little tough meat, and plenty of thick broth! The tall man watched her, smiling.

"Better?"

She glanced up at him, wishing she could scrape the bowl out with her finger to get up the last few drops. "Thank you."

"My pleasure, citizeness. You're well-spoken," he added, turning away from the stall. "Who and what are you, for God's sake?"

"My father was the second son of a gentleman and owned a little land, but we never had two sous to rub together, and we lost the few dues from the property when the Revolution abolished them. Then my father died, two years ago, but not before he'd gambled away most of what we had; and I had to sell our property to settle his debts. I had a fiancé, but he jilted me in the end, because I had no fortune." An old, monotonous story, one everyone had heard a dozen times before. She paused, but he merely nodded.

"So I came to Paris as companion to my mother's cousin, who's married to a rich man. Then her husband made advances, and when I—when I kicked him, he threw me out. That was four months ago. I can't get any work. I don't know any trade besides sewing, and half the dressmakers have shut up their shops and the other half aren't hiring anyone new. I've sold everything I had, my bits of jewelry, my books, even my clothes. So at last I came here, to offer the only thing I had left to sell, but it seems I'm no good even for that." Her stomach rumbled and she clasped her hands over it, embarrassed.

"I think your appetite wants more than some soup," her unexpected savior observed. "There's an eating-house nearby. Come along."

She blinked away tears, so weary she had no strength left to resist. "A favor for a favor—that's it, isn't it? Do whatever you want. You can have me for the whole night if you like. At least the room will be warm."

"You misunderstand me. I'm not looking for a whore. Let's say," he continued, as he steered her down the street and gestured to a narrow alley, "that I think you've had more than your share of ill luck. The least I can do, out of Christian charity, is to give you a hot meal."

"Thank you, citizen," she whispered, wondering how many months it had been since she had heard the word "Christian" used without derision. Many of the brutalized, bitter sansculottes, day laborers, and prostitutes she now saw every day had little love for the Catholic Church which, for centuries, had taxed them and dictated to them while its cynical, worldly bishops flaunted their wealth. Though the Church, in its present state-sanctioned, revolutionary form, was still tolerated, anticlerical feeling had been swelling of late.

"This way—it's not far now."

He gestured her onward and she preceded him into the empty alley, feeling her way along. The closest street lamp was far behind them and the chinks of light from behind barred shutters, and the tiny new moon above, cast only a meager light, barely enough for her to see her groping hands.

"Are you sure this is the way?"

"It's a shortcut. Keep going."

She stumbled on a loose cobble, hearing it clatter like a pistol shot in the silence, and stopped short, heart pounding. She was all alone here with him, isolated and helpless, just as he wanted her.

Fool, she told herself. *You credulous little fool.*

She was going to be raped in an alley, by a degenerate with unnatural desires that a decent woman should not even know of, for the price of a bowl of soup.

She twisted about, but in his dark coat and broad hat he was invisible in the murk.

"Please—please don't hurt me. I said you could do whatever you wanted. Just don't hurt me."

Now she could hear his breath, close by in the darkness. His arm slid about her from behind, clutching her to him until she felt the warmth of his body.

"I told you," he murmured, "I don't want that from you."

"Then what—"

He whispered a few words. She thought they might be "May God forgive me" in the last instant before the knife was at her throat.

Palace of Justice

An Aristide Ravel Mystery

by Susanne Alleyn

In hardcover & eBook from St. Martin's Press (2010)

eBook available at all major online retailers

"A fiendishly clever and compelling mystery set in a grim, gripping vision of Paris where there is no justice, only shades of gray." (*Kirkus Reviews*)

Made in the USA
San Bernardino, CA
09 December 2013